MW01134895

The Lie

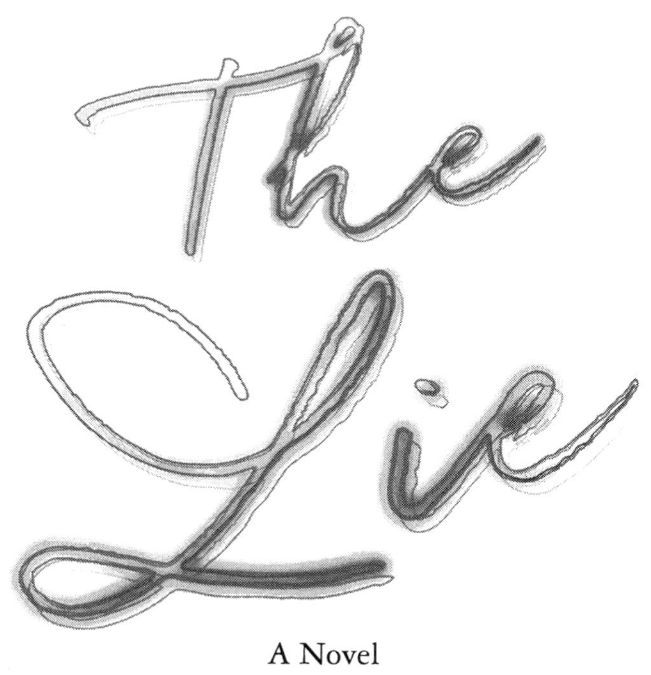

A Novel

KARINA HALLE

First edition published by
Metal Blonde Books February 2016
Publisher's Note: This is a work of fiction. Names, characters, places, and incidents either are the product of the author's imagination or are used fictitiously. Any resemblance to actual events, locales, or persons, living or dead, is entirely coincidental.

Cover design by Hang Le Designs
Edited by Kara Maclinczak
Metal Blonde Books
P.O. Box 845
Point Roberts, WA
98281 USA
Manufactured in the USA
For more information about the series and author visit:
http://authorkarinahalle.com/

ISBN: 1530083664
ISBN-13: 9781530083664

For Scott

Also by Karina Halle

Contemporary Romance Novels

Love, in English

Love, in Spanish

Where Sea Meets Sky (from Atria Books)

Racing the Sun (from Atria Books)

Before the Dawn (from Atria Books)

Bright Midnight (from Atria Books)

The Pact

The Offer

The Play

The Lie

The Debt (Fall 2016)

Romantic Suspense Novels

Sins and Needles (The Artists Trilogy #1)

On Every Street (An Artists Trilogy Novella #0.5)

Shooting Scars (The Artists Trilogy #2)

Bold Tricks (The Artists Trilogy #3)

Dirty Angels

Dirty Deeds

Dirty Promises

Paranormal/Horror Romance Novels

The Devil's Metal (Devils #1)

The Devil's Reprise (Devils #2)

Donners of the Dead

Darkhouse (Experiment in Terror #1)

Red Fox (EIT #2)

The Benson (EIT #2.5)

Dead Sky Morning (EIT #3)

Lying Season (EIT #4)

On Demon Wings (EIT #5)

Old Blood (EIT #5.5)

The Dex-Files (EIT #5.7)

Into the Hollow (EIT #6)

And With Madness Comes the Light (EIT #6.5)

Come Alive (EIT #7)

Ashes to Ashes (EIT #8)

Dust to Dust (EIT #9)

Table of Contents

Prologue

BRIGS

Edinburgh, Scotland

Four Years Ago

"I'm sorry."

I'd rehearsed it so many times that I thought I could just open my mouth and the words would flow out. The whole speech. The entire confession. I thought if I kept saying it over and over again in my head, that when it came time to speak the awful, horrible, liberating truth, it would come easily.

But it doesn't. It hasn't.

I can't even explain myself. All I do is drop to my knees, my legs shaking from the stress of it all, the stress I brought upon myself. It pales in comparison to what she's about to feel.

Miranda is sitting on the couch, like I'd asked her to, the cup of tea placed neatly on the saucer. I keep my eyes focused on the subtle wafts of steam rising from it. I thought I could do the right thing and meet her eyes, but I can't. I'm cowardly at the end of it all, unwilling to see the pain, the deep cuts from my own hand.

"Sorry for what?" she asks in that calm voice of hers. Always so calm, able to weather any storm I've thrown her way. The fact that I'm on my knees, visibly trembling like a fool, hasn't changed her tone in the slightest. Maybe this won't be as hard on her as I thought.

Bloody wishful thinking, that is.

I take in a deep breath and wince when it comes out shaking. I wish the sound of the rain pouring outside would mask it.

"I'm sorry," I repeat again. My voice sounds hollow, like I'm hearing a playback on a dusty old tape. "I have to tell you something."

"I can see that," she says, and now I detect an edge. "You asked me to sit down and now you're on your knees. I hope you're not proposing to me all over again."

It would all be so much easier if that were true.

I finally dare to meet her eyes.

My wife is such a beautiful woman. Grace Kelly reincarnated. A neck like a swan. I remember our first date. We'd barely been out of high school, but even then it's like she held a world of secrets in her poise. She was so put together, so perfect. I showed up with my shitty car and took her to the movies and dinner at the best place I could afford, even though the food was bloody horrible. And she was forever gracious, didn't bat an eye. She made me feel like I was somebody when I was with her, and maybe that's why I married her. She was everything I wasn't.

She's still everything I'm not. That can't be more apparent right now.

"Brigs," she says, frowning. She barely has lines even when she's making that face. "You're scaring me."

I clear my throat but it's like pushing boulders. "I know."

"Is it about Hamish?" she asks, and as that thought comes over her, her eyes widen in panic.

I shake my head quickly. "No, nothing to do with Hamish."

I'm thankful more than ever that the little man has gone to bed when he's supposed to. The rain is coming down harder now, tapping at the windows, and that has always worked on him better than any lullaby.

"I just want you to know," I tell her, putting my palm on her hands. So soft, like she'd never worked a day in her life. I used to make fun of her for that, for being the socialite, the trust-fund baby. Right now they make her seem achingly vulnerable. "I just want you to know that...I've put a lot of thought into this. I never wanted to hurt you." I stare at her, begging with my eyes. "You must know that."

"Oh god," she says with a gasp, pulling her hand away from mine. "Brigs, what did you do?"

The weight of all my choices blankets me.

There is no easy way to say this.

No way to soften the blow.

I don't want to hurt her.

But I have to.

"I..." I swallow the razors in my throat. I shake my head and fight the heat behind my eyes. "Miranda, I want a divorce."

She stares at me blankly, so calmly, that I wonder if she's heard me. My hands are shaking, my heart is about to need resuscitation.

"What?" she finally whispers in disbelief.

To outside eyes we've had a happy marriage. But we both knew this was coming. Maybe she never saw the catalyst, but she knew this was coming. She had to.

"We've both been very unhappy for a long time," I explain.

"Are you serious?" she says quickly. "Are you seriously doing this?"

"Miranda." I lick my lips, daring to meet her eyes. "You must have known this was going to happen. If it wasn't from me, it would have been from you."

"How dare you," she says, roughly pushing my hands away and getting to her feet. "How dare you put words in my mouth? I've been happy…I've just been…I've just been…"

She's shaking her head violently, walking to the other side of the living room. "No," she says, standing against the mantle. "No, I won't give you a divorce. I won't let you leave. You can't leave me. You…Brigs McGregor could never leave Miranda Harding McGregor. You would be nothing without me."

I let her words deflect, even though my belief in them is what's led to this moment. "Miranda," I say softly, and her name is starting to sound foreign, the way it can when you say a word too many times in a row. "Please."

"No!" she yells, and I flinch, hoping she doesn't wake up Hamish. "Whatever foolish ideas are coming over your brain, I don't know, but a divorce isn't the answer. This is just…a flight of fancy for you. You being unhappy at your job. This is you not feeling like a man. This is you not performing like a man."

A dig below the literal belt. I should have known that would be her first line of defense. Our problems in the bedroom for the last year. I can't fault her for that.

"No," she says again. "I can live with that, I can. And if I never have another child, so be it. But my family…my reputation…it will not come to this. We have a good life, Brigs.

This house. Look at this house." She points wildly around the room, a feverish look in her eyes. "Look at these things. We have everything. People look up to us. They envy us. Why would you throw that away?"

My heart sinks further down my chest, to my stomach, and burns there.

"Please," I say softly, not wanting the whole truth to come out, but ready to wield it if I have to. "I'm not...I don't want to hurt you. But I'm just not in love with you anymore. It's the honest truth, and I'm sorry. I'm so sorry."

She blinks like she's been slapped. Then she says, "So? What married couples *are* in love with each other? Be realistic here, Brigs."

Now I'm surprised. I frown. I didn't expect her to fight for us so much. And to fight for a loveless marriage she's okay with.

She's watching me closely, tapping her nails against her lips. Plotting. The rain spatters at the windows, and in the distance, thunder rumbles, the first autumn storm. The room seems smaller than ever.

"We can work it out," she finally says, her voice back to being eerily calm. "This is just a hiccup. We can work it out. You can love me again, and if you can't, then it's okay. It's fine. No one has to know. We both love our son, and that's enough. Don't you want him to grow up with a father, a complete family? Don't you know a divorce would destroy him? Is that what you want for him?"

I take an ice pick to the chest with that one, the cold spreading through me. Because of course, *of course*, that's what I want for him. It's what's held me back and back and back. But kids know, they know when their parents aren't happy. Hamish deserves better than a childhood tainted with angst.

"Separated parents are better than two miserable parents together," I tell her, pleading now. "You know it's true. Hamish is smart, *so* smart. So intuitive. Children pick up on so much more than you realize."

Her eyes narrow. "Oh? What self-help book did you steal that from? Bloody hell, Brigs. Just listen to yourself. Talking out of your arse."

"Do you want him to grow up in a house where I don't love his mother? Is that what you want? Don't you think he'll see? He'll know."

"He won't," she says viciously. "Stop making excuses."

I get to my feet and raise my palms, feeling helpless to the core. Guilty as sin. "I have no excuses. Just the truth."

"Go fuck your truth, Brigs," she snaps.

The thunder crashes again. I pray it drowns out our argument, that Hamish is still blissfully asleep and unaware that his future is changing. Not for the worst, please God, not for the worst. Just changing.

She walks over to the antique bar cart and pours herself a glass of Scotch from the decanter, like a heroine in a Hitchcock film. Playing the part.

Can't she see how tired I am of pretending?

Doesn't she get tired, too?

"Do you want one?" she asks over her shoulder, almost coyly, the glass between her manicured fingertips. Her father gave us those, and the decanter, as a wedding present.

I shake my head, trying to steady my heart.

She slams back the Scotch, and in a second it's down her throat. "Suit yourself. I'll have your share."

She pours another glass, holds it delicately, and glides over to the couch, sitting down in front of me. She crosses her legs and stares up at me, cocking her head, a wave of blonde falling across her forehead. She's buried her emotions again, pretending, acting, as if that will make everything okay.

"You're a fool, Brigs. Always were. But I forgive you. We all have lapses in judgement sometimes."

I sigh heavily and close my eyes. She's not getting it.

"People fall out of love all the time," she goes on, finishing half the glass and putting it down on the glass side table. The *clink* sounds so loud in this room that seems to be growing emptier and emptier. "It's a fact of life. A sad, sad fact. But you can fall back in. I'll try harder. I really will. I'll do anything to make you stay. You know this. You know how I can be. Once I have something, I don't let go. I fight. And I keep what's mine."

I do know that. Which is why I have to give her the truth. The terrible truth. Because only then she'll see. Only then she'll see what I mean.

I wish I didn't have to do this.

"I'm so sorry," I whisper.

"I forgive you." She finishes the rest of her drink, wiping the back of her hand across her lips without managing to smear her lipstick.

"I'm so sorry," I say again, feeling the tears building behind my eyes. I shake my head sharply. "The truth is…I'm in love with someone else. I've fallen in love with someone else."

There.

The truth falls.

Lands on her like bricks.

She jerks her head back from the impact, eyes widening in confusion. Fear. Anger.

"What?!" she exclaims. She stares at me, the fury slowly building and building and building before it's unleashed. "Who? Who? Tell me fucking who?!"

"It doesn't matter," I say, but she's up on her feet, sneering at me, face red and contorted. Unable to pretend anymore.

"Tell me!" she screams, holding onto her head, her teeth bared, her eyes wild. "Tell me! Is it someone I know? Susan? Carol!?"

"It's no one you know, Miranda. It just happened, I—"

"Fuck you!" she screams again.

"Please. Hamish is sleeping."

"Oh, fuck you!" She pounds her fists against my chest and pushes me back. "Fuck you for making me the fool. What is she, some young tart? Did she make you get it up? Huh, did she fix your problem?"

"I never slept with her," I tell her quickly.

"Oh, bullshit!" she screams. "Bloody fucking hell. Brigs. Brigs, you can't be serious. You're in love with someone else." She shakes her head, talking to herself. "You, of all people. The professor. Quiet Mr. McGregor. No. I can't believe it. I can't fucking believe it."

"I know it's hard to hear."

Crack.

She slaps me hard.

Again.

And again.

One side and the other, and I turn the cheek because I deserve this. I knew this was coming, and if she didn't react this way, then I really didn't know the woman I married.

"You arse! You wanker!" She shoves me one more time and runs across the room, to the bar. She picks up the decanter of Scotch, downs a few gulps of it straight out of the nose, then spits some of it up, bent over in a coughing fit.

"Miranda, please."

"You are disgusting!" she screeches after she's caught her breath. "Pathetic little shit! You slept with another woman. You—"

"I didn't!" I yell, my arms flying out to the sides. "I never slept with her, please believe that."

"And even if I believed you, you think that gives you a pass?" She nearly spits the words. "Love is a choice, Brigs, and you chose this. You chose to not love me, and you chose to love her, some fucking whore. Some nobody. You chose to ruin our fucking lives!" At the last word she picks up the decanter of Scotch and hurls it at me. I duck just in time as it crashes against the cabinet behind me, breaking into a million pieces.

"Mummy?" Hamish whimpers, rubbing his eyes and standing in the doorway.

Fuck!

I whirl around, trying to smile. "Mummy is fine," I tell him. "Go back to sleep, buddy."

"Is it storming out?" he says, walking forward toward the broken glass.

"Hamish!" I yell at him, hands out for him to stop. He does before he reaches the glass, blinking at me. I never raise my voice around him. But before I can scoop him up, Miranda is running across the room and grabbing him by the arm.

"Come on, baby. We're going, we're going," she says, leading him out of the living room and into the foyer.

I run after them in time to see Miranda grabbing her car keys and her coat. Hamish is crying now and she's picking him up in her arms.

"What are you doing?" I shout, storming after her.

She quickly runs out the door and into the rain, and I'm right behind her, bare feet sinking into the cold mud, nearly slipping as she heads for the sedan.

She can't be serious. She can't do this.

I manage to grab hold of her arm as she puts Hamish in the front seat and closes the door. The car seat isn't even there—it's in the house, the maid was cleaning it after Hamish spilled his milk this afternoon.

"You can't take him!" I scream at her over the wind and rain.

"Let go of me!" she yelps, trying to pull away. "I'm taking him from you, you bastard."

"No, listen to me!" I tighten my grip on her arm. Hamish is wailing from inside the car, rain sliding down the window. "You're not thinking. You've had the Scotch. It's a fucking storm out there and he needs his car seat. Just listen to me!"

"If you don't let go of me," she seethes, "I'm going to tell everyone that you hurt me and you'll never see your son again." She pulls against me harder, to make a point, my fingers automatically digging into her soft skin. "You can have your divorce, Brigs. But you can't have him."

"Miranda, please. Let me get the car seat. I know you're angry, but please, let me do that! Just let me do that." We are both soaked to the bone now, and my feet are slowly being buried by mud. I'm feeling buried by my own desperation. "Please, okay? Please."

She stares at me, so fearful, so enraged. Then she nods, the rains spilling down her face.

I don't have a plan. But I know I'm not letting her drive away from here, not in her state of hysterics, not in this weather. I look down at Hamish as he's crying, his face pink in the dim light, nearly obscured by the rain.

"Just give me a second," I tell him. "Daddy will be right back."

I turn, running toward the house, wondering if I need to call the cops, if she'll calm down in the time I get the seat. If—

The sound of the car door opening.

I stop and whirl around.

She's getting in her side, slamming the door shut.

"No!" I scream. I try to run but slip, falling to the ground. Mud splashes around me. "Miranda, wait!"

The car starts just as I'm getting to my feet, and I don't feel the cold or the rain or hear the wind or the engine, I just feel horror. Pure, unfiltered, unsaturated horror.

The front wheels spin viciously for a moment before the car reverses back down the driveway.

I start running after her.

I reach the car and slam my hands down on the hood, staring at her through the moving wiper blades. Her face. Her indignity. Her panic. Her disgrace.

His face. Distraught. Confused. The perfect marriage of both of us. The perfect little boy.

Her face. His face.

The wipers wipe them clean.

She puts the car in drive and guns the engine, enough to push the grill into my hips. I quickly leap to the right before I get run over.

I roll over on the ground, out of the way, and struggle to my feet as Miranda whips the car around and speeds off down the street.

"Miranda!" I scream. Panic grips me for one second, freezing me in place, helpless, hopeless.

But I'm not.

I have to go after them.

I run back to the house, grab my mobile, and the keys to the vintage Aston Martin and run back out, jumping into the car.

The fucking piece of shit takes a few times to roll over and I'm looking at the phone wondering if I should call the police. I don't even know if she's legally drunk or not, and I don't want to get her in trouble, but if they can stop her before I can, before she possibly hurts herself and Hamish, then I may just have to. I have to do something.

I know she's heading to her parents' house, the Hardings, across the bridge to St. David's Bay. That's where she always goes. Maybe I should call her mother. Get them on the lookout. Mrs. Harding will hate me even more for it, but not as much as she will when Miranda tells them what I've done.

The car finally turns over. I gun it down the driveway and onto the main road, a winding, twisting artery that leads to the M-8.

"Fuck!" I scream, banging my fist repeatedly on the wheel as my self-hatred chokes me. "Fuck!"

Why did I pick tonight to say anything?

Why did I have to go to London?

Why did I have to choose this?

Why did it have to choose me?

I'm asking myself a million questions, hating myself for letting it go this way, wishing dearly that I had done things differently.

I'm asking myself things I don't have any answers to other than:

Because I love Natasha.

It always comes down to that terrible truth.

I love her.

So much.

Too much.

Enough to make me throw everything away.

Because I could no longer live the lie.

But the truth doesn't just hurt, it destroys.

The road twists sharply to the left as it skirts along Braeburn Pond, and in the pouring rain, the wipers going faster and faster, I nearly miss it.

But it's impossible not to.

The broken fence along the side of the road.

The steam rising from beyond the bank.

From where a car has gone over the edge.

A car has gone over the edge.

I slam on the brakes, the car skidding a few feet, and pull to the side of the road.

I don't let the thoughts enter my head.

The thoughts that tell me this is them.

This could be them.

But if it is them, one thought says, *you have to save them.*

I can save them.

I don't know how I manage to swallow the panic down, but I do.

I get out of the car, rain in my face.

The air smells like burned asphalt.

The pond is whipped up by the storm.

And as I approach the edge of the road, I can see the faint beam of headlights from down below, a misplaced beacon in the dark.

I look down.

The world around me swims.

The hood of the sedan is smashed into a willow tree, the same hood I had my hands on minutes ago, begging her not to leave.

The car is at an angle, leaning on its broken nose.

The steam rises.

And yet I still have hope.

I have to have hope.

I cry out, making noises I can't control. Maybe I'm yelling for them, maybe I'm yelling for help. I stumble down the hillside to the car.

Praying.

Praying.

Praying.

That they're going to be okay.

They're going to be okay.

The windshield is completely shattered, the jagged glass stained with red.

I stare stupidly at the empty car.

Then turn my head.

To the space in front of the hood.

And the grass between the car and the pond.

Where two bodies lay, dark in the night.

Two bodies—one big, one small.

Both broken.

Both motionless.

I have one moment of clarity as the truth sinks in.

My truth.

This real truth.

And in that moment I want to grab the jagged piece of glass lying at my feet.

Put it in my throat.

And end it before I can feel it.

But that would be the coward's way out.

So I stumble forward.

Vomit down my shirt.

Paralysis of the heart.

I cry.

Scream.

Noises animals make.

I stumble past Miranda.

To Hamish.

Fall to my knees.

And cradle my truth in my arms.

And I feel it.

I'll never stop feeling it.

The rain.

The death.

The end of everything.

My world goes black.

And stays that way.

Chapter One

BRIGS

Edinburgh

Present Day

Pop.

A cork flies off a bottle of alcohol-free champagne. The shit isn't Dom Pérignon, but for the sake of my brother and his alcohol recovery program, it will do. Besides, it's not what we're drinking that counts—it's what we're celebrating.

"Congratu-fucking-lations, brother," I tell Lachlan, grabbing his meaty shoulder and giving it a rather rough squeeze. I'm beaming at him, conscious of my all-too-wide grin in his face, but I'm happier than I've been in a while. Maybe it's the real champagne I had with our mum before Lachlan and his girlfriend came over.

Wait. Not girlfriend.

Kayla is his fiancé now. And if you ask me, it's about time.

Lachlan nods, smiling wanly in acute embarrassment, which only makes me want to embarrass him more. That's the job of an older brother, after all, and since our family adopted him when I was out of high school, I missed out on those important torture years of childhood that most siblings experience.

My mum comes over and pours the non-champagne into our glasses, then into Kayla's, who is standing dutifully at Lachlan's side. As usual, she's hanging on to Lachlan in some way—hand at the small of his back—and her cheeks are flushed with emotion. I almost wish she would cry so I could poke fun at her later. She's such a feisty, smart-mouthed girl that a little vulnerable emotion would be wonderful to exploit.

"Here's to Lachlan and the future Mrs. McGregor," my mum says, raising her glass to the happy couple. Before she's about to clink the glasses, she eyes my father, who is standing at the edge of the room, poised to take a picture. He's been poised for the last few minutes. "Well, hurry Donald and get over here."

"Right," he says, snapping one more photo of us with glasses in the air, and then comes hurrying over. She hands him his glass and we all clink them together.

"Welcome to the family, Kayla," I tell her sincerely. I glance quickly at Lachlan before I add, "I've been bugging him from day one to propose to you, you know. Can't believe it took him so long, especially with a girl like you."

The permanent line between Lachlan's brow deepens, his jaw tense. I think I'm the only person alive that can piss him off and not get scared of him. My brother is a giant beast of a man, all beard and muscle and tattoos, and has most recently become the captain of the Edinburgh Rugby team. You don't want to mess with him, unless your name is Brigs McGregor.

"Brigs," my mother admonishes.

"Oh, I know," Kayla says smoothly before taking a sip of her drink. "I'd be lying if I hadn't been leaving out my rings on the dresser, just so it would be easier for him to get the right size."

"Atta girl," I tell her, and clink her glass again, and though I'm suddenly hit by a fleeting memory, about picking out a ring for Miranda, I swallow it down with the bubbles. That's how I've learned to deal with the past—you acknowledge it and move on.

Move on.

Yesterday we were all at the rugby match between Edinburgh and Munster, cheering our arses off. Of course we weren't just there for Lachlan. He had told us a few weeks before that he was going to propose during the game, and it would be nice to have the family there. Even though I just started teaching last week, I flew up from London to Edinburgh on Friday night.

Naturally it was hard for me to keep my mouth shut about the event, but I'm glad I did because it made the moment even greater, especially when Lachlan briefly buggered the proposal part up. It still ended up being romantic as hell.

"This is so exciting," my mum squeals. I don't think I've seen her squeal in a long time. She places her glass on the coffee table and claps her hands together, her bracelets jangling. "Have you given any thought to where the wedding is going to be? When? Oh and the dress. Kayla, darling, you're going to look so beautiful."

I want to keep the grin on my face. I really do. But it's starting to falter.

Move on, move on, move on.

The memories of my mother and Miranda going dress shopping. How long they took—months—before they found the perfect one. How Miranda squirreled that dress home, hiding it in the closet and forbidding me to look at it.

I kept my word. I did. And on our wedding day, she really did take my breath away.

I wish that memory could be pure. I wish that I could grieve like any normal man would. Feel the sorrow and not the shame.

But all I feel is shame. All I feel is shame.

All my fault.

The thought races through my head, lightning on the brain.

All my fault.

I close my eyes and breathe in slowly through my nose, remembering what my therapist had taught me.

Move on, move on, move on.

It wasn't my fault.

"Brigs?" I hear my father say, and I open my eyes to see him peering at me curiously. He gives me a quick, encouraging smile. "Are you all right?" He says this in a low, hushed voice, and for that I'm grateful. My mother and Kayla are talking wedding plans, and they haven't noticed.

Lachlan, on the other hand, is watching me. He knows my triggers just as I know his. But while we can drink alcohol-free champagne for his sake, we can't ignore fucking life for mine. We can't pretend that love and marriage and babies don't happen, just because all of mine were taken away.

All my fault.

I exhale and paste on a smile. "I'm fine," I say to my father. "Guess I'm a wee bit stressed about classes tomorrow. This will be the first real week of school. The first one never counts for anything. Everyone's lost or hung over."

He gives a little laugh. "Yes, I remember those days." He finishes the champagne and checks his watch, managing to spill leftover droplets on the carpet as he turns his wrist. "What time is your flight tonight?"

"Ten p.m.," I tell him. "I should probably go upstairs and make sure I have everything."

I make for the stairs as Lachlan calls after me, "I'll drive you to the airport."

"No worries," I say. I can tell from the intensity in his eyes that he wants to talk. And by that, he wants *me* to talk. The last year, leading up to my new job at Kings College and the move to London, Lachlan was on me to make sure I was handling things, that I was doing okay. Maybe it's because I helped him get help for his drug and alcohol addiction, maybe he's just more aware of me in general, as a brother and as a friend.

Our relationship has always been a bit strained and rocky, but at least now he's one of the few people I can count on.

"It's not a problem," he says gruffly, the Lachlan brand of tough love. "I'll drop Kayla off at home, then take you over."

I exhale and nod. "Sure, thank you."

I quickly go upstairs and make sure my overnight bag is in order. When I'm in Scotland I usually stay in my old room at my parents. It makes me feel terribly old, staring down at my old bed, let alone trying to sleep in it, but there's something comforting about it, too.

My flat in Edinburgh city is being rented at the moment, so there's no staying there. Eventually I'll probably sell it. I accepted my position as professor of film studies at the university with a grain of salt and with no real long-term commitment. I'm renting a nice flat in the Marylebone area now, but until I feel like this job is solid and I'm in for the long haul, I'm treating my new life with delicate hands.

"How is Winter?" Lachlan asks me later after I've said my goodbyes to my parents and Kayla, and we're in his Range Rover, lights flashing past on the A-90.

"He's a handful," I tell him, tapping my fingers along the edge of the door. "And a right bugger sometimes. And I'm pretty sure my neighbors will file a complaint when he barks again in the middle of the night."

"He's not even a year old yet," Lachlan says. "Give it time. He's still a puppy."

"Aye. He's a shitting machine is what he is."

Lachlan's a dog expert and a dog rescuer. When he's not being a hotshot rugby player, he operates a rescue shelter for dogs, especially pit bulls, and tries to build awareness for them. Kayla works for him, and so far the organization – Ruff Love – has been doing really well. He's the reason why I adopted Winter to begin with. I found him as a puppy last Christmas during a snowstorm by our grandpa's house in Aberdeen, hiding out in the neighbor's barn. When the neighbors wouldn't claim the dog, it was either I take the white fluff ball in or Lachlan would take him to his shelter. The bloody dog grew on me, I guess, and now he's a royal pain in the arse who looks like he strolled in off the set of *Game of Thrones*. Still, life would be pretty boring without him, even though I have to hire a dog walker to deal with his excess energy when I'm at school.

"You know," Lachlan says quietly after a few moments. "If any of this gets difficult for you...you can just tell me to shut up. I'll understand."

I glance at him, his face half-covered by shadows. "If what gets difficult?"

He clears his throat and gives me an expectant look. "You know. Kayla and I. Getting married. I know it can't be easy... you and Miranda..."

I ignore the icy grip in my chest and try to relax my shoulders. "She's dead, Lachlan. There is no use pretending otherwise and no point in dancing around it." I look back out the window, getting lost in the darkness and the beams of passing headlights. "Life is always going to go on, that's what I've learned, and I'm making peace with it. Just because some things ended for me doesn't mean they end for everyone else. You're going to marry Kayla, and the wedding is going to be beautiful. After that, I'm sure she'll pop out some giant beast-like children. In no way am I not going to want to talk about it, be there for you, and enjoy it. Life goes on, and so will I. And so I do. Your life and love and happiness isn't going to stop because of the things I lost. Neither Miranda or Hamish would have wanted that."

Silence fills the car, and I can feel him staring at me in that unnerving way of his. I don't turn my head. I just let my words be.

"But it's not just that," he says cautiously. "I can see it in your eyes, Brigs. I always have. You're haunted. And it's not by sadness or sorrow. And it's not by Miranda or Hamish. You're haunted by yourself. When will you finally tell me... why? What really happened?"

I swallow hard.

Move on, move on.

Headlights. Street lamps. Everything is growing brighter. The airport is close.

"Lachlan, I liked you better when you didn't talk so much," I tell him, keep my eyes focused on those lights. I make a point of counting them as they zip past. I make a point of not thinking about his question.

I hear him scratch his beard in thought.

"I don't get any complaints from Kayla," he says.

I roll my eyes, happy to have something else to latch on to. "You couldn't do any wrong in that woman's eyes. That's love, mate. And honestly, I'm truly happy you have it. You deserve love most of all."

A few moments pass. "You know," he says, "we're not going to have any."

I glance at him. "Have any what?"

"Kids," he says. He shakes his head. "We discussed it, but…she's not sold on the idea and to be honest, neither am I. A kid with my genes…isn't very fair."

I have to say, I'm surprised to hear Lachlan say this, only because of the intensity of his love for Kayla. On the other hand, I'm not surprised to hear her stance on it. Kayla has all the maternal instincts of a rattlesnake. I mean that in the nicest way.

"Well, that's too bad," I tell him, "because genes or no genes, I think you'd make a wonderful father. A far better one than I ever was, that's for sure." I sigh, pinching my eyes shut for a moment. When I open them, we're pulling up to the airport. "But you do what is right for you. If you don't want them, don't have them. The last thing the world needs is another child that isn't wanted. You and Kayla have your dogs and each other and very busy lives. It's enough. Believe me."

"I'm pretty sure Jessica is going to lose her mind when she finds out," Lachlan says, calling our mother by her name as he usually does. He pulls the car up to the Departures curb. "I'm her last chance at grandchildren."

"She had a grandchild," I snap, the words pouring out like poison. My blood thumps loudly in my ears. "His name was Hamish."

Images of Hamish fly past me. Ice blue eyes, reddish hair. A big smile. Always asking, "Why? Why dada?" He was only two when he was taken from me. He would be nearly six years old now. I always looked forward to him getting into school. I knew his curiosity would lead him to bigger and better things. Though I wasn't in love with Miranda at the end, I was in love with my boy. And even when I had the selfish nerve of dreaming of a different life for myself, he was always my first concern.

It wasn't supposed to happen that way.

Lachlan is staring at me, wide-eyed, remorse wrinkling his brow. "Brigs," he says, voice croaking. "I'm sorry. I'm sorry, I didn't mean it."

I quickly shake my head, trying to get the anger out of me. "It's fine. *I'm* sorry. I just…I know what you meant. It's been a long day and I just need to go home and get some sleep."

He nods, frowning in shame. "I get it."

I exhale loudly and then try to perk up. "Well, time to go through security hell. Thanks for the ride, Lachlan." I reach over into the backseat and grab my bag before getting out of the car.

"Brigs," he says again before I close the door, leaning across the seat to look at me. "Seriously. Take care of yourself in London. If you need anything for any reason, just call me."

The fist in my chest loosens. I'm a grown man. I wish he didn't worry so much about me. I wish I didn't feel like I needed it.

I give him a wave and go on my way.

...

All the radio announcers keep yammering on about is how beautiful the weekend was, a real extended summer with record-breaking temperatures and searing sunshine. Of course it happens on the weekend I'm in Scotland, and of course as I get ready for this Monday, it's pissing buckets outside.

I eye myself in the hallway mirror and give myself a discerning once-over. I'm wearing a suit today, steel grey, light grey shirt underneath, no tie. Last week was all about making the students feel comfortable—I was in dress shirts and jeans, T-shirts and trousers, but this week is about cracking down. Some of the students in my classes are my age, so I've got to at least look like I mean business, even though I've got dog hair on my shoulders.

My gaze travels to Winter sitting on the floor by the couch, thumping his tail when we make eye contact, and back to the mirror. He's calm for now, but when I leave I know he's going to treat my flat like a gymnasium. Thank god for Shelly, my dog walker. She was watching him over the weekend too and fusses over him like an unruly child.

I smooth my hair back and peer at the grey strands at my temples. I'm wearing it fairly short these days. Thankfully I've put all my weight back on, so I don't look like the weakling I did before. I've been at the gym most mornings, working hard all summer to get back into shape, and it's finally paying off.

After the accident and my consequent meltdown (or, as my old job called it before they let me go, my "mental diversion," as if what happened to me could be so neatly explained, like a detour on the road), I wasn't eating. I wasn't living. It wasn't until I found the courage to see a doctor, to get help and finally stay with it, that I crawled out of the ashes.

I'd like to say it all feels like a blur to me, the years at the bottom of the spiral, the world around me bleak, guilt and hatred sticking to me like tar. But I remember it all vividly. In horrible, exquisite detail. Maybe that's my punishment, my shackles for my crimes.

I knew that falling in love was a crime.

I deserve all the punishment I can get.

And what's worst of all is how on some nights, the darkest ones when I feel how alone I really am, how badly my choices have tipped the world on its axis, I think about her.

Not Miranda.

I think about *her.*

Natasha.

I think about the reason my judgement became skewed, the reason why I chose my own personal happiness over my family's. I think about the first time I really fell in love. It wasn't a stumble into comfort and complacency, like it had been with Miranda. It was cliff-jumping without a parachute, bungee jumping with no cord. I knew, *I knew*, the moment I laid my eyes on Natasha, that I was gone and there wasn't a single thing to hold me in place.

You'd think that memories of love would feel just like the real thing, but these memories never feel anything like love. Love is good. Love is kind. Patient. Pure.

So they say.

Our love was a mistake from the start. A beautiful, life-rendering mistake.

Even if I did let myself remember—feel—what it was like to look into her eyes, to hear those words she once so softly whispered, it would do me no good. That love destroyed so much. It destroyed me and I let it willingly tear me apart. And then I destroyed every last good thing in my life.

Memories of love are a poison.

My therapist told me that I have to embrace it. Acknowledge that people fall in love all the time with people they aren't supposed to, that I was swept away and lost control for once in my life, and no matter what, I can't blame myself for Miranda and Hamish's death. It was bad timing. It was an accident. People get divorced every day and it doesn't end that way.

It's just hard to believe that when none of it would have happened if I hadn't let myself fall in love with another woman. It wouldn't have happened had I not told Miranda that night that I wanted a divorce. They'd still be alive. And I wouldn't be the archaic ruins of a man.

And Natasha is gone, even if the memories remain. In my deep, near suicidal grief, I told her that we had been a mistake and this was our punishment. I told her I never wanted to see her again.

It's been four years now. She listened.

I sigh and observe my expression. I do seem haunted, as Lachlan says. My eyes seem colder, iceberg blue, the dark shadows underneath. Lachlan doesn't know the truth though, only my therapist does. Natasha is a secret, a lie, to everyone else.

I paste on a smile that looks more like a wolf's grin, straighten my shoulders, and walk out the door, umbrella and briefcase in hand.

My flat is on Baker Street, right across from the Sherlock Holmes Museum. In fact, when I'm particularly despondent, I spend a few hours just watching the tourists lining up to go inside. One of the reasons I picked the flat was the novelty of this. Growing up, I was a huge fan of Holmes, as well as anything Sir Arthur Conan Doyle cooked up. I'm also quite fond of the pub next door. It's a great place to pick up women, and if they've just come from the museum, then you know they at least have some kind of a brain.

Not that I've shared more than a few drinks with these girls—I'm mainly there for the company. Then they go on their merry drunk way and I'm ever the gentleman, the man she'll text her friends about and say "Scottish men are so well-mannered. He bought me a drink and didn't expect anything." Though sometimes it does end in the bedroom. The truth is, I'm not ready for dating. I'm not ready for relationships. I'm barely ready for this job.

But you are ready, I tell myself as I dodge the rain and head down into the tube, taking the passageway across to my line. This week I will set the goals for the semester; this week I'll let the students know what to expect. This week I'll finally start working on my book: *The Tragic Clowns: Comedic Performance in Early American Cinema.*

As my thoughts jumble together, I realize the train is about to close its doors. I run half-heartedly toward it, then stop dead in my tracks.

There is a woman on the train, her back to the closing doors.

I can only see her from the shoulders up.

Her hair is thick, half-wet, honey blonde, and trailing down her back.

There's nothing about this girl that says I should recognize her. Know her.

Yet somehow I do.

Maybe not as a blonde, but I swear I do.

I walk right up to the doors as the train pulls away, staring like a madman as it roars down into the dark tunnel, willing the woman to turn her head even a little bit. But I never see her face, and then she's gone, and I'm standing on the edge of the platform, left behind.

"Next train shouldn't be long," a man says from behind me, strolling past with a newspaper in his hand.

"Aye," I say absently. I run my hand over my head, shaking sense into myself.

It wasn't her.

How can you know someone by the back of their head?

Because you spent months memorizing every inch of her that you couldn't touch, I think. *Your eyes did what your hands and mouth and dick couldn't.*

I exhale and stroll away from the edge. The last thing I need is to start the week like this, looking for ghosts where there aren't any.

I wait for the next train, get off at Charing Cross as usual, and walk to school.

Chapter Two

NATASHA

Edinburgh

Four Years Ago

"Natasha, do you have a moment? There's a Brigs McGregor here to see you."

"Brigs who?" I ask into the phone. "Is that a first name?" The line crackles and I can barely hear my supervisor Margaret. That's what they get for sticking me in a closet upstairs and calling it an office. Obviously they were so eager to have an intern here, busting her ass and working for free, that they'd make an office out of anything. I'm grateful I don't have to type on a toilet.

"Just come downstairs," Margaret says before hanging up the phone.

I sigh and blow a wayward strand of hair out of my eyes. I'm piled knee-deep in script submissions which should have been the highlight of this job, but since ninety percent of these submissions for the short film festival suck, my days have become exceedingly tedious.

When I first applied for the internship for the Edinburgh Short Film Festival, I thought it would be a good way to get extra experience before heading into my final year of my

Master's degree, especially as I'm targeting my thesis toward the influence of festivals on feature films. At least, I think that's my thesis. I also thought getting out of London for the summer and checking out Edinburgh would be a nice change of pace, especially from all the dickheads I keep hanging around with at school.

And while I guess those things are true—I am getting good material for my thesis, and I am loving Edinburgh—I didn't expect to be the company's little slave girl. Not that I'm little, not with these hips and ass that can barely fit in this damn closet-cum-office, but I'm literally scrambling around from eight in the morning to seven at night, and sometimes I think I'm running the whole show by myself. For example, now they've put me on script submissions for the contest they have going (the winning script gets all the equipment to shoot it), and they expect me to pick the winner. While I'm flattered with the responsibility, I'm not sure it should fall into my hands.

I'm also not surprised there's some man here to see me, because any time a filmmaker comes in with a proposal or a question or wanting to work with us somehow, they always shuffle them off to see me. I've only been here for three weeks and I'm supposed to act like I know everything.

Luckily, I'm pretty good at acting. I mean, at least back in Los Angeles I was.

I get up and leave the office, walking down the narrow hallway with its rock walls and wood floors, before going down the stairs to the main level and reception where Margaret is busy typing on her computer. She stops her flying fingers and nods at the seats by the door, below the range of shitty movie posters.

"This is Professor McGregor from the University of Edinburgh," she says before going back to work.

A man stands up from the seats and smiles at me.

He's tall and broad-shouldered, in a black dress shirt and jeans.

Handsome as hell, all cut jaw with the right amount of stubble, high cheekbones and piercing, pale blue eyes.

The kind of handsome that depletes your brain cells.

"Hello," he says, walking toward me with his hand out.

His smile is blindingly white and absolutely devilish.

"Brigs," he says to me as I place my hand in his.

His grip is warm and strong.

"You must be Natasha," he continues.

Right. This is the part where I speak.

"Y-yes," I stammer, and immediately curse myself for sounding less than poised. "Sorry, I was distracted by...Brigs, you say? That's an interesting name."

That's an interesting name? Man, I'm winning today.

But he laughs and that smile grows wider.

"Yes, well my parents obviously had high hopes for me. Listen, can I have a minute of your time?"

I glance over at Margaret. "Sure. Margaret, is there a room free?"

She shakes her head, not looking up. Usually I have meetings in any of the other offices.

"Okay, well then." I give Brigs an apologetic look. "Follow me. We'll have to use my office, and I apologize ahead of time because it's literally a closet. They keep me like Rapunzel up there."

I walk down the hall and up the stairs, shooting him a glance over my shoulder to make sure he's following. I expect him to be looking at my ass because it's pretty much in his face, and it's the largest thing in the building, but instead he's looking right at me, as if he was expecting to meet my eyes.

"Here we are," I tell him when we reach the top, stepping inside my office and squeezing between the edge of the desk and the wall. I sit down on my chair with a sigh.

"Wow, you weren't kidding," he says, hunched over so his head doesn't smash into the ceiling. "Is there maybe a bucket I could sit on?"

I jerk my head at the stool that's currently covered by scripts. "If you want to pass me those screenplays."

He starts piling them on my desk, and takes a seat, long legs splayed.

I peer at him over the pile and give him my most charming smile. I really wish I had bothered to look at myself in the mirror before meeting him. I probably have kale in my teeth.

"So, how can I help you Professor McGregor?"

"Brigs." That smile again.

"Brigs," I say, nodding. "Oh, and let me preface our conversation by letting you know I am an intern, and I've only been here three weeks and I don't know what I'm doing."

"An intern?" he asks, rubbing his hand along his jaw. "Not from my program."

"I go to school in London."

"Kings College?"

"No, I wish. I couldn't afford it."

"Ah, international student fees. Are you Canadian? American?"

"You mean I don't sound British?" I joke. "I'm American. And yeah, the fees were too much, even though I have a French passport from my father's side, though that only went through this year. Anyway, I'm rambling. Sorry. I go to Met for film. It was *slightly* cheaper."

He nods. "Fine school."

"That's a very diplomatic teacher answer."

"And I'm a diplomatic teacher."

God, to have a student-teacher affair with him. But I'm twenty-five and he looks like he's in his early to mid-thirties, so it wouldn't be all that scandalous and...

My thoughts trail off when I catch sight of his wedding ring for the first time.

Oh.

Well, that figures.

Still, I can stare at him, married or not.

"So, what brings you here?" I manage to say.

"Well, it's funny," he says, running his hand through his mahogany hair. "I came here for one reason, and now I have two."

I raise my eyebrows. "Okay."

"One reason is that our program at school has trouble competing with the bigwigs down in London, so we decided that perhaps sponsorship of the film festival would give us the right exposure at the right place. In the end, there can only be so many winners, and when the festival is over and the failed filmmakers want to quit, that's when we want to steal them, take advantage of their low self-esteem, and bring them into our program."

I purse my lips. "That's a very pessimistic way of looking at things."

"I'm a realist," he says brightly.

"An opportunist."

"Same thing."

Well, we could actually use some more sponsors. "All right, well I'll have to run this past Margaret and Ted, but I think this is something we'd like to work with you on. What's the other thing?"

"You come work for me."

"Excuse me?"

He looks around the closet office, squinting his eyes at a wet spot on the ceiling where it leaks when it rains (and it rains all the time. I actually have a bucket just for that). "You seem like a bright girl. I'm starting to write my book and I need a research assistant."

"You're an author?"

"No, not yet," he says, looking away briefly. "But that's what professors do in their spare time, you know. Academic papers, journals. Always writing. Honestly, I'm feeling the pressure, but I can't do it on my own. I'm such a slow writer to begin with, and anything extra bogs me down."

"What's your book about?"

"Tragic clowns. Buster Keaton, Charlie Chaplin. Their performances in early cinema."

Could this man be any more perfect? I'm freaking obsessed with Keaton, Chaplin, Laurel and Hardy, Harold Lloyd, all of them, ever since my father got me watching them when I was little. Shit, it's tempting. Really tempting. But Professor Blue Eyes is barking up the wrong tree.

"I'm flattered, I think," I tell him, "but there's no way I could handle two jobs. I literally work here all day long. The intern life. No breaks, no fun."

"You'll only have to work a few hours a day, and if you want more work, that's fine too. I'll pay you forty pounds an hour."

Forty pounds an hour? To do research on Buster Keaton?

It's like a real dream job landed in my lap. And a job at that, not a payless internship.

But I can't exactly leave the film fest high and dry either.

"Can I talk it over with the people here?" I ask him. "Maybe we can work something out."

"Of course," he says, giving me a sly smile, like he already knows I'll be working for him. He stands up and puts his business card on the pile of scripts. "When you have an answer about both questions, give me a call." He peers down at me with a tilt of his head. "It was nice meeting you, Natasha."

Then he's ducking out the door, and he's gone.

Chapter Three

NATASHA

London, England

Present Day

I wake up with that uneasy feeling. You know, the one that tells you your alarm didn't go off like it should have this morning and you're totally fucked.

I open one eye and blink at the ceiling. The light in the room seems a bit off, and I can hear the shower running next door along with 90s gangster rap, which means Melissa is already up. I'm usually out the door way before she is.

I roll over and pick up my phone.

9:50 a.m.

SHIT.

My first class starts at eleven, and I'm all the way out at Wembley.

I leap out of bed, throwing the blankets aside, and quickly search my room for something to wear. I pick up a pair of jeans, but yesterday I spilled tomato sauce all over them when Melissa and I went to the football match. Which makes me think I didn't take a shower when we got home last night, and there's no way I'm showing up for Professor Irving's class smelling like beer and meat pie.

I throw on my robe and hurry out into the hall, pounding on the bathroom door.

"I overslept!" I yell. "How long are you going to be?"

For a second I don't think she can hear me over the blaring of R. Kelly, but then the water turns off and she yells back, "Give me a minute!"

I wait until the door opens and she appears, face flushed from the shower, hair wrapped up in a towel. "I was wondering if you were ever going to wake up," she says. "Here, it's all yours."

"You could have tried to wake me up," I tell her. "You know I have class at eleven."

She rolls her eyes. "Who am I, your mother?" Then she sashays back to her room.

I know she's got a point, but still. Sometimes I think Melissa wants me to fail just so I'll be at her level. She says I care far too much about school, but after everything I've been through, I have no choice but to throw myself into the program. I was gone for nearly four years, and aside from a few credits here and there, I basically have to start my master's degree all over again. The degree at King's College is modeled differently than it was at Met, as well. Meanwhile, Melissa didn't even go to her classes last week because she was at the bars off-campus, searching for prey.

I jump into the shower, washing my hair and conditioning at record speed. Even if Melissa didn't go to her classes, I went to mine, and I learned what a pain in the ass it's going to be to try and get back on track. What if there was no point in coming to King's College? What if I should have stayed in France with my father and just left my education as it was? The fact that I have to do everything over is both disheartening and staggering.

Breathe, I remind myself, closing my eyes and taking a moment to let the water run down my back. My panic attacks are fewer and fewer these days, but I know one has been creeping up on me, just waiting for me to break down.

Oh, that inevitable breakdown.

That's the price you pay for trying to come back to life.

Somehow I manage to shake it out of me and hop out of the shower. I can't even be bothered with makeup. There's just no time. I'm Professor Irving's teaching assistant for Film 100, and even though it pains me to look like a chump in front of a hundred students, I fear my professor's wrath even more. Last week he kicked a student out just for looking at his phone.

"Want some tea?" Melissa asks from the kitchen as I hurry to my room and start throwing things around, looking for a pair of pants that don't have some kind of stain on them. I'd like to say I wasn't this disorganized or messy before the incident, but that would be a total lie. I'm twenty-nine years old and I've only slipped backward.

"No time!" I yell, holding up a skirt that might do if I'd started going to the gym regularly like I promised myself I would. The one good thing about recuperating in France was that I'd lost some weight I needed to lose. Even so, I still have hips and ass for days, and now I have a little belly that wasn't there before. I blame all the meat pies I've scarfed down since moving back to London.

I pull the skirt on anyway, throw on my bra, a light knit sweater, and a raincoat. It's pouring outside and I have to walk a while to get to the tube. Then I run into the kitchen and grab a banana while Melissa sits at the table. She dumps artificial sweetener into her tea, swirling it around and around with her spoon.

"Aren't you going to class?" I ask her. "What do you even have?"

"Eh," she says. "Some class about analyzing film comedy or something."

"Who's teaching it?"

She shrugs and slurps her tea. "I don't know. Someone."

I frown at her. Melissa is a very smart girl, which is probably why it bugs me so much that she's so lackluster about school. She barely goes and she still gets good grades. She's not even getting her master's degree for any other reason than to appease her parents. What she really wants to do—what she does—is acting. I grew up with a mother who was obsessed with it and stardom the same way Melissa is, and I know how it all ends. Even I did my fair share of it when I was growing up in LA, but that lifestyle wasn't for me.

Melissa and my mother are in love with the idea of fame, the idea of being wanted and adored and validated, but not the reality of being an actor. Maybe that's why when I first met Melissa six years ago, we hit it off. She reminded me of my mother, the very person I escaped LA from. How is that for irony? Come all the way to England and then meet pretty much the exact same person you were trying to run away from.

When I first met Melissa, I had gone with my undergrad class to a film set she was working on as a stand-in. We'd got to talking, clicked, and the rest was history. I guess I liked Melissa because even though she was as vain and self-obsessed as my mother—always taking selfies, posting about how much more talented she is than other actresses and that she deserved so much more—she was also a lot of fun, and I needed some of that in my life. She also looked up to me for some reason, maybe because I was a bit older or because I grew up in LA. When she found out I was going to school for film, she wanted to do the same thing. Of course she one-upped me, and by the time I was in the first year of my master's at the Met film school, she was starting her undergrad at King's College—a much better school.

Still, I found it flattering that she wanted to emulate me, and she ended up being a true friend through thick and thin. She hadn't really approved of what I was doing with Brigs, even though she met Brigs only once, but she was by my side after the incident and during my breakdown. When I moved to France to be with my father to get my head on straight and piece my heart back together, we'd lost touch, but as soon as I found my strength to step back into London in May, we reconnected. And when her last roommate moved out, I moved in.

Melissa eyes me like she can hear my thoughts. "Don't worry about me. I'm going. Besides, I haven't seen what guys are in my classes yet. Maybe I'll luck out and get someone with a hot arse."

"Maybe your teacher has a hot *arse*," I tell her, grabbing my bag from the back of a chair. "Text me when you're done with your mystery class and I'll meet you."

She waves goodbye and I run out of the building. The rain has let up for a moment, but it doesn't matter much since my hair is still wet from the shower. Ever since I died it honey blonde, I swear it's gotten thicker somehow.

As I hurry to the tube station at Wembley (we have a view of Wembley stadium from our balcony, which is great for reminding you about all the concerts you can't afford to go to), my mind flits back to something it shouldn't.

Him.

Brigs.

All because I said her teacher might have a hot arse.

Because, fuck, did Brigs ever have a hot *arse*. It's like he was born to do lunges.

"Stop thinking about him," I tell myself. Out loud. Because I'm crazy like that. Luckily there's no one around to hear me, and honestly that would be the least of my problems if my train of thought continues. Brigs is a trigger. He was once the man I loved more than anything in the world. But he was also the man who would never be mine. There was that beautiful, brief period where I thought we had a chance. We were so close to being together, to putting an end to the guilt. Then it all fell apart.

And by falling apart, I mean his life imploded and I was sucked into the blast.

It was my fault.

It was our fault.

And I'll never stop blaming myself for what happened. For what happened to them, and what I did to him.

If I didn't exist, if I had never met Brigs and fallen for him the same way he fell for me, his wife and child would still be alive.

My love killed.

My love ruined that man's life.

I'm shocked to find a tear rolling down my cheek. I wish I could blame it on the rain like the song says, but I can't. I haven't cried over Brigs, over the incident, in months. It's what my old doctor would have called progress. And this tear is what my father would have called "humanity."

"Embrace your humanity, Tasha," he would say to me. "For if you didn't cry, your soul would never heal."

It hasn't healed, and I don't think it ever will. But I don't think crying has anything to do with it. It's just that there are some things in life that you can't walk away from.

But I'm trying. I'm trying.

One foot in front of the other.

Starting over.

As long as I keep focused on the future and not the past, maybe, maybe I can come out of it. This is a new life, a better life. I'm even going to a better school now: Kings College. If I can just keep moving forward, maybe then my soul will have a chance.

I get on the train and head to school.

...

Well that was a fun class, said no one ever, I think to myself, getting out of my seat. The lecture hall is absolutely crammed with students leaving, and I have a feeling that myself and the other two TAs, Devon and Tabitha, will be expected to stay behind and talk to Professor Irving.

The man is such a chauvinistic piece of shit. With his balding head covered in liver spots and the permanent scowl etched upon his wrinkled face, he's the kind of teacher that obviously just crawled out of the stone age. Even though all we had to do during this lecture is listen to him and watch the film along with all the undergrads, the sexist remarks he made to me and Tabitha at the start of the hour were uncalled for. He told me if I want the students to respect me, I shouldn't come to class like a slob. He said the same thing to Tabitha too, even though the woman is wearing a damn pantsuit. I think he said it because Tabitha is borderline obese, and he knows he'd get into some major shit if he commented on that.

Meanwhile, Devon with his penis and his nonexistent chin gets all the praise and glory, just for knowing a few answers.

"What are you still doing here?" Professor Irving says as he spots us standing around. He waves his hands at us. "Go on with your day. I'll email you about the tutorials later."

I turn around, happy to get the fuck out of there, when he says, "Wait, you. The girl who had a break."

I stop and take a deep breath. How did he know about that?

Tabitha shoots me a sympathetic glance, while No Chin Devon looks a bit butthurt that he didn't get called on.

I slowly turn around and give Professor Irving a big smile. "Yes, sir?"

He narrows his eyes at me, raising his chin in appraisal. It's not a good appraisal. "You did take a break, did you not?"

I nod, rubbing my lips together. "I did. Four years."

"And why was that?"

I have a prepared answer for this. It's only half true. "I went to France to be with my father. He was sick."

"I see." He sticks his finger in his ear and wiggles it around. I try not to grimace, keeping the awkward smile plastered on my face. "You went to Met before and completed one year of your Master's. Four years is a long time to mess things up, family or not, don't you think? Do you think you're ready to be back at school, at *this* school in particular?"

My smile falters. "Of course."

He raises his brow. "Good. I just want to make sure we're on the same page here. I expect a lot out of my students and a lot out of my TAs. You see, when I talked about my book, *Iconography in Early Film Texts*, you were the only one who didn't comment. Have you read it?"

Ah, shit. I swallow hard. "No. I haven't yet. I didn't realize it was part of the curriculum."

He chuckles rather nastily. "My dear, when you're assisting my class, you're grading the students. You can't grade them until you know how I think. It's only common sense, don't you think?"

"Yes, sir."

"I suggest when you're done here, you go to the bookstore and pick up a copy. When I see you next, bring it to me. I'll sign it for you. Wouldn't that be a lucky treat?"

Give me a fucking break. But I manage to smile. "Yes, it would. Thank you."

Then I quickly get the hell out of there. I wish my first stop wasn't the bookstore to buy his book, but I know he's going to expect me to read the whole thing before the next class. I stop by the cafeteria to get something for my raging stomach, opting for a goat cheese salad over my usual meat pie and chips, and decide to text Melissa.

Where is your class? Did you make it?

It's room 302. Teacher's not here yet. Maybe I can skip, she texts back.

Stay where you are. How long is it?

It's supposed to be two hours. I hope there's a film.

Cool. I'll meet you in two hours, then. I've got to read a bullshit book in the meantime.

Fun. You deserve a beer after that.

We'll see.

Lo and behold, after I hole up with the book (the crap cost thirty pounds!) in a corner of the library (one of my favorite places), and before my brain starts to bleed from boredom, I think I might need a beer after all. If only the book didn't cut into my beer fund so much.

I head to the third floor just as the classroom doors start opening and people start piling out.

I can see Melissa at the end of the hallway, wide-eyed and walking kind of jerkily toward me like she's just done a line of coke. She's mouthing something to me, but I think it's just, "Oh my god, oh my god."

She probably had a teacher like Professor Irving. So far we aren't having the best luck with teachers this year.

But as she gets closer, hurrying now toward me and shaking her head as if in disbelief, my eyes drift over her shoulder to the classroom.

A man has just stepped out of the door.

Tall.

Broad-shouldered.

Wearing a fine, tailored grey suit.

High cheekbones.

A strong jawline.

And the most haunting blue eyes in the world.

Eyes I never ever thought I'd see again.

I freeze in place, or maybe it's just that my heart stops beating, and I can hear Melissa saying, "Natasha, oh my god, come with me, let's go, you won't believe this, oh my god," as she grabs my arm and tries to haul me away.

But it's too late.

Because those eyes see me.

They see me.

And Professor Blue Eyes looks like he's been hit by a train.

I know the feeling.

It's your heart and soul being smashed to smithereens.

Because of one person.

One look.

"Let's go, let's go, let's go," Melissa says quickly, and I'm turned around as she tugs at me, our eye contact broken.

It. Can't. Be. Him.

It can't.

And yet it is.

I look back over my shoulder and meet his stunned gaze once more.

Brigs McGregor.

The love of my life.

The love that ruined lives.

One step forward and five million steps back.

Chapter Four

BRIGS

London

Present Day

I check my watch. Five minutes until my class starts and I'm still scrambling over the tutorial notes. I made these months ago, but now that I'm here, among the students and in the school, I felt like it has to feel more organic, so I've spent my morning in my office, scrapping everything I was slated to speak about today.

The subject is still the same: analyzing Harold Lloyd's performance in *Safety Last*. But that's the problem with working on things months before you need to. You're often a different person by then. We're all changing, even in the subtlest ways, and now I'm realizing—last minute, as per usual—that I need to make things a bit more dynamic to capture the students' attention. They are grad students, but still, they could have easily chosen another class. In most grad classes, you assign the film for the students to watch on their own, but I want to do things a little differently.

With one minute to spare, I grab my briefcase and head down the hall to the classroom, passing Professor Charles Irving on the way. That man's a real piece of work. He gives me a snide side eye, along with a nod, as if he acknowledges my presence and hates me for it. I guess that happens when you're the new guy at work. And in teaching it's just a little bit worse. Generally, when you have a teaching positon at a prestigious university, you hold on to that for the rest of your career. Turnover is minimal unless you fuck up. Which I did at my last job because of my breakdown. And I'd only been there for two years. Nothing quite like ruining a good thing the moment it's in your hands.

Of course the loss of my job was nothing compared to the loss of everything else.

I heard the man I'm replacing had been here forever, an old but brilliant man with a fondness for hitting on the students until it turned into full-on sexual harassment lawsuits. I'm pretty sure the only reason I got hired is because they wanted new blood, and my uncle Tommy is friends with the department chair, which reminds me I should get in touch with my cousin Keir who said he'd been in London for a few days. It would be nice to have someone to talk to other than Winter and Max, the bartender at the pub.

I take a deep breath outside the classroom door and then stride on in.

I nod at the students, walking over to my desk, throwing my briefcase on top, and taking out my notes. While they're getting settled in their seats, I glance around at them. A few more people here than last week which is what I expected. In a class of twenty students, it's easy to notice absences.

My eyes pause on a girl sitting in the middle. She's staring at me curiously, and the moment I make eye contact with her, her brows raise as if in shock and she quickly looks down at her laptop. She looks strangely familiar, but I can't exactly place her. I guess she kind of looks like every girl. Long dark hair that's been fussed over with a curling iron, a big wide forehead, small eyes, thin lips. She's cute but would be ultimately forgettable if it weren't for the fact that she's eyeing me like she knows me too.

I clear my throat, putting my focus on the rest of the class. "Good afternoon," I tell them. "Hope you all got a chance to get started on *Funny Faces of Celluloid* over the weekend. Anyone catch a good film?"

There's that bloody awful moment where the question hangs over the classroom and I'm afraid no one is going to answer. But one girl, with a red bob and a wide smile, raises her hand. I nod at her.

"The Phoenix cinema was playing a double header of *The 39 Steps* and *The Lady Vanishes*."

I walk around the front of the desk, trying to keep my eyes on the redhead and not the girl who keeps gawking at me. "Some of Hitchcock's earliest work, before he moved stateside. What did you think?"

The redhead beams at me, folding her hands on the desk. "I thought the attention to detail was a bit weak and the actors were stiff, particularly in *The 39 Steps*, but in terms of the cinematography, you could see where Hitchcock got his fondness for shadows and the use of the MacGuffin, as well as comedic timing."

Clearly this girl is a go-getter. "Very true. And your name is?"

"Sandra," she says.

"It's a good observation, Sandra," I tell her, offering her a smile as I lean back against my desk. "*The Lady Vanishes* in particular set the tone for Hitchcock's future films by the use of witty dialogue. However, the film would still be considered a comedy thriller even without the one-liners or any dialogue at all. That's when farce comes in, something we'll be analyzing today as we watch Harold Lloyd in *Safety First*."

Smooth segue, I tell myself, and start asking around the class if anyone has seen it. Surprisingly, a couple hands shoot up and I get them to introduce the film to the class while I go and hit up the computer until the movie is playing on the TV. All the while, I'm trying to place the mystery girl. It's driving me a bit mad.

As *Safety First* starts and a few students start chuckling, I bring out the roster and start going over names. The girl with the big forehead wasn't here last week, that's for sure, and one of my TAs for my undergrad class never showed up either. I check my TAs and see them listed as Ben Holmes, Henry Waters, and Melissa King.

Casually I look back at the girl. She's watching the film now. Maybe she just felt bad because she missed both my classes last week and thought I was going to call her on it.

That must be it. I try and let it drift away from my mind and start going over the next lecture as the movie plays.

When class is over, though, she's the first one to burst up out of her chair and scurry out of the room like she has a fire lit under her arse.

Curious, I follow her out the door and into the hall, seeing her practically run down it, shaking her head and waving her arms at a girl at the end.

A tall girl with long honey blonde hair, who stands out among the passing people, like everyone else is a blur and she's the only thing in focus.

Fair skin, full cheeks, eternally youthful.

And her eyes, those beautiful eyes that used to shine brighter than the stars.

Only now they aren't shining.

They are locked with mine.

Fearful.

She's convinced she's gone mad.

But so have I.

Because how on earth could this be?

To so clearly see a ghost.

Natasha.

My student, Melissa—now I remember where I know her—grabs Natasha by the arm and whirls her away. For a moment our eye contact is broken, and I feel nothing but panic and the hollowness in my chest. I always wondered what I would do if I ever saw Natasha again, and now I'm standing in the middle of a busy hall and she's here.

She's here.

And I am useless, frozen, empty. Because I don't know if I should turn around and get my stuff and lock my office door and pretend I never saw her. Write her off as a ghost from the past, a fading reminder of who I used to be.

Ruined.

But the word fading can never be applied to someone like her.

And I know that I'll never be able to write this one off.

I've seen her, whether I wanted to or not.

The damage is already done.

And so my feet start moving down the hall after Melissa—my TA, my student, god I'm going to have to see a reminder of my past several times a week—and Natasha.

It's probably a mistake.

But I can't help myself.

Natasha looks over her shoulder again and sees me coming closer, a man on a mission with no objective, and she looks like she still doesn't think I'm real. *I'm* not even sure I'm real at this point because I've never acted so on autopilot before with no self control.

"Hey," I call out hoarsely when I'm within touching distance. I'm too afraid to say her name, like if I did it would make her real.

She stops before Melissa does, her friend tugging hard on her arm, but Natasha is standing tall, immovable, a living statue as she turns around to face me.

I'm this close to dropping to my knees. The wind has been knocked out of me, the sight of her a literal gut punch.

My Natasha.

My mouth falls open and I gasp lightly for air, unable to form words.

She doesn't say anything either but her eyes speak volumes as they search mine. It's the same question as mine.

How can this be?

Why?

Finally, somehow, I find the strength to talk. "It's really you," I say softly, my voice ragged as I look her over, trying to memorize her as if I'll never see her again, trying to see the changes the years have passed on to her. Her hair is lighter now but it suits her face, which is beautiful and glowing. She's lost some weight but not too much—she's still very much a woman.

The only major change is in her eyes.

That brightness, that zest for life, that liquid longing for something to surprise her—that's all gone. And in its place is something dark and sad and lost.

I put the shadows in her eyes.

She blinks and tries to smile at me. "Hi," she says unsurely. Her voice is still husky, still makes all the nerves at the back of my neck misfire. "Brigs."

"Professor Brigs," Melissa says, and I briefly tear my eyes away from Natasha to look at her. "I'm in your class."

"Aye, I know," I say to her before looking back at Natasha. I'm grappling for words. What is there to say? Too much. "How are you? I...it's been a long time."

"Four years," Melissa fills in. "Natasha was in France. What were you doing?"

I frown at Melissa, giving her a pointed look. "Do you mind giving us a minute here?"

She raises her brows and looks at Natasha for an answer.

Natasha gives her a quick smile. "It's okay, Mel. I'll text you in a bit."

Melissa looks between the two of us, obviously not believing it's going to be okay. I can't really blame her. It's been four years, and she had to have been there through the aftermath. Bloody hell, I think back to the things I said to Natasha on the phone that night, sick with grief and lashing out at the only person I could blame other than myself.

Finally, Melissa says, "I'll be at Barnaby's getting us our beer." And then she goes, leaving the two of us alone.

"It is you," Natasha says slowly, frowning as she looks me over. "I didn't think you'd be teaching here."

"I didn't think you'd be going here. Are you a student?"

She nods, swallowing thickly. "Yes. Finishing my master's."

She had just started the last year of her master's degree when we broke apart, excited to start on her thesis. I would have thought she'd be more than graduated by now. Maybe working as a teacher already.

"So you were in France for a while?" I ask, trying to learn more, trying to keep her here, talking to me. Trying to pretend that I can do this.

But I can't do this.

Just breathing the same air she breathes hurts me.

I inhale and look down, rubbing my hand on the back of my neck, trying to get stabilized.

"Are you okay?" she asks quietly.

I stare down at her feet. She always said she had clown feet, and I always thought they were beautiful. She's wearing pointed black boots, and I wonder what color her toes are painted. Her toes were nearly a different color every day. I remember trying to write and she'd try and stick her feet in my face to distract me, giggling her head off.

The memory cuts me like a knife.

The memory has a hard time coming to terms with the woman before me.

"I'm fine," I press my hand into my neck, wiggling my jaw back and forth to diffuse the tension. I shake my head once and look up at her, giving her a half-smile. "No. I'm not fine. I can't lie to you."

Though you did once. The last time you ever spoke to her.

"Should I go?" she asks, forehead furrowed. Worried. Prepared to walk.

Let her go.

"No," I say quickly. I straighten up. "No. I'm sorry. This is just...you're the last person I thought I would see today. I just need to process this. That's all. Because...well...it's you. You know? I mean, bloody hell, Natasha."

But maybe she doesn't know what I'm talking about. How I'm feeling. Maybe I'm a fleeting image from her past, dust on a negative. Maybe she hasn't thought of me at all in these four years and I'm just another man she's met on the way.

It can only be for the best, I think.

She nods, her face softening. "I know. I don't know what to say either."

I quickly look behind me at the classroom. Thankfully there isn't a class after. "Do you mind, I need to grab my stuff from the classroom. You'll stay right here? Do you have to be somewhere?"

Her expression becomes pained, torn. But she shakes her head. "No, I'm done for the day."

I give her a grateful smile and move quickly down the hall and back into the empty classroom. I snap up my notes and my computer, shoving them into my briefcase.

Then I stop and place my hands on the desk, leaning against it, and hang my head down. I take in a deep breath through my nose, and when it comes out of my chest it's shaking. My legs are trembling, the world is spinning, spinning, spinning on a terrible axis.

Holy fucking hell.

To rise from the ashes only to have them rain on you from above.

It's her.

Her.

Her.

I try and catch my breath. I know I can't hide in here forever, that she's out there, waiting for me. I need to hold it together, to calm my heart, to ignore the pangs of sorrow, of regret, of guilt, that are trying to rear their mighty heads.

I run my hands over my face and straighten up.

I can do this.

I grab the briefcase and head out into the hallway.

It's empty, save for a short Asian kid shuffling along, texting.

She's gone.

"Natasha?" I call out softly, walking down a few feet and looking around. There's no point in calling out for her again.

She's gone.

Like she was never there at all.

And maybe she wasn't.

Maybe my mind is so battered, so bruised, I conjured her up.

A real life ghost.

A figment of my imagination.

Goddamn it, I'm so bloody fucked up if that's the case, and I wouldn't put it past me.

I don't even know if I'm relieved or disappointed.

All I do know is that for a few seconds, I thought I was looking into her eyes.

They may have been the saddest eyes I've ever seen.

I wonder what she saw in mine.

Chapter Five

BRIGS

Edinburgh

Four Years Ago

A knock at my office door. I grin to myself because I know that knock. Silly, rapid, nonsensical.

She came after all.

"Come in," I say, peering at the door.

It opens and Natasha pokes her head in, smiling broadly.

That smile is better than any bloody drug. I immediately feel the weight on my shoulders lift.

"I have a surprise for you," she says in that adorable, husky voice of hers.

"Well, the fact that you're here when you didn't think you'd make it is enough of a surprise for me," I tell her, though honestly I'm intrigued by what she has to say.

"It turns out Freddie's party was a colossal *bore,*" she says, exaggerating her voice to sound like a high society charmer. "So I thought I'd bring the party here," she says, stepping in the rest of the way and raising her arms. She has a case of brown ale in one hand and Chinese take-out boxes in the other. She raises her chin proudly. "Do I get the award for the best research assistant already or what?"

"You win all the awards," I tell her, grinning as she comes on in and plunks the items on the desk. "I really thought I was in for the long haul here tonight," I tell her. "Though I can't promise you this won't be anything less than boring. Freddie's may have been the better option."

She pulls a chair up to the desk from the other side and sits down, reaching for chopsticks. "Well, you, Professor Blue Eyes, are anything but boring."

I laugh. "I'm sorry, what did you just call me?"

She shoots me a sly grin. "Professor Blue Eyes. Didn't you know it's what everyone calls you here?"

"Oh, that's rubbish," I say dismissively.

"It's true," she protests, grabbing a take-out box and flipping it open. "Whenever someone here asks me what I'm doing, I tell them I'm your research assistant, and they always go, oh Professor Blue Eyes, what a dreamboat."

I narrow my supposedly famous eyes at her. "Bloody hell, stop pulling my leg."

She laughs. "Okay, well maybe I just call you Professor Blue Eyes. In my head. But I promise you, if it's in my head, it's in everyone's head. Girls and guys."

I try to keep smiling but it's hard because, shit, this is flattering. And not in a good way flattering. I'm flattered in a way I shouldn't be. Then again, I've been working with Natasha nearly every day now for a month, and I'm becoming increasingly aware that I'm feeling a lot of things that I shouldn't.

"Sorry, did I embarrass you?" she asks as she shoves noodles into her mouth. She eats with gusto, no restraint, just eating for the pure pleasure of it and enjoying every bite. That gorgeous mouth...

Stop it.

"No, no," I tell her, attempting to snap out of it. I reach for a beer then eye the door. It's open, as it usually is when we're working together. But even though I'm sure what I do in my office is my own business—every professor here seems to have a bottle of Scotch in their desk—I don't want to rock the boat. I've only been here for two years, and people talk.

I get up and close the door. The click of the latch seems awfully loud in the room. I turn around, and she's watching me curiously.

"You want some privacy?" she jokes, but there's something in her voice, a warble that tells me she might be nervous.

I sit back down and raise my beer at her. "I don't want anyone to get on my back about drinking in my office, let alone with my research assistant."

"Why not?" she asks saucily. "Too scandalous?"

I give her a tight smile, ever conscious of my wedding ring. "Something like that." I point my beer at her, and even though I'm starting to question if drinking with Natasha is a good idea, I say, "Now, let's say cheers to a productive Friday night."

She quickly wipes her hands on her jeans, swallows her bite of food, and clinks her beer against mine. "To a wild and crazy night."

But of course things don't get wild and crazy, not with us. We do work, at least for the first two hours—her on her laptop, flipping through books, and me on my computer, typing like a madman as I usually do around her. Having her in my office is the greatest motivator to getting my book done. She's practically a muse.

But eventually, when the both of us have noodles and three beers in our bellies, and I've brought out the bottle of

Scotch from the secret stash in my own desk, the work slows to a crawl.

"So," I say, leaning back in my chair and kicking my feet up on the desk. "You never told me what you were like when you were growing up. High school. That whole thing. Tell me about Natasha."

She takes a sip of Scotch from the bottle and puts it back on the desk. Then she leans back in her chair and puts her feet up on the desk, mirroring me. I can't help but smile.

"I'll tell you my past if you tell me yours," she says, eyeing me slyly.

"Deal."

"Okay," she says, clearing her throat. "I grew up in Los Feliz. That's in Los Angeles. My dad is French, and he married my mother, an American, after I was born. I was actually born in France though, Marseilles, which I got to visit a few years ago. Pretty cool place. But anyway, I know for sure it was a marriage out of necessity cuz my mom got knocked up. I'm pretty sure I'm the last thing she wanted, but anyway. I promise this isn't a sob story. I don't care if I was wanted or not. But I know my dad loved me. He was a cinematographer."

"Ah," I say. It makes sense now.

"Yeah, and he would make me watch so many films when I was younger. Like, so many. All the classics. All Hitchcock, all Preminger. Lots of foreign films, too. He was obsessed with Ingrid Bergman." Her smile fades a bit and her voice drops. "Anyway, he left when I was ten years old. Fell in love with a younger woman. Maybe he was trying to emulate Roberto Rossellini, I don't know. He moved back to France. And my mother became a single mom. She did *not* like that. Her self-esteem problems multiplied, and they were already pretty bad." She shakes her head to herself, her eyes taking on a faraway look. She sighs and grabs the bottle of Scotch. "My mother is quite the character. You'd hate her. Sometimes I think I hate her too, but mainly I feel sorry for her. Which is kind of worse."

"I think I understand that." My relationship with my brother Lachlan has sometimes taken that route.

"You know what my mother used to say to me when I was younger?" she says, leaning in. "She used to say I better not be prettier than her when I'm her age." She rolls her eyes. "I mean, talk about giving me a fucking complex. At the same time, all she would do is praise my looks, along with the daily bomb about how I need to lose weight."

"You don't need to lose weight," I can't help but say. "You're perfect the way you are."

She gives me one of those wry, embarrassed smiles that tells me she doesn't believe it. "Then, at the end of high school I joined the track team and I did start to lose weight. She pushed me into doing modeling, then some acting. The acting was fine, the modeling was a bore, and when track was done and I graduated, the weight started creeping back. I mean, I was never fat. I was pretty much what I am now. But boobs and ass and thunder thighs do not a model make. Nor an actress for that matter, unless you can score a gig on *Mad Men*. No matter what I did, I couldn't please her. When I was thinner, she got jealous, and when I was back to normal, she'd find some way to insinuate that I was fat."

What a witch, I think to myself, feeling protective over her. What I told her was true. I do find her perfect, at least in my eyes. She does have curves and she's not skinny, but her waist is small and her arse is unreal, and her eyes threaten to take me away somewhere. Somewhere new and very beautiful.

Flashes of heat and guilt compete with each other. I take in a deep breath and force my thoughts to behave.

"Did your mother ever remarry?" I ask her.

She starts twirling the Scotch bottle on the desk. "No. But she's tried. She can't be alone, ever, that's her other thing. She always has a man in her life, usually some idiot. When they cheat on her or break up with her, as they invariably do since what man wants to feel second to her narcissism and ego, she moves on to someone else right away. In fact, I don't think I've ever seen her single for more than a few weeks." She sighs, blowing a strand of dark auburn hair out of her face, and stares up at the ceiling. "Man, I wish I smoked."

I tap the desk. "I have a cigar."

She perks up. "Really? Care to split it with me?"

I grin at her. Lachlan gave me a box of cigars on my last birthday, and I usually only smoke them with him or my father on special occasions, though I have a few of them in my desk. It would be nice to share one with her. "You sure?"

"Yeah," she says. "I used to have a few with my dad in Marseilles."

"You sound so cultured," I tell her, opening my drawer. "A woman of the world."

I bring out the box and pick up a couple of them, smelling them and checking for dryness. When I've selected one, I start rummaging for a lighter.

"I got one," she says, reaching into her jeans and pulling out a Zippo. I give her a questioning look and she shrugs, giving me a lazy smile. "A woman of the world should always be prepared."

She tosses it to me, and I catch it with one hand. I smirk proudly at my achievement, glad I didn't fall out of my chair trying to impress her.

"And what else does a woman of the world carry?" I ask her, smoothly flicking on the Zippo and watching the flame dance.

"A notepad and pen, for writing love letters. Or hate mail. Or grocery lists. A mirror because I always have stuff in my teeth." At that she rubs her fingers along her teeth and bares them at me.

"You're good," I tell her.

She continues. "Also floss. For the same reason. And you can use it tie shit together. Gum, because fresh breath, and in case you need to MacGyver yourself out of a situation. Hand cream that smells pretty. A passport in case you fall in love with a foreign man who sweeps you off your feet." She pauses. "And condoms."

I raise my brows. Jesus. I'm both strangely jealous of the idea of her using condoms because it means she's not using them with me, and turned on because...well, now I'm imagining the two of us in a situation that would require one.

"Now, are we going to smoke this thing or not?" she says, straightening up.

I nod, clearing my throat. My cheeks feel hot. "We'll have to take a stroll somewhere. I can get away with some Scotch in my office, but smoking a cigar is something else." I get out of my chair and grab my leather moto jacket. It's late June, but the evenings have been chilly lately. As I put the jacket on, I ask her, "So, what is the Zippo for?"

She wraps a burgundy scarf around her neck that matches her hair and smiles. "In case Professor Blue Eyes wants to smoke a cigar with you."

Fuck.

I'm starting to think I'm in way over my head here.

I swallow uneasily, my throat feeling thick. "Well, I'm glad you're so prepared." I head over to the door and open it for her. "After you."

She sashays out into the hall, flicking her scarf over her shoulder like a bona fide movie star. I can see why her mother might be jealous of her. I can see why anyone would be. How could anyone not be absolutely enamored with her?

I follow her, locking the door behind me, and we head down the halls and out into the Edinburgh night, a light wind making the trees bow. We head to Middle Meadow Walk and stroll down toward the Meadows, pausing underneath a streetlamp as I try to light the cigar without the breeze blowing it away.

Natasha acts as a shield, stepping in as close as she can, and we end up huddling together, trying to get the thing lit.

Her proximity to me is unnerving. I can smell her beyond the tobacco. Coconut shampoo. Sweet. Intoxicating. It makes my heart clench.

I meet her eyes as she looks up through long lashes.

I can feel my pulse in my throat, her gaze completely bewitching me.

We hold each other's eyes and the air between us swirls and spins, a slow tornado changing the pressure until it's hard to ignore. It pulls and pulls, and the magnetism sets my skin on fire.

I don't know what's happening.

But it's never happened to me before.

And it's absolutely terrifying.

The cigar finally lights.

"You're supposed to smoke that thing," she whispers to me, with languid, liquid eyes.

I take a draw, the embers glowing, and she steps back. The smoke billows out, taken by the wind into the dark sky. The thread between us though, that doesn't dissipate. Not with distance. It crackles like a live wire, heavy and taut and so very dangerous.

Miranda's face flashes in my mind. Her laugh, running along the beach in Ibiza with thin, gazelle-like legs.

A warning.

It must show on my face because Natasha asks, "Is it a bad cigar?"

I shake my head and exhale slowly, letting the smoke curl out of my mouth. "Not at all."

I hand it to her, and our fingers brush against each other.

It's electric in a way that can't be ignored.

She holds the cigar like she's been holding one her whole life. Her posture is relaxed, confident, and doesn't at all look like how I feel inside. Frazzled, heart caught in the washing cycle.

But why should she? I know the way she looks at me sometimes, flirtatious and coy with eyes full of secrets, but in the next she's belly-laughing over some crude joke she heard. I'm just a professor, even if I happen to have blue eyes. A man giving her a job.

And I'm married.

I have a son.

I have so much.

So why do I want her to look at me differently?

She passes the cigar back and blows the smoke out the side of her mouth, like a forties film star.

"Very Lauren Bacall," I tell her as we start walking slowly down the pedestrian path, a few people heading the opposite way into town to the bars and nightlife. But we, we're heading to the darkness.

"Bogie and Bacall, they had it all," she says dreamily. "You know, you never talk about your wife."

I cough, the smoke getting momentarily stuck in my throat. "I don't?" I manage to say.

"No," she says. "You don't talk about yourself very often, you know. You'll go on and on about film but nothing about yourself. You're very mysterious, Brigs McGregor."

I roll my eyes. "Frankly I'm the opposite. I guess I don't talk about my life because, well, it's boring."

"What did I tell you earlier?" she says, smacking me on the arm. "You are the opposite of boring. So tell me then. Tell me about your wife. Your parents. Your brother." She pauses. "You talk about your son a lot though, so at least I know that about you. You're a good father."

I give her the same smile she gave me when I told her she was perfect. It's nice of her to say, but I don't believe it.

I inhale deeply and think.

"All right," I say carefully. "I married Miranda when I was twenty-one."

"Wow, that's young. Shotgun wedding like my mom's?"

I shake my head as memories creep on past, most of them unhappy. "No, we only had Hamish three years ago. We met when I was in college. Edinburg University, right here." I gesture back to the school. "Even though we didn't have any classes together, I knew of her. Everyone knew of her. She was the kind of girl that would never give any guy the time of day.

She was a socialite, really. Bred differently. Her parents, the Hardings, they're kind of a big deal around the city. And at the time, my uncle and aunt were here, and they're also part of that scene. We met at one of their parties and somehow I managed to charm her. Still not sure how, really."

"Oh, I can see why," Natasha says, grinning at me. "You have no idea how charming you really are. Which makes you even more charming."

Suddenly, it seems far too hot to be wearing a jacket.

I clear my throat. "Well, I suppose she thought the same. The rest is history."

She stops and studies me. "That's it?"

I stop and stare, passing her the cigar.

This time my finger lingers on hers for maybe a second too long.

God, I wish I had the rest of that Scotch at my disposal. These feelings need to drown.

"What do you mean 'that's it'?"

"You're not going to go on about how wonderful she is, how she's the love of your life? You talk about Hamish that way all the time."

I shouldn't be so floored by how blunt she is, but I am. Or maybe it's not that she's blunt. It's because I don't have the nerve to tell her the whole truth.

Because Miranda isn't the love of my life.

She's just the mother of my child.

And a roommate I've been living with for eleven long years.

"No," I say simply. Even the partial truth is freeing. "I'm not."

She cocks her head, taking a drag. Studying me still, like she's trying to read words written on my face. I wonder what they say. Finally, she just nods and says, "Sorry. I don't mean to pry."

Yes, you do, I think. *And that's what I…*

Bloody hell. I can't even finish my own thoughts without scaring myself.

"It's not a problem," I tell her and start walking again. "As for my parents, they're lovely. Really. My brother and I have more of a strained relationship though. He's adopted, came into my life just after I left high school and put our family through hell. He was a right bastard actually, and I hated him for a long time."

"Why?"

"Well, it seems trite now, but I saw how my parents were with him, giving him the life he never had, and he didn't react well to it. He was a teenager, which didn't help, and eventually he was stealing from them, even me, doing everything he could to get money for crack, meth, whatever it was. Eventually my parents had to kick him out and he was living on the streets. I can't tell you how hard it was to be walking through this city sometimes and see him panhandling. Skinny. On what always seemed to be his last legs. He may have been adopted, but he was still my brother."

"That sounds horrible," she says, shaking her head.

"It was horrible," I say with a sigh, remembering the sorrow and pain Lachlan had caused me like it was yesterday. "But eventually he cleaned himself up, and now he's a lot better. Still drinks too much, and sometimes I wonder if he's abusing some other kinds of drugs. Doesn't talk much."

"Sounds familiar," she says under her breath.

"I swear you'd think we were related in some ways. But now he's starting up an animal rescue shelter and he's a successful rugby player."

"Oh, really?" Her eyes sparkle. "Rugby players are hot. You guys must make quite the sight together."

I resist the urge to roll my eyes. The tattooed beast of a rugby player and the nutty professor. No contest there.

"I've always like the nerds, anyway," she says, passing the cigar back to me, and this time she stops and holds on to it. "There's always more to them underneath."

Shit.

My heart climbs into my throat.

I flash her an awkward smile, trying to play it off. "Are you calling me a nerd?"

She still won't let go of the cigar. Her expression becomes completely serious.

"I'm saying there's a lot more to you underneath."

Her eyes are fixed on mine, and they pull at me, tease me, tempt me, transitioning from want to fear to adoration and back again in a cycle. I'm caught in it, completely mesmerized. Every part of me feels heavier, from my lungs to my legs, like I'm staked to the ground.

This is going to ruin me, isn't it?

The sudden ring of a bicycle bell shatters the heady air between us.

We both break apart in time to see a drunken bicyclist weaving toward us right down the middle, hollering, "Get off the bloody bike path, you wankers!"

I look down to see we were both indeed on the cyclist path.

And now I'm breathless, exhilarated, my pulse running wild at our exchange.

The cigar is in my hand.

I have to do the right thing.

"We should head back," I tell her. "It's getting late and the bicyclists are rampant tonight."

She nods, drawing her lip between her teeth. I really wish she wouldn't do that.

"Okay," she says softly.

Together we turn and head back to the university, back to my office.

I start cleaning up the mess we left with our food and our beers while she slowly puts her laptop and books away.

We work in silence. The vibe of the room has completely changed. Before it was easy and free, and now it's laced with things both said and unsaid, the mahogany bookshelves and dim lighting seeming to push us together.

I keep coming back to that look in her eyes.

The look that said she wanted me.

And whatever I am underneath.

She leaves my office with a small smile and a wave, and I know she feels it too.

The change.

She shuts the door behind her.

I sit back down at my desk.

Finish the Scotch.

And pretend for a moment that I'm not completely screwed.

Chapter Six

NATASHA

London

Present Day

I couldn't do it.

I couldn't stand there and talk to him, look at him, breathe the same air as him.

The moment that Brigs turned around and headed back into the classroom, I did the only thing I knew how to do.

I ran.

I ran down the hall, feeling wild and breathless and aimless, like a trapped animal being set free. I didn't know where to go, only that I couldn't be there with him.

Brigs McGregor.

What stars had to align for that to happen? Two meteors crashing into each other would do it.

But I don't know where to go. I run down the stairs, faster, faster, students staring at me in concern, all the way to the first floor. I duck into the handicapped bathroom, locking the door behind me, and sit on the toilet, head in my hands, my heart dancing with my tonsils.

Breathe, I tell myself, trying to inhale through my nose, but I crave air so much that I'm gasping it in through my mouth, tears burning the corners of my eyes.

Don't panic, don't panic, don't panic.

You're okay.

"How the fuck am I okay?" I cry out loud, my voice bouncing around the cold tiled room.

I try and focus on breathing, getting my lungs full, letting it out.

I'm shaking.

Fucking hell.

Brigs.

He would have come back out into the hall and seen that I'm gone.

The lady vanishes.

I start to feel bad about leaving him like that. But if I've learned anything over the years, it's that I have to protect myself first. I worked really, really hard to get back to London, to get accepted here, to finally pull myself up. I can't let anything or anyone jeopardize that.

And Brigs most certainly would.

He's the reason I fell to begin with.

Shit, shit, shit.

I make fists and press them into my temples.

This isn't a problem I can run away from. Brigs is a professor here. Fuck, he's Melissa's fucking teacher. And I go to this school and will be for the next two years.

Dear god, what if he's my damn teacher next semester? Then what?

It becomes harder to breathe again. I have to force myself to concentrate, to slow my heart rate. I wish I had gotten another refill of Ativan when I had the chance. It's just that I was doing so well. I'm going to need a bucketful to even make it through this day.

I don't know how long I stay in that bathroom, my phone vibrating repeatedly, most likely Melissa wondering where I am and what's happening. I don't look at it. I don't look at anything except my feet and the gross linoleum floor.

My mind keeps tripping over itself, replaying the sight of him.

It hurts, *hurts*, how handsome he still is. More handsome than before. Standing there before me, in that sharp suit, looking every inch the put together professor. Tall, lean, with those shoulders I remember grabbing that one night, digging my nails in when my body and soul went wild with hunger.

The night we almost slept together.

The night he told me he was leaving his wife.

That night that became the last night for us.

How horrible it must have been for him to see me just now.

I ruined his whole life, sent it off the rails.

It crashed and burned.

All because of me.

And that will never ever change. I'll never be able to take anything back and neither will he. We're both doomed to live with our actions, he even more so.

God. The pain cuts deep, to the bottom of my lungs.

Breathe, I tell myself again, and a single tear splashes on the floor.

Eventually, somehow, time passes. The tears stop coming and my heart beats steady and slow. I feel like I've been drugged, the emotions riding me too hard and I've come out exhausted.

I sigh, getting to my feet. My legs ache from sitting for so long.

I check my phone.

Melissa has texted a million times, worried out of her mind. She's at the flat now, with alcohol and the need to talk.

I step into the hallway, conscious that someone might have seen me go in. But the halls are practically empty. Still, in case I run into him again, I don't waste any time getting out of there.

I'm back on the streets of London, the rain having stopped.

I'm back on the tube, crushed against commuters, nobody talking.

I'm back at the flat, going up the stairs instead of waiting for the lift.

Then Melissa is opening the door before I can even unlock it.

"Where the bloody fuck were you?" she cries out, hands flailing all over the place.

I usher myself inside, head down, avoiding her eyes. "I was in the toilet."

"The toilet?" she repeats, while I throw my purse on the kitchen table. She already has the Stoli out, making martinis. "With Professor McGregor?"

"No," I say, sitting down at the table and resting my forehead on it. "I was alone. I didn't...I ran away."

"What? From Professor McGregor?"

I find it funny how she keeps calling him professor. She even did that back then, along with Mr. Married Man

McGregor. The constant reminder of how careless I was being, what a fool I was to fall for someone who wasn't mine.

"Yes," I mumble. "I panicked. I couldn't help it. It seemed he wanted to talk to me, like go somewhere, and I couldn't. I couldn't do it, Mel."

She takes the seat beside me, and I hear her pouring a drink. "Good," she says. "You don't owe him anything. Especially with how he ended it with you."

But I never blamed him for that. He only spoke the truth.

Our love was wrong.

A lie we told ourselves.

And it cost us the world.

As much as it stung to hear it, as much as it made me lose myself, it was well-deserved.

With us, the truth didn't just hurt.

It killed.

"Here," she says, and I look up to see her sliding me a drink. "It's on the house," she jokes. She's the cheapest roommate ever and I feel like I'll somehow have to pay for this in the end.

I take a long sip. It's strong and it burns, but it feels good going down.

After a long pause, I exhale loudly. My shoulders loosen a tad.

"I just can't believe it," I say for the hundredth time.

She brushes her hair back from her face. "Neither can I. It literally took me the whole class to figure out how to tell you. I saw him walk in, and I was like...bloody hell. It can't be. And then I had to look up the class again. Professor McGregor. That's all I saw, and I knew I saw his name before, but we're in Britain. There's a million McGregors here." She takes a sip of her drink. "And you know, he recognized me too. He remembered me. Kept staring at me the whole class, like he was seeing a ghost."

A ghost. That's what his expression said when he saw me in the hall. Like I wasn't really there, that his mind was playing tricks on him.

"And now," she says, "I'm a TA in one of his classes. I'll be working with him closely all year. That's going to be weird."

Something squeezes in my chest. The line "working with him closely" makes my heart burn and I wish it wouldn't.

"That is going to be weird," I repeat quietly. I feel myself sink down into the spiral, the one that robs me of ambition, motivation, and makes me spend days in my room, in the dark, lost in despair.

"Hey," she says, placing her hand on mine and giving it a squeeze. "We're going to get you through this, okay? You suffered for your mistakes enough, and now you're going to move on. You are not your past. He's a teacher at your school—he's not going to pursue you or harass you. You don't ever have to see him again, and if you do, you have no obligation to talk to him. If he doesn't leave you alone, I'll report him."

I give her a dark look. "Don't report him. He's lost enough already."

"I'll report him if he lays a finger on you, if he talks to you or comes after you in any way. I'm serious. I will. You have nothing to worry about. He'll stay away, you'll stay away, and pretty soon things will go back to normal."

But what's normal?

"And in the meantime, I'm going to start dragging you out with me more often and get you liquored up or something, because the past few months you've been here, you haven't hooked up with a single guy. You haven't even flirted with one. You need to get some arse something fierce."

I sigh, not really interested, especially now. "You make it sound so easy."

"It's as easy as you want to make it," she says. "So he's at the school, so what? Does that change anything?"

She stares at me expectantly. I wasn't aware she needed an answer.

"It means I have to see him."

"But you don't have to, and if you see him in the halls, pretend he isn't there. You're his ghost, he should be yours. Keep a wide berth and I'm telling you everything will work out."

Mel isn't usually this optimistic, so while I have a hard time believing her, I'm also grateful for it.

I muster up a smile for her. It's weak, but it's the best I can do.

"Cheers," she says, lifting up her glass. "To going on with your bad-ass self."

I take a deep breath, nod my head, and clink my glass against hers. "To going on."

...

"We will be together, Tasha. I promise."

I promise.

I promise.

Brigs' whispered words float through my dreams, bumping into the fragments of his face.

I reach out to touch them, and they fade.

I slowly open my eyes and stare at my alarm.

I wonder what day it is, what life it is.

Tuesday. I've woken up ten minutes before my alarm.

I exhale and roll onto my back, trying to grab the memories of my dream before they float away.

Brigs, the last time I saw him. In my old flat in London. I lived alone. It was so much nicer. And even though I knew falling for him was wrong, I was happy. Happy in my ignorance, in the naiveté that everything would work out. He was leaving Miranda, finding the courage to leave his unhappy marriage, the strength to choose what he wanted for once.

God, how messed up he was over Hamish. I honestly thought he would stay with her forever because of him, because of how afraid he was of losing his son.

Somewhere along the line though he realized he couldn't live a lie. It wasn't fair to Miranda, to Hamish, to him or to me.

That was the last time I really felt I had hope.

How easily love takes your hand and leads you into the dark.

My alarm goes off on my phone, and I quickly reach over and turn it off.

It's slow going. My mind is foggy from all the vodka I drank with Melissa last night, and I'd be lying if I said I wasn't dragging my feet.

The truth is, the idea of going to school is frightening. I know I should just do as Mel suggested, and if I see him, pretend he's not there. But I'm scared. Scared he'll seek me out. And I'm even more scared that I'll seek him out.

I guess I have reason to be scared, because when I do eventually get ready, I find myself taking more care with my appearance than normal. I'm actually running a brush through my hair, putting on makeup, putting on my cleanest clothes (jeans without tomato sauce, suede booties, and a black v-neck shirt), and standing a little taller.

By the time I get out of the tube and start walking to school, I want to shrink into myself. My eyes are wild, everywhere, searching for him as I approach the stately façade of the main building, my pulse dancing off rhythm.

Somehow I make it to my class with Professor Shipley, whom I really like. Even though the entire time she's going on about gender in war films, I can't help but wonder what it's like to have Brigs there. What's he like at faculty meetings? Do he and Professor Shipley ever have lunch to discuss the students, or perhaps dinner to talk about film? Do they go to the movies together? Even though Professor Shipley is in her forties, she's got this vibe about her, always dressing in capes and long, wide sleeves, her dark hair streaked with grey flowing all the way down to her waist. I could see the two of them hitting it off. If anything, she has to be intrigued by the enigmatic Brigs McGregor.

And then it happens.

Right after class.

I walk down the hall, heading to the bookstore to pick up yet another book I forgot to buy, my mind briefly wondering about the book that Brigs was writing, the one I helped him with.

I've always feared that my mind could conjure up the wrong things, like how thinking about a plane crash while on a plane might cause one, and now I know it's sort of true.

Because I see Brigs walking down the hall in my direction.

He doesn't see me yet, or maybe he's pretending.

His head is held high and he strides forward with easy confidence. He's wearing wire-frame glasses he sometimes uses for reading. A well-tailored navy suit hugs his body, his shirt unbuttoned just enough, no tie. I can see the looks on girls' faces as they pass him by. He stands out—distinguished, quite obviously a professor, but also incredibly, devilishly sexy. None of the other teachers wear suits, except for Professor Irving (though his look like they're made out of a couch). There's just this magnetism about Brigs that turns heads.

He's turning mine right now.

And then he's gone, without our eyes even meeting once.

I'm not sure how I feel about it. I stand there in the middle of the hall feeling relieved at how easy that was. How I saw him again and survived. Didn't collapse into a puddle or lose my head with another panic attack.

And yet, I'm also bereft. Because it feels absolutely wrong to watch this man walk past me and let him go without saying anything, pretending he's a stranger.

A stranger I used to love.

Chapter Seven

BRIGS

It's been days since I've seen Natasha. So long that it feels like a dream.

But on Thursday, when I have the second part of my Analyzing Comedic Film Performance class, I see Melissa again. Proof that the Natasha I saw in the hall on Monday really existed.

I don't say anything to Melissa about her though. I want to, but it doesn't seem like the time or the place, and when class is over, I'm occupied by other students.

When Friday rolls around, however, and I'm in the lecture theatre, teaching Early Cinema to the undergrads, Melissa is front and center. Literally. She and the two other TAs, Ben and Henry, sit in the first row, observing me very carefully. It took me a while to get used to having TAs when I was teaching in Edinburgh, and this is no different. In fact, Melissa seems to be overly attentive, hanging on to my every word, which should be flattering but it's striking me as wrong.

My concern seem justified when class ends and she comes over to me as I'm putting my notes away.

I peer at her over my reading glasses, trying to sound as professional as possible. "Good afternoon, Melissa."

She tilts her head at me, brushes her hair off her shoulder, and smirks. "Nice class. It's going to be a breeze being your assistant this year."

I raise my brow. "I'm glad you think so. I'll try to take it easy on you."

"Oh, you don't have to take it easy on me," she says. "I like it when things are hard."

Was that an innuendo? She didn't say it like one, but still. I think I need to tread cautiously with this one.

I clear my throat and pick up my briefcase. It's taking everything inside me not to ask about Natasha. "Can I help you with anything?" I ask, since she's just standing there staring.

"I was wondering if I could talk to you," she says. "In private."

Is it about Natasha? I want to ask. But it could and most likely is about anything but.

"Sure," I tell her. "Come with me to my office."

We leave the lecture theatre before it starts filling up for the next class and begin a long awkward walk down the hall and up the stairs.

"So," I say, grappling for something to talk about other than what I really want to talk about. "What are your plans for after graduation?"

She laughs, high-pitched, like some Disney princess. "I have no plans at all except to keep on doing what I'm doing."

"And what is that?"

"Acting," she says proudly. "I even had an audition yesterday to be in the new season of Peaky Blinders. Do you watch that show?"

"I do," I say slowly. "So, no plans to use your degree, then?"

"Pfft," she says with a wave of her hand. "This is just to shut my dad and stepmother up."

Well, no wonder she didn't even show up to classes last week. She just needs a passing grade and she's out. Still, a master's degree is a pretty serious commitment for someone who doesn't care. Maybe that's what she wants to talk to me about.

We finally reach my office, and I'd be lying if I wasn't looking for Natasha the entire time we were walking. Still nowhere to be found. I hope to God she's not skipping out on school just to avoid me, but considering all the shit that went down between us at the end, I can't say I'd be surprised.

I put my briefcase on my desk and sit down at my chair, immediately busying myself with the contents so I have something to do. "So, what's on your mind, Melissa?"

"A lot of things," she says, leaning against the desk just enough so that I can see down her top. I immediately avert my eyes, feeling just a tad uncomfortable. "But mainly Natasha."

My head snaps up. "How is she?"

She smirks at me. "Wouldn't you like to know?"

I frown, not wanting to play games with her. I pause and then say, "I haven't seen her in such a long time, and when we last spoke, I'm afraid it didn't end on good terms."

"Well, your wife and child died," she says bluntly.

That was a blow, the icy cold image of Hamish by the pond slicing through my mind.

She continues, oblivious, "I'm sure that would make a man say a lot of things he doesn't mean. But that's kind of my point here. I just wanted you to know that there's no point going after her, no point talking to her. You're in her past and you need to stay there. Frankly, she asked me to ask you to stay away and leave her alone for good."

Her words leave paper cuts on my heart. "I haven't...I haven't contacted her," I tell her, my voice raw.

"But you want to, I can tell. I'm just saying, forget it. She wants nothing to do with you. You should be with someone who doesn't come with a whole pile of baggage." She bites her lip and studies me with sly eyes. "You know what she was doing in France? Having a nervous breakdown. You should have seen her after...well, you know. She couldn't eat, sleep, couldn't even talk. She was a fucking mute for a month. She dropped out of school, dropped out of life. Finally, her father brought her to France where he took care of her."

My stomach churns and I resist the urge to double over.

My Natasha.

Reduced to that.

All because of me.

Melissa continues to look at me, examining my face. I try to keep it as expressionless as possible, but I know she sees the pain there. She likes it.

She traces her finger along the edge of the desk. "You know, Natasha was always a bit unstable anyway. That was part of her charm, wasn't it? Not exactly the type for a professor like you to be involved with."

I breathe in slowly and give her a steady look. "Is that all you wanted to discuss?"

"Yup," she says, straightening up and flashing me a big smile. She might just make it to the movies after all—she's conniving enough. "See you on Monday."

She leaves the room looking awfully proud of herself, sending me an odd smile over her shoulder. I should probably pull out my teacher card and remind her about grading papers or what's ahead for next week, or when she plans to guest lecture, but I don't have the strength.

All of it is being used as I try and process what she said, what happened to my poor Natasha.

I thought I recognized the sadness in Natasha's eyes, that change that happens when you lose yourself. I don't think you ever get every part of you back. She's still missing something.

But so am I.

Closure.

And peace.

I'm not sure I can have one without the other. But I do know there's only one way to get it. I have to get it through Natasha. No matter what Melissa said, no matter how much of it makes sense or doesn't make sense, I can't stay away from her. I can't ignore her. She's a ghost that roams these halls. She's a ghost who roams my heart.

But it doesn't have to stay that way.

I've never really believed that things happen for a reason, and that became even more apparent the night I lost Miranda and Hamish. But this, having her here now, when we've both crawled out of the hole and are teetering on the edge, that can't be for nothing.

We're either here to save each other.

Or one of us is going over.

With that thought, I open my computer and log into the university system. I do a search for Natasha through the student database and come up with her phone number and email address.

I open up my email account, absently noting that my cousin Keir emailed me back, then start to compose a message to Natasha.

I pause, my fingers on the keyboard, but the words refuse to appear.

What do I say? Last time she physically ran away. This time she could see my name and refuse to even open the email.

So then you should write what's true, I tell myself. *If she might not even see it anyway.*

I hate it when I'm right.

In the subject I just put "Please."

Then I type:

Natasha,

I can't explain what it was like to see you again the other day. The only way to describe it is that you gave me hope I hadn't felt in a long time. I have many things I need to say to you, a million ways to apologize, and I can only hope that you'll hear me out. I just want a chance to say these things in person, like you deserve, and then I'll leave you alone.

You know this goes against everything I used to believe, but time can change a man and I believe you're in my life again for a reason.

I don't want to disappoint fate.

Brigs.

Natasha was once thrilled to discover my rather poetic side hidden beneath all the scholarly film talk. I can only hope she still feels the same way.

I take a deep breath and press send.

Then I become obsessed. I try to work, but it's impossible for me to do anything other than check my email. An hour goes by. She hasn't responded and I'm losing my mind.

I decide to check Keir's email and see that he arrived in London yesterday, wanting to meet up. I immediately put his number into my phone and send him a text, seeing if he wants to get a drink today. I need something to get out of this tailspin, anything to distract me.

I'm not all too close with Keir, nor his brother Mal or sister Maisie, just as I'm not close with my other cousins Bram and Linden. I blame the distance. Bram and Linden have been living in the US for a long time, while Keir has been serving the army in Afghanistan. I guess his duty is over and he's in London for a few days for whatever reason. Mal travels all over the world for his job as a photographer, and Maisie has been living in Africa somewhere doing charity work.

Unlike Natasha, it doesn't take Keir long to get back to me. I agree to meet him at the Cask and Glass pub near the barracks and Buckingham Palace for a quick drink, with the potential to turn into an outright bender.

By the time I get to the pub, Keir is already there.

He's sitting alone at a high-top table along the window, peering intently at the people walking past, palming a pint of beer. With his brawny build, grizzled features, and steely gaze, he looks every inch the soldier, even though his beard betrays him otherwise, as does his uniform of jeans, a green t-shirt, and a cargo jacket.

"Hey, Keir," I say to him as I walk over.

Keir grins at me and gets off his seat, pulling me into a hug. "Nice to see you, Brigs," he says in his distinctively low voice. He does an amazing Darth Vader impression. "Thanks for coming to meet me."

"I'm glad you're in town," I tell him, patting the table. "Want another pint?"

He nods, and I quickly head to the bar to get us both one. I sit down at the table and raise my glass. "Cheers."

I nearly down my beer in one go.

Keir raises a brow. "Been needing that one, have you?"

"Like you wouldn't believe."

"Well, I've been having a pretty shit time myself if it makes you feel better," he says, running his hand over his mouth and jaw.

"It doesn't," I tell him. I don't want to pry or intrude on his business, so I don't add anything else. Keir used to be pretty talkative and forthcoming before he joined the army, though that was a long time ago. I don't expect him to say anything now.

He finishes off what was left of his other beer, and I'm about to ask him about how the army is when he says, "I left the army."

I frown, mid-sip. "You mean you're off-duty."

He shakes his head. "No. I left. No one knows." His eyes flit to mine, and now I can see how tired they are. Weary and war-torn, they've obviously seen a lot. "You're the first person I've told. I…I just needed to get it out, you know? Tell someone. It isn't easy living a lie."

Don't I fucking know it.

"Your parents?" I ask. "Maisie or Mal don't know either?"

He laughs sourly. "I don't even know where Maisie is, to be honest. Mal seems to disappear off the earth from time to time. Every time he meets a new woman in a new country, anyway. And this isn't the sort of thing you'd write in an email." He gives me an apologetic smile. "Sorry to burden you with this, Brigs. I know we've lost touch."

"It's okay. Your secret is safe with me." I pause. "What happened? Why did you leave?"

"Because of what happened to my best friend," he says carefully. He swallows. "You know the shooting last month?"

I slowly nod, afraid of where this could be going. Last month we had a terrorist shooting in downtown London, right in the middle of Oxford Circus. Two people died and a few more were badly injured. It made major headlines for a few days and later disappeared—probably because the terrorist wasn't part of an organization. He was Lewis Smith, a Caucasian and a member of the British Army. He'd recently been dishonorably discharged and went mad, gunning people down on the street. The police shot and killed him when he wouldn't surrender.

"Well," he says, suddenly looking a lot older than a man in his late thirties. His face seems to grow pale before my eyes. "That was my best friend. Lewis Smith."

Bloody hell.

He exhales loudly. "The worst part is, I knew how unwell he was. I saw him disintegrate. Some of the stuff we saw out there in the villages…I don't even know how I dealt with it, and Lewis took it hard. But you can't talk about that stuff. We're taught to keep it inside. I should have said something. I should have spoken up. I tried, you know, I did, but…I could have done more."

Well, his week is certainly putting my week to shame.

"I don't know what to say other than you can't blame yourself," I tell him gently.

He raises his brows, his forehead wrinkling. "Oh yeah? And how often do you take your own advice?"

I give him a wry look. "Never."

"Look, I know I haven't seen you much since the funeral," he says. "I heard through my mum that you're teaching now at King's College. I just wanted to say that I'm glad you're pulling through. I don't know how you managed to put one foot in front of the other. I know I couldn't if I were in your shoes. I'm barely dealing with this. Wondering if the guilt, this weight, is ever going to go away."

I'm starting to see why Keir had contacted and confided in me. I might be the only person who knows what it is to be shackled to all the things you should have done. But he doesn't know the whole truth. And even though he opened up to me, I can't bring up Natasha. Not with him or Lachlan or my parents. The moment I tell them is the moment I'm tarnished in their lives forever. I guess I still have some pride left, as foolish as it is.

"I think we can get over the guilt, even if we can't get over the loss," I tell him, my eyes roaming to the window, absently watching the rush of people, suited businessmen heading to the pubs for a pint after work, tourists making their way to the Palace. "Unfortunately, I think it starts and ends with us."

He sighs. "You're probably right. Even so…the reason I'm here is because I'm going to stop by the hospital. One of the victims that Lewis shot was in intensive care there. I'm not sure if she still is or not, but…I need to know if she's all right. I don't even know her, but…I need to do this. I feel I owe her something, I just don't know what."

"You know it wasn't your fault. You couldn't have known that Lewis would do this," I tell him, but Keir's eyes seem to darken, caught in a bad, bad place.

He doesn't say anything for a moment then excuses himself to get us another round of beers.

"So, what's weighing you down?" he asks me when he comes back, obviously wanting a subject change.

I thank him for the beer and try to figure out how much I should tell him. "I, uh, made some mistakes in the past," I say carefully. "Some things I haven't been able to get over. I hurt someone who was once very dear to me, and now that person is back in my life, whether I want them to be or not. Karma has come to bite me on the arse."

"You gave me some advice, so I'm going to give you some," Keir says after a gulp of beer. He wipes his lips with the back of his hand. "You ready?" I nod. "There's no such thing as karma. That only exists in a fair world, and we both know the world is anything but fair."

"That's not really advice, Keir."

He shrugs. "It just means you aren't being punished. Try and make it right, and if you can't, that's on them, not you. Forgiveness shouldn't be stockpiled by anyone. It should be given freely."

I stew on that for a moment. If Natasha never responds to my email, or if she does and wants nothing to do with me, I'm going to have to let her go.

Again.

Without closure.

I clear my throat.

"What a bunch of sad sacks we are," Keir says with a disapproving scoff. "Friday night and we're sobbing into our drinks. I'm going to get us a round of shots before we turn into women."

"Just one round," I tell him, raising my finger in warning. "I've got to get back to my dog. He's probably torn my place to shreds and shit in my shoes."

Keir gives me his trademark smirk. That's more like the cousin I remember. "He's shit in your shoes, aye?"

"More than once," I say with a sigh. "And pissed on my pillow."

That one was a nasty surprise.

"Seems Lachlan is rubbing off on you," Keir says when he comes back with the shots of Jameson. "I didn't know you had a dog."

"Just in the last year."

I explain to him how Winter came about, which then turns our conversation to Lachlan and Kayla, my parents, to Moneypenny, my vintage Aston Martin I never get to drive anymore since the tube is so convenient. With all the heavy stuff out of the way, it feels good to just drink and shoot the shit.

Sounds sad for a grown man to say, but I really ought to make some friends in this city.

Unfortunately, Keir says he's going back up to Edinburgh when he's done here to figure out what his next steps in life are. With the army behind him and his service done, he's starting over.

I wish I could tell him it will be easy.

But I could never lie about that.

Chapter Eight

NATASHA

Edinburgh

Four Years Ago

August in Edinburgh is sublime.

The sun is warm, and even hot some days, sitting high in the sky in the evenings.

People are smiling, biking around the city in droves. Kilted buskers play on street corners. Sometimes there are fire eaters and contortionists just for the hell of it. The ongoing Fringe Festival seems to bring out the free spirits, the wild cards, the crazies.

I feel like I'm one of them.

Because I too have turned into the wild card.

Doing something I never thought I would do.

I've fallen in love.

And I've fallen in love with someone that I can't have.

It's both the most exhilarating and destructive feeling to have ever possessed my body.

And I do mean possessed.

Brigs is all I can think about, all I can see. It's like every part of him, from the crinkles at the corners of his eyes when he smiles, to the suits he wears, to the way he makes me laugh, makes every cell in my body pull toward his. When he looks at me or talks to me, he makes me feel like at that moment I'm the most important woman in the world to him.

And that's the other thing. He makes me feel like a woman. Not a girl, not a student. Like I'm something greater than I've figured out. Like I'm a light that's been waiting her whole life to be switched on and now I'm blinding him and everything around me.

Including my morals.

Including the rules.

Well no, I shouldn't say that.

I may be in love with Professor Blue Eyes, but I'm not going to do anything about it. We've been working together for months, and though I know he's terribly unhappy with Miranda, it's not my style to intrude on a marriage, or any relationship for that matter. I don't ever want to be the other woman. While I feel guilty for my feelings, I won't bend my morals to indulge them.

Love isn't a choice. I can't control how I feel about him any more than I can control the sun in the sky. But what I can do is control what I do with those feelings.

Around Brigs I bottle it up.

It's not so hard.

Okay, that's a lie.

It's terribly hard.

But he's not one to give me an opportunity.

God help me if he ever does.

I'm also lucky that I don't really know anyone in Edinburgh. There's my Vietnamese flatmate, Hang, that I'm rooming with short term, and though we're cordial with each other, we're not exactly chummy.

There's no one to spill my secrets to. I haven't even told my friend Melissa back in London the truth: that I'm in love with not only the professor, who is paying me to be his research assistant, but a married man at that.

Some days when I wake up and my heart gets that warm fluttery feeling, I try and talk myself out of it. Convince myself that it's just a harmless crush, not love, and that when all this is over I'll go back to London, back to school, meet a nice available boy and get on with my merry life.

Other days I sink into that feeling. I drown in it. Because love shouldn't be ignored. Or shunned. Or buried. If you're lucky enough to feel it, you need to indulge it. Give it wings. Let it course through your heart and soul, unfiltered.

And I fucking feel it.

It's Friday afternoon, and the last I talked to Brigs was through an email sent this morning. I wondered if he needed me to come to the office today to work.

He said no, the first time he ever turned down the offer. No explanation why either.

I hate to admit that it stung a bit and got me thinking. Too much, as usual. I started overanalyzing every last interaction. Wondering if my feelings for him were obvious, if I'm starting to scare him off. The last thing I want is to ruin the thing we have now, this easy, fun, light-hearted working relationship.

Well, I guess it's not so light-hearted all the time. I do catch his eyes on me. Not always, but often enough.

The thing about Brigs, that I don't even think he knows, is that his gaze just screams *sex.*

It shouts it from the rooftops, stamps its feet, and makes you feel it deep in your core.

One moment he'll be talking about the virtues of Kim Novak's performance in *Vertigo*, the next he's staring at me with those blue eyes of his with a look that can only be described as carnal.

And every time I catch him looking at me that way, I feel every bone in my body light on fire. I can't even imagine the look I'm giving him back because I'm stripped bare in his gaze, no inhibitions left.

So yeah, maybe he's starting to catch on that I have some pretty mad feelings for him. And I'm too afraid to ask myself what to do next. Keep on pining and have my heart eventually crushed by our separation.

Or?

There is no or.

No matter what happens, it can't end well.

I sigh and stare up at the ceiling of my tiny room. My window is open; I'm trying to get a breeze going inside, and outside people are laughing and talking as they walk to and fro on the street beneath the building. It's maddening that I'm inside, stewing in my feelings, while the rest of the city gets to have fun.

But I've never been one to stay home because of a guy.

I put on a pair of jeans and a white T-shirt with the slogan "Nope," grab my purse and sunglasses, and head out into the street.

I'm flatting in Newington so it's about a twenty minute walk to head into the city but I could use the exercise. Not that I need it at the moment—my appetite is gone these days for the first time in my life, and my ass has finally shrunk a size. So have my boobs. It's so not fair. When a girl loses weight, her boobs go first. But when a guy loses weight, his dick stays the same size. If anything it gets larger in proportion.

I've always wanted to have a picnic in the Princes Street Gardens, and even though you rarely see anyone doing it alone, I won't let that stop me. Fuck the happy couples and families. Why should picnicking be reserved just for them?

I stop by a shop to get some cheese and crackers and two cans of cider, and head down toward the grass, trying to find the perfect spot to have my lonely little picnic. The air smells sweet despite it being late summer in the city, and the sun feels wonderful on my back.

I feel fucking alive.

But damn if there aren't a lot of people here. I guess the park attracts the after-work crowd, and it is a gorgeous Friday after all. It's hard to find the right spot without being too close to a couple making out or a toddler determined to tramp all over your non-existent blanket.

I think I see a good spot, a little too close to the path, but it will have to do.

And then I stop dead in my tracks.

I see him.

Brigs.

With a child on his shoulders.

Walking with a stunning blonde that looks like January Jones. Or Grace Kelly. Someone with the neck of a ballerina and all the grace of a princess.

I don't know what to do. I feel like I'm in *Jurassic Park*, and if I don't move, he won't see me. I can't think of any other option but to turn around and hide my face from his and walk the other way.

But I can't move. I can't stop looking. It's like a horrible car crash.

He and his adorable son and his gorgeous, perfect wife.

How on earth could he not be happy with her? She's turning heads even as she walks through the gardens, wearing a white sundress, her hair done up in a French twist. Shit, she even manages to make an 80s hairstyle look good.

And Brigs is laughing, holding onto his son's legs and staring up at him with the most adoring eyes. I knew from the way he talked about Hamish that he was a father who would do anything for his son, and now I have the proof.

The exact proof why he and I will never become anything, even if he did happen to feel the same. And the odds of that happening now are probably a million to one.

By luck or grace or mercy, Brigs doesn't see me. He walks past, happily chatting with Hamish while Miranda strolls alongside him. I have to say, at least it doesn't look like the two of them are anything more than friends. There are no shared smiles between husband and wife, no looks of lust or love. Both of them are entirely fixated on their son.

But that doesn't change anything, other than the fact that I've been a fool. And even though I've been telling myself it's okay to fall in love with Brigs, to revel in that love, as long as I don't tell him, as long as I don't act on it, I know it's wrong, too.

I had just told myself it wasn't going to end well.

Now I know for damn sure.

I watch them go, walking into the sun, and there's a spear in my chest, my heart bleeding from the inside.

Foolish, foolish girl.

I flop down on the grass and open the can of cider. I drink it quickly, trying to bury the burn. I'm embarrassed and hating myself a little bit. A whole lot.

You're an idiot, I tell myself. A lovesick puppy who ought to be kicked.

I finish the other cider until my brain starts swimming, then start the walk back to the flat.

Halfway there, my feet lead me into a pub.

I sit down at the bar and the rugged looking bartender gives me a wide, welcoming smile.

"What can I get for you?" he asks, leaning across the bar.

"Anything that can make me forget a man," I tell him.

He raises his brow, an eyebrow ring glinting under the lights. "I think that's called Scotch. Or whiskey, since you're American. On the rocks or straight?"

"Straight," I tell him.

"Good to know," he says with a wink, turning around to grab a bottle.

Suddenly there's someone in the seat next to me.

I turn my head to see a big bearded beast of a man wearing a grey t-shirt. His arms are covered in tattoos, even across his collarbone. "Oy Rennie, don't be giving your customers a hard time."

He's drunk but non-threatening in a weird way. I mean, he's huge, and when he turns to face me, he's not smiling. Just observing me with green-grey eyes, the color of the ocean beneath a dock. I don't see any malice in them, nor predatory charm. He's just here as I'm here.

"He's not giving me a hard time," I tell him, sticking up for Rennie who's pouring me the largest shot in the world. "The world is giving me a hard time."

Rennie turns around, giving the tatted beast a wry smile and sliding the drink toward me. "This is on the house," he says. "Since the world isn't being so nice."

"The world isn't being so nice to me, either," the guy next to me says.

Rennie rolls his eyes. "We know, we know. That's your excuse for everything." Still, Rennie turns around and gets him a shot too. And then, to my surprise, pours one for himself. He raises it in the air.

"To the world," Rennie says.

Me and the tatted guy raise our glasses. Theirs go down like water, though even in my heartache and the need to bury the pain, I take it easy and have just a sip.

"I've never seen you around here before," Rennie says, wiping at the bar with a rag, his biceps bulging under his shirt.

"I live in London," I tell him.

The tattooed guy makes a derisive sound. I look at him defensively. He manages to shoot me a sloppy smile. If the guy wasn't drunk, he'd be gorgeous, that much is true. Full lips, a brooding stare, built like he does MMA in his spare time when he's not throwing logs in the Highland Games. The kind of guy I would normally go nuts for, if only my mind wasn't so preoccupied.

"But you're American," the drunk guy says, his brogue getting thicker and thicker.

"I am," I tell him. "But I go to film school in London. I'm just here for the summer, working at the short film festival."

"My brother is a teacher," the guy says.

"Oh really?" I ask, staring at him closer now. He doesn't look familiar. I wonder about Brigs' brother. But other than the fact that he's a rugby player, I don't know anything about him. Though his arms look like they could definitely win a game.

He nods and licks his lips, staring down at his empty glass. Doesn't say anything else.

"So what's ailing you, Miss America?" Rennie says, swinging my attention back to him.

I bite my lip for a moment, wondering if I should tell the truth or not. But these guys are just strangers in a bar. In a few weeks, I'll be gone from Edinburgh. Maybe even sooner if Brigs doesn't need me anymore. His book is moving along at a snail's pace. It used to be he would type so fast when he was around me, but now it seems everything has slowed to a crawl.

"I'm in love with someone I can't have," I tell them.

Rennie whistles while drunk guy twists his lips, giving me the "that sucks" look.

"I'm not sure what's worse," Rennie says. "Being in love with someone you can never have or having someone and losing them."

"You can have both," the other guy says. "That would be worse."

"I don't know," I say, suddenly philosophical. "I think I'd rather know, just for a second, that your feelings were reciprocated."

"You'd rather have that and have it snatched away thereafter," he says, incredulous. "You're a daft bird is what you are."

"Easy now," Rennie says. He gives me a sympathetic look. "You know, I've only been bartending a short while here but I've already given out a therapy session's worth of advice. I think, in your case, you need to tell the man. I have a hard time believing that anyone who learned you were in love with them wouldn't already feel the same."

Normally I would blush stupidly at that. A hot looking bartender with black spiky hair, paying me such a compliment. But I only feel doubt.

"Not this guy," I tell him. "He's…married."

Rennie raises his brows. "Aye. I understand now," he says, gravity in his words.

"And I kind of work for him," I go on. "He's paying me as a research assistant for his book."

"My brother is writing a book," the guy says, his eyes narrowing, sea glass green, as he looks me over.

I swallow and nudge my glass away from me, hoping Rennie will take the hint and fill her up. He does.

"What's your brother's name?" I cautiously ask the drunk guy, noting the tattoo of a lion on his forearm.

"What's your name?" he responds.

"Yvette," I tell him without missing a beat.

"Then my brother's name is George," he says, cavalier.

"Drink up, beautiful," Rennie says, filling up the glass and sliding it back to me. "You keep talking and I'll keep filling."

"You know I'm a poor student, right?" I ask him.

"Aye. And I know you probably need a night out," he says. "It's on me. Just as long as when you think it's time to go home, you let me call you a cab."

I nod just as a pair of pretty girls come to the end of the bar, trying to get his attention. He leaves to go tend to them as I sip the Scotch. Even the drink reminds me of Brigs, of the night we drank in his office and shared the cigar.

"He's got a girlfriend, just so you know," drunk guy says, nudging me with his elbow and nodding at Rennie.

I give him a look. "I wasn't wondering," I tell him.

"Still hung up on the married man," he notes.

I rub my lips together and rotate the glass in my hands, watching the golden liquid spin. "As wrong as it all is, I'm not sure the feeling is going away anytime soon." I glance at him. "Do you have somebody in your life? Ever been in love?"

He smiles and his whole face becomes youthful, like a young boy, even though his expression is embarrassed. "No, and no. But that's okay. I'm making peace with it." He lifts up his drink and has another sip. "Do you want my advice though?"

I cock my head and smile. "Not really."

He chuckles. "Fair enough. But I'll tell you anyway. Take it with a grain of salt because it's coming from someone who doesn't know anything." He leans in close and I'm momentarily caught in his eyes. "Tell the man how you feel."

"I can't do that," I whisper. "He's happy."

You're lying, I tell myself. *Why are you lying?*

"If he's happy, then it doesn't really matter...does it?"

I hate the hope this man is putting in my chest. "And what if it does matter? What if he...what if this changes everything? Not just my life, but his and his wife's and...I can't be a catalyst."

"Better to be a catalyst for change than a martyr for lies."

His words fall over the bar like snowflakes. Soft, but with bite.

I just don't know how to feel.

But I do end up having a few more drinks, and true to his word, Rennie calls me a cab. I don't know what else I told the drunk guy, but when I leave I'm feeling empowered and bold and drunk out of my mind.

I get to my flat, my roommate already asleep and snoring lightly in her room. I flop down on my bed and stare up at the ceiling in that drunken mix of wanting to stay up later and drink but also go to sleep at the same time.

My nerves win out in the end.

In the most terrible way.

I open the email app on my phone and compose a message to Brigs.

Every cell in my body is screaming for me to stop, but all I feel is the selfish need to be heard and heard now. It can't wait. It's now or never.

Dear Professor Blue Eyes,

Do you believe in fate? Of course you don't. You often say you think the universe is made of haphazard events that don't make any sense, that we are the harbingers of our own destiny and doom.

I used to agree with you, though today I'm not so sure.

Today, I had the world make something very clear to me, something you probably aren't even aware of.

I was walking in the park today, wanting to have a picnic at Princes Street Gardens, and I saw you there.

You were with Miranda and Hamish.

Goddamn it if you weren't the most beautiful family.

Now I can understand why you canceled today.

What I don't understand, though, is why you haven't canceled every day before that.

Why have you continued to spend time with me, all day long, day after day, for months now when you have something that graceful and good and beautiful at home?

Miranda is every single thing that I'm not.

And I accept that.

But I can't accept why you bother spending all your time with me.

I'm probably the worst research assistant there ever was.

We laugh more than we work.

You're still the slowest writer in the world.

And yet every day I'm there.

Until one day I'm not.

Tasha

P.S. I'm drunk

P.P.S. I'm writing this because I'm a catalyst for change.

P.P.P.S. I don't think I should work for you anymore.

Probably not the most succinct email I've ever composed, but I figure I'll worry about that later when I send it.

Oops.

I already sent it.

I stare at the "sent" icon just as my phone dies.

Then I shrug. Whatever.

I lay back down on the bed and try and train my thoughts to something worth thinking of. I think about the flat back in London that I had sublet for the summer. I think about going to school, getting up every day without the warm heart and the bubbly stomach and the butterflies, and how fucking boring it's going to be. I think about the pain I'll feel when I won't have Brigs' face to look at every day, the loss of him in my life. The bitterness that will follow. Bitter always follows the sweet, especially when it comes to love. Especially when it comes to forbidden love.

I don't know how long I sit in the dark, but eventually I get up, unsteady on my feet, and wobble out to the kitchen to raid the fridge for a half-drunk bottle of wine I know is in there.

I've just finished pouring myself a glass of the oaky chardonnay when there's a knock at my door. It's faint, as if not to disturb, but that just puts the hairs on the back of my neck up.

I glance at the microwave clock. It's only a quarter to midnight, so not that late, but still. My roommate has never had guests over this late, and I've never had anyone over here except Brigs dropping off books a couple times, or the one time he picked me up when we went to a theatre to see a screening outside of town.

Obviously that thought gives me a jolt of hope as I quickly creep toward the door, peeking through the peephole before the person can knock again.

It's Brigs. Distorted in that fish-eye way, but still him.

Ah shit.

I take a deep breath and undo the chain, slowly opening the door.

"Hi," I say softly, taking him all in. He's standing there in what I saw him in earlier, an olive dress shirt and dark jeans.

I think in the deep recesses of my mind I had hoped he would show up. Isn't that why I wrote the email? A Hail Mary? A last ditch attempt?

He looks pained, his brow furrowed. "Can I come in?" he asks, voice gruff and low. "Sorry it's so late. I tried calling you but it went straight to your voicemail."

"You know I never check my voicemail," I tell him, opening the door wider.

Now he seems larger than life leaning against the frame.

"I know," he says. "But I've never gotten a drunk email from you before."

He walks in and I know I need to laugh it off.

"Well, consider yourself flattered," I tell him, closing the door gently. "Drunk emails are the white unicorn of Natasha Trudeau."

But as he stands in the narrow entryway and turns around to face me, our bodies too close in the dark, he's not smiling. He's staring at me instead, like he's studying a treasure map he knows he'll lose later, memorizing every detail.

"I want to talk about it," he says, and his voice is still on the border between hushed and emphatic.

"The email?" I question, even though it's futile to pretend now.

Every nerve inside me is dancing, waiting, wishing.

He nods and looks around warily. "Is your roommate asleep?" he asks softly.

I nod. "She is, and she can literally sleep through anything." I almost go off on a tangent about our techno playing neighbor and how she says she's never even heard his 90s *oonce oonce* crap blaring through the walls, but I don't because the look in Brigs' eyes is so arresting it makes thoughts fall out of my head.

And I guess because I say that, we don't move anywhere else. We continue to stand in the darkened foyer, feet apart, just staring at each other.

We don't speak for a few moments. The longest moments.

I'm trying to stand still and not wobble, trying to appear as sober as possible, wondering if my breath is okay, wondering if I have mascara goop in the corners of my eyes. Wondering all sorts of little things that have nothing to do with the big things.

Meanwhile, Brigs is still studying me. I can't tell if he's disappointed in me or not.

"So talk," I tell him, but instead of sounding all cool and tough like I thought I would, it comes out meek and quiet. Because I'm afraid, so damn afraid, to hear what he's going to say.

Leave me alone.

Or.

I love you.

One would devastate me. One would make me happy.

But both would ruin me in the end.

"Did you mean it?" he asks gently, eyes searching mine. The hollows of his cheeks look extra sharp in the shadows.

"What part?" I ask. Then I say, "All of it."

"All of it," he repeats. "How you don't want to work for me anymore."

I look away, finding focus on the tops of his black and grey suede sneakers.

"I..." I start but have no idea how to finish the sentence.

"How you're a catalyst for change."

It all seems so silly now. But even so I raise my chin and look at him, immediately absorbed by his presence, by the depth of his eyes.

"I want to be."

"How so?" And he takes a step toward me.

I inhale sharply, trying to steady myself. Only the door is behind me.

"You saw me today," he continues. "Why didn't you say hello?"

I lick my lips, my throat dry, the chardonnay a mistake. "I thought it would be wrong."

His frown deepens, leaning in closer. "Why?"

"Because," I tell him. "It felt wrong."

He looks like he's about to say something else but his lips come together. He tilts his head, observing me deeper. "Why?" he finally says again.

"Because," I say slowly, eventually meeting his eyes. "Sometimes I feel like I'm more to you than a research assistant. Because I know you're more to me than someone who writes me a check."

His brow pinches together as he lets out a ragged breath. His eyes are this mix of fear and wonder that I wish I could bottle because it's leaving a scar on me. One I'll look back on.

He reaches out with his hand and grasps the ends of my fingers.

My breathing deepens, my heart beginning to gallop.

"Tasha," he says, and I delight in the way he says my name. He squeezes my fingers. "You're right. You are more to me than a research assistant. There is no pretending otherwise."

I don't want to be pathetic, don't want to be weak.

Still I whisper, "How much more?"

I wish my voice didn't shake.

He stares at me sadly and shakes his head. "A terrible amount."

Then he winces sharply and turns away, letting go of my hand. He leans against the door, arms splayed as he tries to breathe.

I don't want to intrude.

I want to intrude.

"My whole point of the email," I explain quietly, "was..."

And I trail off because that's the problem with being drunk.

So instead of finishing my sentence I reach out and place my hand on his back.

He's hot through the shirt and his muscles tighten under my touch.

I briefly imagine touching his skin underneath, what it would feel like to run my hands over it, maybe my nails.

"You said you didn't understand why I spend all my time with you," he says, and I can feel his words against my palm. "Why I'm not with my wife instead."

"That's not exactly what I said," I tell him, trying to play it off.

"No, but it's what I heard," he says and suddenly turns around.

I don't have time to back away.

Or maybe it's that I did and I chose to hold my ground.

To be just a few inches from him.

I can smell him, rosemary and soap, see his pulse tick wildly in his throat.

I don't think I've ever wanted something so badly before.

"And?" I ask.

"Tell me what I am to you," he whispers, leaning in closer.

I suck in my breath. Afraid that if I exhale I'll let all my secrets loose.

He's so close now, and the air between us is short and sharp. Maybe I don't even have to say a word. He can just glean it off me, the way an archeologist can pinpoint a year within billions of years because of a grain of ash on a fossil.

"Tell me," he repeats, and I read the urgency in his voice. I dare to meet his eyes again, and they are feverish, like an iceberg melting at a rapid rate.

Here goes nothing.

I lean in quickly.

And I kiss him.

On the mouth. A straight shot that creates goosebumps down my arms, my lips soft and wet and yielding against his.

The soft moan that comes out of his mouth nearly floors me, reaching so deep down into the darkest corners of my very being. It fuels me, like gasoline to a fire. Dangerous. So very, very dangerous.

And then his mouth opens against mine, his tongue softly brushing against the tip of my tongue, and all my body wants is to throw restraint out the window.

Oh god. This kiss.

This is wildfire.

This could so easily consume us.

Until there is nothing left.

We're going to fucking burn this world to the ground.

And there's no better way to go than in the flames with him.

"Wait. I can't," he mumbles, pulling his mouth away, breathing hard. His eyes are laced with anguish. "You don't know what you're doing."

"And you do?" I ask, my lips burning.

Creak.

The door down the hall opens, and we both break apart, no, *crumble* apart, like sand, and my roommate shuffles across the hall and into the bathroom, without even shooting a glance our way.

Now we're left with the heavy blanket of regret as we both eye each other, our chests rising, hearts drumming, utterly aware of how wrong that was, aware that it should never, ever happen again

I want it to happen again.

Immediately.

And yet, the way Brigs is looking at me says he's sad beyond anything, a potent mix of frustration and sorrow.

"I should go," he says, eyes darting to the bathroom.

I know what I want to say, and I know I shouldn't say it.

But still I do. "Are you sure?" I whisper. "You can stay."

Brigs stares right at me—into me—and in his eyes I see a painful battle being fought.

"I have to go," he says again, louder this time, as if he's trying to convince someone else.

Now what?

"Okay," I tell him. "You know I'm drunk, right? What I sent you…just file that under Tasha Being Drunk and we'll be okay." Suddenly some sober part of me wakes up, tapping me on the shoulder, yelling in my ear. I can't ignore it. "I still have a job, right? I mean, I still want to work for you, and I promise I won't kiss you anymore."

Brigs gives me a half-hearted smile that seems more pained than anything else.

"You have a job for as long as you want it," he says kindly.

"And the kissing you part?"

He nods quickly, looking away. "I'll chalk it up to you being drunk and we'll pretend it never happened."

And even though that hurts to hear, to erase that beautiful moment, I'm relieved. I smile at him and awkwardly stick out my hand.

"Okay then, that's great," I tell him. "Thanks for coming by."

He slowly arches a brow but puts his hand in mine and gives it a squeeze. He lets go and turns to open the door. Then he pauses and looks over his shoulder.

"You know," he says. "Drunk or not, I can read you like a book, and I can't say that about a lot of people. Not because you wear your heart on your sleeve, because you, my dear, don't. I can only say that because I know a lot about you and I'm lucky enough to be one of the ones you share your true self with." He pauses. "I hope that after tonight you don't stop that."

I swallow. "Even though my true self may kiss you inappropriately?"

"Even though," he says with a nod. He opens the door and looks back. "See you on Monday."

The door closes with a click that sounds too foreboding for this tiny flat. I exhale loudly and lean against the door, just as the bathroom door opens. My roommate totters across to her room without even looking my way.

As if I'm not here.

As if none of that ever happened.

But I know it did.

I can still feel his lips on mine.

Chapter Nine

NATASHA

London

Present Day

"I don't want to disappoint fate."

I keep reading the line over and over again, refusing to let it sink in, refusing to let it get to me.

With anyone else, any suitor, I would have chalked it up to a lack of imagination or trying too hard in the Lord Byron department. But from the mouth—if not the keypad—of Brigs McGregor, I know how much it means.

Brigs was never one to believe in destiny or fate or anything he believed was out of our control. Even when our brief affair went from hidden to acknowledged, he thought he was in the driver's seat every step of the way.

And I let him think that.

I let him because he was the one with the most to lose. He was the one with the wife he knew he had to leave. He was the one with the son he kept putting before himself, even when it hurt them both.

Fate was never an option.

But for him to think it's the force that put us in each other's path, that says a lot.

And to be honest, I'm looking for every single excuse not to stay away.

I go to sleep and I see his face from four years ago, his eyes wracked with this strange purpose, this truth he believed, that when it was love, it was simple and pure and good.

And then I see it morph into the face I know now, the one laden with guilt and sorrow and hate.

I'm the cause of both of those faces. How strange to be the one to ruin a man in two different ways and so completely.

How terribly, horribly strange.

And so it takes me a few days to come to terms with it, and when I finally embrace the fact that I want to see him, I feel the darkness slipping off my shoulders.

It feels more right than wrong.

"Ready to go out?" Melissa asks, making me jump.

I've been sitting on my bed, and I quickly close the app and put my phone away before she comes in. She's been awfully nosy lately, asking me if I've seen or heard from Brigs. Until recently, I wasn't lying when I'd said no.

Honestly, I wish she wouldn't worry about this so much—it's my life and I can take care of myself, no matter what kind of setbacks I've had. I know she's just concerned that I'm going to backslide, but at the same time I can't hide from him.

And I won't.

"I'm coming," I tell her, not wanting to hit the pub scene tonight, but she's insisting since it's Friday. She says I need to get laid like no one's business.

Well, that part is true. Aside from a drunken, sloppy one-night stand in France, when I was trying everything to purge Brigs from my system, I haven't been with anyone.

Even before I met Brigs, it had been a few months since I'd last been with a guy—some jerk from my class. I don't even want to count how long I've been celibate—it's far too pathetic.

I get up and quickly look myself over in the mirror, my mind flitting to Brigs. I wonder if he's been with anyone since the night of the accident. I assumed he would have found someone. He might even be with someone right now. There was nothing in his email that suggests he wants to pursue me, just that he needs to set things right. And I get that. Even though it terrifies me, I think closure is what the two of us both need. To shut the lid on the past, move on with our lives, and never look back.

Obviously I don't tell Melissa this. Instead I go with her to the pub, filled with drunk boys and surly men and a lot of spilled beer. The music is bad, and even though I get my buzz going, I want nothing more than to be back in my room, alone, watching a Cary Grant film. I can't connect to anyone here, physically or emotionally. Not that it surprises me—I've always been this way.

That's probably why my connection with Brigs meant so much. It was rare. It was something I'd never felt before. I'd always floated through my life, making no meaningful connections to anyone, and then he came around, the first person to ground me, to make me want to stay grounded, so long as he was there.

Somehow I end up surviving the weekend, spending Saturday at yet another bar with Melissa, while Sunday I save for myself, spending the day walking around The National Gallery, trying to distract myself with art and beauty. Then I hit the books that night, trying to finish the godawful book that Professor Irving wrote because I know he's going to ask me all about it next class.

When I wake Monday morning, I feel slightly invigorated. I'm up before my alarm and take my time getting ready—not because Professor Irving told me to last week, but because, well, honestly? I want to impress Brigs. I know I shouldn't even care, but I'd be lying if I said I didn't. Even if it comes to us saying a few words and awkwardly parting—and this is exactly what I'm preparing for—I want to do it looking like a new woman and not the ghost he left behind.

I leave the flat with my stomach a beehive of nerves and get on the tube. The closer it gets to my stop, the more anxious I feel, my fingernails destroyed from me picking off the polish.

It's at the Baker Street station that I actually see Brigs get on the train.

Holy shit. Why does the world make me see him everywhere?

I stand there, holding onto the pole, but as he gets on, giving people a polite smile as he squeezes past them, he disappears into the crowd.

I'm not about to approach him now. This is just life, taunting me with him.

I remain where I am, squished between a guy who keeps sniffing and a man who keeps putting his hand close to mine and "accidently" touching me, even when we get to Charing Cross station, my stop. I know he's getting off here, so I wait it out until the doors close and I'm whisked away. It will take me longer to walk to school from the next stop but at least I won't run into Brigs before I'm ready.

Time seems to crawl on by. In Professor Irving's class, I watch the clock. Afterward, I agree to have lunch with the teaching assistants, Tabitha and Devon, while I wait for Brigs' class with Melissa to be over. I have to plan this carefully or there's a chance I'll either miss Brigs or run into Melissa, and the last thing I want is a lecture from her. Or worse.

I decide to err on the side of caution and go over some of my tutorials until it's been an hour since his class has ended.

This is it, I tell myself as I walk down the hall to his office. Closure.

My palms are immediately clammy at the thought, and I rub them on my jeans as I stand outside his door. It's closed, which means he might not be in there at all. There's a sense of relief in that, that I may be able to ignore this for another day.

With that in mind, I raise my fist and knock gently at the door, breath in my throat.

"Come in," he says from the other side, that smooth Scottish burr sliding through the door. Just his voice alone has the hairs on my arms standing at attention. Thank god my nipples are behaving.

My hand wavers at the doorknob, like if I touch it I might turn to stone, and finally I grasp it and twist, pushing it open.

Brigs is at his desk, writing on his laptop. He looks at me over the top of his reading glasses, stunned.

"Is this a bad time?" I ask him softly, my hand still on the knob.

He shakes his head. "No," he says. He clears his throat and gets to his feet, taking off his glasses. "Please, please, come in."

I close the door behind me and lean against it, my feet refusing to move any further.

He stands by his desk, fingers resting on the surface as he stares at me. "I'm surprised to see you."

I run my teeth over my lip, looking around his office, trying to look everywhere but at him. It's nothing like his old one. His other office smelled like old books and coffee, he had teak shelves with an assortment of torn paperbacks and musty hardcovers. Even his desk was this big old oak thing that was impossible to move. This office is white and clean, with metal shelves and filing cabinets. Sterile. Soulless.

"I haven't really moved in yet," he says, noticing my wayward gaze. "I think it'll take a while until it really feels like mine."

I nod. "How has your teaching been going?" I ask, still avoiding his eyes.

"I'm not as prepared as I thought I'd be," he says. "Or maybe it's that I was too prepared."

"Maybe," I say. I look down at my feet, and he takes a few steps toward me, stopping a foot away. He's wearing black dress shoes, oxfords, along with his tailored suit pants and grey shirt.

Brigs doesn't say anything, but I can feel him, feel everything that's not being said. The space between us is thick with time and longing and regret, just as it always has been. It's almost amazing to be standing this close to him again and to step back in time four years. I thought I'd been thrown down a long dark hole and came out forever changed, but in his presence, it's like no time has passed at all.

This could be very, very dangerous.

But when wasn't it?

"I'm glad you're here," he says. His voice is so low, almost gruff. My spine feels warm from it. "I didn't think I'd ever hear from you again, let alone see you."

My lips twitch into a smile. "I've seen you a lot. You just haven't seen me."

I finally dare to meet his eyes and immediately wish I hadn't.

Those eyes of his burn into mine, in that masterful, carnal gaze that used to slay me over and over again. And like before, I'm hypnotized, and the world around me falls away until it's only him.

"Natasha," he says softly, searching my face. "I..." He pauses and takes a deep breath, pinching his eyes shut. Now he's avoiding my gaze, staring at the floor. "There's so much I want to say to you. To talk to you about. At the same time, it's painful. All of it. And I'm so done with suffering. Aren't you?"

I swallow hard and barely whisper, "Yes."

He looks up at me, his forehead creased. "I just need you to know that the last time we spoke—"

"Brigs," I tell him quickly. "You don't have to explain."

"I do," he says. "I do. Because I wasn't me."

"I know." God, it hurts that he doesn't think I understand.

"No, you don't," he says, looking up at me. Fuck. His eyes are haunted, full of shadows and darkness. "I told you nothing but lies because it was the only way I could get you out of my life. At the time, all I could think was that I caused this."

"And I helped," I fill in.

"I fell in love with you," he says harshly, pain written on his face.

My heart drops like an elevator in freefall.

I haven't heard those words in so, so long.

"I fell in love with you and that was on me. That was my choice. I chose you, Natasha. There's nothing you could have done to stop me." He pauses, running his hand over his jaw. He gives a quick shake of his head. "Everything I said on the phone was a lie. I can't believe I was too fucking *scared* to let you believe it for so long."

I'm sorry too, I think. Because I ruined him. He may say it's all on him, but it takes two to tango. We may not have slept together, nor been all that intimate at all, but when I told him I loved him, I willingly jumped into the deep end. I wasn't naïve. I knew what I was doing and all the risks, and I did it anyway, the whole world be damned, because I loved him.

All because of love.

But I don't want to get into that with Brigs. I didn't come here to find out who feels guiltier. I came here because I wanted closure.

So I take a deep breath and say, "I accept your apology."

It sounds lame but I hope he knows I mean it.

He eyes me. "You're sure?"

I nod. "Yes, I'm sure. Brigs...I'm still trying to figure out what to do with you."

He cocks a brow. "What to do with me?"

"The past will destroy me if I think about it too much. I've worked too hard to get back on my feet. I can't even imagine how you did it. I want to keep putting it all behind me and try to move on, but it feels impossible when my past is standing before me."

Just a foot away. So close I can breathe him in.

"I see," he says softly. "I understand. That's all I wanted to say, really. Just that I'm sorry. And I don't think I'll ever stop being sorry."

"And neither will I." I sigh and press my fist to my forehead. "But at the same time...this can't be it."

A glimmer of hope flashes through his eyes as he stares at me expectantly.

I give him a wan smile. "It's what you said in your email. About disappointing fate. I don't want to do that either. I don't think I can live with you in my life as a stranger. It doesn't seem right."

He takes a small step toward me, his eyes trained so intently on my face, roaming from my brow to my nose to my lips. "What does seem right?" His voice is so low.

I lick my lips and his eyes linger longer. "I don't know."

He continues to study me and I continue to hold my breath.

"Come for a drink with me tonight," he says after a few long, tension-filled beats.

I give him a wary look. "Are you sure that's a good idea?"

"Why not?"

"You're a teacher. I'm a student."

"I'm not your teacher, for one thing. And for another..." He smiles wickedly. "I don't really care."

"I don't know." It's damn tempting. That smile alone is making me weak in the knees. But when I said I didn't want to make him a stranger, I'm not sure hopping to a pub right away is the right solution.

Oh, who am I kidding. It's exactly what I want. I've been in his presence for five minutes now, and though I know the past is a wolf at our door, I haven't felt this alive in years. It's like I'm clicking with the solar system, my body charging cell by cell.

"Where?" I finally ask, giving in.

That smile again. Jesus.

"Any good places near you?" he asks.

I shake my head. "I'm at Wembley and there's shit all."

"Then my neighborhood," he says. "I'm in Marylebone. There's a pub you'd like called The Volunteer. Say, eight o'clock?"

"Okay," I say quietly, stunned at where this meeting progressed. "You sure you won't get in trouble?"

"We're friends, Natasha," Brigs says. "And we were friends before I started here. It's not a problem. It will never be a problem. Friends have drinks together all the time."

Friends.

I'm not sure if that's what we are, but I'll take it. It's better than strangers.

"See you at eight, then," I tell him, turning around and heading for the door so I can go freak out about it in private.

Brigs says goodbye and I'm gone.

...

"Now where are you going all dolled up?" Melissa asks while I stand in front of the bathroom mirror, carefully applying magenta lipstick that I know is going to smear all over my face and clothes in a matter of minutes. I'm so not used to wearing it, and I have a bad habit of getting it everywhere.

I knew I should have closed the bathroom door. I avoid her eyes and concentrate on myself. With some eyeshadow and bronzer, I'm hardly what you would call dolled up, though I have managed to put my hair half back into a Bridget Bardot type look. Hmmm, maybe I do need more mascara to complete the look.

"Just trying new makeup," I tell her. Then I quickly drop a lie to get her off my back. "I'm meeting one of the other TAs for a drink."

She frowns. "Which one?"

Ah shit. I hope to god she doesn't follow up with him about it. She probably would, as nosy as she is.

"Um, he's not in film," I say quickly. "You wouldn't know him. His name is Bradley."

"When did you meet this Bradley?"

"In the library. He's in art history. We got to talking and he asked me out. I'm not really into it, but then I remembered you'd be proud of me if I went. Fingers crossed I get laid."

Wow, I really am a good actress.

"I *am* proud of you," she says. "I just wish you could have told me sooner. I would have put you in a better outfit than that."

I look down at my black knee-high boots, jeans, black long-sleeved shirt. I think I look pretty good. Added bonus—all my clothes are clean.

"What's wrong with my outfit?"

She sighs. "Nothing, if you're going to class or grocery shopping. You're going on a date. Show some skin. A miniskirt would work."

"Not with these thighs," I interject, piling on more mascara.

"Push-up bra."

"Not into false advertising," I tell her. "Besides, he can get a pretty good idea of my body just by looking at me in this."

She looks me over, pursing her lips. Then she says, "What about your bra and underwear, are they matching?"

"Yes," I tell her, even though that's a big fat lie. I've adopted the Bridget Jones way of guaranteeing nothing funny will happen tonight. I'm not wearing granny panties or Spanx, but my underwear have Sponge Bob Square Pants on them. It's insurance for my well-being, not that I think anything like that would happen between Brigs and I, not now, not after so much time.

Then again, if he gets me drunk I can't promise anything. Hopefully Sponge Bob will come to the rescue.

But Melissa needs to think I'm out to get laid and so that's what I let her think. Besides, all this pretending is actually good for me. It's taking my mind off of what's really going on, and I'm afraid that if I think about tonight too much, I might chicken out and not go at all.

I can't hide in my flat forever though. When it's time to go, I say goodbye to Melissa, promising to text her any details, and then I head to the tube. I'm pretty much just as nervous as I was that morning but in a different way, and the only silver lining is that there is a drink at the end of this journey to quench my nerves.

I'm walking down Baker Street, about a block away from the pub, when I really start to flip out. Even the silver lining can't save me. I don't even know why I'm this nervous, it's not like I don't know Brigs at all, and it's not like we're together as anything other than friends. But my heart wants to take flight and my limbs feel like jelly, and the world is taking on this hazy glow, like I'm losing oxygen.

I have to take a moment outside the Sherlock Holmes Museum—closed for the day—and stare at my shadowed reflection in a mirror, trying to get my breathing under control. I keep telling myself there's no reason to feel like this, but my body doesn't care in the slightest.

Eventually I have to pry myself away from the wall of the building and head into the pub next door, otherwise he'll start to think I'm standing him up. I already ran away from him once, I can't let him think I'm doing it again.

The pub isn't all that busy, and I spot him sitting at the bar, laughing with the bartender. His smile is dashing and genuine as always, flooding me with warm memories. He's dressed down, wearing dark jeans, a t-shirt, and his leather moto jacket he always used to wear. I stop and watch him for a few seconds, unobserved, wishing in some ways that this was another instance of watching him from afar. I just want to take in every single detail and hold them in my mind, examine them like precious stones and see just how they make me feel.

But Brigs turns his head and looks at me, as if pulled by an imaginary string, and he gazes at me with wonder. His mouth quirks up into a small smile, his body twisting in his seat to face me.

I will my feet to move and walk on over, suddenly shy.

I stop beside him and rest my hand on the empty stool. "Is this seat taken?" I ask.

His eyes gently crinkle at the corners. He nods. "It's all yours."

I try to sit on the stool as gracefully as I can.

"What will you have?" he asks me, his body still turned in his seat facing me, one foot propped up on the rung at the bottom of my stool.

"A snakebite," I tell him.

"Still have a fondness for that drink," he remarks, looking me over. "You can change your hair, but not your appetite."

I study him, wondering if that was innuendo. He has this way of setting his jaw that makes you think he's struggling to keep all sorts of urges in control.

I clear my throat. "Do you like my hair?"

He reaches out and gently tugs on a strand, rubbing it between his fingers. I freeze, holding my breath, unprepared for how intimate this feels. "It suits you," he says after a moment. "Brightens you up. Not that you ever needed it."

Then as abruptly as he touched my hair, his hand falls away and he signals to the bartender. "Max, a snakebite for the lady. I'll take another pint."

Max gives me a nod and gets to work.

"So, you come here often, I guess?" I ask him since he seems to be right at home here.

He nods. "I live right across the street."

"Really? And the Sherlock Holmes Museum right here. I remember you being quite the fan."

He gives me a quick smile. "And what else do you remember?"

I eye him carefully, unsure of his game here, if there is anything. "I remember everything."

"All good things, I hope," he says as Max slides the drinks toward us.

I exhale. Slowly. I've just noticed his left hand, the absence of the wedding ring that was always there.

Oh my god. I can't do this.

"Natasha," Brigs says, leaning into me. "It's okay."

I stare up at him with wild eyes. "What's okay?"

"This," he says softly.

How? *How?*

He nods at my snakebite, a mix of lager, hard cider, and cassis. It gets you drunk fast which is why I normally just have one, and a lot of pubs won't serve it.

"You're just having a drink with me," he explains. "That's all."

You tried to leave your wife for me, I think. *How could any of this be that simple?*

I take a large gulp of my drink and lapse into a coughing fit like an amateur.

Brigs places his hand on my back, as if to pat me there, but he doesn't. He just presses his palm between my shoulder blades. Warm, even through my shirt. I briefly close my eyes, because god, even that simple contact feels so fucking good.

"So," he says slowly. "Seen any good films lately?"

I almost laugh at how cavalier he sounds. I look at him and his hand drops away, leaving my back feeling cold and bare. He's smiling, waiting for a response, his foot still resting on the rung of my stool, like he needs to be tethered to me in some way.

"Lately, no," I tell him, having another sip and taking it easier this time. "But in the last four years, yes."

"Still on your Christopher Nolan kick?"

"Yes," I say emphatically. "Have you seen *The Dark Knight Rises* and *Interstellar*? He just keeps getting better."

He shakes his head. "Nah. He peaked with *Inception*. Or even before that."

I roll my eyes. "You still don't understand that film."

"Maybe because I haven't watched it a million times like you have," he says. "Ogling Leo and what's his face. You shouldn't have to watch a film a million times in order to understand it. That says something right there."

"It says that you don't become obsessed with anything," I tell him. "Remember when I told you that I saw *X-Men* eight times in the theatre when it came out?"

"Aye. I said you're nuts," he says somewhat proudly. Then he adds quietly, "And I do know what it's like to be obsessed with something."

His eyes become melancholic and I look away. "Anyway," I say, sliding over it, "you've watched *Vertigo* more times than you can count, and you say it's because you discover something new about the film every time."

"Maybe I can relate to Jimmy Stewart's character."

The one who trails the ghost of the woman that he loved.

"Maybe." I'm not sure what else to say. There's so much I want to bring up, and I'm not sure what will send either of us into a tailspin. The elephant in the room is huge and will follow us everywhere.

After a few beats he takes a long swill of his beer and looks me over, his eyes razing every inch of me. He's so bold and open about it, or maybe he's unaware of how blissfully unnerving he's being with his gaze.

"It's really good to see you, Natasha," he says. "Just like this."

Like it was. My memory slides back a hundred frames to the few times we went to the pub together after a long day of compiling research for his book. Those days seem so long ago, and yet they shine in my mind like they just happened yesterday. I would get my snakebite, or maybe a glass of wine if I was feeling classy, he would have his beer, and we'd get a table or a booth and just talk for hours. How easy it was, comforting, just to be in his presence.

And whenever he wasn't looking, I would drink him in like a sponge. All of his features, the lines at the corners of his eyes, the faint cleft at the end of his sloping nose, the sharp cut of his square jaw, the crooked twist to his smile that made you imagine he was planning all sorts of devilish things—I would take them all in with a sense of unbridled fascination.

Even now I feel like I'm losing my footing a bit, because my eyes keep being drawn to that same face, and my fascination is growing into something like hunger. As much as we are sitting here at a pub, just like old times, the air between us dances with electricity much brighter than before. It *hums*. The obstacles are still there—this time it's our mutual shame, the destructive grief, instead of what's right and wrong—but dare I say they are nearly buried by something much more powerful.

Rebirth.

Lust.

Need.

A cocktail more potent than the one in my hands.

Still, I finish the rest of my drink, my head warm and swimming. I'm aware I haven't said anything in response to him, but it doesn't feel awkward. Maybe that's the drink talking.

"Want another?" he asks me while Max hovers around, waiting. I notice Brigs' beer is gone too.

"I'll just have a cider this time," I tell him. "Magners, please."

Max nods, seeming relieved. I'm sure if I ordered another snakebite, he'd cut me off.

"How's your book?" I end up asking Brigs. It seems like a safe topic.

His brow twitches and he gives me a wry smile. "Oh, I'm still writing it."

I want to remark on how slow he is, to make a joke, but I'm sure he hasn't done much writing over the years.

And I'm right. He says, "Honestly, I stopped writing after you left. I haven't looked at it since." He tilts his head at me. "Would you want to be my research assistant again?"

I raise my brows. "Me?"

"Aye, you," he says. "You were practically a muse."

I offer him an apologetic wince. "I can't. I have far too much work to do. So much to catch up on. You know, I can't screw up this year. This is my second chance."

He nods. "No need to explain. I understand."

And yet, the idea of seeing him every day pulls at me like an addiction.

"But, maybe you could bounce ideas off of me," I say slowly. "It might help. I feel I know almost as much about the subject as you do."

"You probably do," he tells me. "Tell me what you remember."

"I remember nights like this, sitting at a bar. Long days in your office, you on your computer, typing furiously. Me being subjected to very dry, boring text describing very funny topics."

I remember the night I kissed you.

I remember the night you kissed me.

A softness comes into his stark blue eyes. "What do you remember about the actual research?"

He's testing me, my knowledge, ever the professor.

I decide to impress him. I remember everything.

I launch into it with perfect confidence. Keaton, Chaplin, Lloyd. I describe their history, their early work, their critics. The rise and the fall. The inevitable tragedies that remind you that no life is safe from pain, even the life of the clowns.

All the while his eyes are transfixed on mine, rapt, cycling between pride and something darker. Deeper. He's leaning in closer, and my eyes take a long drop to his mouth, my mind briefly put on pause, wondering what it would be like to kiss him again. How wonderful would it feel? How badly would it destroy me?

"So there," I say when I'm done, my breath short from talking so much. I take a few big gulps of my cider while he stares at me, rapt. I give him the side-eye. "What? Don't tell me I got any of that wrong. I know I didn't."

He licks his lips then swallows. I watch his Adam's apple move. "No," he says, a quick shake of his head. His eyes light up. "That was bloody impressive."

I grin at him, loving the look on his face. "It seems you've forgotten who you're dealing with here."

"No, no. I haven't forgotten."

After that our conversation lapses into an easy rhythm. We order more drinks, talk, and laugh. I tease him, my favorite thing, and he responds in kind. The world around us seems to drop away, the pub noise diminishing until his voice, that smooth Scottish burr, is all I hear, reverberating in my ears, chest, and bones. Our own little world cocoons around us and it's impossible to count the minutes or the hours.

Eventually though, Max taps the bar. "Closing up, mate," he says.

I turn my head and slowly blink at him. The lights are brighter. My brain is liquid, my face flushed as I take in the rest of the pub. There's no one left. It's only us.

I flash Brigs a shy smile. "It seems we closed the place down."

Brigs looks equally as surprised. He takes out his wallet and puts a few notes on the table. "It seems we did."

"Let me pay for my own half," I say, reaching for my purse on the back of the chair.

"Darling, I wouldn't dream of it," he says dismissively. He slides the money to Max and then eyes the clock above the cash register. "Eleven thirty. You should have kicked us out a while ago, Max."

"Nah," Max says, taking the money. "It was more interesting to watch you two."

Brigs' gaze slides to me, his eyes warm from the effects of the alcohol. I feel a sudden urge to keep the night going, to see where it could go. I'm drunk and comfortable, and I'm not ready to say goodbye to this. It's that kind of combination that makes you keep drinking long after you should have stopped, regardless of right or wrong, good or bad, early mornings or not. Consequences don't matter at this point; they are something fuzzy in the future to worry about later.

I get off the stool, trying to keep my balance, but Brig's hand shoots out and places a firm grip on my arm, steadying me.

"Thank you," I tell him, clumsily grabbing my purse.

He lets go but takes a step forward until I can feel the heat of his body. He studies my mouth and then reaches forward, gently running his thumb underneath my lips.

My heart catches in my throat and I can't breathe.

"Your lipstick is all smeared," he says huskily.

And for none of the right reasons, I can't help but think.

Oh, this is so dangerous.

He drops his hand. "Would I be a good host or a bad one if I invited you into my flat?" he asks.

Oh Jesus.

My cheeks are on fire. I have to be smart about this, but the more he stands there, staring at me, the stupider I get. "I'm not sure if I'm in the right frame of mind to make that decision," I whisper.

He smiles kindly. "Let me walk you to the tube."

I exhale in relief, even though my body is demanding a recount.

We step out into the night, the air cool and crisp, perhaps signaling an early fall, but I'm burning up inside. The station is right across the street, and as we go over, Brigs points up at his building, a stately beast made of brick and white trim.

"I'm just up there," he says, pointing to the third floor. "If I ever get bored, I just stare out the window and wonder what Mr. Holmes is doing."

I see a shadow pass across his nearest wall. "That one? Is there someone there?"

He laughs. "That's just Winter. My dog."

I give him an incredulous smile. "You have a dog?"

"I told you my brother rescues them, right? Well, he kind of rubbed off on me."

Now I really want to go up into his flat. It would be the greatest excuse, too, to pet his dog and maybe, um, other things.

But somehow my willpower is still in control.

I do manage to say, "Maybe I can say hello next time."

That was brave of me. Assuming that there would be a next time and all.

"That would be nice."

We stop walking just outside the entrance to the station. He exhales heavily, brows pulled together, and tucks a strand of hair behind my ear, letting his fingers linger there a moment too long. "I still have to get used to the blonde. I still have to get used to *this*."

I'm not sure if I'm breathing or not. I'm so singularly focused on him, his fingers in my hair, the way his troubled gaze rests on my mouth.

Kiss me, I think. Let's see what else we can get used to.

"Goodnight Natasha," he says, and there's a beat of hesitation, like he's about to lean closer and place his lips on mine. I'm acutely aware of how much I want him, how much I ache.

Then he turns and walks away to his flat.

I watch his tall, lean frame go, admiring his ass beneath that motorcycle jacket, before I head underground.

When I finally get back to my flat, I'm utterly exhausted and still a bit drunk. I open the door and am immediately bombarded by Melissa in her bathrobe and a zillion questions.

"How was the date?"

"Fine." It was better than fine. It was...luminous.

"Did you get laid?"

"No." My conscience stepped in.

"Did he at least kiss you?"

"No." But I wish he had.

"Are you going out with him again?"

"I shouldn't." And I mean that.

She looks utterly crestfallen for a moment then looks me up and down with a one-shouldered shrug. "Maybe if you wore the mini-skirt like I told you."

"Maybe," I concede, even though I know I could wear a potato sack and it wouldn't matter. His soul speaks to me, regardless of what it's dressed in.

I go into the bathroom and wipe off my makeup in the mirror, before getting undressed and glancing down at my underwear. "Well, Sponge Bob," I say. "You did good."

Yet when I crawl into my bed and set my alarm for the morning, my chest feels carved out. Hollow. I knew that seeing Brigs tonight wasn't going to be easy. I just didn't anticipate how hard it was going to be and not in the way I thought. I expected that being in close proximity to him, away from the prying eyes and bustle of school, would have brought on an overwhelming sense of grief and pain, a reminder of the damage we had done together. I thought I would relive his last words to me, that I would remember that epic fall into darkness where I couldn't even save myself.

And while it was there, a potent undercurrent between us, it only came second to what really blindsided me: desire. The overwhelming need to be possessed by him, to have his heart, body, everything. It's like we are picking up where we left off—not on that phone call, but in my old London flat, with hope and promises and the memories of his stubble razing my skin as he kissed my lips and neck. God, even my nipple had been in his mouth.

Before I know what I'm doing, I'm touching myself, sliding my finger along my clit, wishing it was him, needing to burn off this energy that is sweltering inside me.

I come to thoughts of him, trying not to yell out his name, but I'm screaming it on the inside.

And just like that I'm sated enough to fall asleep, and hopeful enough that tomorrow this need will still be wiped clean.

Chapter Ten

BRIGS

Edinburgh

Four Years Ago

"Miranda," I say delicately, standing in the doorway of our kitchen.

She's at the breakfast table, a cup of tea in front of her, the steam rising in the beams of morning light coming through the window.

Her back is to me. She says nothing.

"Miranda," I say louder now and slowly walk closer to get a look at her.

When I'm finally in front of her, only then does she look up.

"Brigs," she says to me. "What is it? Is something wrong?"

I shake my head and pull out the chair, the noise of it scraping against the floor loud and jarring.

"No. Nothing. Why?"

She shrugs and sips her tea, her eyes going to the window.

It's silent in here. I can hear the grandfather clock ticking and the sound of Hamish playing with his toy cars in the other room.

It would be the perfect morning for any family.

But my heart is cold. The room is cold. Everything about this house is laced with ice.

She takes another sip of her tea and gives me an expectant look. She had a manicure yesterday, her nails polished to stones. "What is it?" she repeats, annoyance in her tone.

I guess it shows how often we actually talk to each other. I can't remember the last time we had a conversation that didn't involve Hamish. And that's not good. That's why my heart is being torn in a million directions. That's why I'm feeling everything that no married man should feel.

But it has to stop. I have to try.

"I was thinking," I tell her slowly, eyeing the window. "It's a brilliant day outside. Why don't we drop Hamish off at your parents, or mine, and the two of us go on a drive? Anywhere you want. We haven't taken Moneypenny out for a spin in years."

"Oh, Brigs," she says with a sigh, avoiding my eyes.

"What?"

"I don't have time for that," she says simply. "I've got a lunch date with Carol."

"We don't have to take long. We can go after."

She shakes her head, making the disagreeable little noise she makes when she's fed up with slow waiters at a restaurant or when the maid doesn't dust the china figurines in the sitting room.

"What would we do? Where would we go?"

"Anywhere," I tell her imploringly, leaning toward her and placing my hand palm down on the table. "And we can do anything. You just say the word."

"I'd rather not."

I inhale deeply through my nose, staying silent, hoping she'll see the need in my eyes.

She doesn't. She looks at me briefly, then back down to her tea. "I said I'd rather not," she repeats.

"Tomorrow then," I tell her. "We'll go tomorrow."

She sighs, hastily tucking her hair behind her ear. "I've got plans. You know I'm busy on the weekends."

"You're busy *every* day."

"Well, so are you," she snaps. "And you don't see me on your bloody case about it, do you?"

Maybe things would have turned out better if you were, I think. *If you actually cared.*

"Jesus, Miranda," I tell her. "When did this become okay?"

She raises her brows. "I don't even know what you mean."

I put my hand on top of hers. "This. This marriage. This distance. What happened to us?"

The last time we'd left the house together was a few weeks ago, and that was just to take Hamish to the park. I don't think we spoke more than two words to each other.

It was that night I went to Natasha.

That night that I saw the truth.

Miranda stares at me curiously before slowly removing her hand and hiding it under the table, where I can't touch her. "You are daft, Brigs. Absolutely daft. Nothing has happened to us. This is just us. This is just our life. It's always been this way. Nothing has changed."

But I've changed.

I've changed.

And this won't do anymore.

"Please," I say to her. "Come with me. Forget about your plans and your friends for once. Forget about taking care of Hamish. Forget about everything except your husband. Just this once. For me. Today. Please."

I'm begging. I know she can see it in my eyes, hear it in the crack of my voice. This has to happen. I won't go down on a sinking ship without trying to swim to shore.

She gives me a sour smile and shakes her head. "I told you," she says, voice clipped. Final. "I'm busy."

There's only a table between us but it's a million kilometers long.

I stare at her, hoping that she can at least see that I tried.

But she's back to looking out the window, sipping from her tea with manicured nails, her mind already far away, onto bigger things, better things.

"All right," I say with resignation. I get up. "I'm going to take the car out anyway."

"Be back before twelve-thirty," she tells me. "I'm not burdening Carol with Hamish on our lunch."

"Right," I tell her.

I stride out of the room, say goodbye to Hamish, kissing him on the head, grab my keys, and go.

I get into Moneypenny, the old Aston Martin, and hope she turns over easy. I need to get out of here, fast.

She coughs and stutters.

I slam my fist into the wheel.

"Fuck!"

I yell and yell, my face going red, spit flying out of my mouth. I throttle the wheel, as if I could strangle the car, the key digging into my other hand until finally she gives in.

My heart is racing. Sweat drips from my brow. I gun the car out of the driveway and onto to the road, nearly losing control on the sharp bend by Braeburn Pond. I drive and drive, taking the corners wide, cutting off cars, my mind caught in a whirlwind. Thoughts just tumble into each other without going anywhere, around and around and around.

Without even thinking, I end up in Natasha's neighborhood, on her street. I pull the car over and stare at her building. I can drive off. I can go blow off some steam with Lachlan. I can drive and scream and wish to god that things were different.

But I don't want to do it alone.

I get out of the car and head to her flat.

I knock on her door, wondering if she's even in, if she might still be sleeping. It's still early on a Saturday and we don't see each other on the weekends without it being work related, such as seeing a classic film at the cinema. I hadn't planned to talk to her until Monday, her last week of work as my research assistant before going back to London.

My heart pinches at that thought.

She's leaving me.

What the hell am I doing?

But then the door opens slowly and she's staring at me with wide eyes, her hair piled on top of her head in a messy bun, a fluffy robe around her body.

"Sorry," I say quickly, immediately feeling bad. "Did I wake you up?"

She yawns. "Kind of, but I should be getting up anyway. What's, um, up?"

I rub my lips together. "I...I wanted to know if you wanted to go for a drive?"

"Where?"

I shrug. "I don't know. Far away. But not too far. I have to be back by twelve-thirty for Hamish."

"What time is it now?"

"Eight-thirty."

She rolls her eyes. "And you were wondering if you woke me up. I should still be sleeping for at least another two hours."

I nod, embarrassed at my enthusiasm. I'm being inappropriate. "I should go."

I turn around, but she reaches out and grabs my arm, holding tight. "No, don't," she says quickly. "I want to go with you. Just give me five minutes, okay?"

I turn to look at her and she's flashing me a persuasive smile.

"I'll be in the car," I tell her.

Somehow she's true to her word. In five minutes she's jogging down the steps of her building, dressed in jeans and a tank top that shows off the tawny warmth of her summer tan. She hasn't touched her hair at all; it's still up in that bedhead bun, and there isn't a bit of makeup on her. She doesn't need it. She looks joyful. She looks absolutely beautiful.

"You're fast," I tell her as she slips into the passenger seat.

She giddily drums her hands across the dash and beams at me. "I'm fast when I want to be. I love this car. Where are we going again? Oh right, somewhere far away. Can we get coffee first? I'm dying."

I can't help but grin at her as I turn the key. The car starts on the first turn. She's my good luck charm. "You don't seem like you need coffee."

"I always need coffee," she says emphatically. "You know this. So where to?"

"I honestly don't know. You pick."

"Do you have a map?"

"Of Scotland?"

"Yeah."

I nod at the glove compartment. "In there."

She opens it and it falls open with a clunk. She takes out an old faded road map and starts looking it over.

"Anything strike your eye?"

"I'm looking for Loch Ness."

"That's too far."

"Okay, is there like another lake with a swamp monster?"

"Nearly all the lochs are in the Highlands."

"*Arrrrrrrrr* in the Highlands," she says playfully, imitating my accent.

"Okay, maybe no coffee for you."

"Don't be cruel, Professor Blue Eyes." She goes back to studying the map but the mention of my nickname makes a small fire build inside me. And not one of anger.

She points on the map. "Here. Balmoral."

"That's where the Queen lives."

"I know. I want to say hello."

"It's a two-hour drive," I point out.

"Well, then we better get cracking," she says. "The Queen is expecting us."

She's definitely full of spirit today. It seems to latch onto me and I ingest it like a tonic. She's erasing all the humiliation and pain from the morning.

We head out of the city, taking the A-90 to the M-90 and speed north. After we get her some coffee and we share a couple of sausage rolls for breakfast, I warn her that we literally will see the estate and have to head back. But she doesn't mind.

And honestly, neither do I. I crank the old radio on the car to pick up an oldies station playing a special on Otis Redding. The day is warm and gorgeous, and even though we're going fast, our windows are down, enjoying the wind and the sun on our skin.

About an hour into our drive, Natasha turns to me and says, "Tell me the truth. Why did you come to get me this morning?"

"Was it that unusual?" I ask without looking at her.

"Yes," she says. "The last time you came to my house without me knowing…"

"Back then I was following up on an email. I wanted to know if you were all right," I tell her before she can tell me anything else about that night.

"And now I want to know if you're all right," she says gently.

I glance at her. There's a softness in her eyes that undoes me. I grip the wheel hard, conscious of my every movement and how they might appear to her. A good man, after the night she kissed me, the night I kissed her right back, would have never been alone with her again.

But I'm not a good man.

I'm a man who is slowly but surely falling in the wrong direction.

"I'm fine," I say, but it comes out gruff and broken.

"What happened?" she asks. "It's your wife, isn't it?"

I shouldn't tell her anything. I should let private things be private. And yet, this is Natasha. I can hardly hide anything from her. Not only does she know me in ways I can't even fathom, but I only want to be honest with her. I want to tell her, talk to her, confide in her.

I want her in so many—too many—ways.

I take in a deep breath. "I'm just coming to realize that Miranda and I are entirely different people. And we have been for a long time."

Silence. I glance at her to see her staring down at her hands, her face round and sweet and sad. "Oh. Well, marriages are hard work, I imagine. It must be normal."

"That's what people want you to believe," I tell her. "But I'm not sure I'm willing to settle for that. Not when I know how good something can be."

I let those words hang in the air. I'm not sure if Natasha picks up on it.

She stares out the window. "There's always marriage counseling."

"She wouldn't go."

"You don't know that," she says half-heartedly.

"I *do* know," I tell her. I don't bring up the fact that I'd suggested it last year when I first started having troubles in the bedroom with Miranda. To be frank, I couldn't get it up. She didn't take as much offense as I thought, but even so, I wondered if there was some underlying issue.

The problem still persists, not that I've tried to make love to her in months. It's just...easier this way.

"She's perfectly happy to just let things be," I tell her.

"And you're not."

I knead my hands on the steering wheel and catch a look at myself in the rearview mirror, at how tired I look. "I'm not happy at all."

As Otis Redding plays, we fall silent. Trees and fields and small towns baking under sunshine pass outside the car.

"Are you happy now?" Natasha finally asks. "Right here, with me?"

I clench my jaw. How blunt this lovely girl is. No boundaries. No fear.

I look at her.

She looks back at me.

"Yes," I tell her. I can't lie. "I'm always happy with you."

And yet the truth is so hard to swallow.

Her eyes dance softly, her smile a delicate profession. "I'm happy with you."

My breath leaves me. I can't explain how her simple words make me feel. It's as if my soul has been gently nudged awake from a long slumber and she's the first sight I've seen.

There's nothing to say to that. Just this understanding of how each of us feel. We make each other happy.

I almost reach out with my hand and place it on hers, just to feel her flesh, her warmth, but then the warning bells go off, ringing in my ears.

"You're leaving," I say suddenly. "Next week is your last."

"I know," she whispers. "I've been trying not to think about it."

"I'm nowhere near done with the book."

"You'll find someone else to help you with the research."

"But someone else isn't you."

"I guess I'm irreplaceable," she says smartly, though when I glance at her, her expression is pained as she stares out the window.

Eventually we arrive at Balmoral, only to see the gates are closed.

"Maybe the Queen doesn't want visitors today," I tell her as I put the car in park, engine running.

I expect her to be disappointed but she just shrugs. She takes a sip of her coffee, now cold, and winces at the taste of it.

"Maybe we could find another castle nearby," I suggest.

"It's fine, really. This was never about the destination, Brigs. This was just about spending time with you."

She's slowly undoing me, thread by thread. I stare at her in near awe, this wondrous creature who wants to spend time with me. This rare and beautiful being who says I make her happy, maybe as happy as she makes me.

"Whatever do you see in me?" I ask her quietly. I can't help it.

She tilts her head, frowning at me. "I see you. What do you see?"

I suck in a breath through my teeth, the words hesitating in my mouth. I let them go.

"Everything," I tell her with a pure ache in my chest. "I see Natasha. I see everything I shouldn't want. Everything I do want. Everything that makes the world keep turning on its axis. You have no idea what you do to me. No idea."

She leans forward, eyes pleading. "Then show me what I do to you."

"You're leaving," I whisper.

"Show me," she says more urgently. "*Show me.*"

I oblige her.

I grab her face in my hands, my fingers pressing into her soft cheeks, and I kiss her. It isn't gentle. It is hard and feverish and wet as my lips crash against hers, as our tongues flow over each other, uninhibited. The fire inside is spreading everywhere, filling every hollow part of me. I let out a moan into her mouth as she returns my kiss with wild desperation, her hands holding my biceps tight, her nails digging into my shirt. My cock twitches in my pants, nearly a surprise, and I'm suddenly aware of how acute my desire for her is.

I slide my fingers into her hair and she moans softly, the thread around my heart spinning and spinning.

My lust is growing, unparalleled, and I'm very close to losing control of my body, of my spirit, and just handing it all over to her.

But I'm married and she's leaving me.

And whatever it is I want from her, it can't continue like this.

I break away, my lips aching from her absence, and we both stare at each other, breathing hard.

"I'm sorry," I say, trying to catch my breath and compose myself. "I'm sorry. That was wrong."

"Was it?" she asks softly. Then it's as if she catches herself. She shakes her head and leans back from me. "Yes, of course it was wrong."

"You're leaving," I tell her.

"And you have a wife."

"But I don't want her to be my wife anymore," I say, shocked at my admission. I exhale loudly and rest my head on the steering wheel. "I never wanted it like this. A fucking mess. I would have gone on in my marriage for many more years without knowing I was missing something."

"Eventually you would have woken up," Natasha says. "The human heart isn't meant to be caged by someone who doesn't feed it."

I turn my head, still pressed against the wheel, and manage to smile wanly at her. "That's very poetic."

"It's true. You owe it to yourself to make yourself happy, especially when you're with someone who isn't happy either."

"What are you saying?"

She raises her brows. "Well, I'm saying...what are you going to do when I'm gone?"

I shake my head, staring absently out the window at the trees that line the estate. "I don't know."

"Go back to the way things are with her? You said yourself there is no fixing it."

"There isn't...but...I would do it for Hamish."

"That's not the right answer."

"Well, it's the only answer I have right now," I say gruffly. "You should understand. Your father left you with your mother."

"I was ten," she snaps at me, "and I had to put up with a childhood of fighting and crying and name calling and parents who didn't speak to each other except for yelling. I just wanted my parents to be happy, so I could be happy. They should have broken up way sooner. It's just bad luck that I wasn't whisked off to France."

I sit back and run my hand up and down my face, trying to make sense of everything. I can still taste her lips, feel my fingers in her hair. My first and last glimpses of our desire.

She takes her mobile out of her pocket and glances at it. "It's getting late. We should probably head back now."

"Aye," I say with a sigh, turning the key. As before, it starts without a single cough.

We are both silent during the drive back, the tension between us ebbing and flowing, as if we keep trading thoughts between something wonderful and terrible. The kiss was both of those things.

When we get into the city, there isn't a lot of time for me to say goodbye to her. I wish I could spend time at her flat, talk some more about what happened before I leave. I'm too afraid to leave the words unsaid between now and Monday. Time alone, to think about what happened, could be damaging for either of us.

I park the car on the street and twist in my seat to face her. I want to tell her to email me later, or even text me. Just to let me know she's all right, that I'm not as horrible as I think I am.

I open my mouth but she looks at me point blank and says, "Brigs. I'm in love with you."

A hundred crashing cymbals go off in my chest.

"What?" I whisper, hardly believing my ears. My heart is drumming so bloody fast.

She bites her lip and nods. "I'm sorry. It's true. And I wasn't going to ever tell you but I've got nothing to lose except a week of employment." She smiles as if to herself. "I love you."

Then she gets out of the car, slamming the door and running across the street.

"Wait!" I call after her, but she doesn't stop. And what is there to say?

My precious truth, that I love her too, would only do more harm than good.

Chapter Eleven

BRIGS

London

Present Day

"Professor McGregor?" The voice is muffled and followed by a knock at the closed door.

I look up from my work, annoyed at being interrupted. I've been reading over my manuscript for the first time in years, trying to get back into the headspace of finishing the book. Being with Natasha two nights ago has fueled my creativity, like an energy cell that's finally being charged, and I don't want to lose my momentum while I have it.

Maybe if I don't say anything, don't make a sound, they'll go away.

Besides, I have a feeling I know who it is.

"Hello?" the voice sounds again, and this time they try the knob.

The door opens.

Shit.

I knew I should have locked it.

Melissa pokes her head in. "Is this a bad time?"

I eye her sternly over my reading glasses. "Sort of."

She smiles apologetically. "I'm sorry."

And yet she still comes in the room, walking over to my desk, a stack of papers in her hand. "I just had a few questions about grading the papers."

I sigh and quickly pinch the bridge of my nose. I can't exactly turn her away if it's something to do with being a teaching assistant. "Okay, what is it?"

"Are you okay?" she asks, cocking her head.

"I'm fine," I tell her. "Just a bit of a headache."

Just a bit of wishing you would go away. There's something so off-putting about Melissa. I just can't put my finger on it. It's probably because she told me to stay the hell away from Natasha and I never listened to her. And if I'm lucky enough to see Natasha again, I'm going to have to ask her if it was true, if she put Melissa up to it. Something tells me she didn't, not from the way she was looking at me on Monday night.

Not kissing her was by far and large the right thing to do.

And yet I still regret it.

"Well," she says, sitting on the edge of my desk, her short skirt hiked up to show off her legs. "I honestly don't know what to do. I've never graded anyone before. I'm not sure what's a good essay and what's a bad one."

I cock my brow. "Surely you know what a bad essay reads like."

She shrugs.

I explain. "Well, just think of your essays and the grades you got. Pick your highest grade and work backward. If those essays don't measure up, go lower. Or if you spot the worst essay in the pile, grade all the other papers against that."

"There is just so much power right here." She places her hand at her chest. "I could ruin these students' lives if I wanted to. Absolutely ruin them."

I frown at her. "You could, but you won't. They're undergrads. Just kids. By the end of the semester you'll get a better idea of who is doing good and who's in it to fail, but for now, you're supposed to give them guidance and hope. Be as constructive as possible."

"Don't you think I could better grade them on your teachings if I understood your brain better?"

I crack a sardonic smile and tap my head. "Believe me, you don't want in this brain."

"You'd be surprised, Professor Blue Eyes."

Everything in me stills. "What did you call me?" I manage to ask, my voice hard.

"You remember Natasha's nickname for you, don't you?" she asks, sounding oh so innocent.

I'm fumbling for something to say, and the longer I'm silent, the more smug she looks. "That's fairly inappropriate," I tell her. "Please don't call me that."

"Brings back bad memories, huh?"

A flash of anger burns in my chest. "You told me yourself to forget her. This hardly helps."

She runs her finger up and down my desk. "Oh, I don't think you're ever going to forget her, Professor McGregor. I know what being lovesick looks like."

"Melissa," I say sharply. "If that's all you wanted to discuss with me, then I'm afraid I'm going to have to ask you to leave."

"Then ask me to leave."

I nod at the door. "There's the bloody door. Use it. And next time you need actual help with something, remember to stick to the subject at hand. You may assist me in my class, but that's all you do—assist. I'm the teacher here, and I'm in charge of your grades and your future. Don't forget that."

She raises her brows. "Are you threatening me?"

I shake my head, my jaw tense. "Please, if that's all, just go. I have a lot of work to do."

She narrows her eyes at me and jumps off the desk. "Fine. Last time I ask my teacher for help."

She gathers up her papers and leaves my office, slamming the door behind her.

I let out a sigh of relief.

Bloody fucking hell. Just what the hell was that about?

The first time she came by I chalked it up to her being an overly protective friend. Now I don't know what to think. She either hates me and wants to get under my skin…or it's the opposite. And she wants to get under my skin.

I wish I could talk to Natasha about it. I haven't spoken to her since our pub date, meeting, whatever the hell it was. I've tried, numerous times, to compose an email to her, but I keep erasing the bloody thing. I don't know what to say, I don't know how to express what it is I want from her. I don't even know.

But I know it starts with seeing her again.

And soon.

I bite the bullet and just start to write.

Natasha,

I was wondering when you'd like to come over and see my dog.

He's been on his best behaviour lately and I would like to take advantage of this.

Any night this week works for me.
He'd prefer to see you tonight, and I'm fine with that too.

Brigs

I know for a fact that the whole having a dog thing helps any man with the ladies. I mean, just look at Lachlan. Okay, that's a bad example since the bastard could get any woman without the dogs, but still. I may have not rescued Winter for this purpose, but that won't stop me from using him that way.

I wait for her response, wondering if she's in class. I consider looking her up in the system and seeing her class schedule, but the computer dings as her reply comes in.

I brace myself as I click on it, worried by the quickness of her response. It could be a giant "fuck off" for all I know.

Brigs,

Tell your dog tonight sounds good. I would love to pop in and say hello.

Maybe afterward we could catch a movie. My brain is burning out on all the class requirements, and there's that new Tarantino film at the cinemas I think you'd hate.

Natasha.
PS your dog better be as awesome as he sounds.

I've got the biggest fucking grin spread across my face. I quickly look for theatres closest to my flat and tell her to come over between seven-thirty and eight. It will give me just enough time to show her around before we catch the film.

I understand why she suggested going out, too. Her coming over to my flat without a plan is asking for trouble. Maybe it's just the kind of trouble I'm looking for, but it's still trouble in the end.

I'm positively giddy as I take the train home, like a goddamn schoolboy with a crush. I have to remind myself that I can't get carried away, can't take anything for granted. I guess I'm just happy to have Natasha back in my life, the chance to hear her laugh, to feel every inch of light that she radiates.

Her face Monday night wasn't the same as when I first ran into her in the halls. The fear and the pain were gone, and her eyes were deep with warmth and a certain ease, especially as the night wore on. Of course we were both half-corked, but even so, that only meant the real Natasha was coming through.

The last thing I want is to move too fast, to scare her—or myself—away. The truth is, I don't really know what this is, other than the fact that I have this insatiable need to see her again, to be with her. I haven't been able to laugh, feel joy, or bypass the years of grief in such a long time. To come alive with her is nearly addicting.

I keep this in mind as I do a quick tidying of my flat before taking Winter for a walk around Regent's University. When I get back, none of my nervous energy has dissipated. Winter seems to pick up on that too, running around the drawing room while I quickly jump in the shower.

I pause briefly when I'm done, eyeing my body in the mirror. I may be older than I was four years ago, but at least I don't look it. In fact, I look better than before, the gym paying off, my muscles showcased well by my lean frame. It seems absolutely crazy to think that with everything I feel for Natasha, everything we've gone through, she still hasn't seen me naked. She's barely touched me.

It was for the best, of course, and I have to remind myself not to dwell on it, nor the fact that the future is full of possibility. For all I know, being actual platonic friends may be the easiest—and the smartest—thing to do.

By the time seven-thirty rolls around, I've been sitting on the couch for a while, attempting to work on my manuscript on my laptop, having consumed about two pots of Earl Grey tea. I'm absolutely wired, my leg bouncing, my eyes forever dancing to the door and back.

Eventually I take to staring out the window to the street below, Winter at my side doing the same thing. My eyes are trained to the left, where she would come out of Baker Street station.

Then she appears, jeans and a jacket, and I wish I had binoculars so I could really spy on her and see the expression on her face, if she's nervous, happy, whatever. That would make me one hell of a pervy professor, but I'm fairly certain I wouldn't be the first.

The intercom sounds and I buzz her in without a word. I wait by the door for her to knock, and when she does, I still jump a little. I wait a moment, curling and uncurling my fists at my side, trying to compose myself, before opening it.

"Hi," she says brightly, staring up at me.

I can't help but take a moment to just drink in the sight of her. It does something so unearthly to me, this weightlessness in my chest.

"Hi," I say, swallowing thickly. I open the door wider. "Welcome to my humble abode."

She steps one foot in before Winter is bounding toward her like a fluffy white steam train.

"Winter, sit!" I command, pointing at him to get his arse on the ground.

But Winter doesn't care. He runs right to Natasha and starts to jump on her.

"Winter!" I yell, grabbing his collar, but Natasha is giggling and sinking to a crouch so she can muss with him on his level.

"I'm so sorry, he's such a special case," I try and explain, shutting the door behind her.

"He's lovely," she says as he licks her all over her face.

Lucky fucking dog.

I grab his collar again and pull him back. "I've had him for a year almost and he's pretty much still a puppy. I'm sure he'll outgrow that but I'm not sure if he'll outgrow being a jerk."

She's smiling as she stands back up, wiping her face with her sleeve. "He's beautiful. Where did you get him again?"

"Found him on Christmas Eve. Poor little bastard was left alone by someone in a barn, don't know who. There was a snowstorm and I took him to my grandfather's place. That obviously didn't last one night. He's been with me ever since."

I let go of Winter and he immediately sticks his nose in her crotch.

I smirk at her. "Well, at least he knows where to go."

"Hey," she says, mouth agape as she swats me across the arm. "And *ow*, what's with your bicep?"

"Nothing at all," I tell her, flexing automatically. "Shall I give you the tour?"

My flat is pretty nice. It's not as big as my brother's out in Edinburgh—that's what smart investments and rugby money gets you—but it's still fairly large for this part of London. I actually lucked out, considering it's a rental. And though it's a bit more than what I'm used to spending, the place is starting to feel like home and that says a lot. The last couple of years I've just been adrift.

I take her around, pointing out the maple floors and the white-washed walls and cornices, realizing that aside from a few random women I've brought in here on drunken nights, I haven't shown anyone my apartment. Not Lachlan, not my parents. It's not that they haven't hinted that they'd like to stop by, it's just that I've never offered. It's like I'm scared to let them see this new life and my utter lack of confidence in it.

But now, with Natasha slowly walking in front of me, her boots echoing on the wood floors, I realize I'm not afraid. I want to share this with her, I crave her opinion, and I need her to be part of it all in some way.

"This is beautiful, Brigs," she says in soft awe as we come back to the drawing room.

Unfortunately, I can't beam proudly at her for too long because Winter comes trotting out of my bedroom with one of my shoes in his mouth.

"Oh, bloody hell," I swear, reaching for him, but he bounds out of the way, tail wagging, and leaps onto the couch. When I give it another go, he at least drops the shoe and makes a break back to the bedroom. "I swear, sometimes I think the reason he was abandoned was because some gypsy put some shoe-eating curse on him."

"Now that sounds like it could be quite the indie film."

"It sounds like something Shia LaBeouf would produce." I glance at my watch, wishing we had more time here. Truthfully I want to spend the night talking to her, looking at her, not sitting in silence in a cinema—especially while having to suffer through Tarantino's ego for three hours. "I suppose we should get going."

She grins mischievously, which only cements the fact that I wish we could just stay in. The spark in her eyes is making my blood run hot. "I love the look on your face right now," she says.

"What look?"

She steps forward and taps her finger against my chin. "This one. The one that says you're prepared to be tortured for the rest of the night."

The movie won't be the only thing torturing me, I think, so very tempted to take her finger into my mouth and playfully bite it. Even the slight touch of her fingertip to my skin feels hot and deadly.

I grab my leather jacket and give Winter a warning look before I usher him out of my bedroom and close the door. Then Natasha and I head out of the flat and into the night.

We walk side by side down Baker Street a few blocks to the Everyman Cinema, and with a little bit of time to kill, we order a drink at their bar while waiting for the film to start.

"What are you smiling at?" she asks, eyeing me over her drink.

"Am I smiling?" I ask, and I'm surprised to find that I am. We were just talking about how terrible the UK Netflix is. It's pretty ridiculous that something so benign could have me so enthralled, bent on her every word and apparently smiling like an idiot.

I straighten up, reminding myself to stop acting like such a wanker. What was it that Melissa had called me? Lovesick?

I didn't quite agree with that at the time, and the memory of this afternoon puts a bitter taste in my mouth.

"I'm sorry," Natasha says, putting her hand on mine. "I didn't mean to point it out like that. Please keep smiling. It makes me happy."

The mention of her happiness eases the tension.

I put Melissa on the back burner.

We finish up our drinks and head to the concession stand, getting in line.

"Do you want the usual?" I ask her.

She grins at me. "Of course."

I get us a large bucket of popcorn and a box of Maltesers and hand them to Natasha, who ceremoniously opens the candy and dumps them into the popcorn.

I shake my head, letting out a little laugh. It looks like the least appetizing thing, but I know from experience it tastes rather addicting.

"You love it," she teases me.

"I do," I admit. "Doesn't really help my progress at the gym though."

"Oh? Since when have you become Professor Vain?"

"Since I discovered how awesome I look."

She rolls her eyes, but the way she draws her lip in between her teeth makes me think she'd like to see the evidence firsthand.

With that optimism, we head into the packed theatre. We manage to find a pair of seats together, on the aisle, and within moments the commercials and trailers start playing. There's something so comforting to me about the cinema; it's a place where I can truly relax and unwind. Maybe it's the darkness or the smell of the popcorn and spilled soda, or the feel of the crowd around you, but as long as I can turn off the overanalyzing part of my brain, I'm swept away for two hours, entirely incognito.

But tonight, now, with her beside me, I can't relax at all. I can't turn off my brain. I don't even know what is going on with the movie. The actors on screen are moving their lips, spouting some carefully crafted dialogue, but I don't hear them.

I am completely, singularly, transfixed by her. Natasha. Sitting beside me in the darkness, our shoulders brushing against each other, the planes of her beautiful face lit up in swaths of silver. It's like the most mesmerizing light show, changing with the shots in the film. I can't look away, and I don't want to.

She's as enthralled with the film as I am with her, laughing at the dialogue, cringing at the violence, and I feel my heart swell inside me like a red balloon, pressing against my ribcage. It *was* fate that put her in my path, a chance to get something right that wasn't right in the first place.

But why do I have such a foreboding sense of doom, buzzing like flies at the back of my head?

Because you don't deserve to feel this way, I tell myself. *Not after everything you've done.*

I swallow the shame, refusing to feel it. Just once, *just once,* I want to be unshackled from my mistakes.

I want to be free.

I need to be brave.

Natasha turns her head to look at me, one half of her face highlighted by the screen.

"You're not watching the movie," she whispers.

I lean into her neck, my lips just below her ear. "I'd rather be watching you."

I don't pull away at first, keeping my mouth there, her skin so close, taking in her sweet smell. Thoughts run through my head, heavy and weighted, thoughts I don't dare disclose.

I want to kiss you.

Lick you.

Taste you.

Fuck you.

It's a side of me that's dirty and secretive but completely real.

As if she can hear my thoughts, she stiffens.

I lean back to look at her, feeling my brows pull together. "Was that inappropriate?"

She nods, facing the screen. "Yes."

I stare at her for a few moments. She's not being facetious. She means it.

That balloon in my chest is slowly deflating. The funny thing is, I didn't think twice about it, which only cements how natural it feels to be around her. But she obviously doesn't feel the same way.

I sit beside her for another minute, stiff and awkward in the dark, the embarrassment creeping over me until I abruptly get out of my seat and stride up the aisle and into the cinema lobby. It's quiet out here, both screens occupied, and I head to the washroom to compose myself.

I splash a bit of cold water on my face then shake it off, staring up at myself in the mirror. We've both changed, and as much as it feels like we're back in time, back to the same people that we were, we've both been through so much that it's just not possible.

We can't go back to what was.

But we can go forward.

After I compose myself, I head back out into the lobby.

Natasha is standing there grasping the bag of popcorn for dear life and peering at me with so much worry that it's fucking adorable.

"I'm sorry," she whispers.

"So am I," I tell her, walking right up to her until I'm so close, she has to take a step backward. "I'm sorry for being inappropriate, and I'm sorry for this."

I quickly lean down and kiss her. Her soft cry of surprise is muffled by my lips pressed flush against hers for a long, hot minute. Then my mouth opens and my tongue slides across hers.

The bucket of popcorn drops beside us.

My lungs evaporate in a kind of heady infatuation.

I grab her now, my hand at the back of her head, at the small of her back, pulling her to me, wanting to get deeper, hotter, as flames lick along my skin and my desire is more painful than ever.

It doesn't matter that I'm in a cinema lobby, in public.

We could be on Mars, for all I care; she's all the oxygen I need.

She's feeling it too. I know she is from the way her mouth moves with hunger, the tiny, breathless sounds she's making, the way her body feels underneath me, wild and tense and ready to explode.

With a gasp, she suddenly breaks away, and the bright, effervescent cord between us snaps, leaving me empty and stunned.

"I can't do this," she cries softly. Panic is etched clearly on her face.

She tries to pull away, but I'm grabbing her arms, holding her in place.

"Can't do what?" I demand.

"This!" Her voice is choked, her eyes are growing wet and brimming with pain. "You kissing me, me being with you. Any of this."

My chest grows cold. "Why not?" I manage to say, even though I know her answer. I know exactly why "why not?" because it comes from that same dark place where guilt buzzes like flies.

"Because we're dishonoring the dead!" she sobs. "Don't you feel that?"

I immediately let go of her, sucking in my breath.

She's breathing hard and staring at me like she knows she's done wrong.

I can barely speak. "They were my family, Natasha. Don't think I'm not thinking about them every single day, that I won't be thinking about them for the rest of my life."

"I'm sorry," she whispers, shaking her head, a tear falling to the floor. I'm barely aware that another theatre is emptying, people coming out of the doors. "Brigs, I'm sorry. I just look at you and..."

"You think I'm a mistake," I offer flatly.

"Don't you?" She looks around wildly then closes her eyes. "I just don't know what to do."

Frustration builds at the back of my throat. I want to be patient, I want to be understanding. But if she has more problems with us than I do, I'm not sure what I can do to change her mind. I'm not even sure if it's right for me to feel this way.

But I do.

She bends down to pick up the spilled bucket of popcorn, but I reach it before she does, and walk over to the trash, tossing it in. The lobby is crowded now and people are walking between us. Any chance for a serious conversation is over.

But we can't be over.

I walk back over to her. "Let's get out of here. Let's go somewhere and talk."

"There's nothing to talk about," she says, practically pleading. "Thanks for the movie, Brigs."

She turns and walks away. I stand there for a second, dumbfounded that she's actually going to leave it like this. Then I jog after her, fighting through the crowd until I'm at her side, out on Baker Street.

"What happened? What changed?" I hiss in her ear as I hurry alongside her. "Monday night you were feeling fine, we were doing good, I was the happiest I've felt in years!"

Her brows shoot up. "What happened?! You just *kissed* me."

"So what's the difference?"

She stops, walking back a step to get out of the way of pedestrians. She blinks at me. "The difference is everything. Being friends is difficult enough, but anything more than that..."

I take a step toward her, bearing down on her. "You used to be in love with me. And I was in love with you."

"And look what that love did! It ruined both of our lives."

My pulse hammers against my throat, but I can't look away from her. So much of me wants to agree, does agree, and yet that's not the whole story. It's brutal, but it's not that simple.

"Natasha," I say quietly, my eyes roaming her face, searching for something to latch on to. Her cheeks are flushed, her lip worrying between her teeth. "I'm not sure when I'll stop feeling guilty. I'm not sure when you'll stop feeling guilty. But the fact that both of us have come out a dark hole, to emerge here," I throw my arms out, "where we are now, says we're capable of letting go. Capable of moving on."

"And how can we move on if we're back to square one?"

"Because this isn't square one," I tell her, gently running my fingers under her chin. "This isn't going backward. This is going forward. We get to start again. Now. From scratch."

She closes her eyes briefly, taking in a deep breath. Then she shakes her head. "That's easy for you to say, Brigs," she says sadly, moving away from me, "when I'm feeling everything for you that I felt before."

God, my fucking heart.

She leaves.

"Please don't walk away from me," I call after her, some passerby turning their heads, hearing the hurt break my voice.

But she doesn't turn her head. She doesn't listen. And I know this time that running after her again will be futile.

Maybe it was futile all along.

I sigh, running my hand through my hair. Then I turn and go back into the theatre to finish the rest of the film.

She was right about the movie.

I hate it.

Chapter Twelve

BRIGS

Edinburgh

Four Years Ago

I've gone mad. Bloody fucking mad.

That's what love does to you. Your heart becomes so fucking needy that it siphons energy from everything, including your own brain cells. Your pulse beats to thoughts of her, your veins run hot with need and want. Everything about you becomes so singularly focused on one person that there's no room for you anymore.

And you don't care. Because as maddening as it is, love is the only time you really, deeply feel what it is to be alive. And for that, you'll put up with anything.

I have to put up with a hollow chest filled with hornets. I feel utterly empty because Natasha is back in London, has been for two weeks now. I feel completely ravaged because I still remain married, still lost in what the hell I should do, what the right thing is.

After Natasha told me she loved me in the car, leaving me to soldier the weight of it, I grappled with what to say to her. I texted her that night asking if she was all right and she said she was fine. That was it.

Then on Monday she came to my office as usual. I tried to bring it up but she only raised her hand and said it didn't matter.

I wanted then to tell her how I felt, that I loved her too, that I've been fighting these feelings for months. I wanted to tell her everything.

But I couldn't. I don't know why I held on to my truth like that. Maybe I was protecting myself, protecting Hamish. Maybe I was protecting nothing at all and I was just a chicken shit. The latter is probably true. In the face of it all, I just wanted to run and hide.

I wish I hadn't though. I wish I could have manned up and told her the truth. And because I didn't, the last week of us working together was strained. The joy, the fun, the laughs were all gone. Natasha completely threw herself into her work, saying she needed to do as much for me as she could, but I could tell she was just looking for a distraction. She laid herself bare to me and I couldn't do the same.

Coward.

And then the last day we were together, the last time I saw her, she leaned forward, kissed me gently on the cheek, and whispered, "I still mean it."

And I said nothing.

Fucking coward.

So here I am, in my office at the start of the new semester, wondering how she's doing while trying to go over my course outline at the same time.

It's five o'clock. I should be heading back home but I'm spending more and more time at the office, just like before, only now I'm alone. The only reason I head back early is to see Hamish, but even then I noticed Miranda is being more possessive over the amount of time I spend with him, which is ridiculous.

I can't help but think back to what Natasha said about her parents and how her childhood was tainted with their fighting. I don't want Hamish to grow up with his parents possessive over him and not even speaking to each other. In the last week Miranda said she wanted a bedroom of her own, and what's he going to think when he gets older? We don't talk, we only fight and now we sleep in different rooms? He's going to realize that his family is irreparably broken from the inside out.

I exhale loudly and stand up, stretching my arms above my head. My mobile beeps.

I pick it off the desk and peer at it.

It's Natasha.

I've barely heard from her, with only the occasional email.

Do you ever get lonely? the message says.

My heart sinks as I text back, **Always. Are you lonely now?**

Yes, I miss you. I need you.

I miss you, too.

Do you need me?

Yes. I stare at the phone, wanting to say more. But I don't.

Did you ever love me?

Damn. Damn, damn, damn. I stare up at the ceiling, seeking answers, but there's only plaster.

I can't do this over the phone, I text her.

I wait. There's no response.

I flop down in my chair and stare at the phone.

Please text back, please text back.

She doesn't.

Finally, I call her. It goes to her voicemail, the same one she never checks.

I text her again: **Where do you live? I'm coming to you.**

She texts back her London address.

I'm not thinking properly. I'm irrational. But nothing is stopping me as I look up flights to London. I find a thirty pound shitty Ryanair flight that will get me into the city no later than 9pm. There's no way to get back until the morning, but I can still make my afternoon class. It just means I'll be spending the night in London.

You're booking a hotel, I tell myself.

I then text Miranda, telling her I won't be home until late, knowing she goes to bed early anyway.

She never texts back.

I grab my stuff and go.

It's crazy, and I'm thinking it even as the plane lands at Stansted Airport. But if I don't deal with this now, with her, it will haunt me. If I don't deal with it now, I'll never be able to let it go. I need to be able to see what can be. I need to look down that path, see where it ends, and make a decision.

If only it were so easy.

The cabbie drops me off in front of a modest brick building in Woolwich, above a takeaway Chinese shop and a nail salon. I ring her buzzer, waiting as a group of college-age kids stumble past, drunk.

She answers it, her voice crackling. "Brigs?" Then she buzzes me up.

I rush through the door and take the stairs two at a time. I was trying to be calm and composed the entire flight down here, but the minute I hear her voice through the intercom, every part of me lights up. Now I can't get to her fast enough.

Just as I reach her door, it flings open, and Natasha is standing there, wearing a plain black dress. I've never seen her legs other than in jeans, and I take a moment to stare at them, long, incredibly soft, and curvy, before I bring my gaze to her face.

It's her face that sets my skin on fire.

It's her lips, full and sensual, that make my heart drum against my chest.

And it's her eyes, wanting so much from me, wanting to give me so much, that has me storming through the doorway and grabbing her. My mouth is wild on hers, unapologetic, and thirsty beyond repair.

As I'm cupping her face in my hands, she's digging her hands into my shoulders and kicking the door shut. While my tongue dances with hers, she's pressing her body against mine. I can feel my erection, thick and hard between us, and my hands slide down the silk of her back to her arse, where I grab and squeeze, feeling more savage by the minute.

We walk, stumbling backward through the unfamiliar hall until I have her back against the wall. My lips go to her neck, licking, tasting her. She feels better on my tongue than I ever imagined, and it's nearly impossible not to devour her whole while she tastes so sweet.

"Tasha," I groan into her neck, my hand sliding over her breast as I press myself against her, pinning her to the wall. "I've never wanted you more."

I've never wanted *anyone* more.

She lets out a fluttery sigh, grabbing the back of my neck with her hand, squirming beneath my touch. I pull down the top of her dress, taking her nipple into my mouth and sucking it with one long, hard pull.

"Fuck," she whimpers, tugging at my hair. "Please don't stop. Please don't stop."

But her urging words make me realize I *have* to stop. It's now or never.

I don't know how, but I manage to pull away. I'm surprised I have any willpower, any brain power left. All my blood is throbbing in my cock and I'm inflamed with the desire to finally have her, here, now, in any way possible.

What little is left of my morals, though, is coming through strong.

"Natasha," I say, my voice hoarse. I continue to press myself against her, smoothing back the hair from her face, peering at her intently. Her mouth looks bruised, damp, her eyes glazed by lust as she stares back at me. "I love you."

She seems to melt before my eyes. "You love me?" she asks with soft liquid eyes. "Really?"

I nod and rest my forehead against hers, closing my eyes as I breathe. "Yes. For a while now. Even before you told me."

"Why didn't you tell me then?" she whispers.

"Because I'm a coward. And confused. And I don't know how to do the right thing."

"Love is the right thing, isn't it?"

I sigh and pull back, cupping her face in my hands. "I wasn't sure. But I think I know now. I'm going to ask Miranda for a divorce."

Her eyes widen. "Really?"

I swallow thickly. "Yes. It's going to hurt her, I think. At least her pride. But I have to tell her the truth."

"Don't tell her about me," she says with panicked eyes.

"That's not my plan," I tell her. "But the truth is that I don't love her anymore. I'm not sure I ever did. I want to do whatever I can for Hamish, but staying with her is not the answer."

She studies me for a moment, searching every inch of my face, then smiles. "You love me," she says softly, perhaps finally believing it.

"I love you," I whisper, running my thumb over her beautiful lips. "You've done something to me, awakened a heart in my soul. You have completely enchanted me, my girl, and I am powerless against you. You've taken me from the very start."

"Kiss me again," she says.

I gently press my lips against hers and pull back. I let out a deep breath. "Until I tell Miranda, I can't..."

"I know." Her fingertips trail over my cheekbone. "I can wait. I'll do anything for you. You know that, don't you?"

I give her a wry smile. "Oh, really," I say, brushing the tip of my nose against hers. "Can you suggest where I should sleep tonight? I have to get up early in the morning for my flight."

"Sleep here," she says. I raise my brow and she continues. "Take the couch. I have no flatmates. No one will bug you."

"And if I want you to bug me?"

"That can very easily be arranged," she says, wiggling her fingers in my face. "You know how annoying I can be."

"Hardly," I tell her.

But it's still early. To be honest, I don't think I can sleep at all tonight. I'm flying high and brimming with energy. I'm madly in love with the girl in front of me, and to go to sleep would mean missing out on her face, her words, her touch.

So we go into her tiny kitchen to make a pot of tea, then take a seat on the couch. We stay up until 3am, just talking about everything under the sun, my arm around her as she relaxes into me.

Being with her is as easy as it was before, like we were made for each other, but now we're on another level, another layer. It feels absolutely right, so much so that I can't even question it. We discuss hopes, dreams, the future, and though everything is up in the air, she's not. She's here with me and I've got her.

I'm not letting go now.

When she falls asleep, it's sudden, a ragdoll in my arms. I pick her up and carry her to her bed, laying her down gently. I watch her for a few moments, my chest warmed by the sight, and then head into her living room to catch a few hours of sleep.

The alarm on my mobile goes off at seven, but Natasha is still sleeping, so I quickly jump in her shower. My flight is at 10:30 and I'll go straight from Edinburgh airport to the university.

I put on the same clothes from yesterday and start thinking of when to tell Miranda. I might need a few days to work up the courage, but it has to be done. There will be hell to pay, but for Natasha it's a fire I'll gladly walk through.

"Are you leaving?" I hear Natasha's sleepy voice as I finish my cup of instant coffee in the kitchen. I look up to see her leaning against the doorframe, dressed in an oversized T-shirt and nothing else.

I get up, putting the cup in the sink, and come over to her, wrapping my hand around the small of her tiny waist. "My flight is very soon," I murmur before kissing her delicately on the lips.

She puts her arms around me, holding me close in a hug.

"What if this is it?" she whispers into my neck.

I shake my head, breathing her in. "This isn't it. This is only the beginning. Of us. Of a new life together. It won't be easy, but it will be ours."

"But so much can happen..."

I pull back and brush her hair off her face. "Tasha. Please." I plant a kiss on her forehead. "We'll be together, I promise."

I walk toward the door, my hand on the knob. "I'll text you when I land, okay?"

She nods, biting her lip.

"Everything is going to be okay," I tell her.

I open the door.

There's a girl standing on the other side, about to knock.

I jump back in shock.

"Melissa," Natasha cries out softly.

The girl, dark hair, large forehead, and dressed in workout gear looks between us both with raised eyebrows. "Sorry, uh... Natasha, I thought we were going for a run this morning..."

"Oh right," Natasha says. "I, uh, okay."

"I was just leaving," I tell the girl, hoping Natasha doesn't get in any shit for this. This Melissa is staring at me with an incredulous, albeit slightly disgusted expression.

I walk past her and down the steps just in time to hear Melissa exclaim to Natasha, "Who the hell was that?"

The man she loves, I think to myself. *And the man who loves her*.

I hail a cab and head back to the airport and back to the life that's about to change forever.

Chapter Thirteen

NATASHA

London

Present Day

I've never walked so fast in my life, and it's not an easy feat when your vision is blurry from tears, your chest burning from the desperate need to cry out. Yet if I don't walk to Baker Street station like my life depends on it, Brigs might catch up with me. And if Brigs catches up with me again, I know I'll be powerless in his arms.

I'm already regretting it, regretting everything. The things I said—I lashed out like this was only my guilt to carry, that I was the only who lost something. I was trying to hurt him, and I don't even know why when he's been through so much pain already.

When he kissed me, I felt the world spin back in time, back to when I loved him. It gave me whiplash. And so much fucking fear. Fear that I would fall again. Fear that the enormity of our past would break us apart within seconds of coming together.

And I guess that kind of happened. Only it was at my hand, not his, and not fate's. I'm finally in control.

I wish I wasn't. I don't always move in the right direction.

I get on the train and breathe a sigh of relief once the doors close, knowing that Brigs hasn't come after me. It's fairly empty, and even though my head is fuzzy and my body exhausted, I can't help but watch a couple a few seats across from me.

The girl is petite with a blue pixie haircut and a nose ring, and she's sitting in his lap. He looks like the typical jock you'd see in America, tanned with big muscles and a penchant for polo shirts, only I bet here he's the captain of a cricket team or something like that.

My eyes are drawn to them, not only because of how different they both look, like if they were back in high school they definitely would not be dating, but because of how at ease they are with each other. They aren't even talking, nor are they making out. They're just staring at each other, smiling with their eyes, enveloped in their own beautiful world.

My heart aches so acutely, it burns.

I want that.

I need that.

I could have had that.

Twice already.

The happy couple gets off the train near my stop, so I have to stare at them in jealousy and fascination the entire time. My mind keeps circling over the look on Brig's face when I told him we were dishonoring the dead. It's like I slapped him as hard as I could.

And yet he still stood there, wanting us to move on, to have another chance. After everything I said and all that we'd gone through, he wanted us to start over.

Could we do that? Could we really put it all behind us and start from scratch? Forget the old love and build a new one?

I want to believe that, I truly do.

There's just too much at stake.

It wasn't just the guilt over Miranda and Hamish's death that got me in the end. It was that I never saw Brigs after that. That my heart was shattered like glass while I was burning in shame.

He broke me into pieces.

And that's something that could easily happen again. There's no guarantee that it wouldn't. Brigs could freak out down the line as easily as I just did. And if it became serious, what would happen when we meet his family? If he meets mine? Would we ever be able to tell them how we truly first met?

The other thing is, there's no option for us not to become serious. We may be starting over, but the moment either of us fall into bed with each other, we're all in. I know he is. I know I'd be. There are no baby steps here. It's all or nothing.

I'm just not sure I'm ready for *all.*

And I'm not sure I can live with nothing.

I get back to the flat and Melissa, as usual, is waiting up for me. It's almost like she stops dating and/or sleeping around the moment I start going on these dates and starts hanging around at home, waiting for me. Like my mother. Of course she thinks I'm going out with fictional "Bradley" from the art history program and had high hopes for me before I left the flat tonight.

But when she sees my face, her ravenous expression drops. She comes over to me, cooing, "What happened?"

I need to come up with an excuse, but I feel like I'm all out of them.

"He stood me up," I say, going into my bedroom, dropping down on the bed, and taking off my boots.

"What?" she exclaims. "Why didn't you come home right away?"

"I really wanted to see the movie," I tell her, feeling bad that I'm lying. "I'm used to going to them alone."

"Maybe he went to the wrong cinema. Or," she snaps her fingers together, "maybe you did."

I shake my head. "No. I called him and he said he forgot, that he was busy, and he'd call me back. I heard a girl giggling in the background. He never called back." I add a shrug, so I don't make it into a bigger deal than it is. "It's fine. It got me out of the house."

"But you look so upset," she says "Your mascara is all smudged. I haven't seen you like this...well, since he who shall not be named."

Professor Blue Eyes.

Brig's anguished face fills my head and I quickly shut my eyes, as if that helps him go away. He's shining in my mind more potent than ever.

"I'm just..." I grapple for the right words, words that aren't lies. "Discouraged. And frustrated."

"Yeah, I get that," she says slowly. "I have to say though, Tasha, it's nice to see you suffer."

I raise my brows at her. "Are you serious?"

She gives me a smirk in return. "I'm just saying, you've kind of been a bloody robot for the last few months, ever since you came back to London. I get that you're trying to put up the barricades and move on, but you have to feel some emotion every once in a while, even the bad. It doesn't make you weak."

Holy fuck, she's actually being sweet and apparently sincere. I'm touched.

"Anyway," she says, "I'll leave you to it. But if you ever need to talk, I'm here for you. I'm just glad that you're getting out there and not letting the past define you. You're better than that."

But as I fall asleep that night, I know it's a lie. The only person I can be better than is the one who went to the movies with Brigs tonight and fired barbs at him the moment he got too close, the moment I got too scared.

Tomorrow, I have to find a way to set things right, even if it hurts me.

...

The next day I work up the courage to go to Brig's office. I never got an email from him about last night and I didn't want to email him because what I need to say can't be expressed like that. It's too empty, too cold a way to say that I want him just as he wants me. I want to try again.

But just because I've set my mind to something doesn't mean that I'm not scared shitless. Just like the week before, I practically drag my feet to his floor, and when I find his office door closed again, I know I have a last minute chance to turn and run away and ignore it all to hell.

I also know I can't kid myself. There's no ignoring this anymore.

Before I lose my nerve, I quickly rap on the door. My knock is straightforward, not unlike the goofy ones I would do on his office door back in the day.

I don't hear any response from inside, though. No movement.

Maybe he's not even in.

I knock again.

Silence.

"Brigs?" I say just loud enough for him to hear me, knowing that if he doesn't want to see me at all I'm giving him an easy out. It's about time I make something easy on him.

But at the sound of my voice, I hear a chair sliding back. Footsteps.

The door opens, Brigs peering down at me from the other side.

"Hi," I say to him. "Did I catch you at a bad time?"

He shakes his head, doesn't say anything, and opens the door. As I step in I take a quick glance at his face. His expression is wary. I don't blame him.

He hesitates for a tiny beat, hand on the doorknob, thinking I might want him to leave it open.

"You can close it," I tell him.

He closes it with a little shrug and slowly walks over to his desk. He sits down in his chair, hands gathering his papers as if he's prepared to go back to work. "Are you thinking of becoming my research assistant?" he says dryly.

"Not really," I tell him, walking over to the side of his desk. I take in a deep breath. "I came here to apologize."

He glances up at me. "It seems we're doing a lot of that lately."

I swallow, nodding. "Yes. We have been. And I think we ought to stop."

He frowns and leans back in his chair, studying me, hands folded across his trim waist. "All right," he says. "Is that all?"

Oh god, please don't be like this.

I rub my lips together, feeling desperation course through me.

"No, it's not all," I tell him, my voice sounding so quiet and meek. "I..." I close my eyes. "Fuck. I can't."

Suddenly I hear his chair slide back, and my eyes fly open. He's in front of me, grabbing my forearm, his fingers molten against my skin.

"If you say *you can't* one more time," he warns me, his voice low and sharp and brimming with fury. "You might think you have some right to come here and tease me but—"

I step away from the edge of the desk, not breaking eye contact. "I'm not teasing you."

Our faces are just inches apart. I'm breathing in his air. My gaze drops to his lips, the tense set of his jaw. The tension between us grows thick and heavy, and the back of my neck grows damp with sweat.

"Kiss me," I whisper to him, my lips barely moving, the sound coming out like a last breath.

The tension wraps around us tighter, tying knots. Or maybe it's my stomach that's flipping as my words seem to hang between us with nowhere to go.

"Please," I add. I glance up at him through my lashes and see his expression has changed to a mix of lust and disbelief. He thinks I'm kidding. I don't think I've ever been more serious.

"Fine," I tell him. *I'll do it.*

I put my hand behind his neck and pull him down to me. I kiss him softly, unsurely, worried that he might pull away in some kind of punishment.

But he lets out a faint groan and steps into me.

His hands disappear into my hair, holding my head in place while our mouths slide against each other in a wet, heated dance. It whips up something in my chest, turning coals into flames, want into desire. This kiss reaches down to my very toes and ensures that I can't feel the ground.

But he presses himself against me more, and I can feel the edge of the desk bite into my ass the pressure of his hard chest against mine, the rigid shape of his cock pushing into my hips.

This isn't just going to be a kiss.

Maybe it never was.

Brigs breaks away, holding my face in his hands, breathing hard. His eyes are glazed, hot, carnal, like he's already fucking me with them.

No, this isn't just a kiss at all.

"Are you sure?" he manages to say, his voice coated with this huskiness that makes the hairs on my arms stand up, the space between my legs flush with heat.

My "yes" is caught in my throat. I can only nod.

Please touch me. Touch me everywhere.

My whole body moves toward him like gravity, wanting more.

He gives me a half-smile that borders on predatory. "You have no idea how long I've waited to do this."

"Oh I think I might," I manage to say as his mouth dips toward my jawline, nibbling along it before it slides down my neck, a hot trail of lips and tongue and teeth.

A gasp is pulled from my lungs as my body starts to kick up the adrenaline, and it hits me hard with my heart banging like a drum, my pulse through the roof. I grip the back of his neck harder, urging him to crush me, needing to feel the solidity, the maleness of his body.

His mouth returns to mine, his lips soft and strong, and I'm melting into his mouth, dissolving underneath his tongue. It's just as explicit as sex, and I feel open and bare from just the heat of our kiss, the languid, penetrating way he explores my mouth. It's like he's devouring me, conquering me, and I've never been happier to give in.

"Natasha," he says, our mouths parting for a moment, my name an urgent hiss on his lips. His hands are now moving down to my shirt, sliding over my skin. His hands feel so warm, so possessive as they glide over my waist and stomach, slowly making their way up to my breasts.

I help him out by grabbing the hem of my shirt and pulling it up and over my head, just as he takes a firm grab of my ass with both hands and lifts me up onto the edge of his desk.

Moving like a man with one instinct only—to fuck—he parts my legs and presses his hips between them. He lowers his head to my breasts, kissing the swell of them while he quickly reaches behind my back and deftly undoes my bra, discarding it on the floor beside us.

My nipples tighten in the air, begging to be touched. He cups one breast and brings his mouth to them slowly dragging his tongue around it in circles, over and over again, before giving it a hard flick.

I moan, my head back, as his tongue continues to flick my nipple, hard and fast. It pulls every nerve ending into a tightened knot. I don't even have to guess if I'm wet, I know I am, and I'm growing more turned on and desperate by the minute. My back arches, and I push my breasts up to him, craving more and less at the same time.

I don't have any time in my foggy, liquid brain to think about it being Brigs.

But it is Brigs.

It's his teeth now razing over my nipples, causing me to gently cry out.

It's his hands sliding down to my jeans and unzipping them.

It's his cock that presses against me, pushing against the fabric of his pants.

Lust hits me like a slap. I want nothing more than to come. I want him to make me come, I want my clothes off, his clothes off, I want to be fucked silly on this desk until I'm screaming his name.

If he wants to spank me after with a ruler, I wouldn't complain.

My god, I haven't gotten laid in so long.

"Lay back," he murmurs gruffly, pushing his papers out of the way before putting his hand on my chest and urging me down.

I lie back, the hard finish of the desk pushing into my shoulder blades while he tugs my jeans and underwear over my hips.

With relief I realize I didn't wear SpongeBob this time, but glancing at Brigs as he looks me over, the erotic way his eyes rest on my pussy on full display, I don't think he'd even notice.

"God, you're beautiful," he murmurs. "More than I imagined." He takes his hand and slides it between my legs, his fingers skirting over my clit, before one finger slowly makes its way inside of me. He leans forward, gazing at me, drunk on lust. "And so very, very wet."

His eyes are unnerving. I don't think I've ever been looked at so sexually before. It's almost too intimate. I close my eyes and try to control my breathing as he slowly pushes another finger inside me. I gasp, clenching around him, while the pad of his thumb grinds against my clit.

It's fucking bliss.

"Are you ever going to get naked?" I ask breathlessly, looking up at him.

"When I put my cock inside you and fuck you on this desk, yes," he says, his voice hoarse. "For now though, I want to taste you."

He pushes a third finger inside and slowly drags it out, rubbing my wetness against his lips.

I swallow hard, shocked by how brazen he is.

"Again," he says slowly as his eyes burn into me. "Better than I imagined."

Then he gets to his knees and puts his head between my legs as I'm hanging halfway off the desk. His hands spread my thighs wide before he presses his fingers into my hips, holding me in place.

I'm not ready for this, for him to go down on me. It was something I fantasized about daily, but I never imagined it would happen with me completely naked on his desk in his office, him fully clothed, head between my legs.

I try and sit up to watch, utterly fascinated and turned on by the sight, but as his tongue languidly slides over my clit, washing over my nerves, slippery and wet, I have to lie back down. The feeling is too much and I feel like a sponge trying to soak up stars and lightning and everything beautiful, and it's too overwhelming for this world.

And Brigs is relentless.

I mean, good lord, the man can eat pussy. He's at me with messy precision, his lips, tongue, and occasionally those long fingers of his working me into a wild frenzy.

I can't think.

I can't breathe.

I can only feel as my blood runs hot, my nerves tying up in knots upon knots, pulling, pulling, pulling, until he's groaning against me and I'm digging my nails into his head and his tongue is pushing *into* me in hot, quick stabs.

I'm so swollen, so desperate, that when he brushes his fucking nose against my clit, the knots all come undone at once.

My body is a confetti cannon.

I am blasting through space, groaning, writhing on his desk as the orgasm rips through me, feeling like brightly colored pieces of me are floating down from the sky.

But the relief is short-lived.

As I catch my breath, my limbs still loose, and peer up at him as he stands between my legs, he's taking off his shirt.

Undoing his belt.

Letting his pants drop.

He's just in his grey boxer briefs.

Damn.

Damn.

He might as well be naked.

I can see every hard, rigid detail of his cock.

He said I was better than he imagined?

He's a million times *bigger* than I imagined.

And I imagined him with something just short of a horse cock.

I swallow hard, amazed how quickly I've gone from spent and sated to hungry and, well, a little afraid in a matter of seconds.

Is it too late to change his nickname to Professor Horse Cock?

Somehow I manage to pry my eyes away from his underwear and take in the rest of him. He's all hard angles and long planes, from the wide breadth of his shoulders and chest, to the definition in his abs and the way they lead to the sharp V of his hips. A dusting of chest hair thins out before becoming a treasure trail again.

He's so manly, and his posture suggests he's completely at ease with his body. I had teased him once, when I was drunk, wondering what he was like underneath. I'm not disappointed in the slightest. I want to run my lips and fingers and breasts along every inch of his lean, hard-earned body. I want to feel it press against mine, damp with sweat.

"Are you just going to stand there?" I say to him, feeling just a tad bit vulnerable that I'm still naked and spread eagle and *waiting*.

He flashes me an assured smile and pulls down his boxer briefs, letting his cock, swollen and thick, jut out in front of him.

Damn. This is now an urgent debilitating lust he's stroked within me. The kind that wants it all hard and fast and *now*.

He steps between my legs, the dark, wet tip of his cock rubbing against my sensitive clit as he reaches to the side and opens a drawer. With one hand he quickly rummages through, feeling around, and pulls out a condom.

I look at him questioningly. "Is there a need for condoms in your office?"

"There is now," he says as he tears into the foil packet. "They're handing them out here all the time. Cheaper than buying your own."

I shake my head. "Professor McGregor, I am shocked."

"Then you shock easily, Miss Trudeau. We'll have to fix this."

I love, love, love how normal this all feels, the teasing, the being with each other completely naked, the naughty smirks and innuendo.

But when he rolls the condom over the tip of his cock, slowly sliding it down (and I start to grow more and more impatient), something in his eyes change. The smile disappears. His eyes ratchet up the intensity. Remember how I said his eyes just screamed sex? Well now they scream *fucking*, as in he's going to totally ravage every inch of me until I'm begging him to stop.

And it's more than that. It's something dark and deep, like he's not just after my body but my soul. I can feel it in his gaze, in the way he keeps sifting through the layers, searching for something to satisfy him.

"Sit up," he murmurs, sliding his arms around my waist and pulling me up. I wrap my legs around him, place my hands behind his neck, already damp with sweat. Our faces are inches apart, but he's not kissing me. He's fucking me with his eyes, the way they simmer over my mouth, as if he's thinking of all the things my mouth could do.

I want to show him.

I bring my face closer, take his bottom lip between my teeth and gently suck.

I feel a rumbling groan build through his chest, like he's barely holding his lust in check, a million horses prancing at the gate, waiting to be unleashed.

"I'm trying to have patience with you," he whispers hoarsely, kissing the corner of my mouth. "I can't have this over too fast. I need to savor," he kisses my jaw, "every," he kisses my neck, "part of you."

"Savor me later," I tell him, as a sudden surge of adrenaline rockets through me. I grab the back of his neck, wanting, needing him to kiss me hard. His cock is this hot, stiff pressure rubbing against my clit, and I'm desperate, so desperate, for him to come inside me.

His mouth continues along my collarbone, nipping and licking, and my legs pull him closer. I'm whimpering, his lips ducking down to my nipples, so swollen and sensitive.

"Please," I beg, my voice ragged in my throat. "I need you inside me."

He brings his head up, his eyes wild with this hazy, heavy kind of lust. "I've always dreamed of you saying that," he says thickly. He reaches down, positioning his cock against me. His eyes hold mine at knifepoint, and I'm unable to look away as he slowly pushes himself inside.

I stretch around him, my breath hitching tight in my throat.

"Oh, fuck," Brigs gasps against my neck, his hands dropping to the small of my waist and pulling himself deeper into me. "Fuck. *Natasha*."

My name has never sounded so good.

Meanwhile, my body is still adjusting to his size, feeling absolutely stretched and full. Thank god I'm drenched.

He pulls back—so fucking deliberate, like he's trying to feel every centimeter—and I'm ravenous.

I'm crazed.

An animal.

I need more.

Crave more.

My hands move to his shoulders, and I dig them into his skin, wanting all of him.

As Brigs pushes back in, I expand around him, accepting him as if he's always belonged in me, as if he's always been home. The connection between us is tight and frightening, and the intimacy is nearly too much for my heart to swallow. Our eyes dance with each other, glancing through lowered lashes, through the sweat and haze, searing deep and then moving on to other parts. He takes in my mouth like a glass of water, and the carnality in his gaze snaps a million strings inside me.

He murmurs my name again, his voice sliding over me like rough silk, and I am enraptured by his surrendering, his pleasure, lost in the hot, ragged draw of his breath against my skin and his raw grunts in my ear.

I can't believe this is happening.

Brigs McGregor.

Inside me.

I'm on his desk.

Being thoroughly fucked by a man I had only dreamed about.

How we've gone from what we were then to what we are now...to this.

This.

This.

This.

This is unlike anything I've felt in this world. This is holding fire and stars and electricity in your burning hands. This is magic and light running through your veins, a switch being turned on, turning you into everything primal and basic and real.

This is us.

The desk starts to move underneath me. An earthquake of his doing. My legs grip him harder. I reach down and shrug his toned, round ass between my hands, pulling him into me. His grunts are hoarser now, loud from lust, and I still can't believe this is my reality, that this is my funny, handsome, charming Brigs, and he's so deep inside me I can't breathe. I can't do anything but hold on.

His pace becomes frantic. The desk squeaks as it moves across the floor. A drop of hot sweat rolls off his brow and onto my collarbone. His lungs gasp with exertion, because this is a workout to fuck me like this, so fast, so deep, so thorough.

I never want it to end.

Then his hand slips between my legs, his thumb finding my clit, and now I'm frantically chasing my release until I'm at its mercy, on the edge, ready to fall.

I groan loudly.

I'm opening, I'm opening, I'm opening, legs falling apart, wider and wider.

I'm coming.

I'm coming.

I'm...

And then I'm off like a bomb.

Crying unintelligible words.

My body convulses violently, spasming around him.

It's so good, it's too good.

I never want anything else. Anyone else.

Just this, this, this.

Him.

All the time.

His neck cranes, head back, jaw tense as he grinds his teeth together. He comes, and I watch with a sense of relief and wonderment that I'm doing this to him. His face is pinched in a mix of rapture and anguish, and he's swearing in a low guttural voice, his grip on my hips so hard I think he's going to leave plum-colored bruises.

"Fuck," he swears as he slows his pumping. He's shaking. I'm shaking. His eyes flit over my body in a daze, sex-soaked and spent. I stare up at him, and it's like looking through a dream.

It hits me slowly, like dissipating smoke, what exactly we've done and what it means to me. I hate how sex can complicate things. I hate how it sometimes causes feelings to erupt where there were no feelings.

But I know that's not the case with us. We came upon each other with raw emotions still intact, maybe buried, maybe not, but they were deep and vibrant and waiting. All of our feelings—at least all of my feelings—have a firm root in the ground, and now that we've had sex—*we've had sex*—and he's been inside of me, we've experienced each other in a way I never ever thought possible. Everything is heightened.

And yet I know it's coming from somewhere. I know it's valid. And that's scary. That's terrifying.

He pulls out of me, and I'm immediately hollow. I want to keep him inside. My terror builds as he retreats, brow furrowed as he slips the condom off, and I want reassurance that the world isn't ending. I need to feel that this wasn't a one-time fling, that I'm not alone and adrift. The urge for his contact is unbearable.

Brigs throws the condom in the trash and stares down at me in a mix of worry and amazement.

"Hey," he says gently, his voice thick. He reaches down and slowly pulls me up by my waist and shoulders like I'm a ragdoll. His longer fingers press against my cheeks as he holds me in place, searching my eyes. "Are you okay?"

I can't speak. I can only swallow, though it's like bread crusts are lodged in my throat. I nod.

He rubs his lips together, looking worried. I don't want him to be worried, I don't want him to regret anything.

"Natasha," he says softly. "If...I didn't want to complicate things. I'm so sorry if—"

I clear my throat. "No," I tell him, my hands curling over his biceps. "It's not that. I'm just...it's a lot to take." He frowns, pained, and I quickly add, "In a good way. I'm just... overcome. By everything."

He nods and rests his forehead against mine, still damp with sweat. "I don't want you to regret anything. I feel like I've been waiting my whole entire life for what just happened."

"Was it worth it?"

"Darling, yes," he whispers, kissing me softly. "The last thing I want is to lose you again, not when I've finally had you." He strokes the side of my cheek and stares at me imploringly. "Tell me that meant something to you."

"It meant everything to me," I whisper. "I don't even know how to come down."

The corner of his mouth quirks up in a smile. I can't believe I have permission to kiss that mouth. Impulsively, I lay my lips on his then laugh giddily. He grips my face harder, blessing me with that wide, gorgeous smile of his, and in his eyes I see joy. Pure, beautiful joy.

Then a knock at the door.

Both of us jump, eyeing each other with our breaths in our throats.

I had closed the door, but it isn't locked.

"Just one minute, please," Brigs barks, his voice cracking.

We frantically try and get dressed. I only have my jeans on, and he only has his shirt and underwear when he motions for me to get behind the door.

I quickly scurry over, flattening myself against the wall, while he positions himself behind the door so that when he opens it, the person on the other side can't see anything but his face and a hint of his upper body.

He gives me a look, warning me to be quiet, and then slowly opens the door a crack, poking his head out.

"Yes?" he says. His voice is so calm and smooth it's hard to imagine what had just happened.

"Sorry to bug you." For fuck's sake, it's Melissa's voice. "I was wondering if you had a moment to help me with the upcoming tutorial."

Brigs' whole manner stiffens.

I hold my breath.

"I'm busy at the moment." He says this so harshly I wonder if it's because he's caught off-guard or if he doesn't like Melissa.

"Doing what?" she asks. I don't like the tone of her voice. It's too prying, too casual.

"I'll see you in class," he says and immediately shuts the door, locking it. He leans against it, his head hanging down, taking in a deep breath. I don't say anything, not yet, not until I'm sure she's gone.

If he contacts you, I'll report him, Melissa had said. Just how serious was she? I don't want to find out.

After what feels like an eternity, Brigs moves away from the door, and my eyes focus on his taut thighs peeking out from beneath his dress shirt. The show ends when he yanks his pants back on, his brow furrowed in thought and worry.

"Is she gone?" I whisper.

He nods. "I hope so."

"Does she come by here often?"

He opens his mouth to say something, then rubs his lips together for a second. "How well do you know your friend?" he asks.

I blink at him, caught off-guard. "As well as anyone. She's not exactly complicated."

He gives me a look of mild disbelief. "Very well."

"Why?"

He shakes his head. "No reason." He walks over to the desk and moves it back where it was. The place before he fucked the hell out of me on it.

Jesus.

I still can't believe we did that. On his desk. That it happened at all. But I still feel raw from where he was pounding me, and the skin all over my body feels worn and bruised. I know I'm already different, lit up from the inside like a hot, glowing mess.

But...now what?

Brigs clears his throat, absently looking down at his desk. "Would you be interested in coming over tonight?" His eyes flit to mine, a shy smile on his lips. "Maybe have some drinks at the bar beforehand?"

I grin at him, completely charmed. "Of course."

To say I'm giddy would be an understatement. I'm aware of what just happened between us, but the fear that it wouldn't turn into more has always been skirting around the back of my head. Being with Brigs has the ability to become a full-on addiction, but this shouldn't surprise me. All those years ago I was drawn—pulled—into his office like he was the moon and I was the sea at the mercy of my wild tides. Now that sex has been thrown into the mix, I'm not sure how I'll even survive it.

You might not, a voice inside my head warns. *Think of your therapist. Think of what Brigs is to you. Protect yourself.*

But it's already too fucking late.

"Do you think it's safe for me to go outside?" I ask him, even though it's at least been five minutes. "Or does Melissa stalk you like I do?"

He doesn't smile at that which puts my hackles up for a moment. Then he nods slowly. "You're fine. See you at The Volunteer at seven?"

"See you then," I tell him, heading for the door.

"Wait," he says.

He strides across the room with his long legs and grabs my arm, pulling me around and to him, his eyes simmering before he kisses me.

Brigs' kisses render me obsolete, a hot breeze that threatens to sweep me up and away, to where nothing else matters but us.

"You sure make it hard for a girl to leave," I tell him breathlessly as he pulls away.

He smirks. "Good."

Chapter Fourteen

BRIGS

I can scarcely believe that happened.

One minute I was in my office, alone, licking my wounds, the next I was deep inside Natasha, fucking her on my desk.

Absolutely *fucking* her.

I don't think I've ever been as wild and relentless as I was with her, which doesn't surprise me considering how I used to feel about her. I would have thought there would be a cloud of guilt hanging over my head, telling me we can't and that we shouldn't. Any and all guilt was absolved the moment she said, "Kiss me."

Of course some guilt threatens to raise its head, waiting to come out and play, as it always does. It tells me that I can move on, with anyone but her.

But I only want her.

And I've always only wanted her.

I guess that's where most of my fear lies. Because with Natasha this isn't a fling and this isn't a casual relationship. I was mad for her before, and I'll surely lose myself again if I haven't already.

I mean, it's been only a few hours since I was inside of her in my office and it's not enough. It will never be enough.

I watched her walk out of my door and I immediately felt muted and curiously frightened, as if something dire would happen to her between the time she left my office and the time I'd see her again at the bar. Maybe because I know what it's like to lose so much, it makes the stakes that much higher. The threat of having to go through it all again. Fate might have a target on my back now, loss attracting loss.

But thinking that way won't help anything, so I do my best to bury my fears and get on with my day.

Naturally, my thoughts turn to Natasha at every moment.

The way her lips parted when the passion was too much.

The liquid gaze of her sex-fed eyes.

The little sounds that escaped her mouth, breathless and raw, as she came.

The memory of our naked, sweaty bodies together taints me and I can feel it with everything I do.

I had been with a few girls before Miranda, and it had never been like that. I've had my fair share of passion with Miranda too, especially just after our wedding.

That hadn't been like that either.

What Natasha and I shared surpasses all expectations and dreams. It's difficult for me to wax poetic about it without sounding flowery or clichéd. But I guess the word transcendent could work, even though a single word could never say enough. I doubt all the words could.

At six, I get ready, throwing on jeans, a t-shirt and my jacket, checking myself out in the mirror before I head across the street to the pub.

It turns out I'm nervous as fuck. It makes no bloody sense, all things considered, but it's the truth. I nod to Max and take my usual seat at the bar.

"Alone tonight?" Max asks as he pours me a pint.

"For now," I tell him.

"Same broad?" he asks, his eyes twinkling.

I take the beer from him and give him a wry look. "Broad? Are we in the 1950s? Same *woman*, yes."

"Good," he says. "I was starting to think you were going to be sitting alone here forever."

I cock my brow. Max and I have a strictly bartender-patron relationship, but he does know about Miranda and Hamish. My second night in the bar we got to talking, and when people ask about my past, if I have a family, I'm not one to hold back. I don't give them a lot, but I give them enough to know the truth.

"We'll see," I tell him, ever so cautious.

"Nah," he says loudly, with a big smile that shows his canines. "You know I'm an expert in love."

"Just because you're a bartender..."

"Yeah, a bartender, of course," he says, leaning across the bar. "But I was also a celebrant. A humanist. I still am."

I look Max up and down, nearly spitting out my beer. Max has got to be in his late fifties, with a big beer belly, straggly grey hair and a mustache that looks like it's been ripped off the face of Groucho Marx. He looks more like a grizzled old roadie than he does a celebrant.

"You mean you married people?"

"Yes. Those who weren't religious or who wanted a wedding outside. People would do their paperwork with the register office, but then the ceremony was performed by me. It was my gig long before taking over this place. I brought people together back then, and, well, I hear their troubles now," he adds with a laugh before his expression turns serious. "So believe me when I say I've seen a lot of couples."

How pathetic is it that I want him to continue on about me and Natasha?

"You've known her from before," he notes.

I nod. "Yes. A few years ago."

"I can tell that, too."

I fold my hands in front of me. "What else can you tell?"

He grins at me like he's holding all the cards. "I can tell she's in love with you."

His words send my heart spinning. I shake my head, unwilling to believe it for a second. "I don't think so."

"She loved you once. That doesn't go away."

"And how do you know she loved me once?"

He shrugs with one shoulder, looking around the pub. "It's a skill possessed by whoever isn't the one in love. You can't see it until you're outside of it. And unfortunately, when you're outside of it, you're often too late."

He was right. But the years held too much shame and bitterness for me to ever indulge whether Natasha had truly loved me or not. Here though—now—I know she did.

I know I did, too.

And I know those feelings are rising again, becoming a hard truth once more. There would be no gradual ascent for us. My feelings won't slowly trickle into something. They'll leap all at once, like lemmings over a cliff. With no regard for the future or pain or even if Natasha feels the same way. I'll go over and hope the freefall lasts longer than my years.

I take a swig of my beer and sigh. "You say love doesn't go away. What if it was burned to ashes?"

"Well. Love *is* fire," he says simply, cocking his head. "And fire rises. It creates the ashes. And it rises above them.

Just like any man can come out of something that should have buried him, love can too."

I frown at him, utterly puzzled by this particular man. "Max, Max, Max, I hardly knew ye. A bartender and a celebrant and a poet all in one."

"Yeah, well, don't tell anyone," he says. "And don't write off my philosophy just because it's coming from my mouth. You know it's true. You want love again, well you've got it. She's walking in the door, mate."

His eyes dart to the doorway, and I whip around in my seat to see Natasha walking in.

I'm not sure the feeling of weightlessness in my chest is ever going to get old. The blood rushing to my dick certainly won't.

Natasha sees me and smiles. Everything about her just lights up the room, and I'm surprised she's not turning heads, people wondering where the glow is coming from. This rare and gorgeous creature is smiling at me, for me, walking toward me.

I'll do anything to make her mine.

Keep her mine.

Anything.

Bloody hell, that's such a terrifying thought when you realize the depth of it.

"Hi," she says, stopping beside me.

I immediately get out of my seat and kiss her.

She gasps lightly in shock then giggles as I pull away, my hands in her golden hair and skirting down her soft cheeks, marveling at her.

"How are you real? How are you here?" I ask her softly.

She takes the seat beside me and briefly eyes Max, perhaps shy at the sudden and public display of affection. "Well, I just shared the train with a bunch of stinky people, so I definitely know this is all real. I couldn't pinch my way out of that one."

She quickly reaches over and pinches my forearm, hard enough to make me yelp.

"Hey," I scold her, rubbing at my skin.

"Wuss," she says, grinning happily. "But it's not a dream, is it?"

"If it were, the beers would be on the house," Max says, piping up. "Alas, they aren't."

I eye him dryly, knowing that the longer we stay here, the less privacy we'll have.

"Dream crusher," I tell him. "Give the lady a snakebite and I'll have another. And then I'll settle up the almighty tab."

Max can scarcely believe what he's hearing. It's a long-running joke that I'm slow to pay my tab. But now that Natasha is this close to me, I'm having a hard time keeping my hands to myself, let alone finishing my beer.

Max gives us our drinks and then shoots me a not-so-sly wink before heading down the bar to help someone else.

"He seems nice," she says. "You know, for someone that looks like he was the tour manager for Pink Floyd."

I laugh. "You've been reading my mind today, haven't you?"

She raises her head, appraising me. "Have I? What else have you been thinking about other than the bartender?"

I grin at her, wiggling my jaw back and forth. "Do you want the truth?"

She adjusts herself on the stool to face me more squarely and puts her hand on my knee. "Always," she says with smiling eyes.

I lean in closer, staring at her collarbones. I lower my voice. "I've been thinking about what it was like to fuck you. I've been thinking about what I'm going to do to you tonight."

I wait a moment and then look up. She's staring at me with a hyper-sexual mix of lust and innocence. Her lips part.

"Just that," I whisper to her. "Just your fucking lips dropping open, and I think about all the places you could put them."

Her cheeks are flushed now, eyes glistening. She blinks at me and then takes a long gulp of her drink. I know I'm being too forward, but I can only be honest with her, even if it shocks her. The fact is, I want to shock her. I want to see this side of her with the shy eyes and the pink cheeks. I want to expose her to a part of me she might not recognize.

"Well then," she says when she recovers, quickly brushing her hair behind her ears. She smiles and looks around the bar. "That was unexpected."

"Even after this afternoon?" I ask, reaching out and feeling her silky hair between my fingers, tugging on it gently. I wonder if she'd like to have it pulled later.

"I guess not," she says, her voice becoming huskier. She meets my eyes and chews on her lip. "So, is the bar just a place to have foreplay?"

I smile. "It can be. I wasn't sure how you felt after today, so I wanted to make it neutral. You know, in case you wanted to run for the hills."

She gives her head a small shake. "I'm not running anymore." She picks up her drink and slams the rest of it while darting her eyes to my beer. "Drink up," she says when she's finished.

"Trying to get me drunk?" I joke, but I drink the rest of it down easily.

"Trying to get us out of here," she says, hopping off the stool.

I raise my brows. I wasn't expecting her to be this eager, and I can't pretend it's not the biggest fucking turn-on.

I quickly put a few notes on the bar—plus some extra for Max's sage advice—and we go. I've never been so thankful to have my place just across the street. We're barely on the other side of the road before I'm attacking her, pressing her up against the bricks while my hands fumble for the keys in my jacket pocket.

Her neck tastes like cream, her smell sweet and heady, and even when I do find the key fob, it takes everything I have to pull my lips away from her, to do something else but revel in her taste.

Eventually we do get upstairs and into the flat. Winter is bounding toward us but neither Natasha nor I can even greet him hello. I kick the door shut with my foot, my lips unable to pull away from hers as we move backward into the room. Our clothes are quickly discarded. My jacket thrown across the room, landing on Winter, her shirt pulled over her head. My hands slip down the front of her jeans, desperate for her cunt as her hands try and undo my zipper.

We don't make it to the bedroom. We thump hard against the bookcase, books dropping off the shelf. I'm ripping her bra down, my mouth going for her luscious breast as my pants drop to the floor. Winter is running around us howling, and I'm a terrible dog-father because I couldn't care about anything right now except for Natasha.

But even as I'm taking her nipple into my mouth, nipping it between my teeth until she's gasping and holding me by the back of my beck, I know I can't do a thing to her until the dog is taken care of. Dogs are simultaneous chick magnets and cock blockers.

I break away, taking off my shirt so I'm just in my boxer briefs, and usher Winter into the bedroom, closing the door on him. He can do less damage in there.

He barks what I'm sure are a dozen swears in dog language that only Lachlan or Tarzan knows, but he soon shuts up. Tonight I wouldn't care if he barked nonstop. My heart is beating too loudly in my ears to hear him properly. I have tunnel vision, and Natasha is all I see and think and hear.

"Is he okay in there?" she asks, but I kiss her before she can continue, taking off her bra and helping get rid of her jeans until the two of us are just in our underwear.

I grab her arms and move with her backward over to the couch where I push her down on it, her breasts jiggling as she falls back on the cushions.

"Fuck me," I mutter, taking my dick out and giving it a long hard stroke as I stare down at her. She stares up at me with wide, nervous eyes, her lips parted, her golden hair across her face. Her nipples are hard, tiny pink peaks against the fullness of her breasts. Her torso leads smoothly to her hips and thighs that just beg for me to dig my teeth into them.

The sweet pink flash of her cunt.

"I'll do more than that," she says, pivoting around so she's on all fours on the couch, prowling toward me. "I didn't forget what you said about my lips."

Fuck, I'm lucky.

No. Lucky is an understatement.

I move closer to the couch while she gets on her knees and reaches up for my cock, slowly wrapping her long fingers around it. The pressure reverberates along every inch of me, and I let out a harsh groan, the desire slamming into me.

"Lick me, slowly," I tell her, my words coming out thick.

She flashes me a wicked smile before slowly sticking out her tongue and licking around the dark, swollen tip. My head goes back and my eyes close, giving into the feeling, even though I desperately want to maintain eye contact with her.

Her tongue slides down the bottom of my shaft and everything inside me tenses. I've never felt like this, this white-hot blistering lust that penetrates every last nerve. The tension inside me builds and builds into something more than primal, and when I finally open my eyes, practically panting, her sly eyes glance up at me with excitement. With her honey hair spilling around her lightly tanned shoulders, she looks like a fucking goddess that men would tell myths about.

Only she's no myth. She's nothing but real as she takes me into her mouth. Her lips feel just as wet and plush as her cunt did earlier. I make a fist in her hair, tugging on it just enough for her eyes to widen, and she sucks me harder in response. It would be so fucking easy to just come hard down the back of her throat and watch her swallow it all.

But I'm not about to come now. I want to be inside her again, to feel every hot squeeze of her around me.

"Hold on," I pant, pulling back. My cock pops out of her mouth, a long drop of spit spanning to her lips. God, that's fucking hot. "Turn around," I command.

She does as I ask, and I grab her hips, tugging her back into me, teasing the crack of her arse with my glistening cock.

"I hope you know where you're putting that thing," she says, a slight tremor in her voice.

I can't help but smile at how innocent she sounds. "Don't worry," I assure her. "We have plenty of time for that down the line." But damn, I need condoms regardless. "Don't move." I quickly walk to the bathroom and grab a packet of condoms out of the drawer, heading right back.

"Good girl," I tell her, and she wiggles her arse in response. As I tear open the silver foil, I lean over and take a teasing bite of her cheek.

"Ow," she exclaims.

"Sorry," I mutter, not sorry at all. I lick over the bite marks, making her relax, before sheathing the thin latex on, unfurling it to the end. I want to know how wet and eager she is, so I part her cheeks and stroke my fingertips over her cunt, and I'm nearly salivating over how slick she is. I push my finger into that tight pink hole and bite my lip at how she holds me. Her breath hitches and she lets out a breathless moan that undoes me like nothing else.

Suddenly the urge, the pure need to be inside her is an iron grip, and I'm nearly trembling at the hunger pulsing through me. It's this animalistic, primal drive that surprises me, like I'm being reduced to nothing but basic instinct around her. She's not just Natasha, she's this gorgeous creature I need to claim, to take rough and hard and fast until I can't remember my name.

Without realizing it, I've pushed another finger inside her, rubbing eagerly against her G-spot, feeling her swell around me.

"Brigs," she gasps, her head down, her hair over her face as she breathes heavily, her body pressing back into me, wanting more. "God, you're so good."

Her words are so desperate and urgent and flick on a fiery switch.

I snap.

I have to get inside her now.

Right fucking *now*.

I quickly withdraw my fingers, rubbing them along my lips briefly, savoring her taste, as I hold my shaft, rigid and heavy in my hand and angle it into her. I try to go slow, rubbing my head around her soft opening, getting my tip wet before pushing in just a few inches.

But just a few inches is enough to make my jaw clench, trying so hard to keep myself in control. She's so hot and slippery and tight as a fucking fist that I want to slam myself inside of her, bury myself balls deep. It takes all of me to try and keep on breathing, my fingers digging into her sides that are already tender from the way I was grabbing her earlier.

On the desk was one thing, but here, with her on my couch on all fours, my cock buried halfway into that sweet little hole of hers, this is something else. I hope I have what it takes to bide my time and enjoy every second, but since I'm already struggling to keep it together, I doubt I'll last long.

As long as she comes first. I want her writhing and panting and screaming my name.

"You feel amazing," I tell her, my voice guttural as I push in deeper, watching as my dick disappear into her, her resistance deliciously tight. "You're drenching me."

"You've got quite a mouth, Professor McGregor," she says, moaning.

"Fucking right I do," I hiss through my teeth. "You keep talking like that."

"Call you professor?"

"Call me fucking anything. Tell me what you want. Do you want it slow and teasing or do you want me to fuck that that tight pink cunt, hard and rough?" I pause, sucking in a breath as I pull her hips up, adjusting the angle until my eyes roll back in my head. "Be careful of your answer, I'm not sure how much longer I can hold on."

I pull out in a slow slide and she shudders beneath me before I push back into her, staying cautious. "I want all of you."

I look down where the top two inches of my cock, the thickest part, is still showing. "Are you sure?" I ask her, grinding the words out as I clench my jaw. My body is burning, my muscles tightly coiled as I try to stay still. "I don't want to hurt you at this angle. You're tighter than a fist and my cock can barely fit as it is."

"Yes, give it to me," she says in a shaking whisper. "Please."

"Professor McGregor," I prompt, grinning to myself.

"Professor Fucking *Fuck Me.*"

"Since you asked so nicely," I murmur. She arches her back into me and I slip myself deeper inside her, almost to the hilt. She stretches around me with a loud gasp, her cunt so snug and wet as I roll my hips against her arse. I'm lightheaded, breathless, and the fire inside me builds, licking me until I'm lost in this provocative haze. The world has whittled down to nothing but pleasure.

"Fuck me," she cries out. "Harder. Fucking harder."

A growl escapes my lips and I slam myself into her until she's hugging every throbbing inch. She's yelling my name and I hear nothing but my blood rushing through my head as

I bury myself deep inside her tight hole. My hips thrust into her, hammering in this driving rhythm.

Before I grow entirely selfish, I reach beneath her hips, trying to stroke her clit, so puffy and slick, but I'm pumping so hard into her that it's nearly impossible.

I lean forward, sweat dripping off my brow and onto her back. "Touch yourself," I whisper. "Come with me."

She braces herself on one arm and reaches back, and I straighten up, my hands splayed wide around her waist, gripping her harder and harder as I pound into her with abandon.

She's moaning, then screaming my name and swearing, and I don't hold back. With a guttural groan, I come, the pleasure ripping through me, turning me inside out. I swear and cry out, my cum blasting into the condom as I go into some mindless, hypersensitive state. In this moment, I'm without thought or self-awareness—I'm just an animal, fucking.

I come back down to earth slowly, trying not to collapse onto her lush body. I place my hands on the ripe cheeks of her arse, leaning on them to keep myself up as I try to catch my breath. My skin is damp with sweat and burning hot, and I feel absolutely liquid inside. She's still pulsing around me softly, as if she's trying to milk every last bit out of me.

Natasha is panting too, her back rising and falling, having collapsed into the couch with her arse in the air. She turns her head to the side, her face red and beaded with sweat, her eyes heavy-lidded and completely sated.

There are no words to say to each other. That's the beauty of us. We don't have to speak to know how we're feeling. I sense her just as I know her heart is beating rapidly in her chest.

Slowly, my head heavy, I grab hold of the condom at the base of my cock and pull out. I tie it into a knot and get up, tossing it into the rubbish bin in the kitchen. My legs feel boneless and I have to get a drink of water from the sink, filling up a glass for Natasha as well.

I hand it to her as she sits up, completely natural with me for a moment before she gets self-conscious about her stomach, trying to shield it from my view.

"Don't ever cover yourself up for me," I tell her, making sure she can hear the gravity in my voice. "You know I think you're absolutely perfect."

"That was four years ago."

"And I'll think you're perfect forty years from now."

She stares at me in disbelief and finishes her glass of water just as I hear a bark from the bedroom.

I give her a puzzled look. "Has he been barking the whole time?"

Her lips curve into a smile as she brushes the damp hair off her face. "Honestly, I haven't been paying attention to anything that's going on. Anything other than you."

I slip on my briefs and make my way to the bedroom, slowly opening the door. Winter is sitting on the bed, staring at me with crazy eyes. Thankfully he hasn't pissed in here. Still would have been worth it though.

"Sorry," I apologize to Natasha as Winter bounds out of the room and over to her, his tail wagging all over the place. "I need to take him out. Want to go for a walk?"

She nods eagerly and starts getting dressed, which isn't easy to do when a husky is trying to knock you over. Finally I have to grab his collar and hold him back until she's decent.

We head out into the dark of night. A light drizzle begins to fall and I take off my jacket, holding it over her head as we walk around the block until Winter has done his business. I promise the dog I'll take him for an extra-long walk tomorrow, even though I want to spend every minute of my future with Natasha, preferably with my cock deep inside of her.

"I wish you could stay over," I tell her as we get back to the flat and I shut the door behind us.

"Melissa will notice," she says, standing in the foyer. "She's probably waiting up for me right now. You know how she is." She takes out her phone and glances at it. "Fuck, I should probably head back."

"You sure?" A desperate knot of need starts growing inside me. I don't want to let her go. I'm so afraid I won't have her again. It's just like earlier, only worse now because I know, *I know*, the longer we're together, the more insane my feelings for her will become.

She nods but draws her lip between her teeth, seeming unsure.

"I think I could make you change your mind," I tell her, taking her hand and attempting to lead her away from the door. She stays rooted. "You can just stay there and I'll fuck you up against the door."

She watches me with a cautious curiosity.

"I should go," she says.

I nod and wrap my arms around the small of her waist. "Okay," I murmur before kissing her gently, long and sweet. "But you're coming back here tomorrow. Or I'm coming to get you. Either way, someone is coming."

"You and your innuendo," she teases.

"You and your sweet cunt," I say right back, her eyes widening. A delicate flush appears across her cheeks. "How is that for innuendo?"

"I'll see you tomorrow then."

"Text me, call me, email me," I tell her. "Just please show up here."

"In a trench coat with nothing underneath?"

I groan, hard again, and press my cock against her hips. "Don't do this to me," I whisper harshly into her neck.

"I'm doing nothing," she says, kissing my cheek like she's suddenly chaste and heading out the door.

It closes behind her and I stare at it, feeling a sense of loss and lust like nothing else.

Winter barks from behind me.

"I know," I tell him. "I miss her already too."

Chapter Fifteen

NATASHA

Brigs had said we were starting from square one.

I hadn't believed him at the time. I thought it would be impossible to erase our past and while that still holds true, I think I know what he means.

Square one means a new us, it means an us that can breathe, like wine uncorked. Granted, I think the two of us are still a bit cagey about shouting from the rooftops that the two of us are together. I'm still afraid of telling Melissa (I've had to tell her I'm back to seeing Bradley again), Brigs is cautious about the school. But still – this is, in some ways, so new.

We never got a chance to date before. We worked together and it became something more – briefly – before it was taken away. But we were never able to get to know each other freely, in the ways that we wanted to.

After we slept together – in his office, in his flat – we spent the week together in each other's arms. Every chance I got I was over there. Sometimes we went for dinner or the pub, but most of the time he was fucking me senseless, sometimes in his bed, sometimes in the living room. Pretty much anywhere that the dog wasn't. I know we're making up for years of lost time and I don't have any complaints, even though I'm pretty raw at times and walking around like I've just gotten off a horse. In a way I have. The man is massive and I'm still getting used to his size. I'm pretty lucky that he can get me wet just by gazing at me with those carnal eyes.

Naturally he's clouding my thoughts when we're not tangled together with raw lust and sweat-soaked skin. He's all I'm thinking about and I'm falling back into the rabbit hole, lost in this discovery of a new us, the feeling of finally moving forward. In fact, we aren't just moving, it feels like we're galloping and I can't hold on tight enough.

Melissa has been suspicious and I honestly don't know why. Maybe it's that she sense I'm lying about Bradley, I don't know. She's told me she wants to meet him but I keep making up excuses and I know I can't keep it up forever. Really, I shouldn't be afraid but I have this niggling feeling at the back of mind that I need to keep my cards close to my chest for now.

That said, I still went lingerie shopping with her. I don't need Sponge Bob anymore – he's been regulated to comfy days – and I definitely need a set of bra and knickers that will set Brigs' heart on fire.

Of course, I know he'd rather have me naked all the time and barely notices what I'm wearing, but still. This is one of the sweetest parts of dating – getting yourself all gussied up for someone day in and day out. I love getting to pick out red silk and black lace undergarments, I love getting special exfoliants and body lotions to make every part of me touchably soft, I love putting on the right outfits, the right makeup, doing everything I can to be as attractive to Brigs as possible. I know none of it is needed – he never looks at me so adoringly as when I don't have makeup on and my hair is a mess – but the process makes life so much sweeter.

And to be honest, it makes it all that much more real. Sometimes it still feels like a dream and I have to pinch myself during class when my mind starts to wander. My classes are getting harder to concentrate on and my thesis is totally out the window because my brain just wants to focus on him and my body craves his touch no differently than it craves the air I breathe.

On Friday he texts me during class and tells me to come over at three, that he's whisking me away somewhere for a few hours. There's barely enough time to rush home and slip on my new bra and underwear, even though the elastic band of my hiphuggers dig into my skin too much, causing a muffin top. I sigh, making a note to start working out more, then the other part of my brain kicks into gear and tells me not to worry about it. If Brigs doesn't care, neither should I.

Luckily Melissa isn't home to bug me about where I'm going, so I'm in and out of the flat in a dash and hoping on the train to Brigs' flat.

I buzz the intercom and Brigs tells me to stay put, that he'll be right down.

I wait by the entrance to his building, my eyes drawn to the tourists lining up to get into the Sherlock Holmes Museum. Then his front door swings open and he comes out with Winter on a leash, the pooch's coat looking sparkling white in the autumn sunshine.

Brigs grins at me, eyes bluer than the sky, looking positively dashing in his dark jeans, T- shirt and charcoal waxed cotton jacket. A grey scarf sits around his neck. "There's my woman," he says to me, kissing me quickly. Winter, as usual, shoves his nose into my crotch. Like father like son.

"Are we going for a walk?" I ask happily, feeling so much lighter, brighter, when he's around.

"Going for a drive," he says, slipping on aviator shades. "I even have a cigar. Do you have a light?"

I quickly pull one out of my purse and wave it at him. "Of course I do. Just in case Professor Blue Eyes wants to smoke a cigar with me."

He gives me a wolfish smile. "And what if Professor Blue Eyes wants to fuck you silly?"

I raise my finger to make him pause and then bring out a stack of condoms. "He can fuck me silly as many times as he wants."

"Thatta girl," he says and we round the corner of the building to the back where his Aston Martin is parked.

"I can't believe you still have it," I say, running my hand over the black hood, the finish like new even though it was made in 1978.

"Call me sentimental," he explains, unlocking my side and flipping down the seat so Winter can hop in the back. "I rarely use it anymore but I thought it might be nice to go for a spin."

I totally agree. I get in and we're off, zipping through the city and then onto the motorway, heading in who knows what direction. I don't really care where we're going and I don't ask. The radio plays the oldies, some good old soul, and I've got the wind in my hair. The weather is absolutely perfect for a drive and though the air has a chill these days, the sun has never felt better on my face.

"So how is our date going so far?" Brigs asks randomly as he brings the car onto the A2.

"Date?" I ask, glancing at him.

He shrugs and shoots me his trademark grin. "Well, I thought we ought to make it official don't you? None of this screwing here and there, even though that's a given at this point. I mean, well, sorry to sound old fashioned but I'm rather fond of you and I'd like us to be, you know…a couple."

"A couple?" I repeat. Silly me kind of thought we already were.

"Aye. I want to do things properly with you now," he explains. "I'm going to woo the hell out of you."

I laugh. "Believe me, you're already wooing the hell out of me."

"Good, good," he says, nodding. He glances at me. "But you know, you're something close to magic, Natasha. I'm not going to treat you like you're anything less. You deserve to be wooed and wined and dined."

"And fucked," I add, feeling a bit embarrassed at his proclamations. I don't think I've ever been called *magic* before.

"And fucked, of course," he concedes.

And loved I add in my head but my mouth doesn't dare mutter the words. It's much too soon for that, even though the longer I'm with him, the more that I'm sucked into this heady vortex of feelings I can barely describe. It's not that I believe I deserve his love but, god damn it, I want it more than anything.

"Well, Professor Brigs," I tell him. "Feel free to wine and dine me and do whatever you want. I'm game for whatever you have planned."

And then what? The thought floats into my head. *Where is this going?*

But the thing is, there's only one place for it to go. We're starting from square one and we might be "dating" but as far as I can tell, we're already "all in."

A couple of hours later, we end up near the seaside town of Broadstairs before we're pulling into a parking lot at a place called Botany Bay.

"Ever been here before?" Brigs asks me as I stare out the window at the wide stretch of sandy beach beyond a row of sea grass.

"Never," I tell him. "I barely made it to the seaside. Only Brighton."

"I haven't been here either," he says. "I honestly did one of those point at the map things at home. Well, then I googled the hell out it. But I thought that might make it fun."

We get out of the car, with Winter staying in the backseat for now, and he opens the hatchback, taking out a picnic basket. For a moment I'm reminded of the time I tried to have a solo picnic in the Princes Street Gardens and how lovesick I was and how much I wanted him to be with me. I also remember seeing him and Hamish and Miranda walking past, seemingly so happy, and the memories are kind of killing me as I stand there staring at him.

It's like there was an implosion and the dust is settling and I'm amazed to see we're still alive.

"Are you okay?" he asks, closing the hatchback and resting the basket on the ground.

I nod, trying to swallow. I shake my shoulders quickly, as if to loosen the shame and dust from my shoulders. But even though I can't see his eyes underneath his glasses, I know how good he is at reading me.

"Should we go back?" he asks quietly and I can hear the hurt in his voice.

"No," I say quickly. "No, I'm fine. Really. I just...I was remembering something."

He nods sharply. "Aye. You know you can tell me."

"I know. It's fine. It's nothing." The last thing I want to do is ruin the mood.

He watches me for a few moments, his brows pulled together. "All right. Do you want to get Winter and I'll handle this?"

I nod, happy for a distraction. I put Winter on his leash and we head down a sandy path between waving grass until we're down on the beach. It's strangely desolate here, not even a pier or a boardwalk or a single café, and there isn't a person in sight either, though I'm sure in summer it would be a completely different story.

"All to ourselves," Brigs comments as we stroll down to the end of the beach where giant white cliffs jut out from the sea. A few of the chalky cliffs stand alone, like white soldiers overlooking the sand and with the tide being out, it appears you can wander between them.

But we stop closer to the dunes and Brigs lays out the picnic. I take Winter off the leash since there's no one around and he immediately starts running around, chasing seagulls.

"He'll be all right," Brigs says as he takes out his cigar. I promptly toss him the Zippo and he lights it, taking in a long draw. "Sit," he orders out of the corner of his mouth.

I get down on the plaid blanket he's laid out and stare out at the sea, Winter now playing in the waves and throwing seaweed up into the air. The sun is low behind us and the breeze is growing cooler, the air smelling like brine and salt. I breathe in deep, trying to get some clarity.

I hate that our past has the ability to almost bring me to my knees and I hate how long it takes for me to shake off the guilt. My therapist used to tell me that I wanted to hang onto the feeling because I felt I deserved it and after a while it just became second nature.

Brigs puffs on the cigar in silence and then passes it to me. I hesitate for a moment before taking it, deciding it would probably help me relax. So will the Shiraz that Brigs is opening and pouring into two plastic cups.

"I can tell you don't want to talk about it," Brigs says gently, placing a cup beside me. "But...I just want you to know that you shouldn't hide anything from me. Don't think you have to. Don't think I won't understand."

"I know," I tell him with a sigh before I bring the cigar to my mouth, holding the smoke on my tongue for a moment before letting it drift out of my lips.

"Tell me about your time in France," he says simply.

I stare at him incredulously, passing the cigar back. "You mean over the last four years."

He takes off his shades and tucks them into his jacket pocket. "Yeah," he says, his eyes searching mine. "Before you came here."

I shake my head and quickly slug back some of the red wine. "You don't want to know. It's not a happy story."

"But it's your story. I want to know, Natasha. And I'll tell you mine."

I swallow down more of the wine, not sure if I want to hear his either. Then again, it's Brigs and he's laying his heart bare for me. How can I not take him for everything?

When I don't say anything, he goes on. "After they died, we had a funeral of course. I saw people I hadn't seen in years. It was beautiful, really, the ceremony. Obviously it's something you never appreciate at the time. How can you? But looking back now, it really did Hamish and Miranda justice. It's taken me years, though, to be able to reflect on it with just sadness and nothing more, mind you." He sighs deeply. "Anyway, I, uh...well. I lost myself. Completely. And I still don't know how I'm not down on my kitchen floor, absorbing in the enormity of it all, you know? I really didn't think I'd get out of it. It still surprises me that I'm here."

He chews on his lip for a moment, his eyes pained before taking another drag of the cigar. "I tried to kill myself, you know."

My heart slams against my chest, aching. "What?" I ask in quiet disbelief.

"Yeah," he says slowly. "I guess I should say it was a half-hearted attempt. The doctors gave me pills to sleep. I took a lot. I knew what I was doing too. I woke up in a pile of vomit, halfway to the bathroom. And you know what I felt? Relief at first, that it didn't work, that I was alive. But then the fucking pain...it comes at you so hard. And that was the very thing I was trying to escape." He exhales. "I never tried to do it again but...I often think about it. If I had succeeded."

"I am so, so sorry," I cry out softly, putting my hand on his. My soul weeps for him, the guilt overpowering me once again.

He looks at me with hard eyes. "Don't be sorry, Natasha. They died. And that's independent of you. It's independent of us. I'm learning how to separate the two."

He makes it sound so easy but from his strained brow, I know it's anything but.

"But," he goes on, "I couldn't quite pull myself out of it right away. I lost my job at the university. I lost most of my friends. The suicide didn't work but in some ways I was still trying to make myself as dead as possible. I barely ate. Barely slept. I was barely anything. You wouldn't have recognized me. I was just…a ghost."

I'm staring at him open-mouthed, reeling for him. Reeling for me. The wounds are too fresh and new. "So was I."

"So tell me," he says, passing me back the cigar. He looks me over, like a puzzle he's trying to piece together. "How did you get on after?"

I turn the cigar over in my hands, taking in a deep breath. I'm not sure I'm ready to talk about it but if I can't be ready with Brigs, now, I'll never be ready. "I think…it's hard to talk about it. Not because I'm afraid, or it's too painful, even though it is painful and I am afraid. It's just that, I had two things competing for my sorrow. I had the guilt of their deaths…"

"I wish I never said those things to you," he quickly says, voice choked. "There's not a day I don't regret it, putting the blame on you. I was…"

"You were in shock and you were in pain."

"Don't make excuses for me."

"Don't find something else to feel bad over," I tell him. "It's not an excuse, it's just the truth. I don't blame you. I would have probably said the same, I would have gone mad with grief. I would have lashed out at anyone. It's just that you…you fucking broke my heart, Brigs. You gave me guilt and you broke me in two. I was dying from both."

His Adam's apple bobs in his throat as he swallows hard. "I'm so sorry," he says thickly.

"We're both sorry, Brigs," I tell him. "That's why I don't want us to talk about it more than we have to. We're fucked up. Sincerely, completely fucked up."

He sighs and looks back at the sea. "Aye."

"Anyway," I tell him after a few beats, taking a quick puff of the cigar, feeling my lips buzz. "I dropped out of school and I went to France. My father seemed like the only person I could go to, you know? My mother wouldn't have given a shit about me in LA. She still barely contacts me and I've kind of stopped trying. But my father, I knew he would help me. And you know what? He did. I went to Marseilles and lived with him and his girlfriend and tried to live again. I learned French. I got a job cleaning boats during the summer. I even went to a therapist, in French and all. There was medication and a lot of setbacks. I have bad panic attacks from time to time. But slowly I pulled myself out of the hole. And…I did everything I could not to think about you."

He looks at me, frowning.

"You," I explain, "were my downfall. Eventually I was able to get through the day without thinking about death, without blaming myself. But you…you were something I pushed out of my head. And it worked. I moved on."

"Until you saw me," he says softly.

"Until I saw you," I tell him.

"Well," he says with a heavy sigh. "This is the worst date ever, isn't it?"

I can't help but smile. "In a way. But I'm with you. You're worth everything."

"Even though I'm the man that ruined you?"

I wrap my hand around his. "I wouldn't want to be ruined by anyone but you."

"Thank you," he says.

"I mean it. Brigs, you destroyed me. But you're also piecing me back together. If I hadn't found you again...I don't know if I would ever feel the way that I'm feeling right now."

"Reliving bad memories?"

"No," I say softly. I clear my throat, feeling too many emotions swirling around. "I'm happy." I pause, trying to explain. "It sounds so simple, I know but..."

"I'm happy too," he says, giving me a quick smile. "I know exactly what you mean. It's not simple at all, Natasha. It's everything."

He pours more wine in our cups and raises his in a toast. "To us. To everything."

"To everything."

We drink. We smoke. I lean against his shoulder and watch Winter play in the surf. We talk. I tell him my plans for graduation, that I'd like to start writing screenplays and probably not use my degree at all, he tells me ideas for future books. We discuss movies. We discuss actors. We discuss Europe and vacations and the French. We discuss Professor Irving and how much we both don't like him and we discuss Max the bartender. We even discuss aliens, briefly, as we grapple for the best alien movie (his: Prometheus. Me: Aliens).

Eventually the sun sets and we take a walk along the beach in the lavender twilight. We weave between the white chalk monoliths and I drop to my knees, taking him in my mouth and making him come right there on the beach.

"Quite the date," he says after, as we walk back to the car.

"Quite the date," I agree.

We get in and speed back to the lights of London.

Chapter Sixteen

NATASHA

London

Four Years Ago

"Still haven't heard from him, huh?" Melissa asks as we sit at the bar, pints of beer in our hands. I've barely been eating all week, so a pint of Guinness is as close to a meal as I'm going to have. It's just impossible to have an appetite when my stomach is churning with nerves, my heart fizzing like a freshly lit firecracker. Ever since Brigs told me that he loved me, my life has been turned upside down in the most gorgeous, unruly way.

But, naturally, Melissa doesn't approve.

Why would anyone approve of Brigs and me?

I give her an innocent look as I delicately sip my beer. "What makes you say that?"

She rolls her eyes, brushing her hair out of her face. "Because your eyes keep drifting away and you're not listening to a word I'm saying."

"That's not true," I tell her, pointing the beer at her. "You were just saying how I ought to give Billy the Skid another chance."

"Well, you should," she says. "First of all, yes you said he was a sloppy kisser, but that doesn't mean the sex will suck.

Besides, you hooked up with him before the summer. Things might have changed by now."

When she says before the summer, I know she's reminding me of how I was before I met Brigs. But everything I was before him doesn't seem to matter now. Especially not William Squire, who couldn't sound more British if he tried, a guy from my class that I had a date with but felt absolutely no chemistry. Kissing him was like kissing a very wet, slimy wall. If that wall had long hair and a love of 80s rocker Sebastian Bach. And of course when I didn't go out with him again, he immediately starting dating someone else from our class. You'd think grad school would be miles away from high school, but some people just can't fucking grow up.

"Maybe," I say, my noncommittal answer.

"You know what you're doing with Brigs is wrong, don't you?" she says so simply it makes my chin jerk back.

"I'm not doing anything with Brigs," I tell her in a hush.

"Right. And that's why when I showed up at your door, he was there. He stayed the night. You told me he kissed you."

I swallow hard, my cheeks flashing with shame. "I didn't sleep with him."

"It doesn't matter," she says. "He's married. He belongs with his wife. Not you. I don't care if you say they have a strained marriage, that he doesn't love her. He's scum and he's playing you like some dumb young American."

I shake my head. I look away, blinking fast. Fear leads to tears. "You don't know him or his life or what he's been through or what I've been through."

She scoffs and takes a large gulp of her beer. "You can't have everything, Natasha. That's not how life works."

I stare at her blankly. "I don't have everything."

"Yes you do," she says with a bitter laugh. "You grew up in this fabulous house in LA, spent your youth modeling and acting."

"My mother is insane! If you met her, you wouldn't say that!"

She ignores me. "You have these guys fawning over you in your class, you're smart, you have a father in France, a big deal cinematographer on top of it, you look like a fucking movie star, and now you have some handsome married guy wanting to leave his wife for you. No, sorry, but you can't have that. It's wrong. You need to let him go and just accept that some things are not meant to be. Chemistry is everything, but timing is the real bitch. This is not your time. For once in your life, it's not your time."

I can't believe what I'm hearing. It's not so much about Brigs, it's that Melissa has these preconceived notions about me, none of them being true. I mean, not in the light she's painting me.

"Everyone's lives look different from the outside," I say quietly. "But the truth is there if you're willing to believe it."

"Whatever," she says dismissively. "You know I'm right. As your friend, I have to tell you that going after a married man is pretty low, and the sooner you move on and think about guys your own age, the ones who are available, then you'll have something to be genuinely happy about."

Ouch. Fucking ouch. But I'm not surprised, not entirely. It's just impossible to explain Brigs and me to anyone. If it wasn't for Melissa seeing him that morning, I wouldn't have said anything to her at all.

Am I ashamed? I don't know. Not of how I feel for him. And not of how he feels for me. I just know it's not the kind of thing to ever be proud of. Love is something I always thought of in terms of black and white—you loved someone or you didn't. If you loved them, it was good. How could love be anything but?

But now I'm living in all the shades of grey. How love can lift you up and make you fall all at once. Brigs makes me feel both pure and dirty, carefree and guilty. I can tell myself too, over and over again, that we didn't have a choice in this, at least I didn't, but I couldn't have shut off those feelings any easier than it is to stop breathing.

What we have is complicated. A ball of knots worth unfurling. And if I didn't believe it would be worth it in the end, I wouldn't pursue him. I wouldn't be pining for him, waiting for his call.

I wouldn't be a fucking girl at a bar, wondering when the man she loves is going to leave his wife.

I'm pathetic.

I'm in love.

I guess it's all the same thing in the end.

"Look," Melissa says, gentler now. "I know you're in love with him. I can see it. But you could never be happy with a man who will leave his wife for you. You'll spend your whole relationship wondering if he'll do the same to you."

But I know he wouldn't. He isn't an unfaithful predator. He's just a fool as I'm a fool. A fool with bad timing.

I need us to get off this topic, so I ask her about her date the other night, and things eventually swing in that direction, leaving the complicated mess that is my love to the side.

When I go back to my flat that night though, tipsy from the beer, head swimming with too many thoughts, I wonder why Brigs hasn't contacted me. It's been days. I've been afraid to contact him, not wanting him to feel pressure or to rush something that is so extremely delicate. So I sit and wait and stew, wondering if everything I could have hoped for, ever wanted, will ever be.

It isn't until later, when I'm winding down for bed, putting tea on in the kitchen and hoping a bit of chamomile and a hit of Scotch will put my raging mind to rest, that I get this horrible feeling of dread. It's like a black, swampy shadow makes its way across the room, and I end up pulling my robe tight around me, even though the feeling also seems to come from inside my bones.

I shudder and try to ignore it. I bring the teapot into my room, grab my iPad, and begin mindless scrolling through all the usual sites. Just Jared, Perez Hilton, IMDB, Variety, The Hollywood Reporter, TMZ, US Weekly. Anything to distract me.

I'm half-asleep with the iPad on my face when my phone rings. I jump, blinking at the harsh overhead lights of my room, and quickly grab my phone from under the pillow.

It's Brigs.

My heart was already racing, but now it's hurtling forward, leaps and bounds.

I suck in my breath. Afraid of so many things. Of new beginnings. Of the end. Every way you look at it, it's scary, and I know when I answer this call my life will be propelled in some direction that will forever change me.

I answer it. "Hi," I say, my voice just a whisper.

There is a long, heavy pause.

I hear his breath. Ragged.

He swallows loudly.

"Natasha," he says, and his voice is just so wrecked that a shiver runs through me. That feeling that something is wrong is back, a bony hand hovering at my chest.

"Brigs," I say. "What is it? What happened?"

A few more beats pass. I hear him breathing. Whimpers. Is he crying?

"Please speak to me," I whisper. "Please. Tell me what's going on."

"They're dead," he says so faintly I have to strain to hear.

"Who is dead?" I ask.

"They died," he says, and now he sounds flat. Horribly flat. "Miranda and Hamish."

I'm speechless. Stunned. I blink and try to breathe. It's just a horrible joke. How could they be dead? His wife and son?

"Brigs..." I say. I lick my lips, unsure how to go on. I'm not finding this funny, but then again, and this is big, neither is he. I've never heard him so serious.

Just keep talking. Find out what's really going on, I tell myself. *No one is dead. That can't happen. There's an explanation.*

"They're dead, Natasha," he says, voice cracking. He breathes in deeply, his breath breaking, and in that break I can feel his very real anguish deep into the heart of me. "They're dead. It's all our fault. We did this. We did this."

I can't swallow. My heart has climbed up my chest and I am fighting paralysis everywhere.

"Brigs," I whisper. "Please don't say these things. Miranda and Hamish—"

"There was a car accident," he interrupts, that flat monotone again. God, it feels like a slab of concrete. "She was drunk, driving without a car seat. I tried to stop them but I couldn't.

I was the first at the scene where they went off the road, both of them thrown from the car. It wouldn't have happened if I hadn't told her the truth about us."

"What?" I gasp, unable to take any of it in.

"I told her I wanted a divorce. She wouldn't accept it. So I told her the truth."

"No, no, no," I mutter to myself, my pulse taking wings.

"She lost it. That upset her more than anything. As I should have known. I should have known." He sucks in his breath and lets out a sob that I feel in my very marrow. "If I could take it all back, I would. I would. Don't you see what's happened? We killed them."

I can't even form words. None of this feels real. But I know it's real to him.

"I'm so sorry," I say meekly. So quiet and pathetic because what can I say? How can this be anything but a bad dream? A joke? "Are you sure they're dead?"

Stupid. So stupid. But I don't know what to say. I'm spinning and spinning around this truth and I can't accept it.

"Of course I'm fucking sure," he snaps. "I'm…fuck, Natasha. They're dead! It's my fault. How can I ever go on with this, with what I've done?"

"It's not your fault," I tell him, pleading, tears starting to fall from my eyes. "It's not our fault. You didn't know. How could you know?"

"I should have known," he says. "And now my son, my son—" He stops, breaking down into sobs.

Oh my god.

Oh my god.

"I'm so sorry, I'm sorry," I cry out, my body starting to shake as the truth slowly takes hold. "Brigs, please, I'm sorry."

He's crying on the other end and my heart is being smashed and smashed and smashed with a hammer, and then the guilt blankets me from above, a net to hold me forever in the truth of what we've done.

There is no grey to our love. There is only black. It's sharp and heavy and eternally wrong.

I'm bereft of everything there is. Love, life, soul. In a second everything is gone because of what this has cost.

"I can't ever see you again," he tells me, strength climbing back into him. "We did this. We were a mistake. A horrible fucking mistake and it's cost me absolutely everything."

I can't speak. I shake my head, the tears spilling.

"Goodbye, Natasha," he says. "Please don't contact me. You never existed. We never existed. We can never ever be. I don't deserve that."

The phone clicks and goes silent.

I drop it onto the bed, staring down at it until the tears blur my vision. I try to breathe but I can't. My throat is a mess of tears and my heart wants to leap out of my chest and run far, far away. I can't blame it. I want to run, I want to die. I want to dig a grave and bury myself deeper and deeper.

Brigs lost his wife and child.

His wife.

His child.

His beautiful smiling child that he loved more than anything in the world.

He lost everything in an instant.

Because he had loved me.

He had chosen me.

He had told the truth.

Our horrible, sinful truth.

I collapse back into bed, feeling black hands grab me and pull me under. I don't care what happens next. My heart is broken and reeling from his words, knowing I will never see him again, knowing we were a mistake. My soul is weeping for the lives we cost. My whole being is dying because I know no matter how badly I feel now, however horrible the burden and shame I'll have to carry, it's nothing compared to what Brigs is going to have to go through.

I'm a terrible person.

The worst.

Melissa had no idea how low I really was, how low I would really go.

I hate myself so much. So much.

I weep, silently at first, staring up at the ceiling, then I start screaming, bawling, choking on tears. I bite my fist until I leave deep teeth marks in my skin, little red grooves that nearly break the surface. My chest and heart seem to converge, crumbling steel that makes me convulse and shake, fighting for life and wanting to die all at the same time.

The pain is so much, too much, and I can't stop how loud I scream, how violently I cry, tossing and turning on the bed, this sinking ship.

I did this.

I deserve this.

This bitter, black end.

I'll never move on.

I'll never be the same.

I'll never stop hating myself.

I've killed two people.

And I'll never see Brigs McGregor again.

Chapter Seventeen

BRIGS

London

Present Day

"Daddy?" Hamish says, his voice so soft and curious.

I know it's a dream without even looking at him. But it doesn't stop my heart from expanding, warm and golden, for every part of me to buzz with the feeling of what it is to be alive. I may be dreaming but it's a blessing to know it, to hang on to every scene, every feeling.

"What is it Hame?" I ask him, turning my head.

We're lying beside each other on the grass at Princes Street Gardens. I'm on my side, flipping through a coloring book of his while he's on his back, pointing up at the sky with chubby fingers. I never really figured out where he got them from. Neither Miranda nor I are anything but thin, but I guess this could be passed down from who knows where. And even though I have a few auburn glints in my beard when it really gets going, Hamish is a full-on carrot top. Everyone said that he'd grow dark like me when he got older, but I had a feeling he would hang on to his ginger ways for a long time.

But I guess that's something I'll never know.

"What cloud is that?" he asks, and I look up at the passing clouds he's pointing at.

I squint. "Well, I don't know. What do you see?"

"Is it a consolation?"

I laugh good-naturedly. "You mean constellation. And that's just for the stars. Just for at night when it's dark."

"Why can't we see the stars in the day?"

"Because," I tell him, grasping for a simplified way. "The stars are the same color as the sun, but the sun is brighter. It makes them disappear."

"What are clouds?"

"Candy floss," I tell him. "Cotton wool. God's pillows. They have so many uses."

"Tell me a story about that cloud," he says, pointing.

The cloud had no shape at all, but then before my eyes it starts to transform into a face. Into Natasha's face.

I swallow hard. "That's a girl," I say quietly.

"She's a princess," he offers. "Tell me a story about her."

I stare up at Natasha's deep eyes and high cheekbones, done up in wisps of white. "Well, there once was a princess who loved a man very much. And the man loved her. Swore he would slay dragons for her, walk through treacherous lands for her, do whatever he could to be by her side. He prepared for the moment that she would be his and he would be hers. But that moment didn't come when he thought it would. The man had to lose everything in his life instead."

"Did he get the princess in the end?"

I look at Hamish with tears in my eyes. "I don't know, son. He's still fighting dragons."

"Did the man have a son?"

I nod. "Yes," I whisper. "A wonderful, beautiful son."

"Where is his son now?"

I take in a deep, shaking breath and look back at the cloud of Natasha which is becoming more blurred by the moment. "His son was one of the things he lost. He never found him again."

"Do you think they'll ever find each other?"

I nod, a tear streaming down my cheek and onto the grass. "Maybe just in dreams."

"Why are you crying?" he asks me.

I turn my head and take in his beautiful face. "Because I love you. And I just want to make sure you're okay."

He grins at me, showing off a missing tooth. "You know I'm okay. I'm here with you. I'm never not with you."

I reach across to grab his hand, and I do for an instant. So small and fragile and warm in my grasp. It feels like heaven.

Then, just like the clouds, he begins to fade, turning into wisps of white, until I'm not holding anything but air. My body begins to pull away from the scene, the false reality rushing past me until it's all gone.

I wake up slowly. When I have dreams like this, I hang on to them as much as I can. I don't groan and moan my way into the day. I don't rush. I grab hold of every feeling and every memory before it's lost forever. Dreams are the only way I see Hamish now, and I'd be a fool to waste them.

Today is different though. I can feel it in my bones, this dark matter that seems to leach out of my body and onto the walls.

It's September 26th.

The anniversary of Hamish and Miranda's death.

I should go back to Edinburgh, visit the cemetery like I've been doing every year—sometimes by myself, sometimes with my parents. But this is the first year I've had my job back, the first year I've tried to really pull myself together.

I take out my phone and check the train schedules, wondering if I have enough time to make it up to Edinburgh this weekend. I don't really and decide I need to do something here in London to honor them. I don't know what, but even just getting Miranda's favorite flowers and Hamish's favorite stickers and scattering them in the Thames feels like enough.

But it's never enough. That's the thing. There's not a single ritual I could do to ever make it be enough because nothing will ever convey how sorry I am, and nothing will ever bring them back into my life. My attempts to honor them only serve to bring me peace and nothing more.

Peace, even now, in the throes of love, is still so fleeting.

Later that morning as I'm about to rush off to school, I get a text from Natasha asking me if we should go to dinner together. Aside from a few nights here and there, we've been spending all our free time together, so plans seems like a given. A wonderful, easy given.

But not tonight.

I text her back. **I'm not good for company. Hamish and Miranda died this day.**

There is a long pause from her and then those bubbles appear as she tries to type something over and over again. Finally she says: **I'm sorry, I didn't realize.**

I know you didn't. It's okay. I'll talk to you later.

I don't mean to be standoffish about it, but it's got to be strange for us to be together at a time like this. Besides, I need to be alone. I have to be. It wouldn't be right otherwise.

Though, for the rest of the day, nothing seems right. I grieve for Hamish, and I feel guilt over Miranda every single day, so this day shouldn't feel any different than normal. But it is and it does. I can barely make it through class, and I don't spend any time on tutorials or my book. I can't. I leave and head home, surprising Winter with a long walk around Regent's University, drowning in my sorrows to the point that even Winter is subdued, his head low, eyes glancing at me warily.

When I get back, Winter heads straight to the couch and stares up at me with big blue eyes. I pour myself a pinch of Scotch and stare out the window at Baker Street, trying to get lost in the imagined lives of the people walking to and fro. But I can't. I can't escape the pain nor the life that I chose.

I head out the door, even as the night is growing dark and cold, the sharp chill of fall. I pick up peonies, Miranda's favorite flowers, then head to a toy store. I'm immediately lost within the racks, trying to find something he would have liked. He liked dinosaurs. Bugs. Monsters. Science. I pick up a pack of dinosaur stickers with the T-Rex and Stegosaurus he would have loved, and then make my way down to the Thames.

I don't bother taking the tube. I want to take my time, as if it's a ritual, going over every beautiful thing that I remember. Sometimes four years seems like eons ago. Sometimes it's just like this morning. How could I recall so much and so little at the same time? How can the dead be so close and so far away?

And yet as I walk, with so much pressure on my heart and that heavy weight of time, I think about Natasha. I think about how she should be here with me. I love her. With everything I have. And despite what we were to each other, what our actions may have caused, I want to be with her for as long as I can.

I can't do this alone. I won't do this alone. Not anymore. If she's going to share my life, she has to share every part of it, including the ugly truths that we try so, so hard not to look at. We're both so afraid to bring up our weaknesses with each other, to talk about what we did, even though we never meant for anything like that to happen. We both tiptoe over the very things that burned us both to the ground, the very things that bond us together. It can't be ignored anymore.

There is no true peace in ignorance.

I take out my mobile and call her.

"Hi," she says right away, though her voice is a bit cagey. I hear shuffling and I know she's trying to be discreet about it around Melissa. That's one thing we do have to tiptoe around. She seems to think Melissa has it out for me, and I couldn't agree with her more.

"Listen," I tell her. "Can you meet me at the Embankment Station?"

"Now?"

"Please."

"Of course. I'll come right away."

I hang up and slow my steps, my breath coming easier to me now.

By the time I work my way across west London to the Embankment Station, I see Natasha popping out onto the street. I quickly wave at her, keeping my flowers low.

She strides over to me, and thankfully her face doesn't show any sign of expectation that the flowers are for her.

I kiss her softly and show her the flowers and the stickers. "The flowers are for Miranda," I tell her, hoping it's not too weird. "Peonies were something she always went nuts for. The stickers are for Hamish. The T-Rex and Stegosaurus were his favorite. He always made them battle. I always wondered what would happen when he got old enough to realize both dinosaurs were millions of years apart and never existed together."

She gives me a sweet smile, but I can tell she's been crying. Her eyes are deep, glittering with fatigue. "I'm sure he would have been just as upset over Santa Claus not being real."

"You're probably right."

I take her hand and we walk down to the riverfront, heading under the Golden Jubilee Bridges. The river is dark as sin at night, despite all the shimmering lights. It looks fathomless, the kind of place that holds monsters in its heart.

"I didn't expect to hear from you," Natasha whispers to me as we stroll past a few joggers out for their night run, past the barges and boats that hold drunken laughter from lives that don't have to carry this burden. Light waves lap at the river wall, the air smelling briny and wet, not unlike a damp basement.

"I didn't expect I'd call," I admit. "But I realized something, I guess. That no matter how hard this is for me, I don't want to do it alone. I don't have to. I have you."

"Brigs," she says softly.

"I know," I tell her. "I know it doesn't seem right, but it is right. I want a life with you, Natasha. And both of us have suffered so much for what we've done. Neither of us wanted this. But it is what it is. And we don't have much hope in working through it unless we work together. My pain is your pain. Your pain is my pain. We understand each other, we understand this, unlike anyone else."

She rubs her lips together, nodding. "Are you sure you want me here, though? It's just so private."

"It is private," I tell her. "But darling, you are my private life. I want you in on everything, just as I want to be in on everything in your life. This is deeply personal, and I need to share it with you. It's the only way out. The only way through."

We walk for a bit until we come to the golden winged statue of the Royal Air Force Memorial where it overlooks the river like a soldier on guard. Steps lead down to the water's edge, and across the way, the ever roving wheel of the London Eye looks down on us.

It's private here. It seems as good of a place as any. Hamish would have been enthralled by the statue, and Miranda would have loved the view of London.

Natasha and I stand beside each other, elbows leaning on the railing. We don't talk at first. There's too much to say and not enough words to express them in. I run over in my head everything I loved about them, and when it comes to Hamish, the emotions run away from me, larger than life. Tears immediately poke at my eyes, burning them, and my chest becomes raw and heavy. There's no way I'm getting out of this without becoming a complete mess.

But Natasha reaches out and holds my pinky finger, just enough contact to let me know that she's there for me, and somehow it gives me the courage to find my first words.

"We're here tonight," I say to the black river, my voice cracking already. "To give our respects to Miranda Harding and Hamish Harding McGregor. They were taken from this world unexpectedly and unfairly, far too soon, on this day, four years ago." I take in a deep breath, closing my eyes. The air is salty, oily, smelling faintly of sewage. "I don't think this day will get any easier. I don't think any day will, as they live in more than just my memory. They live in my dreams and in my heart. They live in my soul, and that's a place I will gladly keep them. I just wish...I want them to know how sorry I am for everything I ever did to hurt them. I want them to know that I truly did love them, in one way or another. Though Miranda and I had our differences, she was still the mother of my child and I respected that. I would give anything to reach back in time and prevent it all from happening. I wouldn't have let her near the Scotch. I wouldn't have let her near Hamish. I would have had the foresight to see this unfolding and hidden her car keys. I would have done anything."

I'm very aware that I've never opened up to Natasha about what went on that night, and I can tell from the way the tears are leaking from her eyes, by the way her hand squeezes my finger, that it's hitting her hard.

I continue, my throat thick. "There are so many things I could have done to prevent their deaths and not a second goes by that I don't regret it. That I don't wish upon wish that I could turn back the clock and make things right. But one thing I've slowly, very slowly, learned not to regret is why I talked to Miranda in the first place." I glance over at Natasha who is staring at me with wide, glossy eyes. "I don't regret that. I don't take that back. Because it was the truth and the truth needed to be said. Maybe some things are better left in the dark, but that's never something I believed in. Once I realized what was to never be, I couldn't live the lie. The truth hurts. In this case it killed. But I refuse to be shackled to that guilt anymore. I refuse to live my life in shame because I fell in love with someone else and because I chose to do the right thing, even if it was barely right above a sea of wrongs. I've needed to make peace with this, and I think Hamish, and deep down, Miranda, would agree. Their loss has robbed me of life and soul and irrevocably changed so many lives. But I also know they would both want me to move on, to keep going, to be happy."

I sigh and lift the bouquet of flowers, breaking off a few petals. "I did the wrong thing and tried to do the right thing.

But this is no longer about my own guilt or shame or suffering. This is just about two very special humans who were taken far too soon, whom I miss every single day, whom I wish I could see just once more. This is about the lives of Miranda and Hamish, and the people they loved and those who loved them."

I sprinkle the light petals on the dark water. They look like stars bobbing around in a moving sky. I take out the dinosaur stickers and do the same. "I love you, little guy. And I miss you. Like you wouldn't bloody believe. And I know, I know you're with me sometimes. Or perhaps, like you say in my dreams, all the time. I'm so sorry I never got to know the man you would become. I'm sorry the world was robbed of knowing you, too. But something tells me—maybe it's just foolish hope—that I'll still know. No matter the years that pass, I'll still know you. In here." I press my fist against my heart and try to breathe. It's so fucking hard. "I love you."

Then I collapse to the ground, my legs having had enough.

Natasha goes with me, trying to hold me up, but I can't. I just end up holding on to her, wrapping my arms around her shoulders, like I can't hold on hard enough. I'm crying, sobbing into her shoulder, feeling so much love and so much pain choke me at once. It's a maddening descent into darkness and I feel myself slipping.

But she is light. She gives me light. She holds on and tells me that I'm a good man and that I deserve to be forgiven, deserve to let go. She tells me beautiful things, and I feel her belief, I feel her strength even though I know the darkness has her too. I wonder if it will always be like this, the mutual drowning, the downward spiral of the two of us, holding hands as we go.

And I wonder if we will always lift each other out of it.

But then, as the night ticks on and we lie by the river, huddled together in each other's arms, a desperate and wild embrace, I know I don't have to wonder.

As long as she is with me. As long as I am with her, we will always bring each other out of it.

We are forever surrounded by ashes.

But we are fire.

And fire rises.

Somehow, when all the tears have exhausted themselves and my chest feels numb and my face is leaden with pressure, the two of us get to our feet. The world swirls around us—the dark, lapping waves, the traffic from the bridges, the glittering lights of the Eye, pubs and boats and life going on—and I feel like we were just caught in a passing storm. Horrible and ravaging and merciless at its peak, but then it soon weakens and moves on. It leaves everything behind it both raw and clean.

Natasha puts her arms around my waist and her head to my chest. I cup the back of her neck, thanking God for her, thanking him for letting the storm pass and the light rise. Maybe it won't always be like this, but for tonight, when I really needed it, it is.

I think I finally know what it feels like to have your pieces put back together. It's a shoddy, messy job, but I'm still standing.

"I'm sorry," she whispers to me. "For everything."

"I'm sorry too," I tell her. "But I'm not sorry for you."

She looks up at me and I wipe a tear away from her cheek before kissing her softly on the lips. "Come home with me," I whisper to her.

She nods and we head back through the city, leaving the flowers and the stickers and the tears behind on the Thames.

Chapter Eighteen

BRIGS

"Professor McGregor, you're not looking so hot."

I don't even look up from my notes. I quickly shove them in my briefcase while the class files out of the room, wishing Melissa would go along with them.

"Well, that's not true," Melissa adds quietly, coming closer until she's practically on the desk. Out of my peripheral I can see her red nails drumming along the surface. "You're always pretty hot. And you know it. Why else do you keep wearing these dress shirts, the way they hug your biceps." I can practically feel her leering eyes burn into me. "But you do look tired. Something wrong?"

I close my eyes and take a deep breath. I know I look like shit. This weekend drained the hell out of me. Though it was cathartic to say my goodbyes with Natasha, and my soul feels infinitely freer, it didn't mean that the emotions weren't still running high. The bonds of shame and guilt may finally be slipping from me, but grief doesn't ever let go. It may slacken, it may lie still at times, but it's always tied to you for the rest of your life. I've come to terms with that now too, that I'll never fill the void left behind, but just because you accept something doesn't mean it gets easier.

That said, I haven't yet accepted the fact that Melissa is bugging the hell out of me with her dicey motives every time she's around. The few times I've brought her up with Natasha, she's been supportive of her friend, even though she seems to have her own reservations. Maybe because she's really the only friend I've seen Natasha have, maybe because Melissa—at least in her eyes—is just overly protective.

But there's something more to her. I can tell. And it frightens me to think that it might go undetected until it's too late.

You're being paranoid, I tell myself. *Again.*

But when I finally look up to give her the *Why are you still here?* look, I catch the blatant expression of lust in her eyes. Lust and something ill-natured. I imagine it's the look many girls get when they catch the eye of a man whose intentions are nothing but bad.

"Is there something you wanted to speak to me about?" I ask her, ignoring what she said previously and trying to sound as noncommittal as possible.

"I just wondered what your views were on dating students," she says with false innocence, her giant forehead wrinkling insincerely.

My eyes nearly bug out of my head. "Excuse me?" I nervously look around the classroom to see if anyone heard, but we're alone now, which is both good and bad.

"Oh, relax," she says with a shrug. "It's just a question. You know I don't bite. Unless I'm told to. I'm very good at taking certain kinds of orders."

I frown at her, shaking my head, trying to compose myself. "You know what the rules are about that, I'm sure. How is that relevant to anything in today's class, or any class?"

"I know the rules about fraternizing with students," she says slowly. "But do you? Do you make exceptions?"

"No," I say, my jaw wiggling, trying to diffuse the tension. "Now I'm going to pretend you didn't ask me that."

"Why?" she asks, coming around the desk, stopping just a few inches away from me. "Do I make you nervous?"

I keep my head raised high. "Frankly, Melissa, you make me very uncomfortable."

She tilts her head, appraising me with a smirk. "Because I turn you on, that's why."

Jesus, she's crazy.

"I beg your pardon?"

"You heard me. I make you uncomfortable because you want me, plain and simple. I don't blame you. It's nothing to be ashamed about. And I definitely won't tell anyone."

"Melissa, if you don't leave, I'm going to have to bring this up with the university," I tell her, trying to supress the anger that's starting to flare up. "It goes both ways. Hitting on a teacher is just as frowned upon as the other way around."

The smirk begins to fade. Her eyes narrow. "You would actually report me? Just for talking to you?"

"Yes," I tell her. "Because this isn't just talking and you know it. I'm going to pretend I don't know what the bloody hell you're offering, but between you and me, I don't fucking want it."

Her head jerks back like she's been slapped. I don't feel bad, but as I see the scorn churning in her eyes, I'm starting to regret being so harsh. She's not the type to take rejection lightly, I can see that now.

"What did you say to me?" she whispers.

"I said, get the fuck out." I point to the door. "And the next time you want to speak to me, I'm making sure we aren't alone. And if we are alone, I'm making sure to record it. Do you understand? I don't know what fucking game you are playing here with me, but it ends here and now. I'm not interested in you and I wouldn't be even if you weren't my student. Once you accept that, the easier this semester will be."

She glares at me. "You're a right prick you know that? Fucking wanker."

"I've been called worse by people more important than you." I jerk my head to the door and bring out my phone. "And I have no problems hitting the record button right now if you truly wish to make this more difficult than it is."

She sucks in her breath through her teeth, seeming to simmer, then shakes her head. "You'll regret this."

I give her a sour smile. "No. Don't talk to me about regret. You don't know shit. Now, go."

She blinks at me in some sort of raging shock before she whips around and storms out of the room. I exhale loudly, trying to gather strength and clarity into my lungs and head.

I need to talk to Natasha about her, I just don't know how to bring it up. I don't know what problems it's going to create for her, and the last thing I want is for her to get kicked out. Melissa is in charge of the flat, and if Natasha were to ever tell her something, Melissa's jealousy would rage and Natasha would be gone. She couldn't live with me, not long-term anyway, while I still have a job. I take my chances with dating Natasha in secret, but living together is another risk entirely.

The best I can do is just encourage her to move out on her own at some point, without telling her exactly what Melissa is like. Melissa knows the kind of hell the both of us had to go through. No real friend would then blatantly go after another's man like that, whether things had ended badly or not.

As the rest of the week goes by though, I find myself unable to bring it up with her, even though the sneaking around is starting to feel tiresome instead of exciting. When we go out to dinner together or to the pub or the movies, when we're just strolling around the city, we try and pretend we are strictly platonic. London is a huge city but a small world all the same. Even though we both mess up from time to time, holding hands and stealing kisses in public, we're both always so aware that someone could see us. And no, she's not my student, but it's still a risk.

That's why when Friday rolls around, I'm borderline ecstatic. I'm taking her up to Edinburgh to meet the family, a place where we don't have to be a secret, at least not in the present. I'm also nervous, anxious, and a whole slew of other things that has my heartrate a few notches above normal.

Natasha comes to my flat after her classes, just in time to see Shelly the dog walker take Winter out. She'll be watching him in the flat while I'm gone, but the fuzzy bugger tends to panic whenever I pack up and leave. This way he just thinks he's going for a walk and that I'll be here when he returns, though I swear he gives me the stink-eye when he goes out the door.

Natasha is pacing through the drawing room, wringing her hands and gnawing on her lip.

"Are you a bundle of nerves too?" I ask her, amused to see her like this.

"Of course!" she exclaims. "I'm meeting your fucking parents. And your brother. I've only heard about them all a million times."

"Then you know by now that they're lovely people," I tell her, putting my arms around her waist and smiling down at her. "They'll love you."

"But they don't know me," she says. "They don't know the real us."

I sigh, closing my eyes. "I know. But they can't."

"They have to," she says, and I open my eyes to see hers searching me in a wild dance. "Don't you see? It's not just meeting the family. It's about living a lie."

"We aren't living a lie anymore."

"Then what do we say?" she asks. "When they ask us how we met?"

"I told you. We stay vague. I met you years ago when you were working the short film festival in Edinburgh. That first day we met? That's all true. That's what we keep as our truth."

"And then what?" she says, breaking away and walking to the window. "I..." She exhales heavily and looks down at her hands. "I'm not going anywhere, Brigs. This is just the beginning now. But in a few years? Then what? The truth—the whole truth—will come out."

"Then we'll deal with it then," I tell her. "They don't need to know everything, and certainly not all at once."

She glances at me, worried. "You're afraid to tell them. Why?"

"Because," I tell her.

"You're ashamed," she says softly.

"No. Not of you. Not of this. Just..." I throw my hands out to the side. "You know how complicated this all is."

"But your family is lovely, you said yourself. Your brother sounds like he has more issues than Charlie Sheen. Don't you think they would all understand the truth? They wouldn't blame you. It might even explain a lot to them."

I rub my hand up and down my face in frustration. "When the time is right. This...I just want them to see you the way I see you. The way everyone should."

"You mean not as the other woman."

"You know what I mean," I tell her quickly, coming over to her and taking her hand. "There is no other woman. There never was. It was only you. And I want them to see only *you*. Please. Just this once. We'll figure out the future later."

She nods. "Okay."

I kiss the back of her hand. "Thank you."

"I just hate lying. I could tell Melissa didn't believe me when I told her I was going away."

I stiffen. It's suddenly hard to swallow.

"What?" I manage to get out.

She shrugs. "Well, I can't tell her I'm going off with you. Like I told you before, she's protective and she doesn't like you. So I said I was going up to Glasgow with imaginary Bradley. Imaginary Bradley sure is getting a lot of action these days." She glances at me. "You okay?"

I nod quickly, blinking. "Yes, sorry. I can imagine lying isn't easy. Why can't you tell her the truth again?"

"I guess because of the same reason you don't want to tell your family. I don't think she'd understand. And she wouldn't believe any of it. She holds a grudge against you like you wouldn't believe, and that grudge goes against me too."

"I believe it," I tell her, wondering if now is the moment. But then again, what do I say? Hey, by the way, your best friend has also been both hitting on me and threatening me in her spare time?

"Maybe she'll be more understanding than you think," I say. "She knows we're both adults here."

She shakes her head, wincing. "She's a weird one. She doesn't work like that. I'm afraid it would do more harm than good." She gives my hand a squeeze. "Anyway, it doesn't matter. Is it time to get the train?"

I nod. "We better get out of here before Winter comes back and loses his mind. My shoes won't stand a chance."

...

The train up to Edinburgh is long but I've never minded it. There's something inherently romantic about watching the landscape fly past you. Your mind goes with it, latching on to new thoughts with the new sights. It's an idea generator, a brainstormer, a place to let your thoughts fly away. In some ways it's even better than the Aston Martin (which bit the dust again after our escape to Botany Bay, hence the train ride), because now I can relax and watch the world go by.

I especially don't mind it now with Natasha at my side. Our seats are in first class and the car is relatively empty. We're able to sit beside each other, her hand in mine, my fingertips tracing circles over her skin. We kiss and laugh and share coy smiles, and it's like we're finally free to just be *us*.

It feels good to be home too. London is growing on me, but Edinburgh will always be home, my true love, no matter how many bad memories are locked here. Stepping off the train at Waverly Station and hearing the Scottish accent everywhere makes me feel like another weight has been lifted off my shoulders.

That said, when we call for a cab to take us to my parents' house, a few jitters sneak back in my heart.

It does feel wrong to have to hide the truth from my family. And I won't lie if it comes down to it. But I want Natasha to be judged for who she is and not her past. My parents are as accepting as they come, as are Lachlan and Kayla, but even then if they knew who she really was to me, they'd look at her differently.

Nobody likes the "other woman." No one wants to relate to her, to empathize with her. No one likes a philandering man either, but when it comes down to it, I am their son and they've seen me suffer—they've seen my guilt and grief. I wouldn't walk away from any confession without some form of condemnation from them, but Natasha is the one who would really be burned. They don't know her. They don't know what she's been through. They don't know how she feels about me. I want them to see all of that first before the truth comes out.

I'm protecting her, plain and simple. Protecting us, this fragile, beautiful thing we have growing between us, that gorgeous freefall I couldn't bear to have end for any reason.

"This is it," I tell her as the cab pulls up in front of the house.

"This is so cute," she coos, staring out the window with wide eyes at the house, the iron gate and stone wall, the overflowing squash and kale in the gardens.

We grab our bags and the cabbie speeds off just as my mother flings open the door.

"Why didn't you tell me you were already here? I could have picked you up!" she exclaims with wide eyes, sounding both angry and excited.

"I didn't want to trouble you," I tell her, putting my hand at the small of Natasha's back and ushering her in through the gate.

"Brigs, you know you're no trouble at all," she says, pressing her hands together as she smiles broadly at Natasha. "I'm so sorry we couldn't have met you at the train. My son has an awful habit of being so secretive about things."

Natasha and I quickly exchange a glance. "It's no worry at all," she says smoothly. "It's very nice to meet you. You have a lovely home. And a lovely son."

Now my mother is positively beaming at me. "Isn't she darling?" she asks. "Natasha. A beautiful name for a beautiful girl."

"What is this, another one?" my dad says, leaning against the doorway, hands shoved in his pockets. "First Lachlan brings home a pretty gal and now our other son does. We're going to be the most popular house on the street."

"Don't mind my father," I tell Natasha. "I take after him. See those glasses? He's a nerd at heart who never quite figured out why a woman like my mother took any interest in him."

"Hey," my mother admonishes, walking back up the path to the steps and eyeing me over her shoulder. "A smart woman knows a good catch when she sees one. Seems Natasha is just as smart as the rest of us."

We go inside the house and my father runs our bags up to my old bedroom until we figure out later who is sleeping where.

"Lachlan and Kayla will be here in an hour," she says. "They're doing a fundraiser at the shelter today. A car wash."

"I've heard a lot about Ruff Love," Natasha says as she takes a seat on the couch and my mother starts pouring everyone tea and getting out the ubiquitous shortbread cookies.

"Well, they're definitely influential enough to get Brigs to adopt a dog. How is Winter doing anyway?" my mother asks me as she sits down.

I shrug. "Sheds everywhere. Shits everywhere. Nothing's changed."

She shakes her head, unimpressed.

"You want the truth?" Natasha asks her, leaning forward in a conspiratorial voice. "He's in love with that dog. Treats him like a baby."

"Oh, bloody hell," I exclaim. "I do not."

"You do," she says, eyes sparkling. "You can't see it because you're in it, but you dote on that dog like nothing else." She looks back to my mother. "When I'm not over, the dog sleeps with Brigs, in bed, under the covers."

My mother lets out a laugh, obviously loving this. "Is that true?"

"My flat is very drafty," I explain, busying myself with the tea.

"And he hires this woman to walk him that fusses over him just as much. I'm pretty sure she carries a row of sausages in her purse, just like an old cartoon. Believe me, Brigs may act like he hates that dog, but Winter is spoiled like you wouldn't believe."

"What's this?" My father comes in the room, sitting beside my mother.

"Nothing," I say quickly.

"Oh, Donald, it turns out Brigs is just as bad with Winter as Lachlan is with Lionel," she says.

"Another nut," he mutters under his breath.

Thankfully the conversation quickly changes to all things Natasha. With her accent and her life in LA, France, and London, it's a pretty easy segue, an even better icebreaker than "Where did you guys meet?" I was pretty vague with my mother on the phone when I called to tell her that I had met someone and wanted to bring her up to Edinburgh.

While Natasha talks about LA and film and Hollywood, I can't help but watch her with pride. Just the way she handles herself, she's so different from the girl I met last month, the one with fear in her eyes and the weight of the world on her shoulders. She's charming my parents just as she charms everyone, that glow of hers making everyone around her shine. If she's nervous at all, she doesn't show it, and when she's tired of talking, she deftly turns the conversation to my parents, asking a load of questions.

Before I know it, the door opens and I turn in my seat to see Lachlan and Kayla stepping in.

"You made it," my mother calls out, getting up and going over to them. She takes off their jackets as she hangs them up.

"Brigs," Lachlan says with a nod, his eyes immediately seeking out Natasha. Kayla does the same.

"Lachlan, Kayla," I say to them, gesturing toward Natasha who I can tell is nervous, sitting stiffly. "This is Natasha. Natasha, this is my brother Lachlan and his fiancé Kayla."

Natasha gets up and shakes Lachlan's hand first, smiling genuinely at him.

"Nice to meet you," she says, though there's a flicker of recognition in her eyes. I guess she's recognizing his face from all those rugby calendars. When she moves on to shake Kayla's hand though, who immediately brightens when she hears her

American accent and compliments Natasha on her orchid pink blouse, Lachlan is watching Natasha curiously. What I saw in her was just a flicker, but Lachlan is studying her with a full-on frown, as if they've met before.

Then again, Lachlan looks at everyone that way.

"So you're American," Kayla says excitedly. "I had no idea."

"Well, Brigs hasn't really told us much about you," Lachlan says, an edge to his voice. He glances at me, frowning, and I just shrug, not really sure what he's getting at.

"That's true." Natasha clears her throat. "I'm a bit too awkward to be shown around in public." She adds a dry laugh, trying to make everyone feel comfortable.

"Are you just going to stand there or what?" my dad says. "Sit down before your mother starts rearranging furniture to suit you."

Lachlan and Kayla take the other couch while my mum starts pouring them some tea. Lachlan, though, is still watching Natasha with a peculiar look on his face.

"What is it?" I ask him, getting annoyed.

Everyone looks at us.

Lachlan raises his brow. "Nothing, I'm sure." He nods at Natasha. "Have we met before?"

She frowns, thinking. "I don't think so."

"Ever been to Scotland before?" Kayla asks her. "I haven't even been down to London yet."

"Well, if Brigs invited us," my mum adds, "I'm sure we could all go."

I give her a placating smile. "When my life settles down a bit, I'll make sure everyone comes by."

Natasha looks back to Kayla. "Uh, actually, I met Brigs in Edinburgh. A long time ago."

"How long have you been in the UK?" Kayla asks, which then gets Natasha explaining about her past yet again. But the way she talks with Kayla, I can tell it's not a chore. In fact, with some silly pride, I can tell that the two of them will soon be fast friends. Both of those American girls swept away by the McGregor men. They have a lot more in common than they think, not to mention their easygoing, witty and slightly quirky personalities.

Meanwhile, Lachlan keeps glancing between Natasha and me, deep in thought.

"And when did you and Brigs officially meet?" Lachlan says to her.

She glances at me. "Four years ago." He raises his brows. "I came up here, working at a short film festival during the summer and he came in to apply to be a sponsor. Then I ran into him at school this year and I remembered him."

Such the truth. Such a lie.

"So you're his student?" my mother squeaks, already having scandal written all over her delicate face.

"No," I say quickly. I clear my throat. "She's not in any of my classes."

"Pretty sure that's a dicey area though, son," my dad says.

Right. All this time we were worried about our real past together, we never thought to worry about the real present.

"We'll be okay," I tell him imploringly, splaying my hands in a sign of surrender.

My dad doesn't look too convinced. "Not that I'm trying to tell you who to date because believe me, we would never do that. Just be careful. Both of you."

"We will," Natasha says, nodding gravely. "We are."

"And how long have you both been dating?" Lachlan asks, still on his nosy trip.

I can't help but glare at him. "A few weeks now."

"Really?" Kayla exclaims. "God. Sorry." She laughs and looks at Natasha. "This must be so awkward for you meeting the family already."

"It wasn't awkward until two seconds ago," Natasha says good-naturedly. She's smooth. She's good. Rolling along with everything even though I know it's killing her to put up such a front.

"Oh, don't worry, it's still awkward for me," Kayla says. "I can't tell you the amount of times I've embarrassed myself in front of Jessica and Donald. Still, they don't mind having me around."

"We *love* having you around, Kayla dear," Jessica says. "And when you smeared nail polish all over the wedding dress you were trying on, well, how could I do anything but laugh."

"It seems to me the sales assistant didn't think it was that funny," Donald says under his breath.

"That seems like the kind of thing that would happen to me," Natasha tells Kayla, trying to relate. "Once I was in Rome, backpacking and seeing the sights for a few days, and I was wearing a dress because it was hot and summer and all that. Well, I took the train to the airport and got up, slung on my backpack and walked all the way out of the train, through to the terminal and then onto one of the moving sidewalk thingies. It's like a ten minute journey *at least*. The whole time I had this feeling people were snickering at me and laughing, but I mean I'm super paranoid anyway so that's nothing new. Anyway, finally some girl tapped me on the shoulder—and she was American of all things—and she was like, "I'm not sure anyone is going to tell you this, but your ass is showing." Turns out that when I put on my backpack, it hiked up my dress to my waist and I was wearing nothing but a fucking thong."

I burst out laughing, as does everyone else, since I'd never heard this little gem before.

"Good thing you have a bloody gorgeous arse!" I tell her, slapping my knee. I can imagine her too, strutting through the Rome airport like it's her runway with no idea that her full cheeks are exposed to the world.

With Natasha's admission, everyone seems to relax even more, Lachlan included. While Kayla launches into an embarrassing story of her own, I catch Natasha's eye and give her a wink.

Fucking hell, am I ever in love.

Chapter Nineteen

BRIGS

It isn't until after dinner and dessert, when everyone is settling down in the TV room to have some tea and watch Graham Norton on the BBC, that I run into Lachlan in the kitchen.

"She used to have dark hair," he says, sidling up to me as I grab some honey for Natasha.

I close the cupboard and stare at him, my heartrate increasing. "What?"

"Natasha," he says, keeping his voice low. "Her hair used to be dark."

I stare at him, blinking slowly, and he stares right back at me, his eyes narrow, knowing too much and still wanting to know more.

"It did," I tell him, wondering what's going on.

"I've met her before."

I shake my head. "How? When?"

"At the pub Rennie used to work at. Years ago. Four years ago, I'm pretty sure."

I frown. "Are you sure? No offense, brother, but you, four years ago, in a pub, isn't the most reliable source."

He straightens his shoulders, running his hand over his jaw as his eyes dart to the other room. He nods. "Yeah. I know.

You would think. But I remember that night. I remember a lot more than you'd think. And I remember that girl because I gave her some pretty sound advice that would take me a long time to take in myself." He glances at me sharply. "Natasha isn't someone you forget so easily. She was there, upset, and I was right next to her. We drank on the house and Rennie kept pouring." He pauses. "She told us that she was in love with a married man."

I swallow and try to keep my face from flinching, but from the way Lachlan's eyes narrow imperceptibly I know he sees right through me.

"Is that so?" I whisper.

"She said he was writing a book. Was a professor of film studies. I thought it the strangest coincidence at the time. But I never thought it was you. Not until I walked in that door over there and saw her beside you. And then it all fell into place."

He's got me. Completely.

I lick my lips. "Do you think she remembers you?"

"Maybe," he says. "But she was pretty drunk. She went home in a cab that night."

"What was the advice you gave her?"

He gives me a ghost of a smile. "I told her to be a catalyst for change."

Catalyst for change.

That's what Natasha wrote in her drunken email to me, the email that opened the gates, that led to that first kiss, the first confessions, the first everythings.

Bloody fucking hell. That all happened because of Lachlan.

"So was she?" he asks. "A catalyst for change? Is that what happened? You had an affair with her."

I close my eyes, taking in a deep breath. I didn't expect to be talking about this with my brother, not this way and not yet. "I didn't have an affair with her. Not a physical one."

"And you told Miranda. That's what you argued about the night she died."

I exhale heavily and meet his eyes. "Yes. That's what it was about. Don't you see? It wasn't just an argument. I was trying to end my marriage. And if I hadn't done that, she would still be alive."

"Oh, don't give me that," he says, his tone surprisingly sharp. "Don't try and wallow in that again. You've done enough of it. You don't let me sink into my mistakes and I'm not going to let you sink into yours. I've said you looked haunted by what you've done. Well, guess what. You don't look haunted now. You look like you're bloody in love. Let the wallowing go—it's comforting to hold on to the darkness, I know this. It gives you identity. It gives you purpose. But you're finally getting out of it. Allow yourself to be happy."

I look away and he puts his hand on my shoulder, staring at me. "Hey," he says louder. "I'm not kidding. Did you think I wouldn't understand, that I would judge you, that I would want to push you back into that spot we've all been dying for you to come out of? Fuck that. I'm your family, Brigs. I don't care if you and Natasha have known each other for years or days. I just want you to be happy. That's all anyone ever wants for you, and it's what you should want for yourself too."

"What are you guys talking about?" Kayla asks, coming around the corner. When she sees his hand on my shoulder and the grave looks on our faces, she stops. "I'm totally interrupting something, aren't I?"

"It's fine, love," Lachlan says, putting his arm out for her. She comes over and leans against him, staring up at me. "Brigs and I were just talking about women."

"Good things, I hope."

"Then we definitely weren't talking about you," he jokes.

"Hey," she says, going for his chest with her pointy fingers and squeezing his nipple.

Lachlan buckles over, letting out what sounds like a giggle and a squeal, a sound I've never heard him emit before. Had I known all along nipple pinching was his kryptonite, I could have made some money selling this information to opposing teams.

"Anyway," Kayla says, finally letting Lachlan go. "I just wanted to tell you that Natasha is fucking amazing."

"Well, good. I think so too."

"No, I mean it," she says. "I hate to say this, but I'm starting to look at you like my brother now. Weirdly secretive and strange, but still my brother, and before I met her I had some reservations. I mean, what girl is going to be good enough for you?" She elbows Lachlan. "Right, baby?"

He grunts in response and she continues, "But now I'm starting to think that maybe you're not good enough for her."

"Kayla," Lachlan warns her.

She smiles at me. "I'm just kidding, Brigs. But really. You've done good. And I mean it. Because I hate everyone."

"Oh, you don't say?" I say caustically.

"It's true. My only complaint is that the two of you are in London and I am up here. Doesn't make for easy girl times.

Like when Lachlan acts like a jerk and I need a friend to braid my hair while I eat a tub of ice cream."

"Yeah, that sure sounds like Lachlan." I give him a look and roll my eyes.

She leaves the kitchen after that, taking the honey to Natasha, and before we head back, Lachlan says to me, "I'm not going to say anything to Kayla. I'm not going to say anything to Jessica and Donald. I'm leaving that all up to you. I just want you to know that no one is going to think anything less. Of either of you. But you can't keep this inside forever. You've kept it inside for long enough."

He walks away, and I'm left in the kitchen wondering how a rugby player got so much smarter than a professor.

Later that evening, when it's time to turn in, me in my old bedroom, Natasha in Lachlan's, I knock at her door.

"Are you decent?" I whisper.

"No," she says. I smile, looking down the hall to the shut door of my parents' room before walking in.

She's sitting cross-legged on the bed in her pajamas, flipping through an old magazine.

"Hey," I say, disappointed. "You're completely decent."

"Oh," she says. "I thought you meant in general."

"Well, that too." I close the door and sit on the bed beside her. "Sorry this couldn't have been a bit more romantic. I barely fit on the bed myself."

She gives me a delicate smile, placing her hand on mine. "It's lovely. It's nice to be in a house where you can feel the warmth, you know?" She scrunches up her nose. "So how do you think I did?"

"With my family, are you kidding? You were incredible. They loved you."

"You sure? One moment I'm trying to be all proper and the next I'm telling them that my ass was hanging out at the Rome airport."

I squeeze her hand, grinning. "That story only endeared them to you. And you further to me. I'm a bit jealous of that airport, to be honest."

"You can see my ass at any time," she points out. "In fact, my ass belongs to you and you alone."

"Oh really?" I raise my brow. "Can we get that down in writing at some point?"

"So they really liked me?"

"Yes," I tell her. "Just as I knew they would. How could anyone not be as charmed by you as I am?"

"Well, my mother for one," she says, looking away.

"Your mother doesn't count. Your own family is always complicated. But I bet even your mother thinks you're marvelous deep down. Just as everyone else does."

"Do you think Lachlan liked me?"

"I know he did." I peer at her inquisitively. "Did you recognize him in any way?"

"What do you mean?"

"You've met him before."

"I have?" She shakes her head. "I would have remembered. When?"

"You were in a pub, so I don't think you would have remembered. I'm surprised he does, but that's how much of an impression you leave on people."

"Oh my god. I met him at a pub. What did he say, did he talk to you about it just tonight?"

I nod. "He says you were drunk and upset. About four years ago, here in Edinburgh. You confessed you were in love with a married man to him and the bartender, Rennie, who used to be on his rugby team. I believe Lachlan gave you some advice, saying you needed to be—"

"A catalyst for change," she whispers. "I remember now, though I can't really see his face. I just remember talking and getting that liquid courage. Then I remember writing the email and you came over, and...then I kissed you." She looks down at the duvet.

"Hey," I say softly, hunching over to see her better. "I hope you don't regret that. I certainly don't."

"I was out of line. I should have never said those things, and I should have never kissed you."

"Well, in that way of thinking, I should have never gone over to your flat. But I wanted to see you. I needed to see if you felt the same way that I felt about you. I don't regret a thing. Not me going over there, not you kissing me. It is what it is, and guess what, you were a catalyst and things did change."

She swallows hard. "Not all change is good," she says in a low voice.

"Natasha," I warn her. "I told you that we're done with feeling guilty. I can't move on, move past this, without you moving with me. We're a team, you know that. I want us to discuss what was without feeling any guilt or shame. It's the only way."

She nods, and I hope it's sunken in. I know it isn't easy, but it's really the only chance we have.

"Kayla's really nice," she says after a moment, her voice perking up. "A total firecracker. At first it was hard to see that she and your brother are together—they both seem so different. But it's obvious how in love with each other they are."

Is it obvious how much I'm in love with you? I think. I reach out and brush her hair away from her face, but the words, those words, are stuck in my throat, just where they have been for weeks. I've said them in the past and meant it, and yet now, now in this new phase of us, my feelings are even deeper. They surpass everything at the moment and render those three words nearly obsolete.

She stares at me with big doe eyes, her lower lip pouting, wet and soft. I want to show her how I feel—I just wish we were somewhere else except my parents' house. Not that it's ever stopped me before.

I get up off the bed and lock the door, slowly turning around to face her.

Her brows are raised and she's eyeing me like, *are we really going to do this here?*

I smirk at her, slowly peeling off my shirt as I walk toward her, then I undo my pants.

She doesn't look too thrilled. Not the reaction I was hoping for.

I slip my erection out of my boxer briefs, holding the hard stiff length of it in my hands.

She licks her lips, the pink tip of her tongue showing briefly.

Okay, that was more like the reaction I was hoping for.

"Are you sure?" she asks quietly as I step toward her, still stroking my cock, getting off on the way she keeps her eyes glued there. I watch the hunger slowly build which only makes me harder.

I nod. "If you can be quiet," I whisper to her. "Can you be quiet? Not make a sound?"

She seems to take this as a worthy challenge. Her expression becomes more wanton and she nods. She slips off her pajamas until she's on her knees on the bed, completely naked.

I come over to the edge and she's already running her tongue up my cock, from root to tip.

She pauses. "So, Lachlan knows the truth about us? And he's okay with it?"

I groan. "Please don't mention my brother's name when you have your hand around my cock." I smile down at her. "But yes, he's okay. He's not telling anyone else, and in due time, when we do tell the truth, at least we know what to expect."

She seems satisfied with that and finally throws herself into it, swirling her tongue over my hard shaft before licking up the precum at my tip. It's funny how sometimes her mind holds her back from enjoying sex, like it can't stop wandering enough to root down and live in the moment, even when the moment is in her damn mouth.

I let her lick and suck for a moment, just because I love the look in her eyes, the blazing need for something so sexual. But before she gets too carried away, I pull back and motion for her to move over. I lie back on the bed and beckon her forward with my finger.

"Come over here," I tell her softly, gesturing to my face. "Right here."

Again she looks shocked. She doesn't move, seeming unsure.

"What, you're afraid you can't be quiet?" I tease.

"Of course I can," she says and slowly straddles my chest, making her way up to my face.

I take a firm hold of her hips and position her cunt right over my mouth. With deliberation I snake out my tongue and carefully run it up and down her wet folds. She immediately stiffens and cries out softly, and I dig my fingers into her skin, to warn her again about being loud, to have control over her movements.

She tastes so good, her musky, rich scent filling me up and turning me on like never before, and as I work her with my tongue, greedily plunging it inside her and flicking it over her swollen clit, I'm the one who has a hard time keeping quiet.

The vibrations from my mouth seem to work for her though, and soon she's rocking her hips against my face as I eat her out. I'm lost in this heady desire, enjoying every fucking sensation. This is raw, wicked, primal, a way of experiencing a woman at her purest self. I could do it forever, sucking up every last drop of her, licking her like the sweetest, ripest fruit.

"Oh god," she says softly, and her hand flies out to the wall to stabilize herself as she fucks my face. I press the tip of my tongue to her clit, rubbing in tight, hard circles until she's coming on me. I can feel every pulse as the orgasm tears through her, my mouth drenched with her, her skin blisteringly hot and slick. To her credit, she keeps quiet, keeping her noises to little shuddering moans and gasps that are just as sexy as her usual screams.

When she starts to squirm and fidget, I move my face away and grin up at her, barely seeing her face behind those amazing tits of hers.

"Hi," I say softly, waggling my eyebrows.

"Wow," she whispers in response.

"We aren't done," I tell her. I get up and push her down into the bed so she's on her back. I prowl on top of her, my knee spreading her legs until I'm right over her, my chest pressed against hers. I wrap my fingers around her wrists and pin her hands above her head, holding her in place. Then I trail the tip of my nose down the middle of her face, pausing at her lips to kiss her.

"Fuck, Natasha," I whisper, closing my eyes briefly. "You have no idea what you do to me, how you make me feel."

"You've said that before," she says. "And you ended up telling me."

She's right. It took a while but I eventually told her the truth.

I breathe in deeply and adjust myself, my cock pushing against her wet cunt but not going in.

"And what did I say?" I ask her gently.

"You said I was more to you than I had thought. A terrible amount."

That was one way to describe it.

"A terrible amount," I repeat, opening my eyes and getting lost in hers, so deep, just inches away. Bloody hell, I'm losing myself to her again. No, I'm already lost.

I try to swallow. I rub my lips together, finding courage.

"It is a terrible amount," I say. "It's more than that. Natasha…I'm in love you. Plain and simple. I was in love with you before and I'm more in love with you now. I don't even know how it's possible, but it is. And because it is, it makes me think anything's possible. Even us."

She stares at me, a swirl of emotions behind her eyes, and I wish I could pluck one out and examine it, to see what she's feeling. She's speechless.

I briefly brush my lips against hers. "Talk to me," I whisper. "Say something."

"You love me," she says, almost in awe.

"Yes," I tell her, smiling like a fool. "Yes. Natasha, I love you. More than I'll ever be able to express. Just know it. Believe it. And love me too."

"Oh, Brigs," she whispers, her mouth parting into a wide, glowing smile. "I've never stopped loving you."

My heart thumps. "Even after all these years?"

"Even after all these years. Through the dark and the light, I never stopped. I might have pushed it aside, I may have buried it, put it on pause, but I never, ever stopped."

I feel like a million balloons have been let loose in my chest. I want to laugh. I want to cry. I stare at her, amazed. Just so fucking amazed that we found each other again, and that this us, this us is beautiful.

"I love you," I tell her again.

"I love you," she says.

I kiss her, hot, hard, and possessive as my body kicks into gear, trying to catch up with my heart. This soft tenderness I feel for her is being swirled around with the primal desire, and before I know what I'm doing, I'm pushing inside of her. Her legs widen to let my cock in and I sink into her, so wet and cushioning around my hard length. We fit so well together, like a lock and key, that it's hard to imagine how I survived this long without her.

"You are my salvation," I whisper into her ear, licking along the rim. "You save me from the world. You save me from myself."

I keep her hands pinned above her head with one hand, and thrust into her harder, faster, and infinitely deeper. My other hand goes to her clit, working her again. Even though she just came minutes ago, I know she's still desperate for it. I roll my hips into her, going faster, raw, bordering on violent as the bed starts to shake and she starts to moan, biting her lip hard to keep from crying out.

"You feel so good, so fucking good." I'm moaning, the world slipping away so it's just us in a hedonistic haze. I swivel my hips, hitting the right spot, and soon she's coming again, her body spasming beneath me, her eyes pinched shut, lush mouth open as she cries out breathlessly.

I let go, driving into her in a relentless rhythm, my balls drawing up, my chest tightening as it fights through a rush of feelings. My hunger, my need for her, not for just her body but her mind and heart and soul has never been as razor sharp and visceral as it is right now. I'm lost inside, coming hard, and the world is flipped upside down in nothing but this dark, devastating pleasure.

Fuck.

Fuck.

I collapse against her, trying to catch my breath and not crush her at the same time.

That was surreal.

That was nothing but fucking bliss.

That was love.

Fuck.

Fuck.

We didn't use a condom.

I glance down at her face, cheeks pink, a light sheen of sweat on her brow and above her bruised lips. Her eyes are both languid and anxious at the same time.

"You're not on the pill yet," I tell her.

"No," she says slowly. "I couldn't see the doctor. But we should be fine. I'll just take Plan B."

"Doesn't that make you sick?"

"Not really. I'll get it in the morning. I really wouldn't worry about it," she says, running her hand over my shoulders and down my arm. "That was..."

"Transcendent?" I fill in.

She laughs lightly. "I was going to say fucking amazing, but that works too."

I run my thumb over her lip, grinning at her, and she playfully bites it.

"You know," I say, "I was thinking, even though there's barely enough room to fuck on this bed, maybe we can make sleeping work."

She grabs my biceps. "Like I was going to let you go back to your own room after you told me you loved me."

"I do love you," I tell her.

"I know. And you're staying."

So I get under the covers, and even though sleeping with her on a single bed in my brother's old room is one of the weirdest things ever, I'm with Natasha. And we love each other. And because of that, everything is right.

Chapter Twenty

NATASHA

Weeks ago when Brigs said he wanted to "date" me, I never imagined that one of our dates would be in a pedal boat going around the pond at Hyde Park.

Then again, I never imagined how deeply in love with this man I'd be. And I never imagined how impossibly beautiful it would be to hear him say those words I'd first heard years ago. To feel it again.

Natasha, I love you. More than I'll ever be able to express. Just know it. Believe it. And love me too.

I still melt over that, my heart a hummingbird in my chest. It might explain why I agreed to get into a blue plastic boat and pedal it all over the Serpentine on a chilly autumn day.

"Hey, pick up the slack a bit," Brigs says to me, his legs pumping furiously while I half-heartedly paddle.

"Oh, come on," I say, reaching across the divide, trying vainly to smack him across the chest. "A true lady never paddles."

"That's true," he says. "Though you don't fuck like a lady."

I give him a wry look. "Thank god for that." I look around us. There are maybe five other paddle boats out on the water. I'm grateful I'm wearing a hat and scarf, because today is the first day I've really felt winter might be around the corner. The season, not the dog.

"We should head back," I tell him.

"Why?"

"Because I'm horny," I put it bluntly.

Brigs raises his brows. "All right then." He starts peddling faster, heading back to the green grass of the shore.

"Have you talked to your brother?" I ask him as we get closer.

"I really wish you wouldn't mention him and the word horny so close to each other," he says dryly. "But no, I haven't."

"Do you know when you'll tell your parents about us?" I ask, feeling so impossibly young when I phrase it like that. "You know, how we met?"

It's stupid to keep bringing it up, but I was so nervous over the weekend when I met them. I didn't really have a reason to be though—they were sweeter than can be, and Lachlan and Kayla were absolutely adorable. I still don't remember meeting Lachlan all those years ago—his face is still kind of a blur from that night—but I'm more than grateful that at least he knows the real story. The last thing I want to do is put pressure on Brigs, but it's like a weight on my shoulders knowing that we're not living the absolute truth. I just can't lie anymore.

"Soon," he says to me, and I know he means it. "I promise. I just want to tell them in person. Maybe I'll go up next weekend. I should probably talk to my realtor as well and put my place on the market."

"Are you serious?"

He shrugs. "Why not? I'm liking my life down here. This feels right. This is where you are."

I'm taken aback. Completely flattered. Still…"Don't change your life on account of me. Selling your place is a major deal."

"And being in love with you is a far bigger deal than that. I'm not going anywhere, Natasha. I'm at your bloody feet and that's not going to change."

Damn. This man has a way with words.

"You're getting royally fucked when we get back to your place," I tell him. "And I mean that in a good way, of course."

"I'm glad you clarified that," he says, shooting me a grin.

And I wasn't kidding. Once we get the pedalo to shore and head back to his flat, as soon as we get in the door, I attack him. I know I'm supposed to get my period in a few days, and my hormones are all over the place, plus my heart is on the rampage. Mix that all together and I'm one insatiable girl.

We disappear into his bedroom and our clothes come off, and I'm riding him first, my breasts bouncing, and I thrust my hips, his cock buried deep inside, his face staring up at me in lust and awe, like he can't believe I'm real.

Then I'm on my side, my leg lifted over his hip, and he's driving into me, faster and faster, the headboard slamming loudly against the wall. Sweat drips off his body and onto mine, and the room fills with the thick smell of sex and the intoxicating sounds of my greedy moans and his grunts and his dirty mouth as he fucks me into oblivion. When I come, I'm a dam unleashed, and I'm screaming his name, letting everything go. Every fear, every thought, every darkened part of me. I'm liquid bliss and sunshine and every star in the universe.

"Bloody hell," he swears a few moments later, rolling onto his back. "You weren't kidding earlier. I'm pretty sure Horny Natasha might be the death of me."

I give him a lazy smile. "That doesn't sound so bad."

"It's not." He gets off the bed, peeling off the condom, and I make a mental note to go to the doctor and get on birth control as soon as I can. The other night at his parents' house was too risky. "And now I'm fucking starving. How about I heat us up some pies?"

"Post-sex beer and pie," I say with a sigh, spreading out on the bed and stretching my limbs. "Pretty sure there's nothing better."

"Who said anything about beer?" Brigs says, even though I know he's joking. It's pretty much become a ritual for us, eating pie and drinking beer, naked in his kitchen.

I hear him go into the other room and start rustling around, turning on the oven. I lie on the bed, the orgasm glow pulling me into a soft sleep. But once I hear the beer caps pop off, I drag myself off the bed and join him.

He hands me a beer, and we clink the bottles together, grinning at each other. It still blows my fucking mind that this is my life now, that this man, this gorgeous, special man can stand in front of me totally nude and I can do the same with him, and we can fuck and we can eat and we can love and we can just *be*.

"How long is the pie going to be?" I ask. Brigs' oven is notoriously slow and I possess little patience when it comes to food. My ass is proof of that.

"Ten minutes, promise," he says.

There's a knock at the door suddenly, scaring the crap out of both of us. Winter starts barking.

"Fuck," he says, quickly heading to the bathroom to grab a robe. Since I'm buck naked, I go into the bedroom, hauling Winter in there to shut him up. I close the door and slip on my jeans and his T-shirt, my cheeks going red as I think it could be a damn noise complaint. I was screaming pretty loud as I came, and that headboard was making a racket of its own.

I open the door a crack and poke my head out. Brigs is peering through the peephole.

"Who is it?" I hiss. "Are we going to get in trouble for being too loud?"

"I hope not," he says, hand on the knob. "I can't really see, looks like maybe the girl down the hall..."

He opens it and I duck my head back into the bedroom, shutting the door.

"Where is she?" I hear a familiar voice seething from outside. "Where is Natasha?"

Oh my fucking god! It's Melissa!

What the fucking fuck? I feel myself flattening against the wall, holding my breath. What the hell is she doing here?!

"Melissa," Brigs says. "What are you doing here? How do you know where I live?"

"I followed you from Hyde Park," she snarls, her voice carrying into the room. "I was watching you. I know, I know everything about you." She yells, "Natasha, you come out here!"

Jesus. I'm trembling, trying to catch my breath.

"Melissa, you need to leave right now," Brigs says, raising his voice. "You have no business being here."

"Natasha!" she yells, and I know if I don't go out there, if I don't show myself, she'll cause a scene.

I straighten my shoulders and remind myself that she's the one being absolutely fucking crazy. She followed us here? What the hell is happening?

"It's okay, Brigs," I say, stepping out of the bedroom and into the hall. I close the door behind me and stand there, folding my arms across my chest.

Melissa is halfway inside the door. Brigs has a firm hold on it, trying to shut it on her, and he turns his head to look at me. I meet his eyes and give him the nod to let her in.

He opens the front door wider and she barges inside, hustling right over to me, her eyes flashing.

"What the fuck are you doing?" she cries out, pointing at him while she stares at me. "How long have you been lying to me?"

"Why are you *following* me?" I question in return.

"Because I know you're a fucking liar, that's why," she sneers, waving her arms about. "There is no Bradley in the art history masters. I checked."

"You checked?" I repeat incredulously. "Why? Why the hell couldn't you just believe me?"

"Because," she says, turning to glare at Brigs. "I knew, *I knew* that he was still hung up on you just as you were hung up on him."

"Melissa, please," I tell her, trying to get her to calm down. "I don't understand. Yes, I lied, but only because I knew you wouldn't approve. That's all. You said if he contacted me at all, you'd report him, and that's the last thing I wanted."

"Oh, and I'm supposed to feel sorry for you because you had to lie? All you do is lie, Natasha. When you first met this wanker, you didn't tell me anything about it at all. I only knew about him because I showed up at your door. You kept him a secret from me—your best friend."

Oh god. My heart sinks a bit. Is she really that hurt over it still?

"I'm sorry," I tell her. "I told you I was sorry. I was just so in love—"

"That's bullshit," she says to me. "Love. You don't know love. You said so yourself, you left your mother, your single mom, behind in California so you could come out here and do your own thing! At least you have a mother. I don't even know mine. I was raised by my father and stepmother. And you gave that up and you gave up your acting career in LA. I mean, who do you think you are? That you're so special you can just cast that shit aside? Do you know I'd kill for that? You have fucking everything, and then there are people like me, people who struggle, people who have nothing."

Holy fucking hell. I can only blink, the blood whooshing loudly in my head. I look over at Brigs and he's watching her carefully, seemingly as taken aback as I am.

"Melissa," I tell her, trying to find my voice. "I'm sorry you think that, but you know that's not me. That's not my life."

"Yeah right," she says, tears coming to her eyes. "You've always been better than me in every way. You're prettier, taller, skinnier, more talented, smarter. You've always managed to get by in life, and then on top of all that, you end up having a married man fall in love with you, or so you thought." She glares at Brigs. "He just wanted some young twat, that's all." She turns her vicious eyes back to me, and I'm caught between feeling sorry for her and being completely angry. "And that's what you gave him. Couldn't you just for once have passed him up? Couldn't you have let someone else have him?"

"Who, you?" I ask.

"His wife," she says. "That's when I really knew what you were like."

I shake my head, the tears threatening my eyes, my chest a raging mess. "I don't understand. Why pretend to be my friend then? Why act like you cared?"

"Because I liked that you needed my help," she says almost painfully. "I liked that you were at rock bottom and needed a friend, and you only had me. You finally made me feel useful. I was important to you. I was worth something. You have no idea what you're like, Natasha. You live in your head. You act like you don't need a soul in the world. I see you pretending to care about the world around you, but you have some different fucking world inside you, a place you go to, and that's just not fucking fair. Everyone else has to be out here, suffering, and you can retreat. I wanted to see in you pain, Natasha, because it's the only way I knew you were fucking human!"

"Okay," Brigs says in a stern voice, coming toward us. "It's time for you to go," he says to Melissa.

"Fuck you," she says. "You're just as bad as she is. So single-minded. Nothing else but her matters in your world. And nothing else but you matters in hers. You wormed your way into the toughest of hearts. Congratulations." She looks between the both of us, stepping backward. "You guys deserve each other. Heartless and cruel and too good for the rest of the world. You realize what you did, right? That if you hadn't fucking fallen for each other, two people would still be alive in this world."

Brigs' face turns red, his eyes becoming hard as iron. He points to the door. "Get the fuck out or I'm calling the bloody cops."

"Call the cops, then," Melissa says. "And I'm calling the school. You can't fuck the students, Professor McGregor."

"She is not my student," he says through clenched teeth, the muscles in his neck standing out.

"I don't think that will matter much when I report you," she says. She looks at me, her expression suddenly becoming meek. "I told you, Natasha. I warned you. I said that if he ever looked at you, came after you, contacted you, I would end his career. And you believed me. That's why you hid all of this from me."

God, I feel like everything is slipping away. "That's exactly why," I plead. "So please, have a little compassion. I love him and he loves me."

Her lip curls as she looks me up and down. "And what about me? What about the friend you cast aside, the one you keep lying to? Where's the love for me?"

I stare at her, feeling so fucking helpless. I don't know what she wants. Everything is spinning out of control, crazy. "Melissa. You're the best friend I have."

"Tell me you love me, then."

My chin jerks back. "What?"

"Tell me you love me," she says. "As a friend, as anything. Just tell me."

But I can't. Because I don't. Not as a friend, not as anything else. Until this moment she was just a friend, a person in my life, but no one I had a deep attachment to. God, maybe she's right. It's just me in this world and no one else.

Except for Brigs.

"That's right," she goes on, eyes narrowing. "Because you don't love anyone except yourself and him. Well, you're both fucking perfect for each other. The two most selfish people on earth." She turns around and starts to walk to the door.

Brigs reaches out and grabs her arm, glaring at her with a look that even makes me shrink in place. "If you fucking report me, I'll end you."

She stares right back at him for a few moments and then shakes her head, a sour smile on her thin lips. "You should have gone for me," she says. "It would have been safer."

Then she steps out into the hall and disappears. Brigs quickly shuts the door behind him, locking it, and runs his hand over his face. "Bloody hell," he whispers, coming right over to me. He pulls me into an embrace, but I can barely move. I can't believe what's just happened.

"What the fuck," I say. "I don't…I don't know what that was."

"I guess now isn't the time to tell you that she's been blatantly hitting on me after class."

"What?" I hiss, pushing him back. "She's been what?"

My heart turns bitter, acidic. It adds to the panic.

He nods, looking away. "I didn't want to tell you because I didn't want to cause a rift. She's been hitting on me. Completely inappropriate to the point of harassment."

I'm wounded. I can't breathe. "And you didn't tell me?"

"I couldn't," he cries out. "I wanted to, Natasha. But I was thinking of you. You live with her. What would you have done if I had told you? You would have confronted her about it, and then what? We end up in this same scenario." He growls in frustration, pressing his fist into his forehead. "Can't you see? She wants everything that you have to the point that she's bloody psychotic."

Oh, I can see it now. I just don't understand. I may be standoffish at times, I may be a hard person to know, and maybe I don't let many people in…or maybe I let no one in. Maybe Brigs is the first person I've let see every part of me.

"Natasha," he says to me in a hush, pulling me into him. "Don't listen to anything she's said. *Don't*. She's jealous of you and that's it. Jealousy is almost as strong as love, and definitely as strong as hate. It warps people. It can take the nicest, gentlest human being and turn them into something weak and rancid. She's bitter and she's scared and she's grasping at straws."

"You're making excuses for her."

"No excuses," he says, licking his lips. "Never that. I'm just trying to make sense of it, just as you are."

"She's going to report you," I say. My voice won't stop shaking.

"Maybe not," he says with a sigh. "I think she just wants to be heard, that's all. She still likes you. She's just hurt and envious and it's taking over. You need to go home and talk to her."

"What? I can't go back there," I cry out. "Did you not hear what she said?"

"I know, but that's where you live. I would go with you, but it will only make things worse. Listen, Natasha, you need to try to make things right for now, and hopefully she'll respond to common sense. She wants you to be real with her and vulnerable, so be those things. Then start looking for somewhere else to live, right away. In fact, I'll help you."

"I could live here," I say quietly.

He winces, trying to smile. "I wish you could, darling, I really wish you could. But right now, with her watching us, I don't think we can. I know you're not my student, but I really have to make sure that neither of us will get in any trouble. But I'll help you, and if it costs more, I will pay for it. I don't care. You just can't stay there with her anymore."

I nod. "I know, I know." I turn away from him, knots in my chest. One moment everything was perfect, the next it's blowing up in my face. The last thing I want is for Brigs to lose his job. He can't lose anything else on account of me, I won't let it happen. Fucking Melissa has the whole fucking world in the palm of her hand right now.

"Okay," I say, sighing. My heart feels like lead. "I'll go." I quickly put on my own shirt and grab my stuff. My stomach churns and churns and I've never felt so nervous, as if I'm actually going into battle.

Brigs suddenly cups my face in his hands, his eyes roaming all over me like a wild horse. "I love you," he whispers. "And you love me. Don't forget that."

I swallow thickly. "I won't."

I can't.

I'm out the door.

Chapter Twenty-One

BRIGS

I'm pacing the flat, curling and uncurling my hands into fists. Winter is lying on the floor, staring at me. For once he's completely still, his head down, his eyes following my every movement as I go back and forth.

I don't know what's going on with Natasha. I texted her, phoned her, emailed her. It's been a few hours since she left to go back to her flat and confront Melissa, and I'm worried sick.

I should have seen this coming. I'm a bloody idiot is what I am.

I knew that Melissa was up to something, but my god damn ego didn't realize how duplicitous she was. I thought maybe she was just jealous of Natasha and wanted what she couldn't have. I never thought it could come to this, that she would turn to stalking us, threatening us. I should have figured that out but I didn't and now we're paying for it.

I can only hope that Natasha can talk some sense into her. I know I can't, even though I'm willing to try. If things don't go well, I'll call Melissa into my office after class and try to reason with her. I'm not above bribing her. If she wants perfect grades and to never show up to my class again, I'll give her that. It goes against every moral principle I have about being a teacher but Natasha – and my job – is more important than that. I'll do anything to make this whole thing go away.

But I guess the real problem is that we still wouldn't be out of the woods. We're still hiding ourselves away from the public, because of what could happen if the school finds out. What I need to do is fix that from the inside. Make sure we're safe, that we can be together, whether someone like Melissa tries to ruin it for us or someone else. I should have done that from the beginning, but love plays you like the ultimate fool. Love is a trickster, a joker, and the master of the sleight of hand. She makes you look one way, and only one way, while she makes the rest of the world disappear. Eventually you'll raise your head from the one you love, look around and wonder what the fuck just happened.

I continue pacing, until Winter starts looking anxious and then I take him for a walk, texting Natasha repeatedly.

Are you okay?

I love you.

Did you talk to Melissa?

What is happening?

Please talk to me.

Natasha, please, I'm so fucking worried.

And nothing. No response. I contemplate going to her flat, but even if I knew where it was, I have a feeling my presence would only make things worse.

This is hell. And I've been in hell before, so I know.

I don't know how I go to sleep that night. I write her a few more emails, bordering on becoming stalkerish myself. I check her Facebook but she never uses it anyway. My calls go straight to voice mail.

I know something is terribly wrong.

The next morning I have no choice but to get to school early and plant myself outside of Professor Irving's class in hopes of seeing her.

"McGregor," Irving says to me, looking me up and down. "Trying to learn a few things? I would be more than happy if you joined my class."

"I'm looking for a student," I tell him mildly.

"Oh," he says as the students file into the lecture theatre, giving us curious looks, wondering what I'm doing there. They're all undergrads but I know Natasha is a TA for this class. "What student?"

"One of your TAs, Natasha Trudeau."

He nods, squinting at me. "She's rather bright but hasn't been paying much attention lately. A shame, really. She could do well if she applied herself."

Applied herself. I hate that fucking teacher speak and it's something I try my best not to say to students. But the reminder itself is good, because it reminds me that there is so much more going on in our world than just our relationship. There's a chance that Melissa could mess things up for Natasha too, just when she's gotten her life back.

He pauses. "Is Miss Trudeau one of your students?"

"No," I say and I don't offer any more than that.

"Very well then," he says, thankfully not pressing the issue. He heads inside the theatre. "But she's often late, just so you know."

He's right about that. She's so late that she doesn't even show up at all, even as I wait nearly the entire class. Now I'm worried as fucking hell.

I head back to my office, trying to plan what to do next, my head down, my brain sorting through all the possibilities.

Then I look up. And I see her, standing outside my office door.

I start running down the hall, like if I don't catch her in time, she'll disappear.

Don't let her become a ghost again.

"Natasha," I croak and up close now I can see her red, puffy eyes, her raw nose. She looks ravaged, like she hasn't slept in months. "What happened? I've been trying to call, texting, emailing you. I've been worried sick."

"I know," she says, pained.

I reach out to touch her face but she flinches away from me.

"Don't," she whispers. She pulls away and nods at the door. "I need to talk to you in there."

I swallow hard. My chest grows heavier.

We go inside my office and I lock the door behind us. I immediately pull her into my arms, holding her tight to me. "Fuck. Tell me what happened."

She hesitates and then puts her arms around my waist, leaning her cheek against my chest. I can feel her heart beating against me, wild and crazed.

She takes in a deep, shaking breath. "We have to end it, Brigs."

Unease floods my chest.

"End what? What are you talking about?"

She sniffs and pulls back to look up at me. Her sweet face is torn with anguish, eyes brimming with tears "I tried to talk to her. I really did. She's...she's on a power trip. She's just...

she wants me to suffer, Brigs. She thinks it's all about what's fair in the world. She says what we are isn't right..."

"Natasha," I say sharply, holding her tight. "You're smart enough to know what's right and wrong. What we are is right. You know that."

"I know," she says softly, a tear spilling down. "I know she's wrong but it's what she believes. She says I have to choose – I can either break up with you and be miserable like she is or I can stay with you and she'll make sure you lose your job."

I can't even comprehend this. The only thing I can comprehend is the amount of dread filling me, thick, heavy and sour. "That's ridiculous. Why? Why?"

She shrugs. "I don't know, she's crazy. She's...a...a... cunt. A cuntosaurus."

I would normally laugh at that but there's absolutely nothing funny about what Natasha is saying. "Listen to me," I tell her. "If she won't listen to reason, fine. But I'm not letting you go. That's not an option."

"Is losing your job an option?" she pleads.

"I won't lose my job."

"She said she'll make sure of it."

"Then I'll fight it," I tell her, getting angry.

"She'll make sure you lose."

"Then I'll resign," I say without even a thought. "I'll quit the school before she can do anything."

"You can't do that!"

"I can and I will," I tell her, peering into her eyes, trying to get her to understand. "It's a job and it's my career and I love it. I've worked hard for it. But in the end, it's not who I am. It's just a job and I can always get another one. You, on the other hand, there is no other you. My job doesn't define me but you do, Natasha. Your heart defines mine."

The tears are rolling down her cheek now and I try to kiss them away. She turns her head, shaking it.

"I can't let you do that. I would rather quit school first."

"No," I say to her harshly. "You are not doing that. Think realistically here."

"I am!" she cries out, pulling out of my arms. "We have to break up."

A chill rushes over me in a sickening rush. "Natasha," I warn her.

"I'm being realistic," she says. "I'm trying to not be self-ish for once in my life."

"You're just being stubborn for the sake of being stub-born," I tell her.

"Fuck you," she sneers. I flinch. It's like a slap in the face. "Do you think I have an option here? Do you think I want this? Please, Brigs, you have to know me by now that I'm not being stubborn. This is the only way."

But it isn't, it *isn't.*

"I'm resigning," I tell her simply. "That's all there is to it."

I don't even panic at the thought. It feels right, just as she feels right. It will be hard and I'm sure I'll get a lot of hell for it. People won't understand. It might make getting a new job harder but I will do it for her. At the very least, it will end the sneaking around. We can be together as we should. Free, for once in our lives.

"You're not resigning," she says, her voice becoming hard. Her eyes are dark and gleaming. "I won't let you. And I won't have that guilt on my head. I've had too much already. You're keeping your job."

"But then I'm losing *you*. How is that not going to fucking kill me?!" I yell. My face is burning, lungs so bloody tight.

"It's the right thing," she cries out. "And it's the only thing. I'm sorry."

I blink at her. Unbelievable. I honestly can't believe this is happening.

"Natasha. Please. You'll ruin me. Don't do this," I say softly, voice breaking in desperation. I grab her hand, squeezing it, trying to make her see. "Don't end this. It isn't fair."

She watches me and I watch her and she's being ripped apart just as I am. "I know it isn't fair, Brigs. None of this is fair. But I've already caused you to lose everything good in your life. I'm not going to do it again."

"But *you're* everything good." My jaw is clenches, my skin inflamed, trying to hold it together.

"Yeah, well," she says, pulling out of my grasp. "Maybe I'm not."

I would murder Melissa with my bare hands if I could. The thoughts she's put in her head. She's starting to actually believe it.

"Don't go," I tell her. I want to drop to my knees to get her to stay.

"I'm sorry," she sobs, turning from me, angrily wiping away her tears. "I don't want to hurt you but I can't do this. I can't go through this again."

"Then don't go," I repeat. "Please just fucking stay here and *love me*."

She looks over her shoulder at me. "I do love you, Brigs. I do, I really do. I love you more than anything. That's why I have to do this."

I close my eyes, breathing in sharply through my nose.

"You don't have to do this," I whisper, my nails digging into my palm. Everything in my chest seems to tense and shatter. "Please, please don't do this to me. I am glass and in your hands and I am *breaking*. Can't you see that?"

I finally open my eyes, hoping to see something in her has changed. Whether she chooses to be stubborn or not, the fact remains that she is.

She's shaking her head, staring at me with the saddest eyes.

She's leaving me because she believes it's the right thing to do.

"I'm sorry," she says in a low voice and I wish I could turn to stone. "Please don't hate me."

I stare at her. I am dissolving before her eyes. "I could never hate you," I manage to say. "I love you."

"Then if you love me, let me go," she says. "Let me leave. Let me make things right."

I'm shaking my head. "You're only making things *wrong*."

"Good-bye Brigs," she says with a sob, unlocking the door and flinging it open. "Please, don't contact me. For your own sake. And mine."

Then she's running out the door, her hair whipping around her like a cape of gold silk and I have to lean against my desk to stay upright. The last words I said to her all those years ago ring through my ears and now, now I understand the exact pain she'd spent all this time trying to get over.

My heart is crushed. Absolutely. It feels like an anvil on my chest, pushing and pushing until I can barely breathe.

I want to collapse to the floor. Writhe in pain. I want to sink into the deepest sorrows, be dragged back into those inky depths. The hellish suffering. The turmoil that slices you up inside like poison-laced razorblades.

But this isn't like last time.

Because I don't feel guilt.

And I don't feel shame.

I'm angry.

Really fucking angry.

It's my anger at Melissa, at the situation, at my own carelessness that keeps me from focusing on my water-logged heart. It keeps me moving. I'm not going to roll over and play dead and admit defeat. I crawled straight out of hell – I've been through the worst already. I've come too far to bloody give up because things seem impossible, because someone wants to make my life miserable.

No one makes my life miserable but me.

Natasha told me to stay away, to not contact her.

I'll grant her that – for now.

But if I'm going to get her back, I have to do what I can to change this.

I have to do what's right.

. . .

The week slogs on by like molasses and I stay true to what she asked of me. I don't contact Natasha at all, even though she's on my mind every minute of the day. I'm wondering if she's still living with Melissa, if she's managed to find a place yet or if she's somehow putting up with her and deciding to stay put. That doesn't seem like something she'd be able to do but then again, I didn't think it was so easy for her to leave me either.

I'm trying not to be bitter about it. It's hard though. Because as much as I understand Natasha's reasoning, I don't understand why she thinks losing my job is harder than losing her. Jobs come and go. Love is a million to one.

I don't see her at school during the week and I don't know if that's luck – or bad luck – or if she's even at school. I do see Melissa though, unfortunately. She hasn't said anything to me but she does stare at me with this smugness I wish I could wipe off her face. I don't give her anything though. I act like normal, even happy at times and forever the dorky professor because the last thing I want is for her to take pleasure in what she's done, to enjoy my pain. So I wear a mask and I wear it well.

When the weekend finally arrives, I fly up to Edinburgh to my parents' house, asking Lachlan to be present as well. I wasn't too sure I wanted Kayla there but Lachlan was adamant that she'll soon be my sister-in-law and that she's part of our clan. I had to agree.

On Saturday night we're all gathered around the dinner table, everyone looking at me expectantly. I know they think I have some grand old news and while it's news, it's not at all what they're expecting to hear.

My mum, in fact, looks especially anxious, like she thinks I'm about to announce Natasha is pregnant or we're getting married or something of that nature. I'm sorry to disappoint her.

I clear my throat. "Well, I bet you're wondering why I asked for you all to come to dinner."

"I assumed it's because of your mother's cooking," my dad says.

"That's true," I concede.

"I assumed it's because you miss me," Kayla says.

"Also true," I tell her with a quick smile. "But actually…I have some news. And it's not exactly good news either."

"Oh my god," my mum gasps, hand going to her chest. "You and Natasha broke up."

I tilt my head, considering it. "That is part of it."

Lachlan gives me a heavy look. "I'm so sorry," he says and I can see how much he means it.

I wince. "Well, the thing is. Okay, this is going to be weird to hear and I know I should have told you all this a very, very long time ago. It's just that I was too afraid that you wouldn't understand, that you would judge."

"We would never judge you, Brigs," my mother says.

"Even I wouldn't," Kayla adds.

I sigh. "Okay. Here goes. I met Natasha the summer before Miranda died. We met, as we've told you, at the short film festival office. But it didn't end there. There was something so…enigmatic about her, she drew me in like gravity and it was something I'd never ever felt before. I was a fool and I was lonely and I wanted that around me. So I invited Natasha to become my research assistant for my book." I pause. "And she accepted." I look around and everyone is still staring at me, though I think Kayla is catching on from the sly look in her eyes.

I clear the dust from my throat and push on. "So we worked together almost every day that summer. And I…I fell in love with her." I expect my mum to gasp but still…silence. I can hear the fridge kick on in the kitchen. "And she fell in love with me. I never slept with her. I was as faithful to Miranda as possible but the truth was I didn't love her and I'm not sure I ever really did. Not even close to the way that I felt – that I still feel – for Natasha. I had an emotional affair and it was wrong. The both of us knew it. And I especially knew I had to leave Miranda."

I suck in my breath and close my eyes, hoping it makes the next part easier. "So, I told Miranda one night. It was the wrong night for honesty. I told her I wanted a divorce and when she refused, I told her the truth, that I was in love with someone else. She panicked. She was drunk. Beyond angry. All understandable. There were so many things I should have done in hindsight but I didn't know. I didn't know. I didn't expect her to grab Hamish and then get in the car and drive..."

Now my mother is gasping. I look up to see everyone staring at me, their faces pained. Even Kayla has watery eyes.

"You know the rest of that night," I tell them quickly. "We don't need to go over it again. But right afterward, in my depths of grief and guilt, I told Natasha what happened. I told her it was our fault and that we did this and I ended it with her because I had no choice. I loved her, so dearly, but how could I keep loving the person that brought my world to a standstill? So I never saw Natasha again...until last month."

"Jesus, Brigs," my father says and he rarely swears. He shakes his head, taking off his glasses. "That's more than anyone should have to go through. Why didn't you tell us?"

"Because you wouldn't have understood."

"They would have," Lachlan says gruffly. "We all would have."

"Brigs, you're our son, just as Lachlan is," says my mother, her voice grave. "You're family and we love you. We would have never judged you. And we don't judge you now. To think all this time you were blaming yourself for what happened."

"It explains so much," my father adds with a sigh.

"You're not a bad person just because you fell in love with someone else," Kayla says, staring at me with rare sincerity in her dark eyes. "You're just human. Like the rest of us."

Well I can't say that my heart doesn't feel warm from hearing them say this but that's still not the problem at hand.

Lachlan picks up on this, saying, "So why have you broken up?"

I exhale loudly. "Where do I begin? One of Natasha's friends, Melissa, a student of mine this year, has it in for us. For Natasha especially. She knows we're seeing each other and is threatening to report me."

"Report you for what?" Kayla asks. "You're not Natasha's teacher."

"No, I'm not. And even next year, we would make sure not to be in each other's class. But this girl can do some real damage. She's been hitting on me, trying to mess with me obviously, give her some ammo, and of course I've been trying to be as professional as possible, constantly shooting her down. But she's fragile. No, she's a fucking loon. And now she wants us to suffer. So she threatened the both of us and told Natasha that if she doesn't leave me, she'll get me fired from my job. Who knows the lies she can make up."

"And so she left you," my mum says with disbelief.

I nod. "Aye. She did. She didn't want me to lose my job. She thinks she's doing the right thing but she's not."

"She's trying to save you," Kayla says quietly.

"I know. But she can't save me by losing me. It might work sometimes but not this time."

My dad clears his throat. "It's honorable of her," he says. "But I can tell you're not going to accept it. You do have a very rare teaching position, though, and that's something to consider. That doesn't come around every day."

"No, it doesn't. But neither does she. And if I have to choose, then it's no contest. I choose her."

"So what are you going to do?" Lachlan asks as he begins to cut into his roast. The man can't keep his appetite in check for long. "What can you do?"

I shake my head. "I don't know. Telling you was the first step. The next step…I think I have to tell the school."

"Tell them what?" my father asks. "That you *were* seeing a student?"

"Yes," I say. "And if it works out, that hopefully I will be seeing her again. Look, I can't let her go and I won't let her go. Life rarely gives you second chances like this."

"But what if you tell them and they fire you and you don't get her back," Kayla points out.

"Always the optimist, aye?" I say to her. "In that case, at least I did all I could. I'm not giving up without a fight."

My words fall over the table, bringing everyone into silence where we finally enjoy our meal. It isn't until later, when Lachlan is leaving, that he pulls me into a bear hug.

I have to say, it surprises me.

"What's that for," I tell him, pulling away.

His brow is furrowed as he stares at me, a million creases on his forehead. "It's because I know what it's like to fight. You don't have to do it alone. Go get her back Brigs. I'm with you all the way." He slaps me on the back.

It hurts like hell.

But his words do give me strength.

…

The next morning I get up bright and early, pausing in the doorway of Lachlan's old room and staring at the bed where Natasha and I were last together here. The sun streams in through the window and I can almost see her there, the smile on her face, beaming at me brightly, the moment I told her I loved her. The moment she let herself believe it.

I take it all in and know that I've never been so honest, never been so real with myself than I was right then. That that's something I need to honor.

I have other people to honor as well.

Before I head to the airport, I have the cab driver drop me off at the cemetery where Miranda and Hamish are buried together. I stop in front of their graves and put down a haphazard bouquet of late flowers I picked from my mum's garden.

It's a quiet morning here, almost empty, and the sunshine is golden. Foggy patches still linger and a bird close by sings on and on in a sweetly chirping tune. It sounds like spring, even though we are rushing into autumn. Maybe it's a sign of rebirth. Maybe I don't need any more signs.

I clear my throat and stand above the graves, the shiny headstones. "You both know there's not a day that goes by where I don't think of you. That I don't remember every beautiful detail. That will never change. As long as I keep living, that will never change. Through the good and the bad, you both taught me so much and more than that you taught me what it's like to be alive." I pause, taking in a deep breath. "I just wanted you both to know that I love you. And that I've found someone that makes me very happy. Thing haven't worked out the way any of us thought and I wish I could make it so that you were both here with me. But the truth is, life has other plans for us, greater than the ones we have for ourselves. I think...I think I'm finally ready to move on. I don't know where I'm going but I know what I want and I'm going to fight for it. I just wanted your permission, your forgiveness, before I go forward."

I know the dead can't respond but that doesn't mean I don't wait. I close my eyes, taking in the sorrow and the grief and exhaling hope. I can feel it in my bones.

I feel love.

And I feel free.

Chapter Twenty-Two

NATASHA

It's been two weeks since I last talked to Brigs, that tearful, horrible day in his office where I not only broke my own heart but broke his too. Two weeks and that image of his face crumbling before me, of the hurt and devastation on his brow, won't leave my mind. It's all I see. It's in my dreams, it's when I'm awake. It's my punishment for giving him up, to see how badly I hurt him.

But I'm hurting too. Deeply. Beyond repair. Just like before, I'm on the edge of the black hole and so close to going over. I know that freefall – it's a lot like love. But there's no happy ending.

I don't know how I keep from going over. Maybe it's because I know what the depths feel like. Maybe it's because this was my choice this time. I just know it was the only thing I could do. I had ruined him in the past and it was our love that took so much away from his life. I won't do that again.

And maybe it's because I know I won't survive it in the end. How could he love me, look at me when he knows I'm the reason he's had to give up a perfect career?

He would resent me. I would resent myself.

We would break up.

And once again, he would have nothing.

He's gone through more than anyone should already.

I just can't do it.

The terrible thing is, I know he loves me more than he loves his job. I know that everything he said is true – that he would leave his job for me in a heartbeat, that he would do it for us. I know it and that's why I couldn't let it happen. I couldn't let him make that choice.

So I made it for him.

And I'm dying inside. Slowly.

But so fucking surely.

It's all made worse by the fact that not only do I keep seeing him at school, thankfully at a distance, even though it devastates me to even see his shadow, but I'm still living with Melissa.

It's not for lack of trying. I'm on Craigslist and wanted roommate ads every single day. I'm applying non-stop and I'm visiting flats when I'm not at school. But it's not so easy when you're on a budget and school has just started. I almost accepted a shared room with this angry girl until she made an overly racist comment about someone else who applied, then I had to hightail it out of there.

There is no silver lining here. No saving grace. Melissa doesn't say a word to me but somehow that makes it worse. She's watching me all the time, trying to see where I'm going, what I'm doing. It's like having a fucking private detective following your every move and she's waiting for me to slip up.

But I'm not slipping up. I haven't contacted Brigs and aside from two emails that I quickly erased with all the will-power possible, I haven't heard from him. I'm doing everything I can to keep him out of trouble, to let him keep the life he had before.

I have nothing to hide anymore.

Well, actually.

That's not quite true.

My period is late.

Way late.

I'm usually pretty regular so this scares the shit out of me and of course I'm thinking back to when we had unprotected sex in Edinburgh. I did take Plan B the next day, maybe a bit later than I should have, but that's supposed to work, like, ninety-nine per cent of the time.

I can't be that one per cent.

I can't.

It's just stress, I tell myself as I pick up the home pregnancy test from the chemist and make my way to the flat. *You're under so much pressure, you're not eating, you're crying yourself to sleep every night.*

That's all true.

I'm a wreck. I can barely make it to my classes and at night I can barely grade my papers. My thesis doesn't even exist. It's hard to do anything but wallow in the pain and some nights I can't breathe because my chest is hollow and I'm crying too hard to let anything in.

Those are the nights I know Melissa can hear me but I'm so distraught – so *lost* – that I can't even hide it, can't keep quiet. I know she's loving the pain, the tears, how my supposedly perfect life has been taken down a peg.

But it's not a peg. It's everything.

Brigs was *everything.*

So it's stress, I tell myself once again as I go into the bathroom, grateful that Melissa isn't home so I can do this in peace. *Just stress.*

I take in a deep breath, follow the instructions, and pee on the stick.

I stare at the pink lines.

Seconds pass.

I will the second line not to appear.

But one line does.

And then another.

Two pink lines.

A positive.

"No," I cry out softly. I shake the stick rapidly, as if that will change the results.

But it doesn't.

Fuck.

I'm pregnant.

No, I tell myself. *These kind of tests are faulty so early in the game. Get another.*

And so I do. I run out down the block and I buy two.

Then I do both and the results are the same.

Pregnant.

Pregnant.

No doubt.

Now Melissa is home and I'm in a full-on panic. I have to smuggle the tests out of the bathroom because I don't dare throw them away in the rubbish there. She'll see and then she'll go after Brigs. She would think she has proof that I didn't listen.

I shut myself in my room, hiding the tests in a plastic bag and shove it under my bed for now and I try and plan what to do next. I have to have a plan.

But I don't have a plan.

How could I ever plan for this?

I sit on my bed and try to think but all the emotions have a chokehold on my heart.

I'm pregnant.

With Brigs' child.

Holy fuck.

I'm so totally screwed because I'm not with Brigs, because I can never be with Brigs and I'm going to have go through everything alone. I don't have family here to lean on. I don't know how I can have a baby and still go to school. I don't even know how I can afford a child, period.

But then…then through my racing heart and the impending panic attack and the sense of utter doom, there is something else.

Something I never thought I'd feel before.

Hope.

I'd always figured I'd have kids one day when I met the right person, but to be honest they weren't really on my mind. Maybe because I had such a messy childhood. Maybe because my whole life has been about trying to figure it all out. I focused on school, on film, on the things I thought I wanted. Even relationships were something I pushed aside.

But this…even though I would be alone through it, it's *Brigs'*. The man I love beyond anything. The child would be the product of two people who loved each other so very much. Two people who loved each other so much that they would find each other again, even with the whole world against them.

A wave of fear washes over me, the one that tells me how unprepared I am, how hard it's going to be to go at it alone, that I don't know what I'm doing.

But then I realize how god damn stupid I'm being.

Selfish, stupid and terribly naïve.

The thing is, I can't go through it alone.

Even if I wanted to, I can't.

I have to tell Brigs.

It goes against everything that I set out to do and it risks everything once more.

But I can't have this child without him knowing it.

He deserves to know.

He has to know.

Brigs lost his only child.

This is his second chance.

For me to stand in the way of that…I couldn't do that to him. I couldn't do it to myself. I couldn't do it to the baby.

I have to tell him.

No matter what he says, what I think, he has to know.

My heart bubbles up with urgency, warm at the thought of seeing him again, but I have to do this properly. Tomorrow I'll go to the clinic and take a test with the doctor, just to make sure. Then I'll go to his office and hope to god I'm not seen by Melissa.

Understandably, I can barely go to sleep. I toss and turn all night.

My emotions go in waves.

I think about how Brigs will react. Will he be afraid? Happy?

I think about his job. Will he lose it? Keep it?

I think about being pregnant, about how I don't know anything and how lost I'm going to be.

I'm so scared.

I'm so alive.

I'm buzzing with a million different feelings and in the end they're all wild and warm.

I have Brigs' baby growing inside me.

Too small at the moment to count.

But it already counts for so much.

This changes…*everything*.

Chapter Twenty-Three

BRIGS

"Thank you, Brigs," Dr. Sarah Chalmers, the department chair of the university tells me with a polite smile as I ease myself out of the seat. "We're glad that you told us everything when you did."

I lean over to shake her hand, hoping my palm is dry. "I'm glad you and Phillip were able to see me," I say, glancing over at the dean, Phillip Buck. As usual, his expression is blank, giving me nothing.

"We'll let you know soon what we decide soon," Sarah says and I wish I could read something in her voice that would give me a clue to my fate. But again, I'm blind to everything.

I give them both a nod and leave the office, happy to get out of there.

It took a lot of nerve and a few days to finally get my meeting with the department chair and dean to discuss my situation with Natasha. I'm fairly lucky that Sarah is the one who helped hire me, being friends with Keir's uncle, Tommy. But the dean is the one who made a case out of the last professor. The one I replaced. The one that was fired for sexual harassment. It doesn't exactly look good that my issue follows a similar theme.

But I told them the truth and that's all I can tell them. Even if I don't go back with Natasha, a thought so scary it leaves my chest concave and cold, I'd at least be certain I'd done everything I could.

Still, as freeing as it all is, it's little consolation in a life without my golden girl by my side.

I head down to my office, wondering how long they're going to deliberate for. Sarah had told me that though Natasha isn't my student, she is a student in my faculty and I'm in a position of power over her if she were ever come into my class. Direct teacher student relationships are against the code of conduct because of grade manipulation and academic reputation and the result is almost always the professor losing their job. Melissa was right about that. But everything else is in a case-by-case basis depending on the relationship of student and teacher. The fact that Natasha and I knew each other before counts for something too.

That said, it didn't sound very promising. It's rarely permitted and only in certain circumstances. Basically, it's never happened at King's College. I can only hope that by me going to them and admitting the truth, that might help them see how sincere I am, how much it means to me. I know now, at least, that they aren't going to fire me over my confession. But whether Natasha and are ever allowed to be together is another thing.

Another obstacle between us. Of course the greater obstacle is the fact that I haven't seen or heard from her in weeks. I contacted her recently, two emails, just wanting to know how she was doing. But of course those were never answered.

I'm just at my office door when something compels me to look down the hall.

My head swivels, as if independent, and it takes me a moment to realize that Natasha is standing at the far end of the hallway, motionless and staring at me.

I don't know what to do. Last time we saw each other like this, I ran after her and she kept running.

So this time I take a deep breath and manage to tear my gaze off of her before I run after her again, scaring her indefinitely. I open the door to my office and quickly step inside.

But I leave the door open.

It's false hope but it's still hope.

I sit down at my desk, my nerves misfiring, my heart drumming in ribcage. First the meeting, now this. I'm not sure I'm going to survive this semester in the end.

I stare at the door. I try to busy myself, do something else, but I stare at that damned open door and I hope and I wish and I pray that she'll appear.

Then...

She does.

Like a ghost, she sidles into view and I have to blink at her a few times, trying to drink her in, to make sure she's real.

She's beautiful beyond words. Even in just jeans with what looks like a coffee-stain on the thigh and a white v-neck sweater, her hair pulled back into a messy ponytail and not a lick of makeup on her face, she's the most beautiful creature I've ever seen.

"Hi," she says softly before looking around her, down the hall. "I was looking for you. Can I come in?"

I nod, unable to form words.

She walks in, closing the door behind her and locking it. She walks in front of the desk and stares down at me.

I can't get a hold on her eyes. They're sad. They're afraid. They're…nervous.

"I've been…," I start to say. But there is too much to say and I can barely hold it all inside. "I miss you."

She swallows, nodding quickly. "I miss you too."

Fuck. I am breaking all over again.

"Have you found a new place to live yet?" I manage to say, sucking in my breath.

She shakes her head. "No. I'm trying. I will."

"Bloody hell, Natasha." Even saying her name hurts on my lips. "You can't be around her. She's toxic."

"She's leaving me alone for the most part," she says. "But she watches me. I took a big risk coming here."

"I know," I say, exhaling deeply. "So why did you come here?"

She bites her lip, her brows pulled together. "I needed to see you again. I needed to speak to you." She looks back at the door, as if waiting for Melissa to come through with a key, unlocking it.

"Don't worry," I tell her, eying it.

"If she catches me here…"

"It doesn't matter," I say. "She can't hurt me anymore."

She frowns. "What do you mean?"

I lean back in my chair. "I just had a meeting with the dean and the department chair. I told them everything, Natasha."

She stares at me blankly. I expect her to get angry, to cry out but instead a flicker of hope shines through her eyes. "What did they say?"

I shrug. "They listened. That was pretty much it. They said they'll deliberate about it and let me know."

"You're not fired?"

"No, I'm not fired. But that was never really the point. It wasn't about telling them what I've done and not getting punished for it. It's about telling them what I plan to keep on doing."

"Plan to keep on doing?" she repeats.

My laugh is short and dry. "Natasha. I don't know what you think you're doing trying to save me, save my job. But it's not working. I'm not done with you. You're not getting away that easily. I wanted to know if I can keep seeing you, even if I don't have you right now."

"And what if they say you can't see me?" she asks quietly. "What if they make you choose."

"Then you know what I'll choose," I tell her. "It's you. And that's something you're going to have to accept because I'm not letting go of you. Ever. I love you. You don't seem to realize how your soul belongs with mine."

Her eyes soften and a wane smile tugs at her lips. I expected her to still be stubborn, to fight my decision, to tell me she needs to do what's right and leave me so I can keep my job.

But aside from still seeming anxious, she almost seems… happy.

Her change of heart has me puzzled though I know I shouldn't question it.

"There's something I need to tell you," she says and in one hollow moment I worry that she's going to tell me she's met someone else and can't be with me, no matter how hard I try, no matter how badly I love her.

"What?" I whisper, trying to keep my pulse from racing out of my throat.

She shuts her eyes, licking her lips, as if trying to gather some internal strength. The longer the seconds tick past, the more I'm afraid that I really might lose her forever. The thought is beyond devastating.

The room grows silent.

My pulse rushes in my ears.

Natasha takes a deep breath. "I'm pregnant."

The words hang between us.

That was the last thing I expected to hear. In fact, I'm not even sure I heard that right.

"You're what?"

She opens her eyes, filled with tears. I can't tell if they are happy or not.

"I'm pregnant, Brigs. I checked with several tests. Went to the doctor. It's all positive."

"And it's mine?" I say, even though I feel like a wanker for questioning it.

She gives me the appropriate look. "Of course it's yours. I've only been sleeping with you. It's all you, Brigs." She tries to swallow, looking away. "And I don't know how you feel about it or what you want to do but I just wanted to let you know. Because you need to know. You deserve to know. And I'm keeping it."

I can't move. I can't breathe.

Thinking is out of the question.

The only thing moving is my heart, which continues to race and dance, feeling so light that it might just float away.

"Well," she says, wiping away a tear and folding her arms. "Say something at least."

But I'm dumfounded.

The joy rushing through me is too much to even feel.

I'm numb from fucking happiness.

"I...you're pregnant," I whisper.

"Yes," she says. "With your baby." She sniffs and gives me the most gorgeous awestruck smile. "I'm going to be a mom."

Bloody hell.

Bloody. Fucking. Hell.

"You're pregnant with my child," I say, trying to get to my feet even though I can't feel them, can't feel anything except this light inside me trying to force its way out. "You're pregnant."

"Yes, yes," she says, laughing a little. "This is good, right? Tell me it's good, Brigs, I'm so fucking scared." Her face falls and I can see how damn terrified she must be.

And that's when it hits me. The reality. The enormity of it all.

That's when I kick into gear.

I go over to her and pull her into my arms, holding her so tight, kissing the top of her head hard, over and over again.

"Yes it's good, it's so fucking good," I tell her and now the tears are coming for me. I can't even contain them, I don't even try. "Natasha, I don't even know what to say but it's good. I love you. I love you so much and I am..." I break off, a sob escaping me. "I want this more than anything in the world. Such a beautiful thing. It will be yours and mine. It will be ours to love."

She's holding me as tight as I'm holding her and now she's crying too, soft whimpers into my chest. "I want this, Brigs. I want us again. I want to be with you, I want to love you and keep on loving you. I don't want to do it all alone."

I pull back and cup her face in my hands, smiling so wide that my face feels like it might break, even though the tears keep running down my cheeks and everything tastes like salt.

It's the taste of joy.

Of starting over.

Of life.

"You'll never have to do this alone," I tell her, my eyes searching hers, locked together. "We're in this together. We were *always* in this together, from the moment I met you. This is our child. This is about us. This is our future. We have gone through so much to get right here, right now and you need to know that nothing, not this school, not friends, or family or career or anything will ever get in the way of you and me. We deserve love. We deserve this."

She nods and I brush her hair back from her face, her nose running and eyes puffy but she still breaks my heart. "I promise I won't let you go again," she says. "I promise to fight."

"Just promise to rise," I tell her, my voice hoarse. "With whatever is thrown our way. Promise me you'll rise. Fuck the ashes. You're fire. We're fire."

"We're fire," she says. "We are."

Another wave of joy slams into me and I let out a small, delirious laugh. I kiss her forehead, her cheeks, her nose, her lips. I kiss her and tell her how much I love her and I'll do anything for her. I tell her how much I already love the baby and that I'll be the best father that I can be. I tell her that she's going to be an excellent mother and that this is only the start, that this is the beginning of our whole lives together. A third chance.

But the third time is always lucky.

We stay in the office for a while, cocooned in there. We're no longer afraid of Melissa, of consequences. It feels impossible now that we ever were. The baby – *our baby* – puts everything else into perspective. We stay in there because the news, the joy, feels so new and fragile. I'm afraid to go into the world, that it might disappear.

Someone even knocks on my door at some point but I don't dare answer it and break the spell. Instead, Natasha sits on the chair across from me and I put my feet up on the desk and we talk for hours. We talk like old times, about movies, my book, her thesis, the future, only now one of us will occasionally laugh or cry or burst out that we're going to be parents.

For me, it's the greatest gift I could have ever gotten. Nothing will ever make Hamish come back and no child could ever compare to him. He was a beautiful soul, one of a kind, and the world is less bright without him in it. But I have so much love to give and I know Hamish felt that from me. He would want it to go to another child, while I keep on loving him and missing him in my heart.

I just don't think I've ever felt so much hope before. Pure, raw hope.

It brings me to tears, brings me to my knees.

The realization that life is good – better than good – and it's only going to get better.

It's around dinner time though, and I'm just about to suggest to Natasha that we get something to eat, something to celebrate, when my phone rings.

I pick up my mobile and eye the number.

It's Sarah, the department chair.

My eyes widen and I'm suddenly nervous all over again.

I answer it. "Brigs speaking."

"Brigs," Sarah says. "Am I catching you at a bad time?"

"No, no," I say quickly, plugging up my ear to hear her better.

"I stopped by your office but you weren't there," she says. "I just wanted to let you know that I talked it over with Phillip, as well as Charles Irving since he's most senior, trying to get a third opinion."

I groan inwardly, feeling all that hope dash away. Irving hates me and he doesn't seem fond of Natasha either.

"Because you had a relationship of sorts with her before, we decided that you can be free to pursue a relationship with Miss Trudeau now," she says and I don't think I've ever exhaled so loud before. "Based on the following grounds: she is not to ever take any of your classes, nor can she interact with you at the school in anyway, that means going to your office, stopping by your class, department fundraisers or events, or any action that might give the wrong impression. What you do in your own spare time off campus is none of our business. She's nearly thirty and you're both consenting adults. But the moment any of those lines are crossed and this program's reputation is on the line, we're afraid you're going to have to resign."

"You won't have to worry about that," I tell her. Natasha is leaning forward in her seat, staring at me expectantly.

"I trust you Brigs," she says. "You're a good teacher and frankly you deserve a little good fortune."

Ah. So that's why I was given the exception. The pity vote. Well, I'll fucking take it.

"Thank you so much, Sarah," I tell her graciously. "And tell that to Charles and Phillip, too."

I hang up the phone and Natasha is already grinning at me, her eyebrows raised. "Well?"

"They discussed it with your beloved Professor Irving," I tell her.

Her eyes go round. "Oh no," she exclaims.

I shrug, smiling. "Well, I don't know, I guess the old bastard likes you after all."

"What do you mean?"

"They said I can keep my job."

She nearly jumps out of her chair, clapping her hands together. "Are you serious? Brigs this is amazing! Oh my god, I can't believe it."

"Well, we have to pretend we don't know each other when we're at school," I tell her. "Which means no more office dates like this. But I think we can make up for it when you move in with me."

"What?"

"Come live with me," I implore her. "Today. Tonight. Let's get your stuff and get you the hell out of there."

"Are you sure?" she asks though her eyes are already dancing with the thought.

"Natasha, you're pregnant with my child," I remind her, automatically smiling at the thought. It will never stop getting old, never stop feeling amazing. "And we're free to be with each other outside of the school. There's no one to fear. Unless Winter has any objections, you're moving in with me."

"Okay," she says quietly, blinking at me in amazement. "Tonight?"

"Right fucking now," I tell her, getting up. "Come on, let's go. You're pretty much packed aren't you?"

She nods. "And Melissa?"

My smile is probably wolfish. "I can't wait to see the look on her face."

We leave the school together, both of us anxious, excited, delirious. It's all moving so fast and yet it doesn't seem fast enough. I want her in my flat, I want to wake up to her every morning, I want to live with her shining beside me. The fact that we've just (narrowly) been granted freedom almost feels like we've been pardoned from jail and the way we rush through the streets together, touching, kissing, laughing just cements this.

But we aren't out of the woods yet. When we get back to my flat – our flat – I have to fight against the urge to take her the moment we step inside. We still have something important to deal with and our nerves won't rest until it's put to bed.

Because the Aston Martin probably won't make it across town and wouldn't fit any of her stuff regardless, we have to hire a van. Luckily I've seen Max make plenty of deliveries to and from The Volunteer with his van, so we head across the street and see if he'll do us this favor.

"For you," Max says, tossing me the keys with a big smile, "anything. I'll just add it to your tab."

"Thanks, mate," I tell him and soon I'm in the driver's seat of an aging van from the 80's, heading to Wembley with Natasha at my side.

It's one hell of a nerve-wracking car ride.

Natasha is ringing her hands, biting her lip so hard I fear she'll draw blood.

"Relax," I tell her, placing my hand on her leg. "I'm here. With you all the way. You don't even have to face her if you don't want her, just stay in the van and I'll take care of it."

She shakes her head, exhaling noisily. "I won't hide from her. Not anymore."

We pull up to her building and her face falls when she sees the light on in her flat but to her credit, she gets out and we trudge up the stairs to her floor until we're standing right outside her door.

"Are you ready?" I ask her.

"Nope," she says, trying to smile. She sticks in her key, hopefully for the last time, and the door opens.

We step inside. The sound of the telly blaring comes from the living area.

"Natasha?" Melissa calls out from the room.

The two of us wait in the hallway, staying silent.

Finally Melissa walks out of the room and stops dead when she sees us.

She blinks at us in surprise for a few beats before her face hardens into hatred.

I wiggle my fingers at her. "Hello. Bet you didn't expect to see me tonight."

"What the fuck are you doing with him?" Melissa asks Natasha, though I'm noticing she's not coming any closer to us. I think she's scared of us, that we should be so bold. "Why is he here?"

Natasha and I exchange a glance of who should go first.

Natasha looks back to Melissa and shrugs. "He's helping me move out."

"Move out? You found another place already?"

If I'm not mistaken there's a tiny bit of hurt in Melissa's voice. It makes her human for once.

Natasha swallows thickly but straightens up, head held high. "I did. So Brigs is helping me move."

Melissa is back to glaring, that sliver of vulnerability gone. "Bullshit. You're together again aren't you?"

"Actually," I tell her, walking a few steps toward her. Melissa shrinks back against the wall. "We are together again. Natasha is actually moving into *my* flat. Tonight. We're going to live together. And see each other, as you can imagine."

"You...you can't do that," she says, looking between us. "You can't...I'm reporting you. I told you I would and you give me no choice."

"No, you *do* have a choice," Natasha says, coming over to us and going right up to Melissa's face. I've never seen her so brave. "Maybe we can't choose who we fall in love with but you *can* choose whether to be a total cuntasaurus or not. You don't have to report us but you want to and you will because you're unhappy as fuck with your life." She shakes her head, her tone softening. "You know, I tried to be a good friend to you and I'm sorry I wasn't but I'm not sorry any of this happened. It let me know who you really were deep down. And it let me and Brigs be together in peace."

Melissa is just shaking her head, flabbergasted. When she can't find the words to say to Natasha, she narrows her eyes at me. "You won't find any peace. I'll make sure of it. What's wrong is wrong and you're both wrong."

"Go ahead," I tell her, folding my arms across my chest and looking down at her. "Go and report us. But you should know, I've beat you to it."

"What?"

"I've turned myself in. Had a meeting with the dean, the department chair and Professor Irving. I told them everything, the whole truth. That we loved each other once and we love each other now. And guess what, Miss King? We have their approval."

"I don't believe it."

"Well, you really should. But you know, feel free to take it up with them." I pause, my mouth curving into a smile. I'm about to tell a lie but it's one I feel good about. "I mentioned you, you know, what you've said, what you've threatened me with. So they're kind of expecting you to come by."

Natasha's eyes dart to me, knowing I'm lying, but I keep my focus on Melissa. I can practically see her crumbling in front of us. There goes her plan of attack.

I go on. "Or you know, you could just let it go. Accept that Natasha is happy, that I'm happy. Forget about us just as we will forget about you." I tilt my head, giving her a sad smile. "Because believe me, Melissa, we will forget about you. We have each other. That's all we need. Well that, and our child."

Her eyes bug out. Mouth drops open. She can't even speak.

Natasha fills her in. "I'm pregnant. And we couldn't be happier. So after all this is said and done, I guess we have you to thank. If it wasn't for your bitterness and anger, your jealousy and insecurities, we wouldn't have had to sneak around so much and have all that awesome sex. So thank you for that, Melissa. And thanks for making me move out and giving me a great excuse to be with the one I love."

"Yes, thank you," I tell her, trying to sound sincere. "Especially for all the sex we've been having." Melissa is still speechless, her face flaming pink. I look to Natasha. "Shall we get packing?"

She nods, trying not to smile and we head into her room and get to work while Melissa stands out in the hallway, bewildered and unsure what to say or do. Luckily, it's easy work for us since Natasha had already packed it all up. We take down the boxes and pile up the van in three trips.

During the last trip, Natasha, with hands full of movie posters, calls out into the hallway. Melissa has been in her room the whole time, trying her best to ignore us.

"We're going now," Natasha says, her voice echoing down the hall. "You know, it doesn't have to end this way. We'll be seeing each other at school I'm sure, so if you want to make things easier between us, I'm game."

Silence.

Natasha looks to me and shrugs. I adjust the boxes in my hands and give her a look that tells her she tried her best.

"Okay," Natasha calls out to her again. "I'll take your silence as a sign you want my forgiveness. Well, I forgive you Melissa. Life is too short to hold grudges, guilt, shame or anything other than happiness. One day, hopefully you'll realize I'm right."

"You're bloody right about that," I say, as Natasha pauses at the door, waiting for one last reply. When it doesn't come, she slowly shuts the door. "I'm proud of you," I tell her.

"Yeah," she says. "I think I'm proud of me too." She stares back at the door, a symbol of another life, and sighs. "You know I meant it too. I won't hold a grudge. I've seen what it can do to a person."

"Let's get you to your new place," I say and we head down the stairs, pack up the rest of the stuff, and drive off into the night.

...

Later that night there's a pile of boxes in my drawing room, a dog snoring on the couch and the woman I love lying in my arms. Inside her is a new life, a new beginning, a new chance.

Outside her is a man who loves her more than he can even understand.

And outside us both is a world that keeps spinning, a mad world capable of bringing us to our knees and yet never ceases to be beautiful.

Epilogue

NATASHA

Six Months Later

"Got everything?" Brigs asks, eying me in the mirror as he adjusts his bow-tie.

The man looks disarmingly handsome in a tuxedo and I have to take a moment to drink him in like lemonade on a hot day.

Of course this makes him stare right back at me, shaking his head. "I can't get over how beautiful you look," he says, voice rich and low, all the emotions of the last six months just simmering beneath the surface.

I roll my eyes. "You mean despite the fact that I'm a waddling pregnant woman," I tell him, looking down at my belly. Thank god this wedding dress is empire-waisted and kind of camouflages my bump. What it doesn't camouflage is the fact that my body has turned on me and turned into a fat, bloated monster with an insatiable appetite. You know those pregnant women who you can't tell if they're pregnant or not if you're looking at them from behind? Yeah, that's not me. My ass has only gotten wider, not to mention all the other parts of me. Shopping for clothes has become extremely depressing, so I just schlep about in leggings and baggy sweaters.

Of course the dress is absolutely beautiful and I'm so glad I don't look too horrid. My hair is half up with some height to balance out my lower half, though my roots are coming in like crazy since I can't dye my hair anymore. Or have caffeine. Or drink alcohol. Or enjoy sushi. Or, you know, life.

It might sound like I'm not enjoying being pregnant and I guess that's kind of true. I know it's nature's miracle and all that bullshit but honestly, I'm a sweaty, foggy-headed insomniac now whose hands look like they belong on a Cabbage Patch Kid doll. I just want Ramona (yes, named after my literary heroine, Ramona Quimby – only fair since Brigs would have named him Sherlock if he was a boy) to be born already so I can see her cute face and see which of us she'll resemble. If she could have my boobs and Brigs' eyes, she'll win at life.

Unfortunately, being pregnant has also made me horny as hell. Brigs doesn't seem to mind and neither do I. I mean, I get to fuck him all day so there are no complaints there and even though I feel like a fat, flabby mess, he's turned on all the time. He even makes me feel beautiful – at least he tries. It's hard to feel gorgeous when your thighs look like cottage cheese but luckily my hormones don't care if I'm self-conscious or not.

Even now as we're getting ready to leave, the sight of him in his tuxedo makes my stomach ignite with heat, my legs pressing together to try and relieve the pressure. The only problem is, we don't have much time before we hop in the Aston Martin and drive to Hyde Park for the ceremony.

The truth is, Brigs and I applied for our marriage license two weeks ago. We didn't tell anyone. Everyone – his family, even my family – thinks we're going to have a big wedding in the fall. But really, it just wasn't sitting well with either of us. The minute we announced we were engaged, it was like everyone in his family turned into characters from an episode of Bridezilla. With Lachlan and Kayla getting married in the summer, and those plans in full swing, including all of her friends and their cousins in the States coming over, Brigs and I felt like things were getting out of hand. It stopped feeling like it was about the two of us and we wanted to keep that feeling.

So we decided to elope. Or elope as much as you can in the UK. This ain't Vegas. We went to the register and applied for the license, then just yesterday went back and said our vows officially.

Today though, we're having an actual ceremony – it's not legal, but since we're already technically married, it's just for our own sake. It's just us, Winter, Shelly the dog walker, and Max the bartender, officiating. Who knew the grizzled drink slinger was a celebrant?

I know that all our families will probably be disappointed and hurt by us doing this on our own, but they'll thank us later when that's one less wedding to worry about. Besides, there's a baby on the way and that's taking up enough of their time and energy as it is. It's taking up *my* time and energy and I'm still going to school on top of it.

Plus, we've hired a great photographer to capture the moment and will have a big party next week when we go back up to Edinburgh. For our honeymoon we'll take the train down to Marseilles to see my father and I'm hoping once the baby is born, we can fly my mother out here from LA. Even though we still don't have the best relationship, we're working on it. Being with Brigs has taught me that we have to make amends while we can and that second chances don't come by often. Since I reached out to my mother, and she's been reciprocating, I feel this is as good of a chance as any.

"Are you nervous?" Brigs asks, coming over to me.

"No, are you?" I ask.

He shakes his head. "Not a bit."

"Are you lying?"

"Maybe."

I reach down to adjust my shoes. I'm wearing white Converse. No one will know and heels have been killing my back lately, along with everything else.

"Bloody hell, your tits look fabulous," Brigs murmurs and just the silky way he says "tits" has my blood flowing hot. I glance up at him and he's staring right down my cleavage. My boobs are absolutely out of control, which drives him crazy.

"Don't fucking say tits," I scold him, trying to straighten up.

He puts his hand on my shoulder and pushes me back down to my knees on the plush rug. "No, no. Stay down there. Don't ruin this view. I doubt I'll get to see this again." His voice is so low, sliding over me like butter. "You in a white dress, with those *tits*. So fucking innocent looking."

I know we don't have a lot of time, but I don't really care.

"Only I'm not so innocent," I tell him, playing along. I reach for his zipper and undo his pants, shoving them down his hips. His cock juts out in front of me, thick and long and beautiful. Completely mine now.

I've married this cock.

I take it in my hands and lick him, suck at his precum and let the taste hit my tongue like a tonic. I don't care what any woman says, when you've got a dick as big and excessively thick as his, giving blow jobs is fucking addicting.

He gives off tiny grunts and low moans as I find his balls, knowing exactly where and when to tug, as I bend and lick around his crown and all the way along his rigid shaft, the heat coming through his skin. The desire inside me is building until I'm tempted to slip a hand between my legs, and I can actually feel him get bigger, thicker, inside my mouth as I work at him.

"You're going to ruin me," he groans. He goes to grab my hair and then stops, remembering my hairdo. "Sorry," he says, his voice breaking with lust, making fists at his side.

I suck harder, aching for him to come, to feel his release down my throat. First blow job as man and wife and I don't want to hold back. I want to set the tone for the rest of the marriage. I grab his ass, feeling his muscles flex as he pushes into me, slowly at first, then his thrusts become wild, his voice louder and I want his cum so fucking bad. Everywhere, anywhere.

But he grabs his cock at the base and pulls it out of my mouth, sliding past my lips with a delicious heaviness.

"Turn around," he says breathlessly, stroking himself as he gazes down at me with sex-dazed eyes. "On all fours."

Fuck yes.

I do as he asks, insatiable and trembling with anticipation.

He drops to his knees behind me and flips up my dress until it's bunched around my waist.

Then I hear him suck in his breath.

He lets out a fucking *laugh.*

"What is it?" I stiffen, trying to turn around and see.

"Are you..." he starts, still laughing. "Are you wearing *Sponge Bob* underwear?"

Oh, right.

"Uh, yeah," I admit. "It's one of the few pairs that fit me now."

"Is it wrong that I'm terribly turned on?" he asks lightly.

"If you don't fuck me like you're terribly turned on, then yes, it's wrong."

"Let me see the other side, turn around," he says, grabbing hold of my hips and trying to twist them.

"No!" I cry out but then he grabs my waist and flips me around until my legs are spread and he's staring directly at Sponge Bob's crazy smile.

"That's just…very you," he says, grinning. I can't tell if he's smiling for me or my underwear. He could practically have a conversation with Sponge Bob at this point. "But, sadly for Mr. Square Pants, your pants are coming off."

Impatiently he yanks down them down my thighs and tosses them aside. I'm glad Winter is out with Shelly right now because he'd be making off with them already. That dog loves my underwear as much as he loves Brigs' shoes.

Brigs then slips the straps down over my shoulders and pulls down the bodice until my breasts bounce free. His eyes burn over them and desire pools between my legs, begging for his touch. He cups my breasts, heavy in his hands, and turns his attention to one as he licks in long draws of his tongue, teasing, until he closes his mouth over my nipple and sucks. I feel myself stiffen in his wet, hot mouth, everything so heightened, so sensitive and I'm moaning, wanting more, so much more.

He does the same to my other breast, sucking it so deep in his mouth that my spine arches and I feel like he might just consume me here and now. I grab the back of his head, not caring if I mess up his hair, and dig my nails in, moaning. My breasts spill in his hands, too much for him to handle and he's hungry, frenzied, wanting more.

"Fuck, Brigs," I swear, unable to take it. "Fuck me."

"Yeah?" he asks softly, his voice thick with desire.

I nod and quickly flip back on my hands and knees. This won't take long at all.

But Brigs isn't always one to rush. At least he doesn't rush on the one day he needs to rush.

He places his wide palms on my ass and pulls my cheeks apart before lowering his head. I tense up as I feel this tongue between the crack, swooping down into my cunt and up again. My whole body seems to flinch until his tongue, relentless, tireless, starts to wear me down, skirting over the most delicate areas until my skin swells with need.

"God, you're so fucking beautiful, Mrs. McGregor," he says, taking his fingers and lightly tapping it against me. He blows on me – that's something new – and the ache for him to ram his cock inside me is so acute that I feel like I'm going blind to the world, that there's only him and me and this primal desire for each other. A desire that takes over everything, even a wedding ceremony.

He keeps blowing, the air causing my nerves to dance, my skin to tighten, and then slowly pushes his thumb in my ass while positioning his cock. I'm so open for him, wet, swollen, greedy and, with a firm hold, he pulls me back onto his shaft.

I gasp as he fills me, my body expanding around him, the angle and the wild lust and the hormones and emotions filling me up with so much want and need and joy, that I must be glowing like the sun inside. With deliberation he eases himself back in and bites my shoulder playfully.

"Mrs. McGregor," he murmurs again, in my ear, licking down my neck.

Then the bites are harder and he's holding my waist tighter and with a few hard pumps, he's packed inside me, deep and tight, and I'm clenching around him.

More, more, more.

My lungs ache for air and my fingers dig into the rug and he's pounding me, rough, almost brutal and all thought is gone. I'm just chasing my relief, panting, trying to catch up with my heart which is reckless in my chest.

This is good.

This is so fucking good.

I love, love, love this man.

My husband.

Brigs pistons back and forth, striking deep, like he's forcing the air out of my lungs. Again and again he slides in, savage, and his grunts are louder, his grip slippery on my hips from sweat. His words are dirty, asking me if I like it, asking me if I want his cock harder, telling me how sweet my cunt feels. His accent grows huskier with pleasure.

I'm on the edge.

I shift and his cock hits the right bundle of nerves.

It's like a match is struck inside me.

Boom.

I'm exploding, splintering into sharp fragments that burst again and again until I'm liquid starlight and warm silver that slides through my blood.

Brigs comes immediately after me, a guttural roar ripping from his lips, his breathing raspy as he tries to catch his breath. I'm still pulsing around him, trying to bring reality into focus. My vision is soaked with bliss.

"I guess we should go," he says after a few moments, slowly pulling out.

I love how he feels bare. I guess one good thing about being pregnant is that you don't have to worry about getting pregnant again.

But fuck, even though the both of us are worried, because who doesn't fret about bringing a life into this world, especially in this day and age, I know I've never wanted something more. I know Brigs has never wanted this more. It's beautiful and it's real and it's ours.

It's life.

And it goes on.

Brigs helps me up to my feet and I quickly yank my underwear back on. We both fix each other a bit – I straighten his bow-tie, he adjusts my breasts back in my dress – and then we quickly hit the road.

We're lucky with traffic today and we get to Hyde Park with a few minutes to spare. The photographer is hanging out halfway to the gardens and once she sees us, starts walking over, snapping as she goes.

Brigs turns in his seat and puts his hand up in the air.

I put my hand in his.

"Are you ready?" he asks me, shaking my hand in the air.

I nod, beaming at him. "Am I ever."

He places his hand on my stomach. "Are you ready Ramona?"

We both wait for the kick that doesn't come.

"Not yet," I tell him. "Give her a few more months."

We get out of the car and join hands, walking toward the photographer. In the distance, beyond the Round Pound in the Kensington Gardens, we can see Max, Shelly and Winter waiting for us.

Brigs nudges me in the side as the photographer keeps snapping and jerks his head at the Serpentine. "Afterward, how about we have our wedding photos done on the pedalo?"

"No way," I tell him, laughing. "That's asking for disaster. Especially with this dress and hair and makeup. We survived the pedal boat once, I won't survive it again."

"Oh come on, it's not like you're a walking disaster."

"Hey!" someone yells at us from behind. "Excuse me!"

We both whip around to see a woman coming out of the Kensington Palace. She's waving at me. "Your dress is tucked up into your knickers!" she yells, pointing at her own ass in demonstration.

Oh my god.

No.

I crane my neck, twisting to look behind me, and I gasp. It's true. I see Sponge Bob staring right back beneath a bundle of white tulle.

Brigs bursts out laughing and I hear the photographer snapping away with my ass now on view for everyone to see, including Shelly and Max and everyone else in the park.

"Stop laughing and help me!" I yell at Brigs as he tries to yank the dress out of the waistband but he's doubling over, laughing so hard that he can't. He nearly falls to the grass, and then I nearly fall trying to yank it all out of my underwear.

Finally I'm covered and I'm smoothing the back of my dress frantically, my cheeks flaming hot. There's a lot of fucking people in this park – people who are snickering – and somehow the fact that it was Sponge Bob makes it worse than that time in Rome.

"Oh, I hope the photographer captured that," Brigs says, tears rolling down his face as he grins at me. "That was the best moment of my life."

I roll my eyes, trying to downplay it all. "Well lucky for you, Professor Blue Eyes Brigs McGregor, the best moments of your life are just starting."

He stares at me sweetly for a long moment and kisses me on the lips. "That they are."

He grabs my hand.

And we keep on going.

THE END

Acknowledgments

The minute I started writing The Play, I couldn't wait to write The Lie. I remember walking through Burgoyne Bay on Salt Spring Island, where I live, with my husband and my dog and discussing the plot for The Play and the rich backstory of Lachlan's brother, Brigs. It's funny, even the name Brigs comes from one of my husband's friends on the island, son of musician Randy Bachman.

I knew from the beginning that Brigs' story would be a hard one to take. That it was risky to publish anything to do with infidelity. I knew this already from publishing Love, in English but even so, it was a story that broke my heart and gave me hope. I had to tell it.

Flash forward a few months to San Diego, where my husband, dog and I were renting an AirB&B outside of Ramona and Lakeside (thank you Victoria, Ed and Zena!). I threw myself into The Lie and wrote and wrote and wrote.

Until I got some feedback that screwed me up (they know who they are ;) though I am very grateful for honesty) I started to think that maybe The Lie wouldn't a novel so easily swallowed. I had doubts. Would I be punished for writing such a controversial story? In an industry where so many authors are flogged for writing about infidelity, no matter how unglamorized it is, no matter how much the protagonists suffer, is it wise or safe to publish a book that takes such matters and presents them in a raw, real way?

The thing is, though, I don't care about being safe. And I have to thank my Facebook group, the Anti-Heroes, for having faith in me and insisting I publish the book anyway. This is for you guys. Thank you for believing in me, believing in my stories and believing the world needs more books that are told from the heart, no matter how ugly and real that heart may be sometimes. Love you!